ONE OF THE GUYS

ONE OF THE GUYS

A NOVEL

ROBERT CLARK YOUNG

Cliff Street Books

An Imprint of HarperCollins*Publishers*

HarperCollins books may be purchased for educational, business, or sales promotional use. For information please write: Special Markets Department, HarperCollins Publishers, Inc., 10 East 53rd Street, New York, NY 10022.

FIRST EDITION

Designed by Kim Llewellyn

Library of Congress Cataloging-in-Publication Data

Young, Robert Clark.
     One of the guys : a novel / Robert Clark Young. — 1st ed.
         p.   cm.
     ISBN 0-06-019365-4
     I. Title.
PS3573.0837054   1999
813'.54—dc21   98-52923

99 00 01 02 03 ❖/RRD 10 9 8 7 6 5 4 3 2 1

This book is for Kenneth and Angela, my parents,
and for Michael David Brown, my friend

ACKNOWLEDGMENTS

The author is indebted to the following people, without whose efforts this book would not have been possible:

Lola Haskins, for arguing in the face of propriety at a panel discussion of the Ohio Arts Council that this project was deserving of grant money;

Holly Blake, for rescuing the author from his unfulfilling job in Ohio, inviting him to finish the manuscript at the Headlands Center for the Arts in Marin County, California;

The editors of *Another Chicago Magazine, Buffalo Press,* and *New Millennium Writings,* for publishing excerpts of the work in progress;

Nat Sobel, superagent, for reading the first chapter in *Another Chicago Magazine* and locating the author; for assisting, along with his associates Judith Weber and Laura Nolan, in the revision process; and for selling the manuscript just twelve days after it was completed;

Diane Reverand, for sitting next to Nat (and the manuscript) on a flight from New York to Provincetown, for agreeing to read the book, and for deciding to publish it.

"Ho, good men!" said our host, "now harken me;

Wait but a bit, for God's high passion do,

For we shall have a sermon ere we're through;

This Lollard here will preach to us somewhat."

"Nay, by my father's soul, that shall he not!"

Replied the sailor; "Here he shall not preach,

Nor comment on the gospels here, nor teach.

We all believe in the great God," said he,

"But he would sow among us difficulty,

Or sprinkle cockles in our good clean corn;

And therefore, host, beforehand now, I warn

My jolly body shall a story tell

And I will clink for you so merry a bell

That it shall waken all this company."

Geoffrey Chaucer
The Shipman's Prologue
Translated into modern English by
J. U. Nicolson

ONE OF THE GUYS

1

Possibility and willfulness intersected for Miles Derry, at long last, half a mile from the imaginary point where the U.S. border runs out of land and continues into the Pacific. For this was where, stopped by water and Mexican mountains, he had ceased moving west and south, so completely humbled that it required all of his hyperalertness, at three in the morning, closing time, to come out from behind the cash register and walk past the red neon entrance of the video arcade, up an aisle of shiny magazines, past the salmon-colored dildoes, which stood variously on the shelves like up-pointed weaponry, until he arrived, unhappily, at the mop closet of the Little Pink Bookstore. *Kari, Kari, Kari,* he was thinking as he rolled out the bucket on wheels, knowing this was easier if he concentrated on her name. He hadn't missed a support payment in all three years. The canceled checks came back monthly from Illinois, with Mary Lou's signature on their backs, the only evidence of his responsibility and fatherhood. Last Christmas, when he'd been working at the Laundromat in Salt Lake, there'd been a treat—pictures—and he had them in his wallet, which he kept in a front pocket of his pants because he didn't want those pictures anywhere near the latex gloves he carried in one rear pocket or the hardened sponge he carried in the other.

Outside, in the parking lot, as he used a garden hose to fill the bucket, Miles stared at the loaves of Mexican hills, heavily sugared with light, near and looming. He could smell the fish-and-sewage odor of the confluent waters of the Tia Juana River and the ocean. Between the Little Pink Bookstore and the water there was a night-black, unthinkable swamp, and to the north, too bright and clean-looking and angular to seem real, the lights of downtown San Diego. Kari, Kari in Illinois. It wasn't working tonight, he hadn't seen her in—a year?—a year next month, it was too long, and he focused instead on making a joystick of the mop, putting it into the water-filled bucket, steering it dutifully back into the store.

He added the disinfectant. Sewage outside, cigarette smoke and Lysol inside. When he left this job, it would be for the sake of his nose. And his dignity, whatever would be left of that.

Miles rolled the bucket into the video arcade, where the floor of every cubicle would have to be mopped semen-free, left unsticky, by four A.M., because he wasn't paid beyond that. He pulled the latex gloves out of his back pocket, stretched them on, then took the hard sponge out of the other pocket. He'd forgotten the Windex. He would have to clean the TV screens first, the ones that were streaked with dry or wet semen. It was the worst part of the worst job he'd ever had, the best job he'd been able to find after they'd let him go at the supermarket in El Centro (too many stockers, they decided, so cut the new guy), and he'd come to San Diego, still a man—he wasn't going to let anyone argue with him on that one, not even as he knelt in a video stall to wipe other people's jism off the walls and TV screens— still a man, still supporting himself, still sending $249 a month to his daughter, care of his ex-girlfriend, two thousand miles away.

. . . He'd done four of the booths and was entering the fifth when he saw, protruding from the wall of the cubicle, from the glory hole, an erect purple-headed penis, looking, in the snow-light from the television monitor, as rubbery-false as any of the dildoes in the store. Miles dropped his Windex bottle into the bucket, and the questionable water slapped him on the knee.

"Oh shit."

He stepped out and knocked rapidly at the door of the next booth. "We're closed. Hey!" The red light over the door was off; he tried the door, but it was locked. "Hey buddy, we're closed. Pull up your pants and go home."

He looked again into the other booth, where the erect insult stood out from the wall, curved up slightly, not looking like any human appendage, but like an outrageously inappropriate party novelty suction-cupped to the wall. Miles stripped off the gloves and jammed them into his back pocket and went out to the counter for the keys, giving himself a disjointed, agitated lecture in his mind, that this was the sort of shit the world was always offering him, and yes, he'd made mistakes, many of them, but not everything a man did was a mistake, and so it was still incredibly mindfuckingly unfair for the world to hand him nothing but shit, stubborn idiotic annoyances that he knew other people would never have to imagine, much less overcome. Like the time in the Laundromat in Salt Lake when those kids had poured a gallon of red paint into one of the washing machines when he wasn't looking, or at the gas station in Cheyenne when he was the full-service man and the windchill was fifty below, and he kept breaking off the customers' keys, as though they were made of crackers, in the gas-cap locks, seven keys and much yelling at something that wasn't his fault.

He found Jerry Archer's key ring—for some reason the world was still entrusting him with its keys—in a drawer beneath the cash register, and as he returned to the video arcade, the words of Jerry Archer—Jerry Polynesian-Shirt-White-Chinos-Prescription-Bifocal-Sunglasses-Black-Loafers Archer, the porno entrepreneur who owned eleven adult bookstores in the San Diego area—the words of Jerry Archer repeated themselves, complete with Boston accent, inside Miles Derry's head: *Ah, the thing about it is, ah, you can let them do anything they want to do in the booths, even though it's technically, ah, technically against the law, but the important thing is that they keep dropping those quarters into those machines, the red light over each door lets you know, ah, lets you know the machine's going, and if the police want to send people undercover we're legally clear because we've posted anti, ah, antimasturbation and lewd conduct notices, you get the idea, they can take their chances.*

Miles was supposed to knock and say "Drop quarters!" whenever he found a locked door with the red light off, but he never supervised the arcade, never went back there at all except after closing. He'd surrendered every pretension four years ago, at twenty-nine, when he'd quit the liquor and the drugs and agreed to try working again for his father in Illinois, but he still had enough self-regard (legitimate, he was sure) not to become what Mr. Archer had required of him, a referee of perversion.

To mop the residue was enough. There were even times when he could see it objectively: all of that spent spunk, gallons and gallons over the weeks, was nothing more than an eyedropperful from the human procreative ocean, and his own Kari—who represented the only true and pure expression of himself in the world—was a result of that same overpowering buckling sea of sperm that here, in the video arcade of the Little Pink

Bookstore, washed over the walls and floors in circumstances certainly no more foolish than his impregnation of Mary Lou. After all, who owed his existence to anyone's propriety?

As he approached the cubicle, key extended, he checked the next one quickly, saw again, with disbelief, although he expected it, the red-purple erection coming out of the wall, looking like an upright rope of licorice in an unreal sex world illuminated only by the television snow. Miles wondered at the idiot who would stick his cock through a glory hole without anyone in the next booth to suck it. He didn't want to unlock the door—what would happen next would be pathetic or dangerous or both—so he knocked again and said, "We're closed. Hey! You a deaf-mute? Turn up your hearing aid and put your dick back in your pants."

Nothing. The red light remained off. With the same feeling of doomed resignation that had preceded the snapping of each of seven keys in the gas caps, he slid this key into the doorknob lock—for the first time he wanted a key to break, but it turned instead, and the door swung out with a weight behind it. Miles jumped aside, as though trying to avoid an avalanching closetful of imponderable but undeniable problems, as a half-crouching man in U.S. naval officer's khaki, cap on head and trousers ankle-knotted, moved out of the booth sideways with a death-wide look in his gray eyes, and fell tumble-banging onto the floor, liberated boner wobbling from a black thicket of hair.

"Motherfuck." Miles pranced in terror out of the arcade, razor edges running up the back of his skull. He stood fighting for air, hands on a magazine rack, head down, eyes closed tight and tighter, but unable to obliterate the man's face, a face that was, horribly, almost his own: same gray eyes, same black forelock, same pointed nose, same Miles Derry black-rectangle mustache.

And Jerry Archer had said nothing about hard-on corpses, what to do if.

Yet his mind wasn't paralyzed—horror always made him think faster. What must've happened was this: an officer of the United States Navy, whom Miles now remembered in straight-capped, just-to-the-right-of-his-vision silhouette, requested five dollars in quarters. The Little Pink was patronized by many sailors but not so many officers, and so yes, Miles did remember this one, although he never looked directly at patrons, for he was more ashamed than they at being here. The officer must've followed the basic plot—cubicle, coins, pants down, cock through wall—

Blank. Miles couldn't fill it in. Death, okay, but how?

The lieutenant or commander or whatever-he-was had been jammed (or rather, Miles self-corrected—calmer now—*the body and uniform,* for they were precisely all that remained)—yes, jammed in the narrow booth in a semisquat with the penis through the hole and the hands against the wall and the shoulder against the door.

Miles began a slow pace along the white-lit aisles. Some folks, he realized, might consider this situation unusual. Absurd. He wasn't stupid, certainly not, he'd been to college fourteen years ago for three semesters and could've graduated if he hadn't drunk his way out of the experience. He knew the word *absurdism.* And he knew just as certainly that this situation was neither unusual nor absurd. It was simply itself and nothing else.

Nothing was ridiculous: he could prove this to himself.

Think of x number of generations of no-account, potato-mouthed Black Irish copulating with slick animal heat under rags in cold shanty villages. Think of the first Derry to finagle subwaterline passage to America, Christian name as forgotten and irrelevant as his port of arrival or his trade or his height, weight, color of eyes or hair or, more to the everlasting essential point, his particular striations of girl-conquering passion, which were the sole and pathetic excuse for the continuance of humanity. And the same thing once more and once more and once more, which would bring us to Miles Derry's father, Roger, a man who always said facts were facts and whose own facts were unassailable: born 7 July 1927, Cleveland, Ohio, machinist, learning the electroplating industry in a factory outside Chicago, saving his money, possibility and willfulness coming together for him, moving to Zincville, Illinois, in 1962 and founding, in a leaky warehouse on Lincoln Avenue, Zincville Electroplate, expanding, hiring dozens and then hundreds of people, total revenues in 1990: $12,872,515.97.

And Roger's youngest son growing up with everything and becoming from age fourteen onward a drunk and a drug addict and a dropout and a bum and almost a chowder-brain, and then sober and clean, and then a bum again after all, so that all he had under the bottom line was Kari.

Unusual? Absurd? No more so than anyone's life facts.

Miles regretted nothing and resented no one. This was the result of straightening out, four years ago, in two anonymous groups, Narcotics and Alcoholics, in which his sponsors had called him, respectively, Hardcase and Asshole, and had humbled him out of pot and speed and vodka and self-importance and disregard for the world. His father had given him a choice, gutter or hospital, and he had chosen, with nothing else to cling to, the full treatment. Along the way, he'd relinquished his ambition to be One of the Guys, had finally overcome his vainglorious lack of self-esteem, and had become Miles Derry. He didn't envy the Guys anymore; he knew, for example, that the man lying dead in the arcade was One of the Guys.

His AA sponsor had asked him to make a list of all the guys he hated. This was it:

A Fucking List of All the Fucking Guys I Fucking Resent
Guys who belong to any group or profession
Guys who are "One of the Guys"
Guys with possibilities and willpower
Guys who can spot their main chance and have the guts to take it
Guys who started on my dad's loading dock and became managers
    over me
Guys who reported my using and drinking to my dad and got me
    fired
Guys who make sales quotas and get Bear-Cowboy tickets from my
    dad and get flown down to Dallas for the game by my dad
Guys who pal around with my dad
Guys who drink with my dad
Guys who look like my dad

His father had never called him Miles; he called him Smiles. "Don't smile so much, Smiles. People'll think you're a simpleton—they'll think you're the wrong way—only a woman smiles that much. You're going to go into business. You'll smile at the beginning of a deal, and at the end of a deal, but not during a deal." All of which was curious because Miles could never remember smiling.

The relentless self-exploration of NA and double-A had burnt out most of his anger. Now the list didn't matter as much, and his father didn't matter as much, and nothing at all in Zincville mattered much but Kari, who was so far away she could be anywhere. The past had been extinguished for a long time now, and there was nothing but this moment.

Miles went back into the video arcade.

The officer was curled on his side, legs hairy and knee-bent, rigor mortis erection blue and black now, hands fisted under his chin—they'd moved into that position since death, and this was disturbing to Miles, but not as awful as the face. It was longer and not as dopey as his, but the black mustache and eyebrows and forelock and sharp nose and especially the staring gray eyes were too much like his own. It was his booze-and-drug stare, the catatonic gaze he'd always assumed after the eighth or ninth gin-tonic, the fifth line of coke, the fourteenth joint in fourteen hours. He had frightened himself with this look in any number of over-the-sink mirrors in any number of Illinois tavern toilets over any number of years.

Miles looked away. He saw the man's visored hat on the floor. He picked it up. Hanging it from a finger, he gave it a twirl and tried to think. He paced back into the main part of the store. The police, sure, but that was what he'd done when they'd put the paint in the washer, and when a driver with a broken key had slugged him at the gas station, and these police experiences had been awkward and back-and-forth and wholly unsatisfying. To say nothing of all the times the police had come for *him* (although God knew with full justification)—all nine DUIs, all three pos-sessions, the four months spent on the Zincville campus of the Logan County Jail, and it would've been twelve months if not for his father's lawyers. No, he wasn't going to call the police, not now, not yet.

He gave the hat another twirl. The man's face. It was a message. From the universe to Miles Derry. It was the clearest sign he'd ever received, though the message itself was not yet explicit. Could this be one of those moments? Possibility and willfulness? Coming together, finally, long after he'd given up? He felt excitement washing up the back of his neck, a stiff-ening wave of follicles, a feeling that would make his head and then his body gloriously goose-bumped and confuse his thinking if he didn't stop the sensation soon. All of his hair felt as if it was standing now—he pulled the hat, a half-size too small, tightly onto his head.

Then he went back into the arcade.

Knowing he could replace the wallet at any time, he knelt next to the trouser tangle and felt for the pockets—no keys, he must've come in a cab like most of the sailors—then there was the hard squareness of the wallet, and he wrestled it out, just for a look, just for now. But before he could open it, he noticed another thing, a green duffel bag standing in the corner of the booth. So he slipped the wallet into his back pocket, shoving it down on the latex gloves, stepped into the booth, and brought out the bag by two canvas handles, dragging it over the legs of the dead man and into the bright light of the magazine aisles.

He grunt-hoisted the seabag onto the counter, next to the register. Then he got out the wallet and unfolded it, ignoring credit cards and IDs to thumb open the cash slit. There were fourteen one-dollar bills and six five-dollar bills and four ten-dollar bills and three twenty-dollar bills and a fifty-dollar bill and eight hundred-dollar bills. Miles counted the money three times. It was 994 dollars.

He closed the wallet, with the money still in it, and placed it on the counter. He took the cap off and put it on the counter too. For a long moment he looked at the wallet and the cap and the seabag. They belonged to the dead man. Had belonged. The dead man was nobody now. Miles put the wallet back in his pocket and the cap back on his head and undid the knot at the end of the duffel bag and began pulling items onto the counter. Rolled khaki pants and folded khaki shirts and white briefs and white socks and here was a black leather-bound Bible and here was a manila folder and here was a U.S. passport and here were one, two, three plastic bottles of prescription tablets.

Amyl nitrate. Nitrostat. Nitroglycerine. *Commander James J. Banquette* on all three bottles. Thrifty Drug Store, Norfolk, Virginia.

Miles understood. Commander Banquette, lately of the Atlantic Fleet, a man with a weak heart, had suffered a fatal attack while enjoying the cock-sucking talents of a local queer. Not such a bad way, not really. Hell, it was better than war.

He opened the manila folder. Paper-clipped to the inside was a stiff sheet of stationery with a blue eagle embossed at the top and the words *UNITED STATES NAVY WASHINGTON D.C.* This was the text:

```
PERSUPDEP*ATNAVCOM*WASHDC*051591*06:38*PERNORFVA*XQ72VF9
Cmdr. James J. Banquette
72 Hopwood Lane
McKintry, VA 27292

Commander Banquette:
Per your request for temporary transfer to Seventh Fleet
San Diego you are ordered to report to OOD USS WARREN
HARDING (LST-2282) 0800 hours 6 June 1991 and provide
chaplain services to crew of same for six month duration of
WESTPAC91.
Sincerely,
Adm. J. P. Flowers
COMSUPDEPO WASHDC
```

Miles fingered his mustache. A goddamn chaplain. Well, if that didn't figure.

He took out the wallet and opened it. Besides the cash, there were three credit cards (Visa, Discover, Mastercard) and an ATT calling card and a Virginia driver's license and a naval ID card. Miles took the cards and some photos out and lined them up on the counter to look at them.

The woman was darkly pretty, with straight black hair falling below the border of the photo, and she had bangs stopping just short of smoky black eyes and her nose was small and turned just slightly upward, and her lips were red and full in Mona Lisa mystery. Other photos featured a little girl, three or four years old, a small copy of the mother, but with a face more openly happy, less secretive and knowing, fully smiling, a girl wholly unlike serious-faced three-year-old Kari in her red jumper, the picture in his own wallet. There was a boy, too, tall and bulky-butted and holding the menace of a red Tonka truck over his sister's head. Photo for photo, Miles felt pity. These good simple people did not deserve to know how, precisely, the Reverend Banquette had been transported heavenward.

He looked at the driver's license, seemingly his own face grimacing back at him in all the smudgy glory of overexposed bureaucratic photography, over a birthdate making the man a scant year older than Miles. When he looked at the USN card, he realized that the military photographers were just as bad as the motor-vehicle grunts. That was it, that was what he'd always known, it was a world of grunts, even the guys who were One of the Guys were mostly incompetent grunts, fuck-ups as bad as he was except that most of them hadn't ingested the gallons of booze or fistfuls of pills that he had, and so they were able to retain their positions and advance.

But he hadn't drunk or used in four years. To dramatize this, and to eliminate the smallest possibility of temptation—amyl nitrates would be funfunfun!—he took the medicine bottles back to the rest room and emptied them into the toilet and flushed. Not knowing what to do with the bottles, he brought them back to the duffel bag and stuffed them in.

He was safe, without pills, boozeless. Like One of the Guys, almost. In thirty-three years he'd seen more than plenty, and he not only knew the score, but the score about the score, and the score about the scorekeepers. It was just a matter of becoming One of the Guys and then sitting back and doing zilcho and letting a lot of losers do the work and steadily building one's own little empire. This was dangerous thinking—he knew that—he hadn't thought like this in four years—but he continued with this logic as he adjusted the commander cap on his head.

There were, after all, any number of examples: A) the managers at

Zincville Electroplate, who sat at metal desks and called in subordinates for words and sometimes even toured the labs and put more words in the air and thus sustained their little professional empires; B) the managers at the Laundromats/service stations/supermarkets he'd worked in who sat in offices reading newspapers and occasionally shored up their little empires by making the air a soup of words; C) Jerry Archer of Little Pink Bookstores Inc., an emperor of words and words and words; D) Commander James J. Banquette, USN Chaplain Corps, One of the Guys, the navy not caring about his heart problem—probably only enlisted losers were thrown out for bad hearts—lying dead of a dick-suck in the other room, his Sunday empire of preacher words awaiting a successor.

He went back into the arcade. He looked at his own dead face, wide-open gray eyes. He knelt over it, close to it, unable to name the electric feeling inside him. It was him, it was him, it was himself, this was his time. It was a maniacal moment of self-creation. His hands were agitated, and he tried to control them enough to pull the silver crosses off the collar. He was trembling too much to do it, although he wasn't afraid of touching the cool neck of the corpse. At last he figured out the fasteners on the other side of the collar, and the crosses came free, first one and then the other, and he put them in his shirt pocket. Then he felt for the dog tags. It was a struggle to get the chain unhooked, but he managed, and he put them around his own neck.

He returned to the other room, aware that it would be sunrise in an hour, ninety minutes at the most. He opened the register. He counted the money. Three hundred twenty-seven dollars in bills, and a lot of coins he wouldn't bother with. He stuffed the bills into the chaplain's wallet, then collected all the cards and photos and replaced them. The wallet was so fat with cash it was difficult to fold, but he forced it, then tried putting it in his back pocket, but the gloves were still there so he yanked them out and threw them with satisfaction on the floor.

Miles was moving quickly now. There were three metal barrels of porno novels in the middle of the store. He took the barrels one at a time, rolling them on their edges, into the arcade. Then he tipped them one by one—goddamn they were heavy!—so that the paperbacks landed on the chaplain. Miles had to reach in and help the books come out, there were so many of them, until finally the dead reverend was covered with a hill of titles—*Teenage Lesbians: Breaking Them In* and *Confessions of a Cock Crazy Rickshaw Slut* and *Mom Likes It Both Ways* and many others. It was such a large mound of books that none of the corpse was visible, and they spilled into a few of the cubicles too, which was good.

Miles had given up cigarettes at the same time he gave up pot, so he didn't have matches or a lighter. He went back to the counter area, behind the register, and banged open a lot of drawers until he found a red matchbook with the black outline of a naked woman and the words THE BODY SHOP, HOME OF THE MOST BEAUTIFUL DANCERS IN SAN DIEGO, and there were two matches left in the book, which he hoped would be enough. He wasn't at all worried for Jerry Archer, whose empire, he was certain, was fully insured, nor was he worried about the sirens that would wake the neighborhood, for he suspected that the good Christian white trash and Catholic Chicanos of the area would be happy to see the Little Pink Bookstore become a big red fire.

The perverts of course would be unhappy, but nobody cared about them, and, of course, they were mostly unhappy anyway.

In the arcade he touched the gold diamond of match-fire to the corner of a porno novel, then a second diamond to a porno novel five feet away, and he watched each book begin to shrivel under a broadening sweep of fire. He had an abrupt panic about dental records, then assured himself that no one would know to search McKintry, Virginia, for the files. The hand-sized amber-white flames were moving across four titles now, then eight, and growing arm-length, two living, racing limbs of fire that would soon embrace at the top of the hill of books, and then spread out from there to complete the commander's pyre and sweep into the wooden cubicles and make the arcade a wind tunnel of flames—

get out of here quick

On his way out of the store, running with his hand holding the hat on his head, he stopped to load the duffel bag onto his back, and it was still dark, thank God, and as he struggled along the unpaved block, past the used-car lot, toward his 1984 Mercury Monarch shitbox that still had Illinois plates, which he would have to remove and—what?—throw them into the ocean before abandoning the car somewhere, he was thinking of the time when he had started running, more than three years ago, when Mary Lou had told him she was pregnant. He had been sober and clean for almost a year at that point—his father had taken him back into the company the day Miles graduated from treatment, it was the coldest February in thirty years, and he was working out on the receiving dock, unloading the ceiling-fan escutcheons and the army-shovel flit-handles and the fire-

ladder toggle pins and the bulldozer smokestacks and the helicopter throt-
tle-washers—everything but the industrial kitchen sinks (restaurants used
stainless steel)—that had arrived for electroplating. Because it was too cold
to eat his lunch on the edge of the loading dock, as he preferred to do, and
because he didn't want to be in the cafeteria, since he was embarrassed by
the well-wishing of fellow employees, dozens of whom remembered him
from his get-high-in-the-rest-room-and-throw-up-in-the-office-wastebas-
ket years, he started eating his lunch at an unused desk in a corridor just
outside the chem lab. Mary Lou was quality-control supervisor for the
huge vats of nickel-bath solution into which all metal parts had to be
dipped before the electroplating. She had a break at the same time as his,
and they started talking and joking and eating lunch together and then
dinner at Kane's or Mauger's, and before Miles had the time or sense to
buy rubbers he had his dick in her every night and people noticed them
driving to work together in the mornings.

He threw the seabag into the backseat and fired up the Mercury and
drove up toward Otay Mesa.

Ah, Mary Lou, so exciting: twenty-seven, long brown hair and kind
blue-gray eyes, master's in chemistry, always a lab coat but beneath it a
tight-fitting blouse and hip-and-thigh-defining Levi's, just broken up with
her fiancé, living with two Himalayan cats, responding to the openness and
world-encompassing acceptance of his early sobriety (life had seemed
sharp and brilliant and new to him, yes, he remembered that), and, of
course, she knew he was the president's son. The dirty slushy streets and
snow-covered factory roofs and arctic windchills and lonely clanging and
shrieking freight trains and howling freezing dogs of a February night in
Zincville were not depressing—for the first time in his life were not
depressing—because here came Mary Lou to his small apartment wearing
absolutely nothing at all beneath her ankle-length black fur coat except for
black leather boots, which he could hear crunching in the snow as she
came up the porch steps to his door, and it was something almost like love.

And it might have become love if she hadn't misjudged her ovulations
and he hadn't allowed his exuberance to get ahead of his brains (it was the
first time in five years a woman this exciting had wanted him) and then she
was pregnant. And then his father knew immediately, inexplicably, the way
he knew everything in the town. And then fired him. "I said this was your
last fucking chance. I said that, didn't I? You had to go and knock up the
quality-control supervisor. You have any idea what it's going to cost me to

put in a replacement while she's out having your bastard child? You never think, do you, you always go bumbling along in that half-assed way of yours, you're a completely worthless piece of whale shit, aren't you, Smiles?"

There were no other jobs in Zincville—even the McDonald's, where he had worked a high-school summer and had stolen a hundred dollars for drugs and had been fired—would not hire him, not even when he came to them with an AA chip in one hand and two hundred dollars (the hundred and a dozen years' interest) in the other. He was fighting with Mary Lou. She wanted to keep working till the baby came and stay home for a year— she had some money saved—and then go back to work. Miles wanted an abortion and then wanted the baby and then an abortion and then the baby . . . he had to go to his meetings every day to keep from slipping . . .

. . . He asked her to come west, but no, her family was here, they argued this way and that, a lawyer gave them a formula to calculate child support. He took shit jobs, temporary jobs, and when they ended he took jobs in other towns. He was working farther and farther out of town, he was out of state, he was going farther and farther west, he was still sending that $249 a month, and finally circumstance had pushed him into that corner where California abutted Mexico and the Pacific Ocean, nowhere to turn, cramped-in, kneeling in a video stall to wipe the wall . . .

Miles was almost to the top of the mesa now. It was still dark. In three or four hours, after he had taken a cab to the Thirty-second Street gate of the naval station and reported for chaplain duty aboard the USS *Warren Harding,* he would find the base post office and purchase a USN money order for one thousand dollars and send it to Mary Lou with a note saying, "Go start a college account for the kid."

He parked in a gravelly area near the edge of the mesa. He could see the red lights of Tijuana and the white ones of San Diego and the black endless space of ocean and an evolving fireball where the Little Pink Bookstore would be. He watched for fifteen minutes before the spinning red and purple lights appeared on an otherwise empty freeway below, the sirens tiny in the immense night, and he knew they would be too late to save as much as a condom.

He wouldn't even go back to the shambly hotel where he had a room— nothing there he needed. He would keep moving west—the ocean hadn't stopped him after all—Hawaii, Guam, the Philippines, Hong Kong, Thailand, Australia—the palm trees, bending over paper-white beaches and turquoise lagoons, rustled in his mind. Letters would come from the chaplain's wife, to be sure, perhaps many of them, and he would learn, carefully at first, how to answer them, on a typewriter, without giving himself away—a six-month cruise—

And then? Well, that was a while from now, no need to worry for half a year, maybe he'd meet a native girl in Bali, jump ship, keep moving west in an outrigger canoe.

Watching the porno flame ball, which was surrounded by impotent fire-department lights far below the mesa, Miles knew he could preach. Fire. Hell. Salvation. Drunk off his ass, he'd delivered mock orations in every roadhouse from Zincville to Chicago. He knew he could work for three gods in one for one man in twenty for one day in seven. Words words words words words. For the first time in his life, he would make his way toward it, toward a place in the world, toward possibility and willfulness, toward his own empire of words, toward being One of the Guys.

2

In the naval yard, in the summer haze of a San Diego morning, Miles, wearing the uniform of a commander, silver crosses on the collar, picked a path around the gray barrels and the gray forklifts and the gray USN buses and the Quonset huts with their gray corrugated walls and the blue control cabs of the black overhanging cranes, toward the gray hull of his goal, the USS *Warren Harding*. He could just make out the boxlike prow, 2282 in black numerals, square-blocked.

Getting through the gate had been exhilaratingly simple. With the seabag over his shoulder, he'd followed a line of men, officers in khaki and enlisted in blue denim, all of them with their wallets out and open, IDs ready. He took out and opened the chaplain's wallet and continued toward a boy, standing in a little checkpoint cabin, who was saluting, with a look of overwhelmed concentration, man after man, or rather wallet after wallet. Miles held the wallet out as he passed, and the boy saluted it and he was in. He'd asked an enlisted man for directions to the PO, and the man was happy to help, calling him "chaplain" and "sir" and even drawing him a map, showing the way to the PO and the *Harding*, on the back of a cocktail napkin that said CRAZY EDDIE'S BOOBY HATCH and bore the silhouette of a nude dancing woman. Miles bought stamps and stationery and the thousand-dollar money order and penned Mary Lou a carefully ambiguous note saying that he'd had some luck and to start the college account for Kari.

As he walked slowly among the fast-moving sailors who carried rope coils or gear boxes or blue metal briefcases—frantic with their obscure, last-morning preparations—about a hundred feet from the ship, Miles was close enough to survey the length of the *Harding,* and saw that both ends were square, that the ship was a gray shoebox with an upcropping of port-holed superstructure and a couple of gray smokestacks and—beyond his understanding—a pair of diagonally rising metal arms, each about ten feet wide and rising high over the prow and then over the water. He felt a sharp panic in his chest. He had never imagined a thing like this ship, and hadn't the first idea of what it was. Turn back? To what? Accusations, explanations, jail. He allowed the seabag to slip off his back, like the weight of the dead man himself. Too anxious to go farther or turn back, he just stood there, negatively magnetized against past and future.

An enlisted kid carrying what looked like a small radio with a plastic dial and black metal knobs stopped and said, "Can I help you find something, sir?"

"I'm the new chaplain," he said hopelessly, "on this ship."

"There's the quarterdeck up thataway." He pointed to a long gangway, rails on both sides, that led up to the front of the ship, where two men in khaki stood with clipboards and many others in blue denim were busy carrying boxes away from a large messy stack. "Officers have been getting lost all day."

"We're not very smart, are we?"

The kid, leaving quickly with his radiolike thing, smirked back at him as though the joke were not only as old as the navy but also a well-worn fact.

He hoisted the seabag and marched toward and then up the gangway, feeling, alternately, like a clever thief with the goods on his back and a condemned man with his deeds on his back.

At the top, on the quarterdeck, an officer with a tan face and a sharp-visored cap and, sticking out of his mouth, a pungently burning pipe, passed a clipboard from one hand to the other and saluted and said, "Fresh meat. Five new officers and none of them have ever been to a Filipino whorehouse. We're gonna rock, welcome to FUCKPAC-91. You're the new"—glance at collar—"*chaplain?*"—quick inspection of clipboard— "Commander Banquette? Well, the goddamn chaplain, that's my luck, forget I said anything. Got your orders around?" He was still saluting.

Miles made a hasty attempt at a salute, careful to keep his fingers and thumb straight, as he dropped the seabag on the deck. Although he was confident that everyone was too busy to monitor small deficiencies in anything as routine as a salute, he was worried about his orders—were they, in fact, the letter in the manila folder? If not, wouldn't they be somewhere in the seabag?

"My orders," he repeated, a switchblade of fear springing open in his gut, and he undid the bag and found the folder and handed it (a plausible mistake, he hoped, if this were the wrong item) to the pipe-smoking officer, who opened it for a glance at the letter and handed it back, then thumbed his way through the sheets on his clipboard until he found the right one and made a check mark on it.

The officer grinned at Miles and offered his hand. "I'm the DISBO, usually I'm down in the disbursement office helping the squids bounce their checks for my poker games, but I've pulled OOD like a motherfuck all week. Well, excuse me."

"Jim," Miles introduced himself.

"Ever ridden an LST, Reverend Jimbo?"

"No," he said, wondering if it were true for the dead man.

The grin widened. "Well, you'll be riding this one. Flat-bottom boat, forty-five-degree rolls, three hundred jarheads and three hundred of us, are you ready for it?"

"I don't know. I hope so."

Setting the clipboard on a wooden podium, crossing his arms, the DISBO said, "Ben Franklin's been in church more recently than I have, so you probably won't be seeing me at services, but the last chaplain we had was one hell of a poker player—maybe we can get up a game sometime in the wardroom."

"Maybe so," said Miles. He'd learned poker from his father, one of the best in Illinois.

"I don't mean for money, of course."

"Of course not."

"That'd be against regulation. But if you lose enough, I'll just keep your paycheck. That's one of the privileges of running the disbursement office." He laughed, and Miles made himself laugh with him. Then the DISBO said, "I'm just kidding. I know how you chaplains like to play cards and drink. If you ever need a cash advance or need a shot from my private stock, just let me know. Our skipper looks the other way on a lot of the slack-ass shit that goes on around here."

"That's good," said Miles.

"Welcome aboard, Reverend. If you're a true Christian, you'll forgive everything you see over the next six months. Atkinson, throw that fucking cigarette over the side and show the commander to his stateroom."

An enlisted man, moving so fast that Miles didn't see his face, just the back of a blue denim shirt with the seabag suddenly on it, started away and he followed. It was a narrow strip of deck with the superstructure to one side and the lifelines to the other, and when he looked down it was a long way to the dock and even longer to a dark ribbon of water. Under his feet there were cables and ropes and black tubing to be careful about. He could hear machinery whirring with a pitched insanity and he could smell diesel and oil and an aroma, shipwide and delicious, of fried chicken—somebody cooking for six hundred. Enlisted men hurried toward him and around him and then the man he was following stopped at a hatch door, released it by pulling down on a handle that was like a metal club against the breast of the door, and Miles followed him in. They went down a passageway with a green tile deck and gray walls festooned with red all-metal axes and red fire extinguishers and brown coils of cable and countless up-and-down and diagonal pipes. Then they climbed a ladder that was almost straight up and looked as though it were constructed from an Erector set and then up another and another and Miles was careful not to slip, hands on the rails. He wondered at the man now six and eight and ten feet above him, flying away in black polished shoes without using the handrails, eighty pounds of duffel bag riding like nothing on his back.

Finally they turned up a passageway stencil-sprayed OFFICERS' COUNTRY. There were gray doors with shiny brass doorknobs right and left, and one of them on the right was open. The man, whose face he still hadn't seen, said, "This must be you," and led him in.

And dropped the seabag and turned and left and went facelessly down the passageway, saying "Welcome aboard, sir."

Miles shut the door and stood with his back against it. All at once he was exhausted, his arms and shoulders feeling empty in his shirt, his feet aching from climbing all the ladders, even though the dead man's shoes were a comfortable half-size too large. The bookstore job had required Miles to be a day sleeper, and he was past his bedtime; he imagined he could stay awake only long enough to survey his quarters.

Everything was gray—the metal wardrobe running deck-to-ceiling with its twin locked doors, the naked bunk-bed frame, the skeletal arm-chair with its dun-colored butt cushion, the rectangular ventilation shaft and pipes of all diameters running across the ceiling, the industrial tile of the deck, the bulkheads—a gray metal world—

—no porthole—

To his right there was a dark doorless entrance, and when he took a look, he saw it was the head, with a shower cubicle and a sink and a toilet—all stainless steel except for the toilet seat, which was black plastic. He was happy to note that nothing in his metallic suite appeared to have been electroplated. He was standing in the head, cock in hand, anticipating the pleasant ring of his urine against the steel toilet bowl, when somebody knocked.

"Uh-oh." He put it away for later and went to the door. *Military police, so soon, so soon, military police.* He bit his lip, then opened the door with a trembling hand.

"Officer of the Deck confirmed you were aboard, Commander Banquette," said a white-stubbled man in khaki, a man with a tanned skull face, a man older, certainly, than Miles's father. "I'm Chief Ditchfield, wardroom crew. Welcome to the *Harding*." He had the kind of voice lowered and thinned by forty years of cigarettes. "I brought you your keys." With a liver-spotted hand he held them out, two little brass-colored keys on a ring, and Miles took them.

"Thank you."

"Breakfast for all duty sections is oh-six-hundred and oh-seven-hundred, lunch at eleven-hundred and twelve-hundred, dinner at seventeen-thirty and eighteen-thirty, midrats at oh-one-hundred hours, and the captain likes his officers on time. You met the CO?"

"No, not yet." Miles was studying the little keys, wondering what they opened.

"Well, he ain't exactly a religious man, but he'll be wanting to meet you at chow tonight. He gives a big talk to all the senior officers and JOs at dinner the first night under way for WESTPAC. It don't matter which one you go to, seventeen-thirty or eighteen-thirty hours, it's the same speech each time. Much as your sermons, I would suspect." Ditchfield smiled at last, his tobacco-brown teeth looking like seasoned wood.

Miles laughed deliberately. "You've known a lot of chaplains."

"Only ones are any good are the Mormons, they take it serious. The others are just—you a Mormon?"

"No," said Miles. He didn't know what he was, he realized with a fearful pang.

"I thought maybe you was a Mormon, they all have mustaches, black ones like yours, for some reason. I put my foot in it, and you'll have to forgive me. Seeing it's your job to."

Miles laughed again, though Ditchfield wasn't smiling now. Then Miles said, "You've been in the service long?"

"Since the war."

"The war?"

"I was one of MacArthur's valets on the *Missouri,* Japanese surrender, got a framed picture over my rack. Your sleep gear's in that dresser, I'll send a boy later to set it up."

"Well—you know, I just got in. I've been up all night—I mean, been traveling all night from, uh, Virginia. I was thinking of maybe getting a nap—you think I could set it up myself, and get some rest? I mean, do you think that would be all right?"

Ditchfield shrugged. "First thing a chaplain does," he said, "is take a nap, that's always the way. Suit yourself, Commander." And he smiled again, those long tobacco-brown teeth. "I'll wake you up for dinner, sir, so's you won't be missing the captain's talk."

Miles had been holding his pee throughout this conversation and was grateful when the old man was gone. Now, urinating loudly against the steel toilet, he told himself never to act deferentially around men of lower rank. He didn't know how many levels a commander stood over a chief, but he guessed it was a lot.

In twenty minutes he'd hung up the dead man's uniforms—and a white-collared preacher suit—in the wardrobe and filled the wall drawers with socks and underwear and prayer book and Bible and address book and stationery and computer discs and framed diploma (Bachelor of Divinity, Maryland Methodist College) and shoes and shoe polish (a round tin with a raised-relief anchor and a ring of words on the lid: SHIPSHAPE SHOE POLISH—*A MIRRORED SHINE FROM PORT TO STARBOARD AND FROM KEEL TO MAST IN WAR AND PEACE SINCE 1812*). He'd thrown sundry sundries into the metal cabinet over the metal sink. He'd found a thin rolled mattress tied with string and with it some sheets and a blanket and pillow, and he'd assembled them on the lower bunk, which had a detachable steel guardrail, designed to keep a man from rolling out of his rack, he decided as he climbed over it naked into bed.

He was so limply exhausted that he had only a moment's inclination to notice that he was enclosed tightly on three sides: mattress beneath him, bulkhead to his right, the long gray shelf of the overhead rack just twelve inches over his nose. But it was heaven. It was sleep.

Although not one of his best. Yes, it was a seductive, lulling kind of falling-away from the world, a rocking sensation taking him all the subconscious way to his mother's arms in Chicago, before they moved to Zincville and before his father was anyone, a time that Miles couldn't recall when awake—but this rocking was also disturbing, for it soothed him only to jangle him, calling forth splintered dreams, images caught hideously and without narrative in a kind of overexposed hot white stop-action clarity: a red erection poking out of the wall; his own face, open-eyed, dead on the floor of the video arcade; a mound of porno books and a small fire and the threat of a larger fire and then a very large fire indeed, viewed from a height that made his legs panic-twitch—the fire was another wall between him and Kari, another wall upon the walls between him and Mary Lou. He'd done something too horrid to think about, and yet there it was, the fire and the face, the fire, the face. It was like the nagging half-dreams he used to have when he took pills and drank. *You did something awful last night, here's a picture of part of it, something terrible, really ghastly, and when you wake up it won't go away, it'll just get bigger and fuller and you'll have it in color and it'll be your inescapable life.*

And then his eyes were open, and there was a gray metal shelf twelve inches over his eyes, and he realized that the world was moving.

Moving—the room was moving, this entire hermetic ship, not merely up and down and side to side, not in straight lines, but zigging up-left and zagging down-right, as though passing not over water but over boulders and rocks of all possible irregular surfaces. The metallic components of his stateroom were creaking and more things were creaking out in the passageway and updecks and belowdecks, as though the ship were straining against contradictory forces to keep itself from coming apart. Aside from this universal creaking, there were no other sounds but the buzzing of the yellow-grimed fluorescent tube running between two pipes on the ceiling, the grinding of engines far below, and, nearby, a door going bang-shut, creak-open, bang-shut. He could've been the only person alive.

"You act like you're the only person alive," Mary Lou had actually, finally, concluded in one of the last arguments, and it had hurt him as badly as anything, because he was trying, wasn't he, he was trying to work the steps of NA and double-A and be honest and not self-centered—but he didn't want a baby! Or rather, he did! It was a big deal, drunk or sober, and now that his father had fired him, what could he do but go wherever he could and do whatever he must in order to send those support checks? There were men who did less.

The ship moved down-left, upward-right.

He wondered what she would think when she got the money order. What she would think if she knew. He had done an awful thing, and if he were unlucky it would put him in federal prison, but this was his way, at last, to make himself into something. "Rationalization, Asshole!" he could hear his NA sponsor say. And yet, he wasn't entirely selfish, Mary Lou had been wrong about that. He was protecting Mrs. Banquette and her children from a dead cock sticking out of the wall, and he was helping Kari and Mary Lou, and he would find a way to do this job, to help the men on this ship. Although it was true that he was no minister, it was also true that he'd gone through his bottomless personal hell and he'd come back, and he knew that the world wasn't just earth and ocean, not just the minerals and elements seasoning the land, not just the winds and tides moving the water, but a metaphysical place where the personal will, acting on absurdity and tragedy, was the only thing defining a man.

Metaphysical your ass, Hardcase, you'll never fool anybody. They're gonna come for you, yeah, get scared, get real scared, because you deserve to be.

He had time to torture himself with as many disaster variations as he liked, and he did so, augmenting them point by point until he was able to console himself with a parody: Jerry Archer and the San Diego Police, toeing their way through the ashes of the Little Pink Bookstore, would of course assume the charred skeleton was his, and hire investigators to trace his crooked path back across America to Zincville and inform Mary Lou that he'd died in the early morning hours of June 6, and she'd tell them about the money order, and they'd call it up on their Super Postal Cop Computer and find that it was time-dated *three hours and twenty-seven minutes* after the last jar of K-Y jelly had exploded in the flaming bookstore, and the navy postal clerk would of course remember him instantly and in flawless detail: "He was wearing chaplain's crosses, but he didn't look like no goddamn U.S. Navy chaplain to me, no siree sir, that man was an *impostor,* I could tell from his shoes, they looked like they hadn't been shined in three or four hours," and the Seventh Fleet would be alerted and come steaming after him and he'd be arrested for the homosexual murder of an officer-minister-family man and tried under the Law of the Sea and convicted, and strapped to the hull, at the waterline, where the salt water would eat into his eyes and the barnacles would skin him raw and hundreds of little fish would pick at his armpits and genitals—

After an unknowable length of time, there was a *tatatat* which startled him into sending his forehead painfully against the undershelf of the top rack and he said to the door, "Yes? Who's there?" although he knew with a beatless heart that it was the military police with an impersonating-an-officer warrant—he'd been an idiot to think it was doable, he saw that now, and military prison would be far worse than county jail . . .

"Dinner's in fifteen minutes," said Chief Ditchfield through the door. "Just so you don't miss the CO's little speech, Reverend."

"Thank you!" For not being the military cops.

He climbed out of the rack and fell back in and realized he would have to learn to walk against the rising turning swinging dropping deck. He climbed out again. He moved his hips and feet to find his balance, then began hop-dancing into the commander's uniform, first the pants and then the shoes, then the shirt and the cap, falling backward into the chair a few times. Then he went to the head and had a look at himself in a steel-rimmed square of mirror just large enough to hold his face, and decided he had enough black stubble, when combined with his mustache, to make him look Turkish, so he took off the cap and the shirt and got out the reverend's shaving cream and razors and mustache scissors and did a quick tidying, dancing against the ocean to keep his face in the mirror, nicking his Adam's apple and making the left end of his mustache perhaps too short. He toweled himself and put the shirt and cap back on and went out the stateroom door, entering a maze of rocking passageways, wondering how to get to dinner and frightened of being late and frightened of what would happen even if he were on time. He walked with his hands out, hitting the right bulkhead and the left and the right.

The passageway turned left, and there were some bulletin boards, and then it turned left again. He saw a pair of officers, hatless, going through a door. He took off his hat and followed them into the wardroom mess.

A long paneled room—officers sitting and standing around a white-clothed table glittering with symmetrical placements of embossed plates and stemmed water glasses and shining knives and forks and spoons and steel-ringed fluted napkins, and everyone was talking. There was a group speaking and approaching from his left, toward the table. He did a quick-step against the rising deck to avoid falling into the passing men—they'd come from the lounge end of the room: blue vinyl couches and chairs, bulky, roll-resistant furniture set in a rectangle with a television bolted to the wall in one corner. His eye swept the length of the room. At the other end there was a long opening in the paneling, very much like the cafeteria counters at Zincville Electroplate, and through the opening he could see enlisted men moving steaming bins of food. He smelled chicken and it was so delicious and he hadn't eaten in so long that his stomach went weak with hunger.

"Chaplain, you're third from the captain's right," said an enlisted man with a clipboard. Miles realized that they would be sitting according to rank and that he was senior to most of these officers, for it was a long table and he would be only three seats from the most important chair. The enlisted man, with a weary but patient expression that told of directing lost and helpless officers all day, pointed out the chaplain's place setting with a thrust of the clipboard.

To get there, he had to pass between men already seated and a row of portholes, one of which he stopped at for a look. It was the bright-hazed sky and the faint ocean-horizon of the Southern California coast in early summer, and when he looked down—straight down a rising-falling, slip-ping-rolling, plated-riveted wall of ship—he had to fight for balance to keep his face in the porthole, but was able to see that the ocean was a purple violent animal made of seamless waves that covered an area exactly the size of the sky but would never be tall enough to harm it, hating instead the man-made can called the *Warren Harding*. The waves exploded against the sides and bottom of the ship now and now and now, leaving white foam streaking down the metal wall as they retreated, then crashing back. It was making him dizzy, and twisting his grumble-hungry stomach, and he was afraid of the eyes he felt at his back, so he decided to sit down, but before doing so, he scanned the ocean one more time, farther out, and discovered the black silhouettes of four more ships. He was in a flotilla.

He pulled out a heavy blue vinyl chair and seated himself with his cap on his knee (no, none of the others had brought theirs, he must assimilate a thousand details). The other men were settling around him, conversations dying, and he examined with pleasure the stemmed water glass and silver-ringed blue napkin roll and his knife and fork and spoons, all of which were lined up with naval precision to the sides of his china plate with its blue trim capped by a blue anchor pointing parallel with the utensils.

Looking around the table, making careful eye contact with those who were willing, nodding hello when they did, he saw that most of them wore khaki while four or five wore green. He had the guilty feeling of not belonging among these men, who were welcoming him with their earnest nodding faces; he was afraid. Each of them appeared, in his open convivial way, to be One of the Guys. This was his father's factory, male and metallic, set upon the water, with the added variation of uniforms and a slanting-dropping-rising deck. He had never fit in—how could he here? And yet, they were accepting him without hesitation: he hadn't had a chance to fuck up. The old Miles could fuck up, but the new Miles—Jim Banquette—mustn't fuck up because the penalty this time would be—don't think of it—

The smell of fried chicken was rumbling his stomach and dizzying his mind. Or was it the movement of the ship? As they waited, there was little for Miles to consider but the irregular rolls and slanting corrections of the ship, movements that, if he closed his eyes, were once again lulling to him. He compared them, with dreamy satisfaction, to the miserable roller-coastering of the fishing yacht of his father's wealthy friends in the Gulf of Mexico when he was fifteen, when they'd ordered him endlessly to bring up beers from the bar and mix martinis, and his father had said, "Pay your dues, Smiles, this here's a working vacation—*you* work, and *we're* on vacation." All he'd wanted was to sit with his ears between his knees and his face in a bucket. With an abrupt feeling of command, he knew that the *Harding* was a larger vessel than that fishing yacht—he'd have to be alert when walking, but wasn't afraid of getting sick.

A door opened, and before he could see who it was, everybody was standing. By the time he was up, a hoarse voice was saying "Sit down, sit down, sit down," and they did. The captain, hurrying to his end of the table, was a tall, pallid-faced man with breasts and a potbelly and a thick stand of white hair that was combed—arbitrarily and haphazardly, as though it had no natural part—mostly to the right.

"Many of you who've worked with me before know I pick and choose from the wardroom code—never stand, but do ask permission of ranking man to join or leave." He stopped at the galley counter to incline his head and say, to no specific person, "I don't know, ten-fifteen minutes, boys," and there being, of course, no opposing view, he knuckle-rapped the counter and took his seated position at the head of the table, a man of fifty or fifty-five, with owl-ringed eyes, smiling with trained professional cheer, the arbitrary part in his white hair having shifted slightly, Miles thought, as the speech commenced:

"Well we've got some new faces and some old faces and we'll get to the introductions after I've given the overview. The Fifty-seventh Amphibious Ready Group pulled out of SDNS at zero-nine-hundred hours, five ships, three thousand marines and four thousand navy, twenty-nine helos and seventeen AAVs and five floating parking garages full of armored vehicles—yes, a jeep did break loose on the tank deck about an hour ago and ran over one of your corporals"—he nodded at a green-uniformed marine sitting next to Miles—"but he's all right, just a tire track on the back of the head, did more damage to the jeep I think"—laughter—"and that's the last goddamn accident we're going to have on this WESTPAC, you're going to guarantee me that. This gal's the one Groucho Marx was talking about, the one with the flat bottom, so we're going to secure everything that's not smaller than a nail clipper, and you'd better secure those too. A couple of WESTPACs ago one of our hull technicians was working on his big toe when we had a forty-five-degree roll and the instrument took off his eyelid."

"Ouch, sir," somebody said.

"So let's leave the mishaps to the carriers in this man's navy, to the bacon boys who step behind an F-15 at the wrong moment. This is going to be a long deployment, and we're understaffed in a few departments, and I can't spare the manpower, especially with a couple of R&Rs scheduled for Sodom and Gomorrah." Laughter, laughter. "What I'm saying applies to the mail, too, which they're going to airlift to us from Alaska just before we pass the Aleutians on the Great Circle—"

"The Aleutians, sir?" said one of the marines.

The captain blinked three times, not with annoyance, Miles thought, but with confusion at having his arbitrary thoughts interrupted. "Yes," he continued, "the Aleutians, the Great Circle—you have to go north and south to go west—you marines are apparently unaware that the Earth is round." Laughter from everyone. "I could show you on a globe, a straight line from San Diego to Okinawa passes two hundred miles off the Aleutians, so I hope you brought your thermals." He paused again, licked his lips, found his place: "*The mail*. We always get a few Dear Johns, most of them go to the marines for some reason—sailor boys aren't quite that monogamous, I would guess—and the temptation is for that marine to have a cleaning accident with his M-16, even though no real marine, no real man, would clean his rifle with his mouth . . ." The captain was lost. He blinked. Then: "So you officers—navy and marine—give those poor bastards a lecture, I mean all your duty sections before each mail call, tell them the good Lord has made a special lady just for them, has her waiting in their future, some such crap like that, the chaplain can help you, I can't afford to lose any personnel to the adolescent emotional suicide syndrome."

"Any of you seen the paperwork on suicide?" said a toad-faced naval officer sitting at the captain's right. "Weighs more than the body."

"Now," said the captain, "now—we're going to have a good cruise. Battle-ready at every waking and sleeping moment, that's our mission, to be able to respond wherever and whenever our commander in chief may require, but we'll have plenty of time to wriggle our toes in the sand, too. One-day stop at Okinawa, the Philippines for a week, Thailand for a few days—Pattaya Beach, Thailand, by the way, is the home of the black clap, completely resistant to penicillin, I want zippers *welded shut* in that fucking place, down the ranks—then maybe on to Hong Kong or Singapore, Australia for sure—unless the Persian Gulf heats up again. Ship's movement is classified, I remind you, so no letters or telegrams or portside telephone calls betraying our location—you don't really want your wife to know you're calling from the Jacuzzi Room in Caligula's Orgy Palace in beautiful downtown Bangkok, anyway."

Though the other men laughed, and though Miles wanted to fit in, he kept quiet, trying to be the proper chaplain.

"Now, to the naval staff: when these marines are having onshore maneuvers for a week or two at a time, up to the backs of their shaved necks in Filipino mud, things're going to get real quiet on this boat, but that doesn't mean we're going to get lax. I don't care if you're out scrogging whores till zero-seven-fifty-nine on a Monday morning, you're at your goddamn duty-station at oh-eight-hundred, even if you're still wearing the dingle glove." He put the flat of an index finger on the bag under each eye and rubbed, then rubbed some more, distractedly, as though he hadn't been talking at all for the past five minutes and they were merely waiting for the food. Then, without warning: "Introductions!" and he started with the man on his right. "This frog-faced gentleman is the XO, Steve Jarvis," and so on around the table, giving names and bantering with each man about physical characteristics, some of which brought laughter. When he was halfway round the table, when he had described the supply officer's potbelly and the disbursement officer's pipe-stained breath and the chief engineer's left-eyebrow twitch and the doctor's anemic thinness and the lawyer's slanted nose, he stopped to say, "That's the way I like to introduce people, if you make fun of them they'll be remembered," and he continued around, discoursing on the puniness of the navy JOs compared to the muscularity of the marine JOs (Miles couldn't figure out what JOs meant—jerkoffs? junior officers?), the lip wart of the quality-assurance officer, the tiny ears of the marine CO, the mustache of the chaplain—

"Now about that black mustache. You're not a goddamn Mormon, are you?"

"No sir."

"Thank God! Those Mormons they send us never let us have any fun. What's your denomination?"

Miles was frightened. *Don't pile your pants, Hardcase.* He remembered the dead man's diploma. "Methodist, sir."

"Methodist? Shoot pool? We had a Methodist three WESTPACs ago who cleaned out the entire Subic O Club. We ran out of money and had to pay him off in drinks, on our goddamn tabs."

"I don't drink, sir."

"A chaplain who doesn't drink? You sure you're not a Mormon?" Laughter all around; he could feel the burn in his cheeks. "You take your mission seriously, that's good, you work for God."

"Yes sir."

"Only one problem with that."

"Yes sir?"

"On the *Warren Harding,* I'm God."

"Yes sir," Miles said and was again surprised and embarrassed at the eruption of laughter, then realized it wasn't the competitive kind that dominated his father's factory, but warm and comradely.

The captain left him alone, went on to the blond overweight communications officer and the chinless security officer, then toss-turned his head—so that his half-standing white hair acquired yet another part—toward the galley and said, "We're ready for the grease parade," and winked at nobody specific, whereupon a door in the wall swung open and out came blue-denim sailors in a line, carrying coffeepots and serving tongs and steaming bins of chicken and vegetables and gravy. Though the ship fell and rolled and straightened and shuddered, nothing fell out of the bins, and soon a boy was asking Miles, "Coffee, sir?" and filling the blue-anchor-embossed cup, and another was tonging a golden-fried wing and a breast and a drumstick onto his plate, and others came asking which vegetables he wanted and he chose green beans and mashed potatoes with white gravy. Then everybody was waiting for the captain, who at last said, "Padre?"

Miles realized with an electric jolt to his heart that he was being addressed.

"Yes sir?"

"I run an efficient ship, so this is the first and last time I'll require it, but I think it's appropriate for our first night of deployment."

It took a moment for Miles to understand, with a quick drying of the throat, what the captain meant. Looking around the table he saw that everyone, including the captain—his hair parted along a new line—was bowing his head, and with reckless courage, Miles pressed his hands together and closed his eyes, knowing it was possible only with eyes closed, and, feeling slowly for the words, began: "Dear Lord our God in Heaven . . . we ask You . . . to accept our thanks . . . our gratitude for this food . . . the food we are about to eat . . . and . . . and we thank you for allowing us to be on this ship . . . I mean . . . we ask you to give us strength . . . to serve you, and to do our duty on . . . uh, this deployment . . . and we pray for the knowledge of Your will for us, over the next six months . . . Amen."

Everyone said "Amen," and a few men crossed themselves, and then everybody was eating and talking—everyone except Miles, who, hungry as he was, could only stare at his food in a sweat, hugely relieved that he'd succeeded, yet at the same time not believing it, as though he'd jumped over a hole in the ground only a moment after noticing it. Gradually he relaxed. It was okay. The food was here, and it smelled good, and nobody could stop him from eating. He started in. Yes, yes. He was ravenous. He ate with his hands, with his fork, with his fingers, in a delirium of hunger and fear and relief and satisfaction, until there was nothing left but bread and butter and coffee and an expanding feeling of triumph.

"Second helping, sir?"

"Thank you."

More than triumph. It was *the life*, he could be served and eat like this for six months, for six and sixty years, no problem. His father had always said This-is-a-great-country, and Miles had always retorted Yeah-for-hot-shits-like-you, but now he could see—feel—what the man had meant, was aware of the country's promise even as he drifted farther away with every roll of the ship.

He thought of his years on the outside, the poverty and jails, the alcohol and cocaine and marijuana—the happy but stoic time of getting sober—the wanderings and crap jobs and the still sometimes maddening desire to drink or get stoned. He remembered that during the first year his toothpaste had inexplicably tasted like gin, no matter how many times he changed brands. There were a thousand absurdities, and now all of it had been washed away into the harmless insipid past, and an enlisted man was saying, "Chaplain, we have vanilla or rocky road or chocolate ice cream or apple pie for dessert tonight."

"Is it available à la mode?"

"À la mode, yes sir, what flavor?"

The only thing missing, he thought as he sat back after his coffee and dessert, was a cigar.

And then there *was* a cigar, an open boxful of them proffered by the man sitting next to him. As he selected one and passed the box along, men were thanking the captain for this first-night-underway gift. Miles, taking a matchbook off the table and lighting his first cigar since his abortive college career of fourteen years ago, abandoned his private thoughts to listen indolently to the conversations around him.

"You know that wardroom chief? Ditchfield? Gives me the creeps."

"He must have a million years' worth of NAVRETBENs. Why the hell doesn't he cash out?"

"It's for the LBFMs in Subic."

"LBFMs?" said one of the JOs.

"Little Brown Fucking Machines, kid, you'll meet your share." Laughter. "It's the only way an old pencildick like the Ditchman can scrog." Laughter. "Seriously, those little girls say he's quite a CDSOB, cockdriving son-of-a-bitch."

"MINPAC could use a ward CPO like that."

"NAVWARCOL too."

"NATOPS at fifteen-forty-five, by the way."

"Get your NATRI chit from NAVPERS?"

"NAVORDFAC intercepted."

"What time are those NCOs PTing?"

"Zero-four-hundred."

"I think that SN-3 will make LDO."

"You know, CONVEX is up in two weeks. You think COMTACRON COOP has a chance?"

"Like hell."

"Got an RDO chit from FICPACFAC on the CONVEX."

"That so?"

"I wouldn't bullshit a bullshitter."

The marine officer sitting next to Miles, a triangular-faced man about his own age, with dark hair (short, but not buzz-cut) and a pair of dark eyebrows molded in a perpetually inquisitive slant, as though all of life, not just this conversation, were a riddle to him, turned and asked through the cigar smoke, "Ever been on a T before?"

This is it, thought Miles, his heart ready to split open with anxiety—he would have to confess everything. He muttered hopelessly, "A T?"

"An LST."

LST. Okay, ah. This ship, LST-2282. "No," he said, not caring if it were true for Commander James J. Banquette, and anyway who would know? "I've never been on an LST before."

"That's too bad," said the marine. "I was hoping you'd be able to explain some of this T terminology to a dumb marine like me. I can't understand a damn thing these people are saying."

"I guess we're in the same boat."

"You might say that. Makes me wish I'd brought my DICNAVAB to dinner."

"Your DICNAVAB?"

"*Dictionary of Naval Abbreviations,* Naval Institute Press. I'll loan you mine, Reverend, if you start to feel really lost."

"Thank you."

"I'm Major Frank Lebedeen, by the way, marine CO." An extended hand.

Miles moved his cigar to his other hand and they shook. "Commander Jim Banquette," he said. "Chaplain."

"That's not a bad billet, you'll never have the watch, work on Sundays and as needed, probably never share a stateroom. That's not bad at all."

"No, it's not too bad."

"Now me, I'm responsible for every marine on this ship. Professionally, personally, even spiritually. I've never had this much responsibility before—I was on a few WESTPACs when I was a lieutenant, but mostly I've been pushing a pencil in San Diego, I've never been CO, I missed the Gulf War and all that. So I'll be coming to you for help when I—when I need your expertise with—with people issues."

"Of course," said Miles, relieved and agitated, once again, at a successful interaction. "I'll be happy to help."

The door from the passageway opened and then slammed, from a roll of the ship, before anyone could come in, and then opened again, and the person who came into the mess—a determined lurch into the room, against the incline of the deck—the person who regarded them with pop-rounding eyes, as though not expecting to see anyone, was unlike anyone Miles could've predicted—was wearing a white T-shirt and a pair of tight blue shorts—was a person with red-brown hair falling past the shoulders—was saying "Oh" in soft surprise—was causing stillness and silence—was a woman.

"I thought it was six-thirty," she said. "Captain," she added.

"Next feeding is in ten minutes," said the captain without looking up from side-forking his apple pie.

"Oh, excuse me," and she reopened the door, and the roll of the ship carried her out, and the door slammed. Miles was so amazed that he didn't notice the ash until it fell off his cigar and landed hotly in his lap, where he brushed it off, and then returned his gaze uselessly to the door, which was still closed.

Nobody resumed speaking. Discomfort pollinated the air as men finished desserts and drank down coffee and mashed cigars into heavy glass ashtrays and said, "Permission to leave," and got up, dropping napkins onto the table and going one by one out the door—after the woman, Miles couldn't help thinking—then decided they were returning to the pitching compartments that required their administration, for they moved with the resentful quickness of men who had work.

Miles knew if he were One of the Guys he'd be feeling the same tension, but as aware of it as he was, it didn't churn within him as it must in the others. It had been four years since Mary Lou, and there'd been no women since. Sex, to him, meant the grunting-exhaling sounds coming from behind the doors of the video arcade, sex was the odors of Lysol and Windex, sex was a puddle he wiped away with sponges and mops, sex was a dead thing, sex was a matter that made him wonder if he would ever again feel like other men.

Unable to continue sitting with his thoughts in the woman's electric field, which remained in the emptying, rocking room, he said, "Permission to leave," presumably to the captain but actually to no one, as the others had done, and went with a feeling of loneliness and unease out the door, putting the cap on his head, step balancing step balancing step across the moving deck. He found an open hatchway filled with a sliding picture of limitless purple ocean, and stepped outside to stand with his hands on a lifeline cable taut between girders, alone with himself and the sea wind and the pinking sky and the glittering mauve water fifty feet straight down and fifty miles straight out whichever way he turned his eyes. *I'm at sea, and not only that, but I'm at sea,* and he grimly enjoyed the truth of the riddle. He became aware that the ship was not merely being hurled boxlike by the salt-winded muscular ocean, but possessed, deep belowdecks, a powerful heart and lungs. He realized he'd been hearing the mechanical workings for hours. Their force was driving the ship in a real and relentless and somehow straight direction over the loose skin of the tossing animal sea, and no matter how hard the ocean slapped them side-to-side and up-down-up, they would always be safe, they would never be lost.

"Here's an extra one," somebody said right next to him, and he thought the speaker meant *him*. The fright almost sent him overboard. Oh, it was the marine, Major Lebedeen with the triangular face and questioning eyebrows and nearly flat head with caesarlike bangs—Miles figured only the enlisted marines were jarheads—and he was holding out a blue paperback white-stenciled with the word DICNAVAB.

Miles took it. "Thanks."

Hands on the lifeline, they looked out at the sky, which was turning the color of an open watermelon. Then Major Lebedeen said, "It's just terrible."

Miles was eager to agree, not because he found anything immediately terrible, but because he wanted to show that he understood, that he belonged. But he was afraid to agree without understanding. "Terrible?"

"The captain's woman."

"Ah," said Miles, confused and unaccountably jealous. "Who is she?"

"She's the PACE instructor."

Miles opened his DICNAVAB.

The major laughed. "Program for Afloat College Education. She's the math teacher, civvie of course, special contract with stateside colleges so that our guys get the same educational bennies as the men ashore. Trouble is, women aren't supposed to serve on amphibious landing vessels, not even civilians."

Miles slid the book into his front trouser pocket. "So," he said, "she's a kind of stowaway."

"Her name's Robin, the computer in Washington thinks she's a man. That's how the captain gets her aboard."

"He's done it before?"

"Every WESTPAC, that's what I hear. Not that anyone could get her thrown off. She'd have every women's-rights lawyer in D.C. suing the navy."

They studied the reddening sky, the water darkening everywhere except near the horizon, where it glimmered silver-blue.

"I hate this," said the major. "I miss my family. I guess you're the one I should talk to about it."

Miles realized he was on the job. He made himself say, "I understand."

"I cried on the plane—I cried in the cab—I cried in my stateroom this morning—"

"Nothing you say will go beyond me."

"I'm responsible for three hundred men, I've never had this much on my shoulders, and I'm lying in my rack at three in the morning, crying over my wallet."

There was an open wallet, a flutter of color photographs, in front of his face, but Miles was afraid to take the billfold lest a lurch of the ship make him drop it—would the major dive after it? The woman was Asian, a large, short-haired, bullet-headed woman in a red muumuu, and the boy was light-skinned with Asiatic eyes, wearing a yellow shirt with a black Charlie Brown stripe zagging across it.

"That's my wife and boy." Major Lebedeen put the wallet in front of his own face, his mouth quivering into a smile. "Boopsy and Pogo, that's what I call them, and they call me Cookie." After a moment he closed the wallet and returned it to the back of his pants, his face taking a tight-mouthed angry look. "Everybody thinks my wife was a bar whore, just because she's a Filipina."

Miles manufactured a shocked and inquiring look.

"I didn't meet her in Subic, I swear I didn't, I'm not one of those guys who takes advantage of the people there, my wife's never even *been* to the Philippines, her family came over in 'forty-seven. She's a high-school vice principal, and I met her at a Toastmasters convention in Philadelphia when I was studying leadership skills. She's a remarkable woman."

"Women," said the DISBO, passing by so unexpectedly that, again, Miles would've dropped overboard if not for the lifeline, "are like equity funds. You have to diversify." The man's pipe, held in a thin mouth in his tanned face under his large cap, puffed its aroma into the salt air. They watched him weave across the moving deck, his hands in his pockets, leaving a white trail in the air, until he disappeared around the vinyl-hooded five-foot shaft of an antiaircraft gun.

Major Lebedeen said, "That's the DISBO, don't look it up, it means disbursement officer. What an asshole, there are some stories I've heard about *him*. There was three thousand dollars missing from their last WESTPAC, never turned up. Rumor is he knocked up some whore in Korea and had to pay off her family." The major looked straight at Miles: "How do you put up with it?"

"Up with what?"

"The low morality of the U.S. Navy, top to bottom? If a marine wanted to marry a whore, or was caught stealing money, or . . . we'd break his balls, but these sailors. You say this was your first WESTPAC?"

"Yeah."

"Never been to the Philippines, Subic, Olongapo? Pattaya Beach?"

"Never."

"Reverend, you've never been to hell."

"Well," Miles said too quickly, "I guess I'm going."

The major's triangular face, with its questioning eyebrows, gave him an unsure look, just for a moment, then the major laughed and looked out again at the darkening sea and sky. "This is my third deployment, but I'm not interested in any of those places. There's just one place I want to see again, it's an island off the coast of Malaya. There aren't too many people on it, no whores or drunken idiots. Just peacocks, you never saw so many peacocks, it's their natural habitat. We use the uninhabited half of the island for reconnaissance. Virgin beach, snorkeling, coconuts you can break on a rock. Peacock Island, that's the only place I want to go. Besides home." He looked again at the chaplain. "You didn't say, Jim. You got a family?"

"Yes," said Miles. "I do."

"Pictures?"

"Sure." He reached for his back pocket, for the dead minister's wallet, then changed his mind and went into his other back pocket, for his own wallet. He opened it carefully, so that the major couldn't see into it, and extracted one of the photographs of Kari smiling with diamond-bright eyes, standing in front of a Christmas tree, in her red jumpsuit, holding a pink-and-white stuffed rabbit upside-down by its foot. "That's Kari, she's my little girl."

"Just the one girl?"

"That's right." A continent away, soon an ocean and a continent, she hardly knew him and would hardly know him, yet she was all that he'd created, a cipher to him, but alive in faraway Illinois.

"And your wife?"

Miles panicked, then remembered—yes, it was probably still there—a finger probe in the plastic sleeve containing his social-security card and Illinois driver's license, between the two, found something slideable and yeah, it was the brown-haired crown of Mary Lou's head. He slid it out quickly, the wallet angled away from the major's eyes, and he handed him the picture without looking at it and said, "That's my—my wife—Mary Lou."

"Very pretty." The major gave it back. Miles looked at her for the first time in two years. She was an attractive stranger with long brown hair, a forelock draped across her right temple, blue-gray eyes, a slightly parting smile. He looked at her too long, until the major said, "You must miss her a lot."

I don't know her anymore.

"I guess the thing to remember," the major said, "is that we're here for *them,* for our families. The rest of it is all bullshit."

"Yeah," he said, though he didn't feel the familial pull as strongly as the major did. Mary Lou was a myth; Kari was a little more than a myth, the outline of a playful big-eyed ghost-child whose image twisted his insides with love and loss.

"Well, there are probably some lieutenants looking for me, so I won't take any more of your time. Thanks for listening, Reverend."

Miles waited until he was gone and then got out the chaplain's wallet and switched all the photographs, putting Kari and Mary Lou into the dead man's wallet and exiling the dead man's family into Miles's own wallet, which he then released over the lifeline, watching it drop like a dying bat, flapping weakly straight down into the water. Then he looked out to sea—at the sister ships, tiny silhouettes with their masts and antennas precisely defined by the sunset—at the sky, a hot red sheet torn by the white intensity of the falling disc with its horizontal rippings of amber fire—at the water, whose violence wasn't false like the sky's, but palpable in every deck lurch that vibrated up his legs and rocked him into and away from the life cables he kept his fists around. The ocean was the true mystery, for if the sky was the face of God, the waters hid the powerful hands—the enormous purple waves rose and fell seamlessly, suggesting a strong and depthless power that he took to be creation, and that he knew had erupted life onto the land only a moment ago. He felt insignificant in the hugeness of time and sea and sky—he wasn't very significant even in the creative triangle of himself and Mary Lou and Kari—and he wondered how he could ever pretend to talk to others about God when he knew so little about the power of this ocean, so little about the few people he'd been close to, so little about anything of religious or philosophical importance—he'd have to admit that when it came to everything, he understood nothing.

Later, back in the metal cubicle of his room, he tried his little golden keys in the only lock he could find, opening a rectangle of metal down from the wall, creating a desk and revealing an inserted area with a built-in safe, a wire memo basket, and a small gray computer. He sat in front of it with the discs from the seabag, recalling, from working in the invoice department at Zincville Electroplate, how to access files. He realized one after another with burgeoning excitement that they were all sermons.

They had titles like "The Holy Ghost Amongst Us," "The Trale of St. Paul," "The Biblical View on Warfare," "The Man Who Woke Up at the Age of Twenty-Fore, and Found Jesus, in His Bed," and "Keeping a Pure Manly Body in a World of Sin," the fifth paragraph of which transfixed Miles to the point of reading it three times:

Satan is alive and well in the Filipines. When we visit such towns as Olongapo and Angeles and Manila we should never take advantage of the poverty of the people there to satisfy our own selfish desires. When we are in a Philipino port, we are already in The Lake Of Fire. The garbage hills burn, the children go naked, the people eat rice in the wooden sheds which are there homes, and we come amongst them like giants with gold. We are already in Hell. The sex that goes on is the most exploitating imaginable, taking advantage of the most corruptable innocence of the poorest people on this Earth. How many times must the soul of a thirteen year old girl be destroyed for seven dollars?

This struck at things he didn't know and didn't want to know, but he feared he would come to know them well. With dread of the future and remorse for the burning past—for having worked at the Little Pink Bookstore, and for the way he'd discontinued his employment there—he put the discs away and tried studying his DICNAVAB—*ARG, Amphibious Ready*

Group, usually consisting of an LST (see), LPH (see), LPD (see), LKA (see) and LSD (see), deploying between 3500–4000 USN and 2500–3500 USMC personnel—but he couldn't concentrate. He was troubled by the idea that he hadn't escaped the adult bookstore at all, but was floating toward a porno world larger and more disturbing than anything he'd ever seen, and that he, as chaplain, would have duties far more unpleasant and challenging than mopping a jerk-off booth.

He took off the uniform and hung it in the metal closet and, wearing nothing but the dead man's briefs, he lay in the rack, on top of the blanket, and switched on the plastic-encased rack light. He tried to concentrate wholly on the DICNAVAB in an effort to feel sleepy—***LST***, *Landing Ship, Tank, an amphibious assault vessel displacing 8400 tons and having an overall length of 517 feet, a beam of 68 feet, and a rated speed of 20 knots, and deploying up to 750* . . . but his eyes wandered up and down the columns of words. The rocking failed to lull him, and he worried about adjusting his day-sleeping life to the ship's schedule in three days' time for Sunday morning services.

The door opened, and instinctively he was on his feet, just beginning to think he might have to salute, but it wasn't an officer, it was Robin, it was the woman, standing there in her white T-shirt and tight blue shorts, her eyes surprise-popping at him as she said, "Oh, sorry, all the doors look alike, guess I'm the next one," and then her eyes traveled down his nakedness to his briefs and back up again. She smiled and nodded, pausing just a moment before she shut the door as she left.

3

The next morning he overslept and missed breakfast, but if this were a breach of any kind, nobody came rapping at his door about it, and he had the sense, from footsteps and clanking mechanical sounds appearing in his dreams throughout the night, that the ship, like his father's factory, was a twenty-four-hour operation where people's comings and goings were too complex and techno-specific to be of general interest. As he luxuriated in his own private shower, flex-learning his sea legs as the deck rose and fell, soaping and resoaping himself as though to scrub away the salt-sweats of his now unbearable former life, he felt an electric happiness in his chest, which reminded him of holding Kari twenty minutes after she was born, and more distantly and vaguely, the few times he'd been happy as a child. He had purpose. Toweling off, he resolved to be industrious today about his DICNAVAB and his prayer book, more interested in study than he'd ever been during the vodka-weed-pill party known as school.

When he was done toweling, he found the dead man's blow dryer and plugged it into the socket over the metal sink and thumbed the switch, and a spark exploded from the plug and then the world went dark. He could hear men swearing in other compartments. He yanked out the plug by the cord and, after a moment, the lights flickered back on. There was distant applause. Sheepishly he dried his hair with a towel. Then he got into a fresh uniform and sat at the desk that folded down from the bulkhead, got out the DICNAVAB, and began to read.

During this time there were several announcements over an address system with speakers in the hallway. The DICNAVAB told him it wasn't an address system but a "1MC," not a hallway or passageway but a "P-way"—how would he ever learn this language? The acronymic 1MC announcements echoing in the P-way may as well have been in Sanskrit. Then there was one in English:

"This is the captain. I want to thank the dumb-ass who blew out circuit breaker W3 about twenty minutes ago. You darkened five decks before backup clicked on, you pea-brained son-of-a-bitch. CHELECT tells me I've got two possibilities: a blow dryer or a microwave oven. Since even the marines aren't stupid enough to bring their own microwaves for that dehydrated rat shit they like to eat in the jungle, I'm declaring all blow dryers contraband. I've said it a thousand times—use those goddamn things for port calls only. I want every man with a blow dryer to take it down to the tank deck by fourteen-hundred today and turn it over to the CHELECT for tagging. If you want to use them in the Filipino whorehouses you'll be moving into when we hit Subic, you can have them returned at that time. I catch anyone with a blow dryer before then, I'll ram it up your butthole and run it full blast. That goes double for the dick-brain who did this. That is all."

Miles felt like crawling back into his rack and pulling the blanket over his eyes. Instead, he inspected the blow dryer, found no burn marks to incriminate him, then went out to find the tank deck. Not wishing to admit he didn't know where it was, he asked no one, carefully going down the Erector-set ladders, through humid compartments crowded with shirtless men running deafening machinery, walking among enlisted and NCOs and the occasional fellow officer, minding his balance in the up-swing down-drag world of gray metal, the pitching less severe as he arrived middledecks, the fulcrum of the ship. He passed offices full of blue-denim clerks bent over typewriters and computers and copy machines; machine shops full of half-naked black men and white men; a long crew mess with rows of chairs and tables bolted to the deck—empty now, but the hot beefy smells of lunch were coming from the galley; enlisted quarters mazing this way and that way with three-tiered bunks, a few filled with the humpforms of sleeping men who'd had the duty all night; rubber-matted showers large enough for a hundred men; a small carpeted library, just a table and four chairs and five metal shelves of trash paperbacks with cracked and illegible spines; honeycombs of P-ways lined with doors identified only with stenciled numbers. Every ten or fifteen minutes, there was a

DICNAVABic announcement over the 1MC. Lost, but not afraid, since the ship, in its mechanical affinity to Zincville Electroplate, was feeling oddly like home, he opened a hatch and stepped into a softly lit, less humid place, cavernous, high as a hangar and long as the Mount Logan Tunnel back home. He'd been drunk there, secretly and endlessly, as a teenager, daring himself to step into the headlights but never having the guts. The tank deck, like the tunnel, was full of vehicles, though these were asleep, headlights protected by green metal eye patches, the dark outlines of the hulks tethered by steel cable to the shifting deck, all of it creaking monstrously, trucks and jeeps and canteen wagons and long-nozzled tanks, a tied-down bestiary groaning to tear free and go headlong over the extending metal tongue of the ship's causeway to blow a firestorm through beaches and jungles and cities. The number and variety of vehicles, their towering shapes and shadows, frightened him as though he were a child alone in the immense world.

He walked through the aisles, high-stepping over the cable tethers, following a shouting voice: "What in hell do you need with a blow dryer, marine? A Velcro-head like you?" He encountered a half-dozen young men, enlisted sailors and marines, being berated by the officer who was the CHELECT—chief electrician, so said the DICNAVAB. The CHELECT took the blow dryer from Miles, tagged it, dropped it into the cardboard box full of blow dryers, and handed Miles the tag stub, saying throughout, "This man's an officer, makes sense he'd have a blow dryer, he's allowed to have human-length hair, but you lousy jarheads, you squids . . . "

He felt bad for causing the abuse of these boys, and for being used as an example to abuse them further, so he left the tank deck, out a hatch and up a few ladders, lost again, then he was through another hatch and in a weight room, men wearing nothing but red shorts insigniaed with the eagle-on-globe of the marines, working black stacks of rectangular weights up and down, standing or crouching around a Universal machine. Passing through the wet-sock smell of the locker room, Miles opened the next hatch and stepped into the lesser humidity of a classroom. Dozens of black desks, bolted down, were filled with the blockish shoulders and buzzed heads of naval enlisted blues and marine greens. Standing at the front of the compartment, before a white board made brilliantly illegible by the yellow light, was Robin, the civilian college instructor, her red-brown hair ponytailed down her back, her breasts nipple-pointed in a khaki T-shirt, her hips and thighs roundly packaged in khaki shorts. Her brown eyes were glimmering with intelligence as she wrote on the white board with a squeaking grease marker and said, "An Aegis-class cruiser has crew's rec compartments that measure sixteen feet by sixteen feet, twenty feet by eleven feet, seventeen feet by ten feet, and fourteen feet by twelve feet. If the carpet selected by the procurement officer costs fourteen dollars and thirty-seven cents per square yard, and padding and installation cost an additional eight point seven-five percent, with sales tax of seven point five percent, find the cost of carpeting all four rec areas."

The men were hunched as they copied the problem, eyes looking up to follow the shifting tones of her khaki-painted buttocks and naked legs, and as she turned to and from the board, the contours of her breasts were also of interest. The only sounds were her voice, throatily mathematical, the squeak of the grease marker, the whisper of ninety pencils, and a roomful of breathing.

"Questions so far?"

Pencils quiet, a world of eyes.

"Come on, I know you have questions."

"We have to do these by when?"

"All solutions are due by midterm, just after we pull out of Subic. So if you think you're going to be—to be busy in the Philippines, you should complete your work beforehand."

No one spoke. An insect was buzzing against a fluorescent tube.

"Well then, problem twenty-two: A shipboard filtering system has a nineteen-gallon-per-minute pump filter on a water tank that holds twelve hundred cubic feet of water. Assuming a backwash ratio of zero point five eight percent per hour, how long will it take the pump to circulate all of the water through the filter?"

As he walked along the rear bulkhead, across the long compartment toward a hatch, he felt as though he were moving through the sexually tense air of Zincville High School. He was grateful that Robin was ignoring him: "Converting into its metric equivalent the mass pressure of two hundred and twenty pounds per cubic inch . . ."

When he'd escaped from the room, working the hatch quickly and quietly, he found the first ladder and went up-decks from the belly of the ship, toward the towers of Officers' Country, where he knew he would find his lunch. The blue masses of men—the first duty section—were filling the enlisted mess as he passed through it, their din creating a buzz-vibration in the metal room, and their talk was youthfully earnest and profane, and the smell of hundreds of hamburgers was almost tearfully delicious in a world stripped of every civilian comfort. As he went up one skinny ladder after another, learning his confidence on the narrow steps, he passed compartment after compartment of men who were still sweat-laboring in their offices and machine shops, and for the first time in his life he felt what it was like to be involved in a great collective effort. He'd never been on any teams in high school, he'd never been on the team in his father's factory, and twelve-step groups weren't so much teams as they were psych wards. Reentering the high decks of Officers' Country, he was proud to have a place—*his own place*—in the pitching beehive of men.

Going down the P-way toward his stateroom, he stepped around a boy sponge-mopping the deck on his knees, turned a corner, and came nose-to-nose with the tanned skull face of Chief Ditchfield.

"Oh, excuse me," said Miles and tried to step around the old man, who intentionally blocked him, raising a big-knuckled finger: "Just the man of God I'm looking for. Sir."

Total alertness and rising apprehension: "Yes?"

"You took a shower this morning."

"Yes?"

"Or to put it more accurate, what was left of the morning."

"Yes?"

Miles was walking backward now with the roll of the ship, and the old man coming forward right on top of him: "But was it a navy shower?"

"What?"

"Wet-down water-off soap-up rinse-off water-off."

"I—"

"Didn't sound like one."

"It didn't?"

"I don't like to contradict a man of God, but it didn't sound like no goddamn navy shower to me. Sir."

Thinking fast, walking backward, sweating down his back: "This is my first deployment, and I haven't—"

"Figures. Goddamn OTS, so full of techno-hackers it's a miracle the officers they send us can take a crap without falling off their asses. I have to report all resource waste to the RBO, but I'm going to let it go this time with a—with an *information session,* which is now concluded. I'm happy we got this opportunity for up-the-ranks communication. Commander, sir."

"Thank you." In fifth grade, in the cafeteria, they'd caught him inhaling CO_2 from an empty whipped-cream canister and his heart had beat as quickly as this, and not only because he'd been high.

"Now you'll probably be wanting to get to your stateroom on account of the holier-than-thou waiting in front of your door. Reverend."

"Yes—of course—yes and thank you very much."

He went down the sliding P-way to his room, feeling that everyone could see his nakedness, even though he wasn't naked and passed no one. His rank was superior to Ditchfield's, why did he cower before the chief? He determined to be more authoritative with the next enlisted he must interact with, who was leaning cross-armed against the door of the chaplain's stateroom, probably thirtyish but looking fortyish with his black flap of hair combed thinly over his baldness, with his too-white face and black-framed navy-issue glasses and thin red mouth. The man came alive and straightened with a mad smile.

"Reverend?"

They shook hands, although the man wore enlisted blue.

"Jim Banquette."

"Pete Kruger." The handshake lasted longer than Miles was comfortable with, as did the smile—it would remain, in fact, throughout the conversation—and there was a contented insanity in the dark blue irises with their hot-yellow streaks. "It's common knowledge all over the ship you've come to preach to us from the Methodist tradition." The man licked his lower lip.

"Well—"

"I'm Pentecostal but that shouldn't be a problem so long as we both take a Scripture-based approach. I assume you'll follow the standard Protestant military service, with the doxology after the offertory? Of course you know you can vary it by placing it just before the invocation? Which would be more in line with my own beliefs although it's common knowledge that your way is the proper way at Pentecost."

"Well, I—"

"But the real reason I'm here is for Bible study. When's our group starting, and who else is gonna be in it, and what place and time are we gonna meet? We need to get the times and location into the POD ASAP before ship's routine is too rigid in the guys' minds. It's common knowledge that sailors have to be disciplined on Day One, and of course the closer we get to first port call the harder it's gonna be to get the men focused on the spiritual stuff that really matters."

"Well, I—"

"You see, what I'm real curious about is what you have planned for the first study night. Romans three is good for starters, but so is Galatians six. Of course, if we've got a more advanced group we can always start with Isaiah twenty-two or even something from Revelation, maybe seven or nineteen. But what do *you* think? You're the chaplain, and it looks like you're a real quiet one. I've known a lot of chaplains and it's common knowledge they always start with something simple-dimple, like Genesis. What kind of place is *that* to begin?"

The black-framed glasses were magnifying the blue eyes, and the skinny lips were magnifying the smile—its mad Christian love—even as the words came out. Miles had a stomachache, and he knew it wasn't from the dipping and tossing of the ship. "You go ahead and do it," he said.

"Sir?"

"Galatians, the POD, whatever you want. I'm putting you in charge. In fact, you can run the first meeting. All the meetings. Just give me a progress report." *Progress report*—two big words from his father's factory.

"But it's common knowledge that it's the chaplain's duty to—"

"It's common knowledge," said Miles, "that the Lord wants me to delegate according to men's talents. I'm delegating to you."

"Where's it say that?"

He felt light-headedly drunk with his audacity: "Exodus. Moses let his brother Aaron do all the talking and the Lord God was pleased. Look it up." It was an Old Testament story that he remembered from third-grade Sunday school. "Now run along, and look sharp about that POD."

From the DICNAVAB: *POD, Plan of the Day, a listing of general announcements, including duty schedules, drills, port-call information, mishaps, and relevant miscellany, compiled daily by the executive officer and distributed to, or posted for, all personnel . . .*

Free-associating religious bullshit with Kruger, he'd felt onrushingly drunk. It was a feeling that had been born long before the first sneaky drinks from his father's wet bar when he was nine—by the time he could talk, he could con his way around his mother, who was a nervous staring pigeon married to a man who was married to money, a woman who'd lost her two older sons to their father's world (they were both vice presidents today, one of sales in Chicago, the other of customer relations in Detroit), and so she'd clung to two things: Miles, her baby, who was permitted everything, and an alphabetic array of prescribed tranquilizers that permitted her nothing, not even the built-in motherly lie detector that was biologically common and might've curtailed her son's elaborate scheming—booze, pills, shoplifting, endless high-school truancies, check forging, other guys' girls in other guys' cars, all-night hejiras of sensation.

So his parents had been complex people, and he could read them. With enough preparation—unlike today with Ditchfield—he could successfully lie to anyone. It had served his alcoholic career. And now, four years after the fogs of self-medicaiton had dissolved, his faults, his perverse assets, were still here, were sharpened even, were all he had available from which to try to fashion a brave functioning self.

He went to lunch, anxious, doubting his talents, hoping his ability to tightrope-walk his way over people and situations would appear when needed.

As he approached the wardroom mess and opened the door with difficulty against the sliding weight of the ship, he was surprised to hear the twangy country-music version of a familiar melody, unnervingly unplaceable due to the alien rendition, then he realized with horror that it was a male-female, harp-and-banjo duet of "O Little Town of Bethlehem."

It was still ten minutes before the first seating—Major Frank Lebedeen, the marine he'd met last night, was the only officer in the room. He was sitting rigidly, with his hands on his knees, on a vinyl couch in the TV corner, his ever-questioning eyebrows arching up in agony at the screen. Without looking at Miles he said, "*The Dolly Parton Christmas Special,* in the middle of June, for Chrissake. I'm writing a poison memo to the goddamn video yeoman." When he looked over at Miles, the major's face colored up like the flesh of a cantaloupe, vividly pigmented against his marine greens.

"Oh, sorry."

Confused at the major's embarrassment, Miles looked around, saw only a pair of enlisted boys arranging utensils and water glasses on the table, then remembered that he was the chaplain. "I've been known to swear," he said. "Jam my toe, blue streak."

The cantaloupe face, turning back to the TV, didn't relax. "I can't handle it."

"It's pretty bad," Miles agreed, watching Kenny Rogers and Dolly Parton, in matching red overalls, segue into "I Saw Mommy Kissing Santa Claus." "Is that the only channel we get?"

"That's not what I mean." Voice and eyes lowering: "I'm talking about the deployment." Eyes rising, almost pleading: "I'm lucky I keep running into you."

On the clock again, Miles seated himself in the vinyl armchair across from the major, took a gangly open pose with his hands clasped between his knees, and tried to make his expression as receptive as possible. This wasn't easy, given the saccharine stupidity of the country vocals, but the major, in an earnest voice, began right away:

"I know you're sworn to confidentiality, that's why I'm telling you this. I abused my position today. During PT. It's *hot* out there on that helo deck, I'm running laps in a circle with three hundred marines, and I'm responsible for all of them, I have to set an example for each of them, but I couldn't concentrate on our PTing. I've been keeping this to myself—I didn't tell you about it last night—my wife found a lump last week. She's supposed to go in tomorrow, and there's no one I can talk to about it. I'm thinking to myself, Here I am running circles on a fucking helo deck— excuse me—running circles with three hundred guys in the middle of the ocean when I should be at home. But I'm not a hardship case—not yet, not that I want to be—and my mission is important, I'm responsible for each of these three hundred people, but it's *hot* out on that goddamn helo deck and I can't get my Boopsy out of my mind. That's when I abused my position."

"It won't go beyond me."

"Just before the aggression-training exercise, I told my XO I was expecting an important QSW in the radio shack, and I told him to take over for me. It was a lie, I never went there. Instead I've been sitting here, sweating for an hour."

"It's not a sin to delegate."

"I've abused my position. I could be court-martialed."

"Who's going to know? You're a man of authority, but you're only a man, and God's the ultimate authority." He felt drunk again with words. "Moses had a weak voice, and he delegated his authority to his brother, and that was pleasing to God." He shrugged; these words would either help the major or he would decide that chaplains understood nothing of the real world, that religion was an antique irrelevancy; either way, Miles felt safe.

"Hmm," said the major.

"It's okay to slack off—not all the time, of course—but every now and then. God understands that; He doesn't expect perfection. He knows you deserve your position. You worked hard, didn't you, to get where you are?"

The major shook his head, although he said, "Yes. What's that got to do with it?"

"You probably had to study hard, and train hard?"

"I was one hundred and twenty-third in my OTS class. Nobody knows that, not a single man serving under me. Most of the time, I feel like an impostor."

"There are times when we all feel that way."

"That's probably true."

"When will you know the results of your wife's test?"

"In about a week."

"Please come talk to me then." He wasn't looking forward to the kind of conversation that would be necessary should the test be positive, but there seemed nothing else to suggest.

Major Lebedeen nodded with resigned gratitude. "I just can't stand being on this ship, y'know? This fucking—excuse me—floating tin can, floating metal prison. I've never been a CO before, I don't like being in charge and making decisions. I like being at home. My wife decides everything there. The only thing I'm interested in is that island I was telling you about—just stretch out on that white sand with some coconut milk and forget everything about the goddamn—the world. Peacock Island. We're going to be there in four weeks."

The major paused, then started to say something more, but the door opened and the DISBO, pipe in mouth, came into the mess, regarding Dolly and Kenny with a banker's long-chinned disapproval, and he said, "Those morons down in MEDIACOMMSERV. I donated two of my finest videos before we deployed. *Car Wash Sluts,* and *Spit, Swallow, or Hang It on the Chin.*" He looked at the questioning face of the major, then at the intentionally neutral face of the chaplain, then took his pipe out of his mouth and said with droll contempt, "I beg your pardon, Father. Minister."

"That's all right." Miles could've told him that although he'd never seen the videos in question, he'd been selling both of them for the past several weeks.

Other officers were now entering the mess, including a pair of marine lieutenants demanding Major Lebedeen's attention, which arranged itself on his face by means of narrowing eyes and straightening eyebrows and tightening mouth. His conversation became as acronymic as a naval one.

Dolly Parton was replaced by David Letterman, and one of the marine lieutenants looked up long enough to say, with the bitter curiosity of a man who'd never stayed up past nine o'clock, "What's this guy's name?" and the other lieutenant said, "I can't remember, but I've heard of him, he used to do the weather when I was growing up in Indianapolis," then he addressed the major again in technicalese.

Miles seated himself for lunch.

The major sat next to him again but didn't speak to him, needing to discuss JMTs and AAVs and APCs with his lieutenants. The captain's chair was empty and remained empty throughout the meal, which was salad and hamburgers, same as for the enlisted. Still the woman did not appear. After lunch Miles went to his room. With only three days before Sunday services, he was determined to study the prayer book, and was soon at his desk with it:

An Order of Sunday Service Using the Basic Pattern

He studied the general structure—Prelude, Greeting, Ritual of Friendship, Opening Prayers, Invocation, Offertory, Doxology—and was contemplating the blank space beneath the word *Sermon* when there were five quick knocks.

"Yes?"

The knob was impatiently tried but it was locked so Miles reached over from his desk, wondering, with a gathering apprehension, which rule he'd broken now.

It was Ditchfield, and his ancient skull face wasn't friendly or unfriendly. He dropped two letters, addressed to Commander James J. Banquette, on the desk. "Mail call. Sir."

Miles stared at the letters as though they belonged to someone else. They did. "But how? So soon? I don't understand."

"Got here before we pulled out. Anyone else would be grateful, you know. There won't be any more till we pass Alaska."

Anyone else—what did that mean? "I am grateful," he said. Grateful there wouldn't be any more till Alaska. The old man gave him a slow appraising look and left him alone with the letters. Return addresses: Father Tom Tuttleman, 81st Support Depot (Naha, Okinawa), FPO San Francisco 95998; and Mrs. James J. Banquette, 72 Hopwood Lane, McKintry, VA 27292.

Shit. He'd thought it would be weeks before any mail from the missus found him; he certainly wasn't ready to work his brain about her now. He tore open the other letter.

Dear Jim!

Hope you don't mind, but I asked one of my buddies at COMMPAC about your next deployment and I can't believe you're actually on a WESTPAC and coming to Okinawa.

I know you remember me, I'm the big guy with red hair you met at the military ecumenical conference in Washington last year. I sure remember you, in fact I think of you quite often. You have the tightest asshole I've ever been fortunate enough to penetrate.

I'm thinking about you right now. I'm sitting here in my room wearing nothing but a cock ring and a pair of green high heels. I'm rubbing lubricant all over the big purple helmet of my boner and I'm thinking about forcing it past your bitchy little sphincter . . .

With a revulsion rising so fast he was afraid it would bring up his lunch, he scanned the rest of the letter, the sucking and fucking explicitly described in loopy black ink, and the revulsion became a resentment around which he could feel his anus tightening. He realized, with a cold numbness traveling his skin, the full implication of the letter, of the fact that this priest would be waiting for him—for Commander James J. Banquette—as the *Harding* anchored at Okinawa. He stared at the final line:

See you soon, and so happy happy happy that you're cumming cumming cumming cumming—to Okinawa!
—Father Tom

Disaster! The orders had read "temporary transfer to Seventh Fleet San Diego"—Banquette had been an Atlantic chaplain, nobody should know him on the Pacific—but the bastard had gotten around, damn him. The sweat was collecting on his back and beginning to roll down as he shoved the letter back into its envelope.

Fucking shit, what am I gonna do?

The other letter. Could it be as bad? Could anything? But he was afraid to open it. He held it up, feeling it with his thumbs and forefingers, a soft, unpresuming thing, and he opened it carefully.

Dearest Jimmy,

You're asleep in our bed and I'm writing this in the den at four o'clock and I don't know what to say to you. I love you. I HATE you. Even though you won't admit it, I know you're picking WESTPAC because it's the first deployment available and it will take you furthest away from me and that's how much you hate me.

I'm so sick of all the fighting I could scream.

You're aloof, you're mean, you won't touch me. I still think you're seeing some woman you've met through the ministry. Though even that doesn't make sense, because, if so, why would you be so eager to go? So it must be something else but you won't really talk to me, just the same old fights about me being in your face.

I've prayed about us but have not found an answer.

By the time you get this, your ship will be getting under way. I'm so afraid it's going to be like your Med cruise when we didn't hear from you but three or four times. You're not hurting me—I mean, you are, but you're hurting Laura and Teddy the most.

I don't want to say any more right now, because I know how delicate the problem with your heart is and how it flutters when you're upset. I don't like you lying to the navy about it and sneaking around with private doctors even though I know if you were forced to leave the navy a church ministry wouldn't pay as much. I just think it's wrong to sneak behind people's backs and lie to them.

Still loving you,

Michelle

P.S. Please don't forget the doctor said to take your heart pills <u>with a meal</u>.

The wife's letter, despite its injured tone, had calmed him, perhaps because he had more information than she did. He was sorry for her, but was glad to know he could wait a while before writing back and she wouldn't think it odd.

But the other letter. There had to be a way to neutralize Father Tom Tuttleman, some gamble. He turned to the computer and began playing with an idea.

Dear Father Tom,

Thank you for your letter, but please do not write me again. Also, please do not wait for my ship in Okinawa, because I do not wish to see you.

After a lot of soul searching and prayer, I've decided that I've allowed my obsession with my secret life to harm my relationship with my wife and family. Therefore I have sworn off forever the activities which you describe.

I hope you will not take this personally. I wish you all the best.

Yours in Christ,

Reverend Jim Banquette

He studied it, wondering if it would work. Father Tom's letter had revealed an aggressive personality. Miles would have to keep the priest's letter for counter-blackmail purposes, of course, just in case the man threatened to—well, expose him—on Okinawa. The priest might be determined to meet the ship, given the detailed testimonial to Reverend Banquette's sphincter. Miles bit his thumbnail. He really had no choice but to mail the letter, hope it worked, and find a good hiding place on Okinawa.

When he explored the print commands, he learned that his letter would appear in Yeomanry 2-B on Deck O-3, and he went looking for the compartment, which was on the same deck. He told the clerk, a pimpled enlisted boy, that he was the chaplain and would have a confidential letter printing out soon, went back to his stateroom and typed in the commands, then rushed back to the yeomanry to watch the letter come out of the machine with a spit-typing sound, took the letter to his room and put it in an envelope, which he stamped and addressed, then went out and asked the first enlisted boy he saw about the ship's PO and found it four decks down. Miles held his breath and put the letter through a slit in the bulkhead.

4

There were less than seventy-two hours before Sunday services, and these hours were so completely filled with the frantic routine of study and meals and more study that the time passed too quickly. Despite his growing confidence with the DICNAVAB and the prayer book, the rushing-by of hours led to a pretest panic he'd never experienced in his doped-up schooldays, a panic that drove him back to his stateroom immediately after meals, even when the increasingly unhappy-looking Major Lebedeen lifted his questioning eyebrows at him in a silent plea for counseling. It was a panic that made Miles forget about the matter of the captain's woman for a few days, even though at mealtimes she was situated, because of her civilian nonrank, at the end of the table in view of everyone, where she said little but attempted wry flirtatious eye games with anyone willing, especially when the captain was absent. It was a panic that had Miles walking a terrified circle one morning when an alarm like an electronic hyena crying a hysterical note over and over filled the ship, interrupted by a man quick-announcing "Generalquarters generalquarters." Miles was ready to climb back into his rack with the pillow over his head when Ditchfield burst in demanding to know why the chaplain wasn't at his GQ station, and he answered that nobody had told him where it was, which was true enough, and Major Lebedeen going down the P-way with a helmet in his hand had rescued him by yelling, "Down to the tank deck with the marines!" Miles spent an hour in a helmet and life vest, huddled next to a jeep, until the drill was over and he could return to the more manageable panic of practicing the doxology in his head, a panic that so engrossed him that he lost his balance for the first time, on the way to lunch, when the ship jerked violently aft and he fell forward and collided so violently against the back of the DISBO that the man's pipe flew out of his mouth, and Miles landed painfully on the steel plate on his elbows and knees, and the DISBO said "Ah—you—trying to hump me in the P-way, huh? You a queer or something? Masquerading as a priest?"—an arbitrary reproof, though it grew his paranoia in several new directions.

On Saturday afternoon, Ditchfield, his eyes looking out from deep in the skull face as reproachfully as during the shower lecture, was at his door wanting to know about hymnals.

"What hymnals?" said the chaplain.

"The ones that been in my WARDCO locker since San Diego. We only got so much space. Sir."

"Oh. I'm sorry."

"Tomorrow's Sunday and it's about time you got them out of there and down to the crew's lounge."

"The crew's lounge?"

"Ain't that where you do services, oh-eight-hundred and ten-hundred?"

"I—don't know—I was waiting to see what it said in the POD."

"Tomorrow's goddamn POD just been posted. Reverend."

"I'm sorry—every ship's different—"

"Every ship's got limited WARDCO storage. I got five thousand Styrofoam cups I been having to keep under my rack. Hymnals ain't even on my TSRB list."

"I'll move them right away."

"And something else."

"Yes?"

Ditchfield pulled a laundry slip out of his shirt pocket and Miles recognized his own handwriting as the old man said, "You ordered starch on your minister collar?"

"Well—it looked a bit limp."

Ditchfield's eyes trained on him with sunken, binocular contempt. Miles didn't breathe.

"Reverend, your collar's plastic."

"Oh—yeah—well—of course it is." He'd hung the clerical clothes and a uniform outside his door yesterday and filled out the laundry slip without looking carefully at the items. "I—I must've thought I brought my other collar."

"Uh-huh. McComas, the laundry chief, he ain't so understanding and patient as I am. He bounces these fucking things back to me if you got errors."

"I'll write out a new slip right away."

"By the way, when was you planning to pay your wardroom fees?"

"Uh . . . soon."

"Hundred thirty-seven for the first month." The smile, the tobacco-brown teeth: "Just if you want to keep on eating, sir."

"Of course. I'll take care of it today."

"Just bring it to the galley." The old man went out the door, then turned and came back to stand in it. "How long you say you been in the navy?"

"In the navy? . . . uh, a few years."

"A few years. Was just wondering who taught you to shine shoes. Commander."

For the next hour he was too busy with his penances and emotions to think like a con man. He was a humiliated child as he went to the ward-room locker and a seaman opened it for him. Miles balanced the stack of prayer books—not hymnals, but prayer books like his own so the men could follow services—balanced them in a tall stack against his chest as he snaked along the seesawing deck. Bemused, not having known that officers, unlike enlisted, paid for all their meals, he went to the galley and counted out six twenty-dollar bills and a ten and a five and two ones from the bookstore wad, leaving him with 181 dollars, enough for next month, but what about the one after? Were the chaplain's paychecks going to the wife in Virginia or coming here? He couldn't ask the DISBO anything that basic. He filled out a new laundry slip, hating himself for the way he'd allowed Chief Ditchfield to lecture him. He couldn't find the handle to the man. It was like dealing with his father, who always had one more reason to make Miles feel foolish.

He did have an insight about chiefs, though, based on his observations of ship life and confirmed by his interactions with Ditchfield: the chiefs, the ones in khaki who were neither commissioned officers nor seamen— the oldest men on the *Harding*, often fat—actually ran the ship, supervising the enlisted men, nominally reporting to ensigns and lieutenants, younger men who accepted the opinions of their more experienced inferiors. With officers, then, Miles decided his behavior must be collegial; with chiefs, deferential without being as passive or cowering as he'd been with Ditchfield; with enlisted, as arbitrary as he'd been when he'd told Kruger to start the Bible-study group himself.

This left the marines, who, despite his evolving friendship, if that's what it was, with their commander, Major Lebedeen, were still mysterious men to him. They were passengers—he'd seen them do little so far. He'd be walking through a compartment and find twenty of them sitting on the deck, polishing helmets and boots and disassembling intricate machine guns with the many parts scattered around them. And the DICNAVAB had revealed a maddening complication: equivalent marine and naval ranks had different names. A private in the marines was the same as a seaman in the navy, a sergeant was a chief, a first lieutenant was an ensign, a second lieutenant was a lieutenant junior grade, a captain was a lieutenant senior grade, a major was a lieutenant commander, a lieutenant colonel was a commander, a colonel was a captain, and a ship's commanding officer was always called "Captain" regardless of his actual rank. Miles couldn't understand how any work could be accomplished in such a byzantine hierarchy—they should be walking into each other all day, unable to determine their relations.

He got out the tin of polish, found a rag in a drawer, and took off a shoe. Sitting with it in his lap, he tried to shine it so it would look like the other men's. He looked at it. It wasn't good enough, not mirrored like the other men's. He did it again but still no good, then the impossibility of the task had him in a fresh panic. He held the shoe between his knees and flailed at its stubborn dull tip with the rag with all the manic energy of his fear and his frustration and it still wasn't mirrored, so he dropped the shoe and was trying the other one when he realized—with a bile crawling up from his stomach so acidically that he allowed the other shoe to drop, unaware of the symbolism of doing so—that he'd contradicted himself in front of Ditchfield, had claimed during the shower lecture a couple of days ago to be on his first deployment, but had asserted just an hour ago that "every ship is different." Ditchfield was putting it together, assume the worst.

After stepping back into the dead man's unshinable shoes, he went out to the weather deck to walk along the lifelines and examine the sky and sea. He was worried, but the caliber of his worry, in the four years since he'd quit the booze and pills, had become narrower than most men's. By the time his father, in a controlling fury, had thrown him into the treatment center, Miles had been stripped down to nothing—no job, no money, no woman, no apartment. His ensuing existence, though better, had barely skimmed the surface of street life. He always lived with the nervous knowledge that everything could come apart in sixty minutes. He looked out at the glittering water and hot blue summer sky, immense in their beautiful indifference, and he knew that he was still prepared for his life to devolve to zero—but it wouldn't, not even if he died in Leavenworth, because he'd created Kari and would at least leave some piece of himself on this earth. He took out the stranger's wallet and pulled out the photo of his own little girl, who was also a stranger, but would someday, perhaps, come to know him.

Then he was ready to go back to his stateroom and continue studying.

By nightfall he was intellectually prepared for the next morning, if emotionally unsure about standing in front of a roomful of men and leading them through the rituals of doxology and response to the word and prayer for illumination. Study had taken him as far as it could; the ability to perform the things he'd learned would have to come from another place.

He lay in his rack, yawning, allowing his mind to empty. When he returned at length to his concerns, it was with a childlike distaste for them. Like the petulant boy he had always been—not wanting to go to school, to work, to a fucking treatment center—he angled the inner microphone of his ear-for-trouble against the white noise of distant gears and pulleys and rotors and air hoses, and his ears filtered out from the soup of nautical noise the soft rhythms of a conversation in the next compartment. Out of his boredom, he pressed the side of his head against the bulkhead and heard Robin saying:

"Density is defined as the ratio of weight to volume, seaman. Styrofoam is less dense than wood, and wood is less dense than steel. All I'm asking you is this: if the density of an aircraft carrier's hull is five hundred ten pounds per cubic foot, convert that figure to kilograms per cubic meter and find the desired thickness at a depth of twenty-two fathoms, using the water-pressure calibration formula we discussed in class."

"It's very confusing," said the sailor. Miles imagined instructor and student sitting at the fold-down desk, going over a problem sheet.

She said, "You want to up your rating to Hull Technician Three, don't you?"

"I don't know if I really want to be a hull tech. Do you have to know calculus to be in Supply?"

The rest of it wasn't very interesting, a lot of one-sided talk about conversion ratios and hull volumes and acceleration curves. Miles would've turned away except for a quality in Robin's voice, a slow throaty intelligence that emerged as she calculated the specific gravities of soluble volumes. Again, he wondered what it would really be like to be One of the Guys, to be wholly interested in everything a woman was, to have that interest returned.

"Uhm," said the boy, "I'm gonna need more time with this."

"It's due Monday morning."

"Yeah—uhm, I know—I talked to SN-3 Zilensky."

A silence. The silence continued. Miles didn't know how to interpret it. All the mechanical sounds of the ship seemed very loud as he strained to listen for the next words.

The woman said, "You talked to Paul Zilensky. Good. I was hoping he'd talk to you."

"Yeah. He told me that."

"Did he tell you anything else?"

"Yeah—a lot else."

"And that's why you came to see me, not really for help with these problems."

"Well—"

"But that's okay," she said. "I think we can get you extra time on that assignment—if you do something for me."

"Yeah?"

"Yeah. Wait, I'll be back."

There were the muffled sounds of a chair being pushed back, someone walking, and Miles guessed she was in the head. It was perhaps two minutes before the same sounds occurred in reverse order and Robin said, "I want your opinion. I'll be wearing this on the beach on Okinawa."

"Yeah?"

"Yeah. So what do you think? I have a blue one too. Maybe you'd like a blue one better. I just need someone's opinion."

"This is—uh. This is good."

"You sure about it?"

The boy's voice was nervous and uncertain. "Well, yeah, I mean—it's good."

"You don't sound so certain. Maybe you'd like a closer look. I shaved here . . . looks like I missed a spot."

"Oh God."

"I wonder if I shaved the back of my leg well enough. Does it look smooth?"

"Oh God, I have to go."

"Wait a minute—"

"No, I gotta go, I got the duty." Papers rustling.

"Wait—"

"Excuse me—and thanks—I gotta go now, I really do." Chair-scraping noise, quick footsteps, the door opening and closing.

"Damn," Robin said.

Miles sat up and started rearranging his rack so that his pillow was now at the other end. If he was going to live on this ship for the next six months, he didn't want to listen to the kinds of sounds that might soon be emanating from Robin's cabin. It'd been so long since he'd been presented with the fact of female lust—the *fact* of it, not the porno fiction of it—that he wondered how he'd react to it, what would happen if he indeed became One of the Guys and allowed himself to want a woman—Robin?—in the blind uncompromising way of sex, which had so often meant trouble. Robin would be a mistake. And yet her heat, her aggression, her sultry intelligence were hooks upon which to hang any number of imponderables. Was he beginning to want her? What would happen? Either she would come to him as she fucked her way through the ship—would she stop at a chaplain?—or he'd have to break through his better sense, which would be more difficult with sobriety, and approach her—and how would it be? Quick and hot and awful, as it had been in the boozy, drugged-up years?

He'd lost his virginity at fourteen at a "cocktail party" at his parents' house, when they were out of town and his brothers at college. Cocktail party: get a big bowl, take all of your mom's pill bottles and pour them in, invite half the freshman class and have them bring their mothers' pills too, eat 'em out of the bowl like pharmaceutical M&M's and down 'em with generous gulps of tequila milkshake, then—SEX TIME! That night, after he'd crawled off Laura Steeby, his second virgin, he bled more than both girls when her father busted down the door and busted open the nose of the host . . . police . . . suspension . . . first trip to juvihall . . . his father's sulfurous contempt, his mother's shaky exploration of the remains of the party bowl.

Then had come, again and again and too often, the exquisite misery of falling in "love." Michelle. Jennifer. Anne. Lucinda. Maxine. Yes, even a Violetta. The loves of his teens and twenties had taught him that he was insanely fucked up and couldn't do anything about it. First would come a romantic longing as weakening and consuming as that of the most sensitive twelve-year-old girl, making him feel freakish and starved and out-of-control, leading to a frenzied seduction, a booze-and-pill fuckfest, a purging that would momentarily send his pain to the moon and also jettison—permanently—his interest in the girl. The next one would be standing right there . . . it was a hamster wheel of fever and self-loathing.

It had finally stopped turning—to his bottomless relief—when he'd sobered up. He hadn't been in love since, and he hoped never again. It was an anxious burning feeling, after all, a youthful dissipation. He wondered if he could someday love a woman without falling in love—it would be the best way for him—and he'd almost achieved it with Mary Lou, but this new woman, this Robin, she threatened to rip open the scabs of his sobriety and bring back the insanity of those years . . .

Robin . . .

Now stop that, he knew exactly what this feeling was, this stirring in his crotch; he was going to regret it the way he had a hundred times—okay, so think of the worst examples, may they deter him from further folly—

1. Lorelie. This was from his first and only year of college. He was regularly fucking and getting high with a brunette named Lorelie, but he didn't tell anyone. He was supplying her, and she did anything he asked, so each Friday night he set her up with a different jock, because he hated jocks, and this was how he'd humiliate them: she'd go out with the jock and do everything possible to turn him on without letting him get as much as a finger wet, then she'd ask the jock to take her to a party at Miles Derry's apartment, where she'd lock herself in his bedroom and she and Miles would fuck very loudly—"Bang me, Miles! Do it to me, do it!"—and the jock would be standing outside horny and angry. This was lots of fun. Until the night when he and Lorelie had just finished fucking and they were passing a joint back and forth and the door came splintering open. When Miles stood up to protest, he felt immediately through the marijuana haze what it was like to have his jaw cleanly broken. He wasn't able to smoke or talk for a month and stayed drunk for the whole miserable time . . .

2. Rosie. One of the secretaries at Z.E. Every spring, every summer,

every fall and winter too, there'd be a new secretary at the factory whose pants would be open to him—he used to think of each girl as This Season's Girl. Some were married, some single, some he'd knock up and all of them would abort—his father would yell at him whenever he got a call from his golfing pal, the abortionist. Sometimes there'd be a threat from a jealous boyfriend, a husband, even a geeky brother or two—but Rosie was his worst secretarial experience. He was upstairs in his apartment smoking dope naked on his mattress with the Wild Turkey–swilling blond roly-poly elf named Rosie, and there was a knock downstairs. He put on the robe she'd given him, the red one with his initials in gold, M.A.D., over the heart, and he went downstairs. Opened the door just a crack, just wide enough for the big-nosed anger of a man: "I think this bullshit is over, you tell Rosie to get her hanky-panky ass the hell downstairs." Miles almost laughed; he was comfortably stoned; this was very funny. He went upstairs and said, "Your husband's here." "Shut up, that's impossible, I have the car." "Well, he's downstairs right now and he wants you to get your hanky-panky ass the hell down there." He laughed again, and then they were both laughing. She lit the second joint. Glass breaking downstairs. "Oh shit, oh shit, it *is* my husband, it is, oh shit," and Miles was laughing very hard, although Rosie, glaring ahead in a pot paranoia, wasn't. The man yelled up, "Rosie, get your hanky-panky ass down here," and then Rosie was laughing, was trying to tell Miles something as the footsteps came up the stairs, but she was laughing too hard, and at last she managed to say: "That's not my—not my husband—that's—that's just my other boyfriend!" and they were both rolling naked on the mattress, laughing without breathing. When the man came into the room, Miles stood up to shake hands with his fellow cuckolder and felt immediately through the marijuana haze what it was like to have the break in his jaw reopened. He wasn't able to smoke or talk for a month and stayed drunk for the whole miserable time . . .

    3. Cathy. He wasn't working for his father, this was between his second and third firings, or was it just after the single time he'd quit? Yes—he'd sold enough coke in a one-time deal to drink for a year, and he'd gotten himself an apartment over in State College, Illinois, a town full of pretty girls. It was the Fourth of July. He'd spent the day with Jose Cuervo Especial, watching *The Ten Commandments,* making up his own Egyptian language as he drank, and he decided to go out to a bar and find some college girls and teach them his new language. On his way to the parking lot, he came upon the doubled image of a short-haired blond in a T-shirt and

cutoffs, and the image spoke: "We're having a shindig!" "Gun-tu-rah!"
"What?" "That's Egyptian language, kam-bot-khan." "Cool! Apartment
Twelve-H." The doubled image swayed away—he dimly realized how
drunk the girl was—and he went back to his apartment and put on his
wildest Hawaiian shirt and his strongest cologne and he made sure he had
his rubbers and he scooped up a mystery mix of pills and grabbed his bottle of Cuervo and went over there singing in Egyptian. The girl's apartment was even messier than his, every surface and most of the floor covered with plates and bottles and wineglasses and assorted garbage—
there'd been quite a party all day, and now there was no one left but the
girl, who said her name was Cathy, and two fat chicks sitting butt-to-butt
on the couch. Cathy took him into the kitchen, and he saw the uptilting
face with half-closed eyes, the drunken invitation to kiss, and they kissed
sloppily but intently for a while and then he pulled out the pills and said,
"Take some of these," and she did and he did too. More kissing, tight hug-
ging, the beginning of the animal trance of sex, which he broke long
enough to say "Get rid of those fat chicks." She tried to, but they couldn't
find their keys in the post-party mess, and he said, "I'll find your goddamn keys," and he did, too, they were lying in a long tray with a demol-
ished lasagna. Then he and Cathy were alone, kissing again, and the
clothes were coming off item by awkward item, and then he and the girl
were humping on the couch among the debris. They moved to the bedroom, the furious animal trance had fully taken over—she riding him,
then 69, doggy, even the old-hat grinding missionary—and this girl was
actually scratching his back and legs and ass, and looking straight up at
him to say, "What is your wildest sexual fantasy?" and he'd responded
through the velvety sexlight of the drugs, "My, yeah, biggest sexual fantasy
is, one night, I'm walking out to my car in the parking lot, see, and I meet
this girl who . . ." but they were too hot and hopped-up to laugh, and he
had a blackout shortly thereafter. When he came to—whenever that
was—not only was the animal trance gone, leaving him as it always did,
alone with a stranger, but this time the stranger was lying on her side
throwing up into her hands and shitting a stream of diarrhea right into
her bed, and she was crying furtively. When Miles opened his mouth to
say something, only vomit came out, burning drug-hot, and he had the
hot shits like he couldn't believe, and they were both lying there puking
and shitting and crying and it wouldn't stop, it went on, they were hyper-
ventilating and losing gushes of fluids at both ends, unable to move.

Finally, the girl was able to roll off the bed and drag a phone over by its cord and dial 911, and then there were uniforms and flashlights and stretchers in the room, and the police were picking up pills from the carpet and asking a lot of questions in Egyptian, and out of the noise-and-light came a bulky man, the goddamn apartment manager, who was distinctly yelling, "Pig pig pig!" though he didn't seem to be addressing the cops. "She's only nineteen, I promised her parents she'd be okay here." When Miles tried to stand to explain, he knew immediately through the drug haze what it was like to have the break in his jaw reopened. He wasn't able to smoke or talk for a month and stayed drunk for the whole miserable time.

Miles lay in his rack, rubbing his jaw, grateful he hadn't had to live like that since he'd quit drinking and using. He wondered darkly what would happen to the chaplain if he got caught fucking the captain's woman. If he got caught.

Stop that shit, you would *get caught, you always get caught, you dumb-ass.*

The healthiest sex relationship of his life had been with Mary Lou, but even so, the last memory of making love with her was not happy. She hadn't been showing with Kari yet, and they'd been fighting a lot about what to do. He went over there at five in the morning after being up all night brooding, and for the first time, he had to seduce her. She was willing and unwilling—there was no sex trance, no animal part of it—finally she shoved him aside and said, "Get the fuck out of my house." She was crying. He was all jangled and morose, and when he stepped outside it was just dawn, a cold April morning, a rusty light on the factory roofs, which were jagged against the pale sky. He'd turned up his jacket collar and withdrawn his head turtlelike and turned round the corner, and knew he was walking away from the closest thing to love he'd ever known.

Their conversations were all legalistic after that, except for one. She hadn't allowed him to participate in the birth, but he was allowed, about twenty minutes later, to come into the room in a green smock and plastic hairnet and to hold Kari, who was wrapped in a pink hospital blanket. She was wet-haired and squinty-faced and not crying, and she was the tiniest softest thing he'd ever held. *Wow,* he was thinking, *wow*—he couldn't make his mouth do anything but smile. Then Mary Lou, who was lying there with a washed-out happy look, reached out, wanting her baby back, and as he carefully transferred Kari he said, "Wow. She's really beautiful."

And Mary Lou had said with weary pleasure, "I know," and for an instant they were a family, and he'd felt like a father, no matter the distances, ever since.

And so Kari, tiny as she was outside his mental life, was the only good thing he'd ever gotten out of sex.

He'd have to forget about the captain's woman. He resisted the pull of his curiosity to turn the other way in his rack and press the side of his head against the bulkhead. He hoped nothing would ever happen between them, because if it did, it might very well be like the old days and that would mean a disaster.

5

Alaska was only a hundred miles to starboard, so it was a chilly morning when the 0600 announcements woke him. He took his navy shower and shaved and put on the black preacher suit with its stiff collar, and his molars were grinding, and he didn't know if it was from the fear or the cold or both. Because his overhead ventilation unit was giving no heat, just cold air, he went looking for Ditchfield and found him in his little office off the galley and said, "There's no heat in my room," and the old man said, "Comes out cold in the Arctic, hot in the tropics, how many goddamn ships you been on, anyway?" Miles, terrified it was a test question, pretended to be insulted and said, "This isn't the Arctic," and Ditchfield said, "Close enough—you coulda fooled *my* scrotum—Reverend."

Miles went down the P-way, which was windswept cold from an open hatch, and he remembered the captain's geography lesson, how you had to go north and south to go west, due to the curvature of the earth. Passing the open hatch, he felt the wind of the Aleutian morning like a knife slicing into his shirt and the air was salty and raw and the water was whitecapped in its purple undulations.

Going down the ladders to the crew's lounge with a prayer book and Bible in one hand, the index finger of his other hand trying to work the tightness out of the collar, he was unsure of himself, a feeling from the first day of school: new clothes, new people, new expectations of him. The kind of feeling that had caused him to skip the first week of high school. When he'd finally shown up, he was so drunk he spent the free period in the boys' room with his head in the toilet, and didn't come out till they found him and sent him home, where his father, showing a Chrysler executive the taxidermic big-fish collection in the den, came out long enough to whisper, "You'll never be anything, Smiles, you know it? Keep smiling, 'cause someday you'll see I was right—get away from me." On this goose-bumpy Alaska morning the two feelings were still with him—the fear of having to go among others and perform, and the hatred for his father. The mix of feelings resurrected an old resolve that had never been fulfilled: *I'll show you I'm not a loser.*

"Smiles" because he never smiled in that house. He was going to smile as much as possible during services no matter how he felt.

It was hard to keep smiling, but he did, as he walked into the crew's lounge and saw that it was jammed with men. All of the red vinyl couches and metal folding chairs were occupied with men who were talking, reading, napping, or watching the large TV bolted to the end of the compartment as they apparently waited for him. It looked like a hundred men, and there were only forty prayer books in four stacks in the corner. He looked about helplessly; no one had noticed him. Then Kruger, the man who'd come to see him about Bible study, was at his side saying, "Want me to throw them out, sir?"

"What?"

"I'll get rid of them," said Kruger, and his smile was thin-lipped and too red against the pale eagerness of his face. With a bone-white finger, he pushed the black-framed glasses up the bridge of his nose and went to the head of the compartment, near the TV, and got up on a chair and snapped off Arnold Schwarzenegger in mid-machine-gunning.

"Hey, what the fuck you doing!" "Put it back on!" "Put that fucking thing back on, asshole!" "Kruger, you fucking freak, you put it back on right fucking now or I'll kill you!" "PUT IT ON!" All of them, white, black, whether they'd been watching TV, reading, talking, or sleeping, were shouting, many of them standing. Miles knew he was the ranking officer, the only officer, but he was afraid to speak. He kept smiling.

Then Kruger, unperturbed, even enjoying this, started yelling back. "Listen up! Listen up, you guys! That gentleman over there is a minister, he's Commander James Banquette! And he's requisitioning this facility right now for Sunday morning services. Which are now five minutes late and I doubt he's happy about it."

Miles felt like a schmuck. He knew there was nowhere else for the men to relax. At the sight of his black-garbed, white-collared presence, they were quiet and sullen and gathered their magazines and Walkmans and filed out the hatch. But in the P-way they were vocal: "Fucking shit." "Fucking religion, man." "Goddamn chaplains, don't care about no one but theyselves." "Fuck that chaplain, man, he probably thinks we was just sitting there waiting for *him*."

Counting Kruger, this left five men, three white and two black, scattered throughout the long compartment, but looking attentively at Miles. Kruger said, "Show time, Reverend."

When he spoke, he was alarmed that his voice was a squeak of anxiety, that the words had a clipped awkwardness as he strained them one by one through the sieve of his smile: "Okay, everybody take one of those books in the corner, and move in a little closer." My God, his voice was that of the vice principals, the scoutmasters, the middle managers he'd always resented. He spotted a podium in a corner and went over to get it and pulled it to the head of the compartment and stood behind it, happy to be hiding most of himself. "The responses begin on page five," he said, cringing at his nasal authority. The men, as though they'd been obeying such a voice for years, were settling into the couches and chairs nearest him, books open, Kruger looking up at him with beaming expectation.

Miles raised his hands, palms upward, as he'd seen many pastors do— on TV—and he said, with as much confidence as he could put into the traitorous weasel in his voice, "The grace of the Lord Jesus Christ be with you."

Scattered responses, Kruger's the loudest: "And also with you."

"The risen Christ is with us."

"Praise the Lord," said the men.

"Almighty God," Miles said, his hands still up, his voice continuing to trick him, his face red and his armpits damp, "to You all hearts are open, all desires known, and from You no secrets are hidden. . . ." He concluded the opening prayer, hoping he was just bad enough, just boring enough, to be convincing. He dropped his hands and segued into the prayer for illumination, which he droned out in what he hoped was a preacherly monotone. Then he opened the dead man's Bible by the ribbon marker, which he'd placed along the column containing Mark 4:19, identified by the lunar calendar in the back of the prayer book as one of the gospel choices for Sunday number fourteen of the liturgical year, and he started reading to them, "'The cares of this world, the deceitfulness of riches, and the lusts of our bodies choke the Word, and it becometh unfruitful . . . '" When he was done he said, "This is the word of the Lord," and the men weakly responded, "Praise be to God," except for Kruger, who said it loudly, and then Miles was ready for his sermon.

He'd selected the Banquette homily against prostitution in the Philippines, as well as the gospel passage he'd just read about "the lusts of our bodies," in hopes that a stand against sex would make him more credible as a chaplain. He pulled the sermon, computer-printed on gray paper, out of his Bible, unfolded the sheet, and began to read, in as full a voice as he could, the sole sentence that was his own composition: "The Gospel of the Apostle Mark holds an important message for us as we approach our ports of call, especially the Philippines—our bodies and our money have led us too often into sin." He looked up, inspecting the rock faces, then back down, speaking in a voice that became squeakier with every paragraph, even as he struggled to speak with authority. "Let us remember, as we prepare to meet human beings far less fortunate than ourselves, that just because we earn more money in a week than they do in a year is no justification for us to take advantage of the least of God's children, just to satisfy our own selfish lusts. It matters little to the Lord our Judge that this degradation is legal in the Philippines or Thailand. Unless we turn our lives over to the higher law, the lusts of our bodies will destroy both ourselves and those around us. . . ."

As he spoke, he became aware that a person was entering the compartment far off to the right, taking a seat away from the men, as though present only to observe. Miles was afraid to look at this person, and didn't glance up as he lectured against the whorehouses in the Philippines, the twelve-year-old girls sold into sexual slavery by starving families, the "uncles" offering "nephews," the Lord's judgment in the mark of syphilis or gonorrhea or AIDS, the lake of fire that God our Loving but Angry and Disappointed Father has reserved for sexual sinners.

When he was done, when he'd read them the final line—"How many times must the soul of a thirteen-year-old girl be destroyed for seven dollars?"—he looked again at the rock faces, but only one of them had changed. Kruger was staring beyond the podium, in dissociation, his mouth crooked and shifting, as though it were fighting back a churning weight of pain. Miles didn't know how to interpret any of the men's faces. Finally he looked where he didn't want to look, toward the person who'd come in late and was still sitting far to the side, and Miles was stunned to see that it was another chaplain, a big, jowly man wearing gold-and-purple Roman Catholic vestments—and this intruder was nodding and smiling at him, and then winked! *Father Tom Tuttleman? Here for a roll in the rack but finding instead this impostor?* It couldn't be—Okinawa was thousands of miles away—yet, how had this portly cleric, not before seen on the *Harding,* appeared?

The silence drew long. Miles looked down at his prayer book and stumbled into the doxology: "Father Almighty, creator of heaven and earth, You formed us in Your image, and breathed into us the breath of life. When we turned away, and our love failed, Your love remained steadfast. And so, with Your people on earth, and all the company of heaven, we worship Your name and join their unending hymn of praise"—this was where the men joined him—"Holy, Holy, Holy Lord, God of power and might, heaven and earth are full of Your glory, hosanna in the highest." The words felt like peanut butter in his mouth as his tongue worked around and beneath them. Was he credible? Was he doing anyone any good? He was unsure of everything but his name, a word he could say to no one. Without the breath of the hundred men who'd been warming it, the room was growing cold. The ship lurched sideways and he quick-stepped to find his balance.

Then he read to the men, "Let us now take a moment to offer up to the Lord our joys, our concerns, and our thanksgivings. Let us all share." He turned to the nearest man and smiled his invitation.

The sailor spoke up: "I want to pray for the weather. Navigator says there's a fifty-eight percent probability of a jet-stream depression, could be heavy swells. They could rock us into forty-five-degree rolls, and I'm sure nobody wants that."

Everyone said, "Lord, hear our prayer."

The second man said, "I want to thank the Lord for letting me make RM-two. It's a good rating, and on account of it I can buy Jamie a new truck. Jamie, that's my wife."

"Lord, hear our prayer."

After a moment a third man said, "Let's pray for a safe deployment. Let's pray for no mishaps on deck, and no arrests in Okinawa, and no STDs or guys getting their heads bust open in the Philippines. Also, no drug or alcohol violations while aboard ship."

"Lord, hear our prayer."

Miles nodded at a fourth man and the man said, "I ain't got nothing special to say."

They all responded, "Lord, hear our prayer."

It was Kruger's turn and he took off the black-framed glasses and shut his eyes and wrinkled up his face and squeezed the bridge of his nose with a shaking hand as his mouth twisted its way around the words that were cracking his voice: "I have a special intention that I'm going to keep to myself. But I want the rest of you guys to pray for me. I'm *lost* unless you guys pray for me. I need you to pray that I stay on the righteous path."

"Lord, hear our prayer."

Kruger put his glasses back on and became marble-faced again, though the marble had a blue vein bulging across the forehead.

Everyone turned to the Catholic priest. It was his turn, if he wanted it, and there was no guessing what he would say, and Miles, sweating again though the room was colder, wouldn't be able to stop him. The priest was balding, but he ran both hands over his head as though palming back an unruly stand of hair. He straightened in his chair and adjusted the gold-and-purple vestments over his large stomach and said, in a piping voice, which attested to the years of his own uncertain authority, "Let us pray for sexual sinners everywhere."

"Lord, hear our prayer."

Who the hell is this guy and how'd he get here and why'd he say that?

He ran through the rest of the service, the Lord's Prayer, the prayer of thanksgiving, the prayer of pardon and peace, the final benediction—"May the blessing of the Lord Jesus Christ be with you"—"And also with you"—"The service is now concluded, let us go in peace"—and all he wanted was to get out of there.

He was almost out the hatch when a hand tightened on his arm. When he turned he was terrified to see the fat, smiling, balding priest who, he was now certain, was Father Tom Tuttleman, miraculously transported from Okinawa.

"Lovely service, Reverend."

"Uh—thank you."

"I'm Father Bernard Ogleby." The breath was bad, like spoiled milk.

"You are? How'd you get here?"

"Helo'd over from the *Natchez* this morning. I'm the only Catholic chaplain in the ARG, so I have to helo up and down all day Sunday." He made a weary face.

"Jim Banquette. Methodist." They shook hands. The other men had filed out, except Kruger, who was pacing between the couches and chairs with his hands in his pockets, looking down.

"I especially enjoyed," said the priest, "your sermon against the sex lust. There is no greater sin"—he shook his jowly face—"than the sexual one. I think we can say it is surely the one deadly sin."

"Well—"

"Absolutely," said the priest, "but absolutely. You know, the sex sin is something that gives me a lot of anger. But being chaplains, we're in a unique position to help these people. Do you enjoy being a chaplain?"

"Well, I—"

"You know, as I was heloing over here and I saw the flags on your masts—that beautiful white chaplain's flag, with the gold cross on it, flying over the American flag—did you know, by the way, that's the only flag that ever flies over the American flag, and only when services are under way aboard a U.S. Navy vessel? When I saw that flag—whenever I see that chaplain's flag flying—it fills me with a lot of pride. Doesn't it you? A lot of pride?"

"Well now—"

"But I have to say I envy you, you Protestant chaplains, staying on your own ships, never having to helo around the way the rabbi and I do. Not that we should be complaining, of course, lying in our racks till noon the other six days, and being quite slothful."

"Well—"

"I've enjoyed our talk, Reverend, and I hope you'll be joining me and the other chaplains of the Fifty-seventh ARG when we dine at Norio's All You Can Eat in Naha, Okinawa, the night we land ashore. All you can eat!" The priest laughed in self-mockery, patting the underside of his robed belly. He offered his hand and they shook again. Then his gaze alighted on something on the podium. "What a fine Bible! Polished leather, is it?" He picked it up, handling it, flipping its pages. "You know, I really covet this, all they issued me was a big paperback." He replaced the Bible, a bit regretfully. "Well, if you'll excuse me, I must prepare for Holy Mass."

Miles was happy to pick up his books and papers and get out of there, but in the P-way he was aware of someone following him and Kruger said, "Chaplain, can I talk to you?"

Miles turned, already resenting the criticism he was expecting, but Kruger looked sad. His Christian smile was gone.

"What's the problem, Kruger?"

Kruger looked up and down the P-way. "Can we talk in your state-room?"

"All right."

Completion of his religious duty was giving him a curt confidence. Without looking back at Kruger, he led him up the nearest ladder as sprightly as he himself had been led on the first day aboard. He couldn't guess what Kruger wanted, but had a creepy sense of it, as though the huffing behind him on the ladder were the desperate sounds of copulation.

In the stateroom, Miles sat on the edge of his rack and motioned impatiently at the chair as Kruger locked the door.

"So what can I do for you?"

Kruger sat down, gripping the armrests, searching the bulkheads as though doubting their security. Then he folded his hands and leaned forward, his black-framed glasses a little cockeyed, his mouth turned down. "Nobody knows this."

"It'll stay with me."

He licked his lips. "It's about the Philippines—Subic Bay—Olongapo."

"The Philippines. Okay."

"How many times have you been to Subic Bay, Reverend?"

"The Philippines? This is my first WESTPAC." Contradiction, damn it: why'd he just give a sermon about the Philippines if he'd never been there?

"It's common knowledge," said Kruger, "that the things you said are true, even if you've never visited there . . . "

"Just tell me what's bothering you."

More lip licking. "It's about your sermon—the topic of it."

"Yes?"

Head down: "That sermon was about me."

"About you?"

"About me."

"I see," said the chaplain.

"It's common knowledge that a man like me—a man who's made the decision for Christ over ten years ago—shouldn't be paying twelve-year-old girls for—for that sort of thing." Kruger looked up at the ceiling, his glasses reflecting light, his mouth open in a kind of spiritual exhaustion. By the time he looked down, his eyes were watery. "You ain't never been there, you don't know, it's *worse* than what you said in your sermon, the things you said are only common knowledge, you guys must be borrowing each other's sermons or something. When you walk down the Strip—the

Magsaysay Strip—the girls just come out and grab you, they physically grab you, they rub your crotch and everything right there on the street, they try to pull you into the—into the clubs—these are *young girls* doing this—" He put his hand up under his glasses and massaged his eyes. After a moment, his voice skittering a sob, he said, "It could happen to anyone, that's just common knowledge, they don't care who you are so long as you're American, 'cause we're rich to them, all of us, it don't matter, they could approach *you*, they could put their hands down a chaplain's pants, right there on the street, I seen it happen."

Kruger was sitting with his elbows on his knees, the fingers of both hands under his glasses, and Miles withheld judging him in order to consider Banquette: he'd been an Atlantic chaplain, not Pacific, so he would've known nothing about Filipino whorehouses. He'd probably traded sermon files with other chaplains. Banquette's actual views were a mystery. This was of no practical import, since Miles, in the middle of the ocean, was free to create almost any kind of Banquette he chose, but he felt freer to do so now.

"I'm going to tell *you* something in confidence, Kruger."

"Okay."

"It has to stay between you and me."

The hands came off the reddened face, adjusting the glasses; the eyes looked wetly at him.

Miles said, "I've committed fornication myself."

"You have?"

"I have."

"Does your wife know?"

"It was—it was before I knew my wife."

"Oh."

"Kruger, God wants to forgive your sins. But first you have to stop having sex with teenage girls."

"I know that, I know, that's just common knowledge."

"Now, what about Bible study?"

"What about it?"

"I put you in charge of the Bible-study group, right?"

"Yeah, there's three guys signed up. We're going to meet on Thursday nights."

"That's fine. I want you to throw yourself into that. It'll keep your mind occupied. When we get to the Philippines, I want that group to keep meeting."

"What if—what if I go with—bad women?"

"Then come tell me about it."

"That's all? Just come tell you about it?"

"That's the kind of thing that seems to help druggies and alkies. Maybe it'll help you. Promise you'll do it."

"Okay."

"Maybe now you'll be ashamed to take advantage of those people."

"Oh, I am, I am, sir." He stood to go. "Thank you, Reverend." He went to the door, but he turned as though recalling something, and there was nothing on his face to suggest he'd been having an emotional crisis moments before. "I almost forgot. It's common knowledge that the doxology is always sung."

"Well, seaman, I'm not known for my singing voice."

"Just common knowledge, that's all I'm saying."

"Thank you."

When Kruger was gone, Miles made sure to give Father Ogleby plenty of time to say mass and clear out of the crew's lounge, and didn't go back till he heard the helicopter. There were seven men at his second service and he did everything as he'd done it the first time, gaining confidence, though his voice continued to find authority only squeakily or nasally. Then he decided to go up to the wardroom mess to watch another six-month-old David Letterman tape on ship's cable while waiting for lunch, but when he got there Major Lebedeen was watching *Hee Haw* by himself, or rather, staring at *Hee Haw* from beneath his questioning eyebrows while he twisted his twined fingers worriedly on his stomach.

Miles hoped to escape but it was too late: the major saw him and said with relief: "Thank God it's you. We've got a real situation here."

Miles created a smile and took a seat. "Is it your wife?"

"No, no, I haven't heard about that yet, though it's got me plenty worried, I can tell you that, plenty plenty worried, which is why I don't need this damned—excuse me—situation. In fact, if my wife was here I wouldn't even have this problem, because she would know how to deal with it. She would just tell me how to proceed and I wouldn't have the stress of trying to figure out what to do. I'm not good at dealing with a situation like this, there's nothing in regulations that covers civilians, I've got no leadership training in it, not the kind you have, I can barely deal with the situations I *do* have the training in. I've got a heck of a situation to deal with here." He looked around. They were alone; no one was preparing the table yet and none of the other officers was here. "It's that woman, the captain's woman."

"Yes?"

"I had to skip PT again, because this's been bothering me so much. I mean, I delegated, the way you said?" He made a clenched mouth and shut his eyes and raised his head and shook it *no no no,* as though life were unbearable and this latest matter would undo him. Then he leaned forward, looking directly at the chaplain. "This woman is starting to mess with my men. I can't have it. We marines have to take a lot of crap—excuse me—from the navy, but we don't have to live according to their so-called morals. I can't have my men messed with."

"Messed with, I see."

"I don't need this kind of shit, my wife's sick and I'm responsible for three hundred men and I have to help organize maneuvers in the Philippines, and I've never organized anything that size, and this first mail call is coming up—that first mail call is always real hard on the guys—and now I have to worry about *this,* the captain's whore—excuse me, but that's all she is—the captain's whore trying to—trying to do all the unmentionables with all the marines. It causes jealousy and dissension and destroys morale and I just can't have it. Aren't there enough squids for her? Why's she have to pick on the marines? If my wife was here she'd go have a talk with that woman."

"Do you think the captain suspects?"

The major gave an exasperated shake of the head. "The captain's a bureaucrat, he could take a lesson from you and me, he doesn't know how to delegate. He shuffles papers all day and then he's heloing over to the *Natchez* for staff meetings. Getting in good with the admiral, all that kind of crap. Meanwhile, the woman starts to feel ignored." The major shrugged. "I guess I can't blame her, I guess if I were a sexy woman on a ship with six hundred horny young guys, I'd act the same way. But as marine CO I just can't have it." Again he lifted his head and shook it with his eyes closed.

"You'd think," said Miles, "someone would tell the captain."

The major looked at him sternly. "Who would dare? Ship's CO is like a god, this is his little magical kingdom floating on the sea. What I'm leading up to is this: somebody ought to tell this woman to stop harassing my men."

"So why doesn't somebody?"

"It has to be a person of impeccable uprightness."

Uh-oh. He looked away.

"In my view," said the major, "it has to be you."

"It has to be me?"

"It has to be you. There's no one on this ship more qualified, or with better personal morals."

Miles looked down at his badly polished shoes. "Well—I don't know—"

"I do. A thing like this can tear a command apart."

"I wouldn't—wouldn't even know how to approach her."

"Don't worry about all that, I'll make sure she gets word that you want to see her. Didn't they teach you in—in minister school—how to deal with, you know, an oversexed woman?"

Miles was afraid—afraid of—what?—all the unknown destinations a sex discussion with Robin might arrive at. "I just wish—if there were some other way—"

"You're not afraid," said the major, "are you?"

"Of course I'm not afraid."

Major Lebedeen's face went crooked with panic as he lifted his legs to one side, staring at the deck as he said "Gross! See that? It was a cockroach." Then he lowered his legs and said "It's so cold," rubbing the short sleeves of the green uniform he wore every day, as though he were commanding troops deep in the jungle. "We must be near the Aleutians. I hate the thought of being here. My wife is being tested for cancer and I'm out here. I hate Alaska. I hate Okinawa and I hate the Philippines. Just one place I want to go. Peacock Island. Kick back on the beach and close my eyes and forget everything . . . no responsibilities . . . just delegate everything." He sat back with his eyes closed.

Miles stood up. He was feeling a mild contempt for the major—and a stronger contempt for the musical idiocy of *Hee Haw,* which was stridently awful even with the volume way down—and he thought he'd skip the first lunch seating, return to his room, and wait for the second lunch.

He was almost to the door when the major said, "Sorry I missed services."

"That's all right."

"I'm a real busy guy."

"I can see that."

"Maybe next week."

"Major Lebedeen, can I ask you something?"

"Shoot."

"Just how do you get your shoes that way? That mirror shine."

"I use a little cum."

"A little what?"

"A little cum. I put a little cum on the rag, before I buff."

"Are you kidding?"

"Go try it. Next time you're winging the willie—or aren't you chaplain guys allowed to do that? That's the kind of advice I'm always giving my men, it's part of being a leader, it's part of being a professional. As WEST-PAC continues, the longer we've been from home, you'll notice the shoes getting a lot shinier. I figured that little trick out on my own, by the way, by accident once."

Back in his stateroom Miles shrugged and took off his clerical clothes and hung them up and sat in his chair and, trying to think up an erotic fantasy, unable to come up with anyone but Robin, he gave in to images of her hips and thighs and breasts as he masturbated into the shoe rag. He sat there feeling dazed and vaguely unclean. Then he picked up a shoe and buffed madly. His face looked back at him no matter how he turned the shoe, as though he were looking in a black mirror. He did the other shoe, then put on his commander uniform, including the jacket, happy to have something against the cold. Then he stood there, abruptly aware that he had nothing to do. There was nothing left to study for; the next lunch seating wasn't for another hour.

Idly, he sat before the computer and clicked it on. Maybe he'd look at the sermons again. He read the list of files. Nothing interesting, nothing he hadn't read five times. He switched to the hard drive. *PETNOB. RAMPAC-COM. SUBPAC. LATCOMNAV.* Just a lot of DICNAVABic shit, left by officers from other deployments. *NORLONG. SUPDEPPO. DEPTH CHARGE.* Check that one out. The screen filled with a picture of white sky and gray ocean and sitting on the jagged horizon was a ship and he could move it left-right and now there were some submarines entering the screen from the margins, at various depths, and he could drop a kind of bomb on them. Boom! It was fun. After an hour he was pretty good at it. 3600 . . . 4500 . . . 9800 points. But he couldn't crack the top scores, which were in the hundred thousands, held by a player named Mike, an officer who'd obviously been very good at delegating.

Miles missed lunch.

Maybe he could get one of the galley boys to bring him something later. Play a few more games. Annoyingly, at 87,000 points there was a knock.

Eyes on the screen: "Yeah? Who is it?"

The knob was tried and found to be unlocked and the door opened and the person came right in—all of it done so aggressively that Miles thought it was Ditchfield—and the intrusion had him so unsettled that he failed to move his ship out of the way of a torpedo and there was an explosion on the screen, and before he could click off the game so Ditchfield couldn't see it, he heard Robin saying, "You're as bad as Mike was. Nice guy, but he wouldn't even look at you, just sat on that stupid game all day. Chaplain."

Helpless, he shut off the computer. He could feel her moving across the room behind him and when he turned to look she was sitting on the edge of his rack, a woman in her late twenties, blue shorts and white T-shirt clinging to her compact figure, her red-brown hair falling over one shoulder, her eyes shining and her lips a pink bow, mischievous, smiling, barely showing teeth.

"Marine CO sent word you wanted to see me, Reverend."

She'd closed the door on her way in and he couldn't decide if he should open it wide or lock it. He sat there too long wondering. He left it unlocked and positioned his chair toward her. His heart was working with a heavy apprehension; he didn't know how to begin. Services had been easy, the words written out.

He was relieved when she spoke: "Actually I'm kind of surprised that you wanted to talk to me."

"You are?"

Her legs were crossed; now she uncrossed them and spread them a little, and ran her hands down her thighs, capping her knees. She caught his eyes and held them: "You never talk to me in the P-way, you never look at me at meals, you never make eye contact, it's like I don't exist."

He freed his eyes and studied the air five inches over her head. He could feel himself coloring—damn this!

"So what did you want to talk to me about, Commander?"

"Uh—this was Major Lebedeen's idea, actually—the whole thing was."

"It was?"

"He didn't tell you—tell you what it was about?"

She shook her head. Then her eyes looked to the side, large with exaggerated ignorance. "I can't even guess." Did she know exactly what it was about, was she going to make it hell for him?

"Let's just forget it," he said. "This is really a bad idea."

"I bet I can figure out what it is," she said.

He tried staring her down, but her eyes were alive with a self-assured humor, and slid away from his. Any strength he had fell apart—was it the first thrust of desire? He said what he thought: "You're really, very—different."

The sides of her mouth lifted just perceptibly, just enough to show that she knew it was a compliment and she knew it was true and she answered, "I'm the only kind of woman who can survive in an environment like this."

"You're not afraid of anything."

"Not much."

"That's the way, the only way to become One of the"—he didn't say *Guys,* though he supposed it appropriate enough; instead he said, "It puts you in the better position."

"What can they do?" she said, bringing a hand to her chest in false modesty. "I'm just a little ol' civilian, I'm not in their chain of command." Then, more seriously: "Don't have to live by their stupid rules and double standards."

"I admire that."

"None of the other officers will talk to me. They're afraid to."

"You can't blame them."

"I *blame* them, I do. Men are ridiculous people. At least the enlisted guys are nice to me."

"Aren't you afraid the captain will find out?"

She gave him an appraising look with her mouth open and her tongue probing the side of her cheek out. "That marine's been telling you a lot."

"Aren't you afraid?"

"Have you ever been to the captain's cabin, Reverend? It's five times the size of this, it's carpeted, it's paneled, it's heated. It's very nice for one person—very cozy for two. Except he's almost never there, and when he is, he's tired. I don't need that shit, there are a lot of other ships I could be on, better ships—tenders, you know, that don't rock like this and have a ship's store that isn't just a window in the bulkhead—I don't need this crap, I don't need Captain John Shepard and his fucking LST."

"So you're trying to get back at him."

Her brown eyes went molten with an emotion too brief to be studied, then they were sly again. "Don't try to analyze me, Chaplain. The best have tried, little people with little minds, with tiny ideas of what life is supposed to be like."

"But don't you think it's going to end badly?"

"Not for me. Civilian, remember."

"There are others involved."

She shrugged, she raised her hands, she filled her cheeks with air and blew it out all at once. Her eyes were dead, and for the first time he got the sense that the things he appreciated about her—energy mixed with intelligence mixed with ego mixed with a matter-of-fact sexuality—were maskings for a core that wasn't easily known.

"I won't analyze you," he said.

"Good. So why'd you call me here?"

"The marine CO wants you to leave his men alone."

The smile was to one side of her mouth. "All right. Anything else?"

"That's all he wanted."

"But was there anything you wanted?"

"That was all."

She stood up. Her naked legs were tanned, her T-shirted stomach flat, her breasts roundly up-pointed, nipples obvious. Her hair was shining and her eyes were malicious and sexy and smart, and for a moment he felt the hot craziness of wanting her.

"Are you sure?" she said. "There's nothing else I can do for you? Chaplain?"

His rational mind—the only cool part of him still operating—overruled all other possible responses, leaving him with the blatant, "I *am* a chaplain, you know."

"Oh, I know," she said. "I've known *lots* of chaplains." She looked at him a moment, then went to the door and out of the room without saying more.

When she was gone he bit his lower lip and thought of all the other ways he could've responded, but was glad he hadn't, and was determined to stop thinking about her, and turned on the computer and found Depth Charge and was recommencing his assault on the hundred-thousand level when there was a knock. He was in a panic that she was back, but when he asked, "Who is it?" the person answered "Lebedeen."

The major's agitation as he came into the room was so severe that no part of him was still: he paced, he twisted his hands together, he shook his head and opened and closed his eyes, he frowned and exhaled, he arched his eyebrows and slanted them in a torture of uncertainty: "What happened? Did you tell her? What she say? It better be good, because there's more bad news. I need some good news now."

"It's okay, it's all right."

"It is? It is?"

"I think she'll be limiting herself to the navy from here on. She'll leave the marines alone."

"She will? What'd she say?"

"I told her what you wanted and she said okay."

"You brought *me* into it? Oh my God."

Miles was annoyed. "If you'll excuse me, I have some important work to do on the computer."

The major was antsy-pantsy about something else now, and continued to pace.

"I just found out, I can't believe it, we're due for VERT-REP. *This afternoon.* I had no idea, I thought I'd have more prep time, I thought we'd have two or three more days, but they say there might be a storm, and the Aleutians are right out there, the supply stations, we're VERT-REPping at fifteen-fifty hours."

Miles reached for his DICNAVAB, next to the computer. "VERT-REP?"

"VERT-REP! Vertical replenishment." Discussing it was making the major even more agitated, and he rubbed his eyes with the knuckles of his forefingers, and shook his head so that the hair, short as it was, flew here and there as though he were shaking off water.

"Ah," said Miles. "Vertical replenishment." Whatever *that* was.

"I have to spend the next two hours organizing work squads, twelve of them, the most I ever organized was two at a time when I was a lieutenant. On top of everything we'll be getting that first mail call, and ten or twelve of them are going to be Dear Johns—that's always the percentage, never fails—there's going to be a few of my men thinking about having a cleaning accident with their M-16, and it's my responsibility to make sure they don't do it."

"Yeah? How you supposed to do that?"

The major stopped pacing long enough to put his hands in prayer position and aim them at the chaplain: "With your help. Now that you mention it. Remember? First night under way? The captain said we should use you as a resource in these situations."

"Yeah, but I don't—I don't know what to—"

"Wait," said the major, "just hold on there, I don't have time to talk to you now. We'll have to talk about it later. I can't spend the whole afternoon in here listening to you and your problems. Those helos are going to be here in two hours and there's a lot—I have a lot to do. I have to find those lazy lieutenants and tell them to organize work details for this goddamn— excuse me—for this fucking VERT-REPping . . . "

When the major had gone, Miles had two hours to worry what his own mail call would be like. The letter he'd written to Father Tom Tuttleman, he knew, was still lying in the ship's PO, since there'd been no chance to offload it—it would probably go out during VERT-REP. Even so, he wondered if he might actually beat the letter to Okinawa. And there might be more letters from Tuttleman, and from Mrs. James J. Banquette. He caught himself pacing, in the same tight figure eight as the major.

He got a lunch of warmed-over chicken and potatoes from a galley hand and ate in his room and went back to the computer game. As he played, he became gradually aware, as though he were half asleep in a field of grass, of a faraway insect strumming the air, and the sound doubled and redoubled, as though more insects were awakening, and then the sound vibrated over the entire field, metallic in its implications. When he looked up out of his trance he knew the air outside was being whipped by more helicopters than he could imagine in a dream.

And yet this harsh and beautiful music couldn't prepare him for what he saw when he was out of the stateroom and down and out of the P-way, through a hatch, onto a ladder landing. The wind slapped his face, and the ship was rocking, and he held the railing: the bright cold sky was full of helos, some of them circling the *Harding*, others buzzing the gray silhouettes of the other ships. The choppers were navy gray and marine green, each dangling a spider thread with a mesh-wrapped bundle at the end. The water looked as purple-cold as the sky, and the other ships were heaving, and the helo chopping was thrumming everywhere. There were still more helos coming in three distinct lines from three points on the watery horizon, the farthest ones were blips on the shimmering band of light where sky met water, the edge of the world, concealing, just beyond the curvature of the earth, a thing stretching out larger than the sky—Alaska. Miles watched as one of the copters, a long green machine stenciled USMC with two invisible horizontal blades, one at each end, approached the *Harding* with a Chinese puzzle of crates bundled at the end of the tether. The ship

and the helo did a dance, the ship diagonal-up and straight-left and diago-
nal-right and straight-down, the helo forward and aft and higher and
lower, the pilot obviously afraid of striking any of the swinging falling rising mast-crosses or stacks with his bundle of cargo or the helo itself. For a
moment, Miles was afraid, because the cargo was swinging close to a stack
that was billowing up a lot of diesel-black smoke, threatening to blind the
pilot. Then, as though by mutual awareness, the helo and the ship were in
synchrony, and the bundle of cargo landed with a bang on the fantail.
Immediately sailors and marines were all over it, unhooking it and undoing the net before the whole thing could lift again and carry them into the
sky, and the helo buzzed away starboard, rolling up its tether. Navy chiefs
and marine sergeants were yelping orders, managing the disassembly of the
bundle and the disposition of the crates, which the men began to carry
away in teams, crates stenciled CALIFORNIA TOMATOES, CALIFORNIA LETTUCE,
CALIFORNIA GREEN BEANS, CALIFORNIA ORANGES. Major Lebedeen was
nowhere to be seen. By the time the men were dragging away the pallets,
the next helo was already swinging its two-ton bundle over their heads.
Then the next bundle of crates slammed onto the fantail . . . they were
stenciled FPO SAN FRANCISCO***UNITED STATES MILITARY MAIL. He felt a clench
of anxiety in his stomach.

He returned to his cabin and took a nap and had a dream. Robin had
come to see him in his stateroom, and she was wearing her blue bikini. The
blue went very nicely against the gold-brown of her shoulders and tummy
and legs. He was sitting on the edge of his rack, and she was standing in
front of him, and her eyes were giving him a sly and slanted look as she
said, "Do you think I shaved well enough?" She put one leg forward for his
inspection. "Is it smooth, Miles?" In the false logic of his dream, he was
happy that she knew his real name. He reached out and touched the inside
of her thigh with his fingertips, ran his palm down to her knee, and her leg
was smooth and warm. When he looked up, she was regarding him with
wry humor and proprietary lust, and he was so scared and happy his chest
was hurting, because it couldn't contain his feelings.

"What's your wife's name?" said Ditchfield.

He thought he was only dreaming.

"Hey, sailor, I said what's your wife's name!"

"Mary Lou," he said, knowing it was nonsense but still living in his
dream. He didn't know if he'd said it aloud.

Then he was awake and Ditchfield was standing in the open doorway—had he opened it himself?—Ditchfield with his gray skin and gray uniform, standing with a bulging canvas bag to his side, almost as tall as he was, and he was holding a brown package lacquered shiny with tape. "That ain't it," he said.

"What?" Miles stood up at once.

"I asked you your wife's name and you got it wrong." He was showing his tobacco-brown teeth, and there was a malicious narrowness to his eyes—either it was *You goddamn chaplains dream about other women too, ha*—or, more horribly, *You ain't no Chaplain James Banquette, don't know your own wife's name.*

"Of course I know my wife's name."

"What is it?"

Okay, what is it? He wasn't quite awake and he couldn't go to his desk and check her letter and he was damned if he could remember her name. He resorted to bluster, to rank: "CPO, her name is Mrs. James J. Banquette, now give me my package."

Ditchfield laughed so hard that he accidentally drew a long snot wad back from his nose and began coughing and choking on it. He threw the package at Miles and continued hacking as he dragged the mailbag away.

Catching the package, Miles looked immediately for the return address. Michelle. Of course. And there were two kids, a boy and a girl, what the hell were their names? Open the package and find out.

The damn thing was certainly well taped. The tape wound round and round the package, apparently one piece, invisibly turning corners, running in mysterious perpendicularity to itself, no beginning or end, so there was nowhere for him to begin to peel. After two minutes with this maddening cube, he had a fuller sense of the kind of stalwart and meticulous woman Mrs. James J. Banquette was than had emerged from her previous letter. He'd have better luck ripping up corsets and chastity belts with his bare hands. He opened and slammed drawers looking for a penknife, a razor—anything—then he went cursing into the head and came back with the mustache scissors. He was about to stab them into the heart of the package when the door, which Ditchfield had left open, and which had been swinging in the P-way, hit someone in the face and he heard Lebedeen saying, "Ow, ow!"

"Sorry," said Miles.

"Goddamn it! Secure your door!"

"I said I was sorry." The scissors were tangling in the layers of tape.

The major came in with both hands over his nose. "That was a real owie."

In his chair, working on the impossible package, Miles watched the major walk across the room and get down into the rack and lie there with his hands over his face. Stretched out on his back he was a short man, thin, his two-inch hair worn in bangs, which made him look like a rock star next to the Velcro-heads he commanded, and his skin was pale against a green uniform that was too clean, too sharp-cornered, to look like anything having to do with battle. Flat on his back with his hands covering his face, the major looked like a boy.

"Nobody has the worries and problems I do," he said. "They can watch where they're going in the P-way."

"Hear from your wife?"

"Letters, yeah, but they're too early for the cancer test, that'll come by radio message. I just can't seem to concentrate on my job, what with everything at home. Listen, I've got those poor bastards assembled, you better go now."

"What poor bastards?"

The major looked up. "Hey, are they delivering packages already? All I've seen is letters. My wife usually sends me the ingredients for oatmeal-and-raisin cookies and I whip them up in the galley and share them with my lieutenants, they appreciate a thing like that, you know, from the command. It shows you care, even though you're of superior rank. I know that most wives would just bake the cookies on their own and send them, but then they're not fresh. And besides, my wife is pretty busy with her job and everything, so she and I have agreed it's better if I bake them out here. We have equality in our home."

"*What* poor bastards?"

"Poor bastards? Oh, the Dear Johns, the poor bastards you said you'd help."

"I didn't say I—"

"Those guys've got to learn that whatever's happening at home, they can't let it interfere with their professionalism as marines. That's what I'm trying to teach them."

"How do you *know* they got Dear Johns? What do you do, read all their mail?"

Major Lebedeen sat up on the edge of the rack. His nose was still red from running into the door, and his eyebrows assumed their questioning slant—features incongruous with the pride in his voice: "Hey, we're *the marines*. We're different from sailors. We have higher standards and we take care of our men. If a man has trouble managing money, the lieutenants take over his bank account, we balance his checkbook for him, and we make sure his wife and kids have enough to live on back home. If a man has a drinking problem, we have a DAAPA—that's a Drug and Alcohol Abuse Prevention Administrator—who takes him to AA meetings and forces him to drink Antabuse every morning. If a man who works in the laundry goes into town and gets his hands all cut up in a fight and then visits a prostitute and comes back with digital gonorrhea all over his fingers and thumbs—this is a true story, by the way, this really happened—if that marine comes back with the digital clap and he's working in the camp laundry, we don't let him wash any more clothes. We force him to go to the doctor and we reassign him to scrubbing out pots in the kitchen or something, some job where he can't infect people's clothing. That's the way we are, we're *the marines*, we're responsible for one another. Do you think the naval command gives a shit if a sailor is broke, or sick, or his girlfriend dumps him? We have a great retention rate in the marines. It's because we *care*. My men were *ordered* to read their mail out loud today, in front of their sergeants, and the ones with Dear Johns were *ordered* to turn in their M-16s, to prevent any 'cleaning accidents,' and those poor bastards were *ordered* to report to the library, where they're sitting right now, around a table, with their letters in front of them, waiting for you, Reverend."

Miles shook his head, giving in. He threw the unopened package, with the scissors still in it, onto his desk, and said "Okay, all right, I guess I can talk to them, it won't cost me anything. I can probably help—I know what it's like to be young and to have—well, love problems."

The major's eyebrows leapt in surprise. "Yeah? What they do, give you a special class in minister school?"

"I had a life before the ministry, Major. I've been around."

"You mean, you dated girls and stuff?"

"And stuff."

The major scrunched up his brow as though thinking, *Well, if he says so.*

Miles went to the door. "So okay, let's head down there."

"Oh, I'm not going," said the major.

"What do you mean you're not going? Aren't we talking to them together? I thought you had some big speech you wanted to make, how they're marines first, can't let what's happening at home bother them, have to concentrate on their jobs and all that."

"Oh, I've got too much on my mind to give a big speech like that." The major looked at his watch. "I'm going to have to delegate all of that to you. I'm due in the radio shack in ten minutes."

"For what?"

"Clear-channel hour. If I'm going to be getting a message from my wife today, it'll be soon. There's rumors of a storm, you know, and that disrupts transmission. I can't miss a message from home because I'm out talking to some group of marines." The major stood up, dragging his hands down his face. "This has been an exhausting day. I really feel depleted, you know? At least we're headed for Peacock Island, at least we can say that. Okinawa, the Philippines, then Peacock Island—only twenty-three more days. I know I'm going to feel renewed there. Sunshine, swimming, a little volleyball—I love being on maneuvers. It rejuvenates you. Well, look at me, I know I don't have to explain spirituality to you."

The ship was starting to rock harder as Miles went down the ladders toward the library. The ship jumped and skidded and shuddered and rolled in sudden new directions, and he could hear things slam-banging everywhere, and he held tightly to the ladder rails. He guessed that outside, in the darkening sea and sky, the storm rumors were evolving into fact.

He tried to decide what he thought of Major Lebedeen, a man apparently near his own age, but who seemed ten years younger. Miles had been the baby of the family, and his two brothers, Purvis and Lamar, had always treated him as though he were an annoyance left underfoot, an object to be occasionally tortured with physical and verbal jabs, but otherwise to be as fully ignored as one would ignore any demanding, unbathed, chocolate-mouthed, whining, wall-coloring, snot-running pants-pisser of a five-year-old. He realized these were exactly the feelings he had toward the major, as though the universe, having forgotten to inflict upon Miles the bother and indignity of a younger brother, were making up for it now.

Miles entered the little room that was used for a library and there were six men waiting for him, four white and two black, wearing green T-shirts and camouflage pants. They were sitting around the rectangular table, their letters lying in their envelopes before them. The men who were chewing tobacco were using Styrofoam cups to spit into, which they had to hold on to, lest the rocking of the ship send the brown tobacco-sputum spilling across the table.

The Velcro-heads were turned in the direction of a lance corporal who was saying, "Then you put a lighted match to the sauce. You wait for the flame to die down, see, then you add the lemon-and-orange mixture. You drop the crêpes into the boiling sauce and pour in a shot glass of curaçao and a shot glass of maraschino liqueur and a shot glass of kirschwasser. You set the whole damn thing on fire again, then you serve it right away, makes enough for four people. That's crêpes suzette, that's all there is to it. . . ."

Then the men noticed Miles, and they stood at once and were quiet, their hands raised in salute, their chins up and their eyes focused on imaginary points. They stood that way even though the ship was rolling and their faces were pinking from the workings of their leg muscles to keep them standing bowling-pin straight. "At ease," Miles said, returning their salute, and they sat down, each with his hands clasped in front of him on the table.

He took a seat among them, as though he were their equal, and assumed what he hoped was a warm, inviting look. "I'm Chaplain Banquette."

"Sir," they all said.

"I understand there were some problems with the mail."

"Yes sir," they all said.

"I want everyone to speak openly," Miles tried. "I may be a minister, but you can say anything you want in front of me. You can say what you feel."

"Thank you, sir," said one of the men. "I lied just now."

"You lied? You haven't said anything yet."

"I lied when I said there was a problem with my mail. There's no problem with my mail, sir. I'm here because I'm ordered to be here, and that's all." The marine crossed his arms and gave Miles a superior look.

"I don't understand. Isn't that a Dear John lying in front of you?"

"Yes sir."

"Well, that's a problem, isn't it?"

"No sir. I've got three girlfriends at home and I've been trying to shake this one for six months. I finally worked it so she got pissed at me before I deployed, and she wrote me this letter. I'm glad she did, you know? The girl's trouble. She's always wanting to get married and start having babies. She's a pain in the butt, sir."

"I see."

"I can manage my own life just fine, I don't need 'sensitivity sessions' or any shit like that, I don't need my weapon taken away. I still got two women at home and more waiting in Subic Bay. So I ask permission to be excused, Commander."

Miles didn't know what to say. This boy was obviously more self-assured than he himself had been at eighteen—or maybe even now. "There's always a special case, permission to leave is granted."

"Thank you, *sir!* Can I please have my weapon back? Only a pussy kills himself with his weapon because some bitch writes him a letter."

"I'm going to try to get all the weapons back. I'll talk to the major."

"Permission to speak in confidence?" said the self-assured marine.

"All right."

"Sir, somebody ought to take the major's weapon away. I think we all feel the same way—he's a girl, he's a paper pusher, he's a little flower, I wouldn't follow him into battle against Munchkin Land."

"Is that all?"

"Yes sir. And thank you, sir."

The marine picked up his letter and left and Miles addressed the others: "Well, who wants to go first? You'll feel a lot better if you just get the stuff out." It was what his old NA sponsor always said.

Nobody spoke. They sat there with their hands clasped in front of them. The ship took a roll and one of the tobacco spit-cups moved diagonally and dangerously across the table, but one of the marines grabbed it before it could upend.

"Well," said Miles, "I guess I have about as much time as you do."

"Okay, I'll talk," said the man who'd been explaining crêpes suzette. "The way I see it," he said, picking up his letter and gesturing with it, "it's like this: Julie wants to fuck my best friend? Fine. She's good-looking enough to get anyone she wants, that's pretty damn obvious. But you know what? When she's in her thirties she'll be divorced from some clown, maybe have a kid or two, and her looks are gonna start to go, and she'll be lucky if any guy looks at her at all—you ask any woman in her thirties, they'll tell you all the good guys are taken—meanwhile, us guys just keep getting better. We go up in rank, we get richer, and if we're not married—or even if we are—we'll have women practically attacking us. So I'm just gonna sit back and wait fifteen years. We'll see what kind of time Julie's having, and we'll see what kind of time *I'm* having."

As the man spoke, Miles looked around at the others. One of the black marines, no older than twenty, his head shaved around the sides with an oval mesa of hair up top, had taken out his letter and was reading it. He sucked in his lips and blinked, and blinked again, and Miles realized with a pang of sympathy that the boy was trying with all his being not to cry.

The crêpes-suzette expert was still talking: "You know what's wrong with women? You want to know what their basic problem is? They grow up with this fucking fairy-tale idea of what life is really supposed to be like. They're supposed to be princesses, they're supposed to meet a fucking prince—some guy who's perfect and doesn't have any human flaws or any shit like that—some fucking *knight*—and he's supposed to take her to some fucking castle somewhere and make babies with her and give up anything else he's interested in and basically become her slave. Whenever a guy falls short of that fairy tale in any way, man, there's trouble, there's a fight, he gets a fucking letter like *this*."

"You're not being fair," said the black marine, still blinking.

"I'm not being fair? *I'm* not being fair?"

"Some of your ideas," ventured one of the others, "are a little bit sexist."

"Yeah," said another man, "it sounds like you think women are only good for one thing."

"All right, all right," said the crêpes-suzette guy, raising his open hands in angry defense, "you think I'm a sexist, you think I hate women, you think I just want to use them. All right, all right, what if I do? I'm not saying I do, but what if I do? How'd I get that way? Huh? How'd I get that way, I'll tell you how, I'll tell you how a lot of us get that way. See, the first time you're in love, the very first time, when you're fifteen or something like that, you fall in love with this really great girl. Trouble is, she doesn't give a shit about you. She really doesn't care about you. What she really wants is some older guy, some guy with a car, some guy with whatever it is you don't have. Every guy has a girl like this in his past—the first time he was ever in love. And this girl just completely treats him like shit, fucks a lot of older guys, or if she fucks younger guys, she fucks his best friend. What does this do to a guy? What does it do to him for the rest of his life? The next time you fall in love, it's not the same, it's not like the first time. Each time you meet a new girl, you get more cold-hearted about it. You gotta be, else you don't survive. So these women who complain about the way some guy is treating them, they have to look back into their own pasts, see, and admit that they're a part of it all, think back real hard and try to remember that guy in high school that they made feel like total shit, wouldn't give him the time of day or nothing."

"What do *you* know?" said the black marine, his eyes shining-wet, blinking. "You're just an ignorant cook."

"I may be just an ignorant cook, okay, I'm just an ignorant cook, but this is the second time in my life I got a letter like this, and I'm not ever going to forget it, you never do, and I swear to you"—he picked up one of the tobacco spit-cups—"I'll drink this damn thing if this isn't the truth—I'm just going to wait till someday I'm a colonel and I'll have all the women I want, I'll get transferred to the White House detail and I'll cook for the president and the queen of England and I'll have all the babes I want, when I'm cooking for the queen I'll meet some royal princesses and have love affairs with them, and the fucking bitch who's fucking my best friend right now—my *ex*-fucking best friend—she's going to be nothing, she'll just be nothing to me, she'll be fat and divorced and ugly and old, the way they all get."

"It's hard to believe how anyone like you," said Miles, "ever got a Dear John." But nobody laughed. They were all looking warily at the black marine, and when Miles turned, he saw that the boy, who was carefully folding his letter back into its envelope, had a tear moving down one side of his black shining face. He did nothing to wipe it off, just let it fall off his chin onto the table. Then he clasped his hands in front of himself and lifted his chin and refocused his eyes on that point in the air that all good marines could imagine.

Nobody was looking at him now, and everyone was quiet.

"Well," Miles began, but wasn't sure what to say next. "Anyone have anything else to share?"

No one.

He felt that he'd failed, that he'd let the discussion get out of control, that he wasn't any kind of chaplain. He felt guilty. Most of all, he felt infinitely sorry for these boys, even the cook. "Well," he said, "I see—I see it's almost dinnertime. I want you to know that you can always—you can always come talk to me, if you need to." Could he do them any good? "Uh—everyone all right?" Silence. "Will you men give me your word—I mean, if nobody's going to do anything crazy, if you can go back to your quarters and not do anything like that—uh—if you give me your word, I'll have the major return your weapons to you. How's that? Would that make everyone feel better?"

"Thank you, sir," they said together in their monotone.

"All right then. I'll speak to the major." He stood up and they all stood up, rigid-straight. "Dismissed," he said and they picked up their spit-cups and letters. On his way out, the cook, showing both rows of teeth as he spoke, told Miles, "What do you know, anyhow, Chaplain? You're an officer, you got your wife at home in your big-assed house, she never fucks around on you, she's always there for you. Sir, you're not one of *us*."

Miles stood there as though he'd been hit square in the mouth with a two-by-four and he watched them file out. The black marine was the last one and he turned around in the doorway and said, "Thank you very much, sir."

Miles found his voice just in time to reply, "I guess I didn't help a whole lot."

"It helps to know somebody cares."

Miles felt a little better, but still wished he could've led a more effective discussion, and painfully felt his lack of training for the job.

Hanging onto the ladder rails with both hands as the ship jerked one way and another with the intimations of rougher weather, he continued to feel inadequate, and this feeling turned to one of peril when he unlocked his door and found Ditchfield leaning over the desk. Miles had forgotten to close and lock it, and the package was still on it, scissors sticking up. Ditchfield jumped and dropped some papers and gave Miles the fierce look of a surprised but dangerous dog. "Chaplain's back," he said, "come out." An enlisted man came out of the head with a round toilet brush. The old man composed himself and said, "We was just finishing up, Reverend. Sink, terlet, some light dusting too." There was a pail on the floor and a broom against the bulkhead and Ditchfield picked them up and went clanging past Miles, saying, "Come on, Sylvester," as the boy hurried after him with his own bucketful of cleansers and brushes. And the boy was saying, "But we ain't done yet, Chief," and Ditchfield was saying, "Don't matter, we're in the commander's way." And they were out the door.

Miles went over to his desk. He felt sick. The letter from the gay priest was sitting slantwise in a cubbyhole, apparently undisturbed. But there was no way to know.

He picked up the letter, which he'd been saving to counter-blackmail Tuttleman with, should the priest discover his imposture when the ship arrived at Okinawa. He looked in some drawers and found a matchbook, took the letter into the head, dropped it into the sink, struck a match, and applied it to a corner of the envelope. He watched the letter take flame, gradually lift and ball up into an orange meteor of fear in the shining steel sink, a fire like a tiny coda, a punctuation mark to the conflagration that had transformed him into the man he now thought he was, hoped he was. Then there was nothing left but the black-wad curl of paper, which could not hurt him or help him now.

6

The storm exploded against the ship from above and below, the rain-driving gales tilting the superstructure too far toward the capsize line, and the helmsmen would furiously correct it, and a mountain of ocean would rise beneath the ship and send it sloping downward where it would crash into a valley of water, all decks shiver-shaking as though the flat bottom had fallen on rock, then up and sideways again. All the while the screaming madness of the storm was whistling into the tightest rivetings of the ship, making the P-ways and compartments sing and moan like wind tunnels, as if the storm, even as it blasted the ship from above and earthquaked it from below, knew that the quickest way to destroy the ship was to send a million filaments of sound into its cracks, each whistle uniquely pitched—the drowned voices of sailors from the wooden schooners and whalers and men-of-war that had struggled this far years ago, but only this far, and had been waiting quietly, a mile below, for the night when their crews would come flying out of the sea to circle and mock ships of metal and sing them to pieces.

Miles was able to reach the wardroom mess only by allowing himself to be thrown up against one bulkhead and then the other, his hands out, his feet fighting for progress against a deck that rose when he thought it would fall and fell when he thought it would rise. Too many things had gone unsecured, and he could hear file drawers rolling open and smashing closed, chairs skittering and overturning, medicine chests flying open and spilling their contents into steel sinks with the sound of pachinko machines, and the more mysterious and perhaps serious disasters occurring belowdecks with profound and echoing booms. The singing was everywhere, the creaking was everywhere, as though the *Harding* would go popping at its joints.

Miles fell into the room with such force he was afraid the door would come off, as he had to hang onto it to avoid landing on deck. The Dear John meeting had made him late, and everybody was already at table. He was surprised to see the captain—the storm must've made it impossible for him to eat with his dinner companion of preference, the admiral, on the *Natchez.*

Miles took advantage of a starboard lurch that sent him across the room and held him against the bulkhead, which he inched along until he came to his empty chair, between the COMMO—communications officer—and Major Lebedeen.

Bracing himself against the table as he took his seat, he was planning to ignore the major, but Lebedeen was gripping his salad plate so fiercely that Miles looked at him inquisitively. All the men were holding their plates to keep them from sliding, but the major wasn't eating, just staring at his salad. The major wouldn't look back at him, and Miles knew the man had received bad news from home.

All at once, the ship rose twenty feet and fell violently to port, and the line of officers sitting across from him fell backward and out of their chairs, showing eight pairs of soles, and their food was flying after them. Miles and the others on his side were thrown across the top of the table and everybody was swearing. As the ship righted itself, the captain, whose position at the head of the table had allowed him to hold onto its corners without falling out of his chair, grabbed his salad plate as it started moving back the other way and said, "Holy fucking shit!"

Robin had the seat at the other end of the table, and she too had avoided falling. "Who the hell's driving?" she said. "W. C. Fields?"

The captain's white hair was standing erect, partless. His face was purpling, and the more it colored the more he looked like W. C. Fields. "Shut up," he said.

"Shut up and drown?" she said.

"Just shut the fuck up," said the captain, and he got out of his chair and waited for the ship's movement to propel him toward the door and out of the room. In the P-way he collided with a seaman who danced him backward into the room. The captain landed back in his chair while the seaman grabbed the galley counter to keep from falling into the captain's lap.

"Message from the *Buchanan,* sir! From the CO!"

"Yeah? What in hell's that little faggot want?"

"Shall I read it to you, sir!"

"Read it fast, ain't got all night."

Clipboard up: "The message reads: 'Hey, Johnny Boy: We're sitting here on the bridge smoking cigars and watching your flat-bottom ass get kicked all over the goddamn Pacific Ocean. Thanks for a great show. Benny.'"

"That's not fair," said Major Lebedeen so loudly that Miles, who'd just climbed off the table and into his seat, almost flew out of it again. "That's not fair at all, we're a tank ship, we have to pull in close to shore and roll out the tanks, that's why we're flat-bottomed, they know that, they know it, it's not right. We're in danger and they're making jokes about it, where's the esprit de corps?" Lebedeen looked around the table, manic-eyed, for support, but the others looked at him warily. He dropped his eyes to his plate and gripped it again.

"You send that little faggot a message back," said the captain to the seaman. "You tell him—"

"I haven't got a pencil, sir!"

"Goddamn it, yeoman, memorize it! You radio that little faggot with the following message: 'Benny, I'll not only beat your syphilitic ass all the way to Okinawa, but you'll be eating my shit-foam all the fucking way to Australia AND all the fucking way back to your flat-titted wife in San Diego.'"

"How many *f*s in syphilitic, sir!"

"Five, goddamn it! Now get the hell out of here!"

"Aye-aye sir!"

The boy turned, and the captain, holding onto the sides of the table, was rising to follow him out when Robin said to him, "If the hold needs pumping, remember that you have to calculate the cubic area affected and then divide by one hundred and twenty gallons per minute—"

"The hold doesn't need any damn pumping," said the captain.

"That's what you said last summer in the Straits of Taiwan and we almost sank. Captain," she added.

"Straits of Taiwan was a completely different ballgame, it was a fucking monsoon, this is a divergent tropical depression."

"But if the hold fills with—"

"I said the hold doesn't need any goddamn pumping, now shut up."

The ship struck a wall of water, headlong as though running into a shelf of rock, and the hull vibrated and screamed as though it would accordion. Everybody had to finger-hang to the table edges to keep from falling over, and two or three men did fall over with spectacular cries and the frenzied arcs of knees and feet in the air.

"Goddamn that helmsman," said the captain. "I'm going right up there and relieve that son-of-a-bitch. I could drive this boat better myself, drunk and blindfolded with a broken beer bottle up my ass."

"Put in someone gentle," said Robin.

"I don't know anybody gentle. And if I did I wouldn't put him in."

Miles couldn't help imagining that Robin was sticking her tongue out at the captain, but when he looked down the length of the table, she was looking at her food, watching the plate slide left, then right. Her eyes had the same dull emptiness he'd seen in his stateroom, and he wondered how far the vacuum widened within her, how empty she might be, or whether her detachment was a stoicism he could admire. He didn't know what he felt about her, about being a chaplain, about the Dear John meeting, about anything, as though the metallic earthquaking of the ship, combined with his trip halfway across the table, had scrambled him completely.

Watching the captain weave out of the doorway, he didn't even know if he should be afraid. Then Major Lebedeen kissed him on the ear. Miles jumped. The major had been leaning over to whisper something and the ship had lurched. The major said, "I don't care if we die."

"Have you heard from your wife?"

"She has cancer."

"I'm sorry."

"I don't want to talk about it." The major's eyebrows were as questioning as ever, and his mouth was adolescent in the bitterness of its pout.

For the rest of the meal, Miles and the others played a nervous eating game; the servers came swaying out with the bins, aimed food at the shifting plates, sometimes hitting them. The diners would eat when the plates were near, chew when the plates moved to the center of the table, eat again when the food had slid back . . .

The tablecloth was mottled with food and so were the men's uniforms and Robin's T-shirt. Ditchfield stuck his head over the galley counter and said, "Due to inclement weather, we ain't gonna have no goddamn dessert operation tonight, no coffee neither. Also no midrats tonight, and first breakfast seating is postponed till oh-nine-hundred hours. The wardroom staff apologizes but we can't be chasing egg yolks across the deck with our snouts all morning. That is all!"

"No fucking midrats tonight," said one of the JOs in his young piping voice. "What're you supposed to do if you got the duty all night and get hungry at oh-one-hundred?"

"That's what it means to be a junior officer in the navy," said the DISBO, trying to align a burning match with the bowl of his pipe and failing. "You want to raid the kitchen all night, join the army. You want to eat jet farts all night, join the air force. You want to polish your tools all night, join the marines. You want to get laid nineteen different ways in a Siamese whorehouse, join the navy."

"Siamese whorehouse?" said one of the JOs. "What's that, two whorehouses joined together?"

Another JO wanted to know, "Do Siamese whores charge you double?"

The DISBO had succeeded, with a series of puffs, in lighting his pipe. "Don't worry, gentlemen—there's a two percent chance we won't drown tonight. We might just live to see Pubic Bay again. Excuse me, *Subic* Bay. Forgot there was a minister and a lady present."

A minister, thought Miles. *A lady*. And then he was afraid of these ironies, for the DISBO, squinting at him now, pipe held judiciously in his mouth, was, like the most accomplished of cynics, a man of hostile probity.

It was time to leave. He asked his permission and went across the mess and down the P-way, and it was like shambling around drunk. As he landed against one bulkhead, then the opposite, he remembered with an antinostalgic, sickening feeling how he used to fuck himself up until the world moved exactly like this, the floor pulling out from under him, the walls collapsing on his shoulders and head, and he was nauseated, and terrified at the joke of having cleaned himself up and contrived a new life and come thousands of miles only to die as he would've anyway, the world spinning and folding in as he drowned, not in alcohol, but in water.

He struck his head against a big water gauge sticking out of the wall, and the fireworks exploded in his brain. He went down on his knees with his hands over his head and he was unable to see for a moment.

Getting up was hard. His hands found nothing but wall and deck. When he could see again, the lights were flickering and he didn't know if it was his jangled brain or the jangled *Harding*. There was an oval of dullness where he'd hit his head, then the pain began to twitch to life with hot electric needles. He had to shut his eyes against it as he gingerly felt the swelling under his blood-wet hair.

He realized with a numbing apprehension that if he was going to die tonight it wouldn't be all at once. There were no such deaths at sea.

Walking-crawling-dancing into his stateroom was like falling into the exploding soup of existence, a book sailing here, some papers shuffle-flying there, the overturned chair skidding here and there. He went tripping over these items and into his rack, where he kept a hand on the throbbing lump on his head. He rolled left, right, hitting the bulkhead, hitting the guardrail, without which he would've been on the deck. He watched the possessions of James J. Banquette flying and thumping across the room as though they were his weightless remains, free, now that he was dead, to disattach themselves from reality, from gravity, an abrogation of every relationship a person could have to an object. Among these items, rolling and skittering across the deck, was the unopened package from the minister's wife, the scissors stuck more securely into it, driven more deeply by the violence of the storm. Miles fantasized that the package held the dead man's bisected heart, and felt a morbid pity, for the thing was just as irrelevant as the shaving-cream can or the deodorant stick rolling alongside it. Miles watched the package bounce and land and go bouncing away again.

The captain's voice crackled into the air, coming out of speakers in every P-way on every deck, and his voice overrode the screaming storm: "This is the CO. Well—goddamn it—*this sucks.* I'm ordering every man to stay in his rack. And the one woman, for that matter. Repeat, every man not on bridge duty is to remain in his rack until further advisement. And needless to say—even though I'm going to say it, because you never know what some anchovy-brain is gonna do—stay off the goddamn weather decks. If you go outside, there's not a goddamn thing I can do for you. The *Buchanan* reports a man overboard—don't be next. That is all."

The knowledge that somebody was already dead—or at best, getting thrown around in the cold ocean, waiting to die—depressed Miles to a breathless extent, and he raised his hands to his throat, and swallowed, and his eyes were wet. A man was dead, a man was dead. He didn't know why he was more moved by this abstraction than he'd been by the actual corpse of Chaplain Banquette, then he realized it was because the man who'd gone overboard was any man, and therefore himself. Banquette, though real in his memory, though looking enough like him to make a smudgy photo ID passable, was not Miles. The boy now dying, or just dead, represented

Miles's own death, and so his depthless pity wasn't for the boy, nor was his growing terror for the boy. As the storm rolled him quickly left and right he could think of no one but himself.

He could die tonight. Ships went down in storms all the time. He'd be erased. The idea was so intolerable that he couldn't bear his selfishness or self-pity, and so he forced himself, as he always did in difficulty, to think of Kari. It was a paradoxical way of forgetting himself and remembering the small part of himself he would someday leave behind.

The last time he'd seen her it was winter, a year and a half ago . . .

He'd been working in a grocery store in Salina, Kansas, and he hated it there. He couldn't understand why people said Kansas was the Midwest—there were no factories or woodlands or real cities or Victorian neighborhoods or covered bridges, just a flat winter-whiteness suggesting that the character of the place was eternal vacancy. The Kansans, paler than Chicagoans or even Hoosiers, walked around in their gray parkas with expressions of blue-eyed simplicity or, more strangely, an unfathoming kind of shock, as though they'd just woken to find themselves in this cold flat place that had no identity, this nonplace on the plains. These same strip malls you would find anywhere else, but you got the feeling that the malls and modular neighborhoods had no reason for being here, had been accidentally dropped by the Devil on his return trip from Los Angeles, were a graham-cracker front less sturdy than anything in a studio lot. The Kansans drove around the place in Chryslers, big-eyed, or ate their way through racks of pork in mall diners, lazily, or stood in plaid lines in groceries, silently, as though their idea of being human was simply that they were better than hogs, the only other mammals in the state. His conclusion: these folks were innocent, but they did not wonder.

He would die on this ship—he expected to hear the explosions of water as it broke into deck after deck on its way up—he would die and be returned, for his sins, to the snow-winds of Kansas, the dirt-winds of Dakota.

Kari—

So he'd cashed his paycheck and bused himself the hell out of Salina, Kansas, going, for the first time in his wanderings, eastward, back home. He hadn't thought he could miss home so much, especially in winter. As the bus went bouncing down the snowy interstates of Missouri, he hugged himself in the cold of his cheap overcoat and fantasized what it would be like:

He would get off in front of the one-room Greyhound next to the coffee shop in Zincville, and he'd be on Broad Boulevard—how he used to joke about that name!—and yes, the Illinois sky would be the color of wet newspaper and the streets would be full of dirty slush, but he'd feel fortified because there were activity and purpose here. His father's trucks would be going down Broad Boulevard, kicking up salt wads and snow as they carried electroplated solenoids to Detroit, air-conditioner casings to Chicago, microphone stands to Nashville, gold-plated dinnerware to New York and Houston and Boston and Atlanta. In the blue shadow of his father's factory, he would walk down the street with his hand grip and turn onto Lincoln Avenue, thickly lined with naked oaks, and go straight to Mary Lou's white clapboard house, and give her this month's support money in person, in cash, and they'd talk, and they'd both be with Kari. He'd see her again and pick her up—and then perhaps—maybe—

But of course his arrival had been utterly different. From the moment the door had opened, at his third knocking, everything had gone askew. Mary Lou, tousle-haired in a housecoat, had looked at him as though he were a killer, and their conversation as they went down the entry hall into the living room was anxious and stilted, and the television was on, some dreary soap opera, and when he first saw Kari—walking, she had learned to walk!—a little dark-haired person, penguin-walking quickly in a pink jumper—when he first saw her she looked like someone else's child. What did this impression mean? Kari was a miniature Mary Lou, same dark hair, blue-gray eyes, full lower lip and gently tapering chin—was there anything of him in the child?

. . . Was she in fact his child? . . .

The ship tossed. He rolled in the rack, the universe in a spin. Remembering was painful, yet Kari was all he would leave behind. She was his, of course she was, she had to be.

He wondered how many other men were rolling in their racks, fearing the end, thinking of families and the unresolved pain of marriage and fatherhood. He wondered what was happening in Major Lebedeen's head. He felt his own head, and there was no blood now, but the swelling was still tender.

He'd picked up Kari and put her down and spoken stiltedly to Mary Lou and picked up Kari and put her down—Kari Winslow, of course she wasn't Kari Derry. Mary Lou had explained again and again from the beginning how silly that would be, as though he were an idiot. The memories were agitated and unfocused—he'd picked up the child, in absolute awe of the child, loving the child as though she were a paramour he'd been corresponding with for months in his head and had finally met. He was happier and sadder than he'd imagined he would be. This was his child, of course it was, no one had ever suggested otherwise. He'd even wondered (stupidly and not seriously) how many other men were bringing or sending checks to this address—had he only thought that or had he actually said it? Finally, he gave Mary Lou the money and she said he'd better go, she said a lot of things he'd since forgotten, most of them intentionally forgotten, hurtful things, it was coming back to him, Mary Lou had said he was still a child himself, that she was no longer impressed with his sobriety, that he never acted like a real man. Mary Lou had yelled at him, "You're sober, but all it means is you don't drink."

No, he wouldn't think about these things anymore. Don't think about the walk back to the bus station—or wait, did he go to an AA meeting that night? Yes, of course, it was either that or drink, so great was the pain—and then it was the bus in the morning, and he'd gone west, west, farther west than he'd ever been, losing himself in the shit jobs that provided his sustenance, his survival, that required all of his attention, and this was good, because the luxury of a wandering mind, free to think and feel, would have only made life more unbearable.

And he had survived. And he had never returned to his hometown again.

There was a gradual easing of the storm, a dropping of the waves, and a weakening of the winds, interruptions of the howling and whistling, and he knew he was going to survive this too, and that he was a man who could lie awake in his rack for any number of hours having any number of thoughts without going insane.

Because now he was the chaplain . . .

"Hey, Chaplain!"

It was morning; the ship was rocking to its usual degree. Ditchfield was knocking and talking: "Hey, Chaplain, you gonna miss the date-line wogs."

"The what?"

"The date-line wogs! Get going, you're gonna miss them."

"What? Come in!"

Ditchfield unlocked the door with his own key; Miles wondered what the point of having keys was. The old man was happier than Miles had ever seen him, not an old man anymore, but an ancient boy, dusty-looking and knobby-boned, bright eyes in a dead face, ready to go triking away if his legs held out. "You're gonna miss the fun, Commander."

Climbing over the guardrail of his rack: "Sorry, I don't understand what you mean."

"I'm talking about the date-line pollywogs, goddamn it."

Date-line pollywogs, what were they, it wasn't an acronym so he couldn't look it up.

"Ain't you never crossed the date line before? Ain't you a date-line shellback? What are you, a friggin' wog?"

Was it a trick? "I've never crossed the date line," he said, truthfully for himself and Banquette. "I told you, I was in the Atlantic."

"Well, come on out and watch the wogs anyway, it's the most fun we'll have before port call."

He'd slept in his uniform. No matter, there was another one hanging pressed and ready. As he dressed, he surveyed the mess in his room—the chair was overturned, there were papers all over the deck, and the package from Banquette's wife, still unopened, with the scissors still stuck in it, lay in a corner. He was bending over to pick it up when the captain made an announcement over the 1MC, the crackling voice echoing metallically throughout the ship:

"This is the CO. I have a special announcement for all you wogs making your first WESTPAC. Navigator tells me we'll be crossing the international date line in seventeen point two minutes. So all you pollywogs who've never crossed it before, but want to get a picture, show up on the starboard weather deck, O-3 level, with your cameras and camcorders by oh-eight-twenty-two hours. That is all."

Miles put the package back on his desk and went out to the ladder landing, where he could observe the O-3 level of the weather deck on the starboard side. The ocean was gray, made up of broad active waves, and the ship was rocking comfortably. The only vestige of the storm was the humidity; the sun lit everything with a summer intensity. Miles felt a calmness in the aftermath.

Eventually two sailors came along, far below on the O-3 level, and they both had cameras. They shielded their eyes and looked out to sea. One of them checked his watch. They were joined by two others, also with cameras, and another boy came by with a camcorder, and then two more boys with camcorders, and soon there were about a dozen. On the bridge-level weather deck, about thirty feet above Miles, a group of chiefs and officers had come together to watch. A couple of them were laughing, and somebody told them to shut up, not yet.

The boys with the cameras were growing confused: "What time did he say?" "Shoulda been a minute ago." "So what is it, a buoy?" "Keep taping, keep taping, we'll miss it." "It must be a long line of buoys." "How long a line of buoys do you think it is?" "Must go all the way from the north pole to the equator." "Mullins, you're so fucking stupid, those buoys wouldn't stop at the equator, they'd go clear down to the south pole. Maybe even back up the other way." "Well, I don't see nothing." "Just keep looking." "Shit, I dropped it!"

One of them had dropped his camcorder over the side.

"Goddamn it, Mullins, you have to be pushing on my goddamn ass all the time, and I fucking dropped it."

The laughter of the officers and chiefs finally cascaded downdecks. "You dumb-fuck squids!" "Stupid wogs!" "The international date line is an imaginary line, you can't see it from a ship, you fucking morons!"

The young men's faces were going scarlet—even the tops of their heads, which Miles could see through their peach-fuzz haircuts, were red. The officers laughed deliriously, stomping feet, punching one another, almost crying, all of the storm fear releasing itself in a gush of superior hilarity. Everything was fine, everything was better than fine, not only were they still alive, but they were still in control, each of them was still One of the Guys. The pollywogs shuffled away, hunching, the one boy looking ruefully over the lines after his fallen camcorder.

Miles went back inside, shook his head, felt sorry for them. Almost immediately he ran into Kruger, whose born-again eyes seemed even more largely magnified than usual in the black-framed glasses. He licked his thin lips and said, "I cleaned out the crew's lounge, sir."

"Yes?"

"Cleaned it right out."

"Well—was it dirty?"

"I told everyone to get out, sir."

"What for?"

"For your services this morning."

"What services?"

"We've crossed the date line, sir, it's Sunday morning again, so I cleared out the crew's lounge so we can have church again."

"The hell we will," said Miles, too upset at the thought to notice, at first, Kruger's mute horror at a swearing chaplain. "That can't be true, I'm going to ask somebody."

The XO was coming down the P-way, his froggish head still shaking and grinning at the stupidity of the wogs.

Miles said, "Excuse me, sir—"

"Man, did you hear those fucking squids? *Buoys* across the equator—"

"Excuse me, Seaman Kruger here tells me it's Sunday and that I've got to give services again."

The XO became very serious. He looked suspiciously at Kruger and then back at the chaplain. He crossed his arms, then raised his hand to his chin. "Sunday," he said menacingly.

"Is it really Sunday again?" said Miles.

"Don't you wogs know what fucking day it is?"

Miles and Kruger looked at each other, then back at the XO.

"It's *Tuesday*," said the XO, "Tuesday, Tuesday, Tuesday. Doesn't anybody read my fucking POD anymore?" The XO looked from Kruger to Miles and hooked his thumbs into his pants pockets, fed up.

"Thank you, sir," said Miles, and he tried to get away, but the XO took his arm.

"Wait a minute, Padre, wait a minute here, you've taken Basic Navigation? In officer training?"

"Yes—of course—"

"Then you should have been able to straighten this man out on his seamanship."

"Well—"

"If you're traveling west across the date line on a Thursday," said the XO, "what day does it become?"

"Wednesday?"

The toad face hardened and the thumbs came out of the pockets and for a moment Miles expected to be struck.

"What day?"

Kruger tried to help: "Saturday, sir?"

"Quiet, seaman, I'm not addressing you."

"Friday," said Miles, "Friday."

"And if you're traveling the other way on a Monday?"

"Uhm"—Miles thought hard—"Sunday?"

"All right." The XO looked at Kruger again, then at Miles. "Bad as those stupid pollywogs," he said, going out the hatch. "Too much to ask chaplains to be sailors . . ."

"I just want you to know one thing," Kruger told Miles. "I was ready to meet the Lord last night, during the storm, I really was. I know I have a lot of problems, but I think I'm going to be okay. If the Lord can make a big complicated world like this, with date lines and equators running all over it, I'm sure he can help a little guy like me stay away from—well, you know. That's just common knowledge. The thing that really helped? Was when you said you'd been through the peter Olympics a couple of times yourself." And then Kruger gripped him on the upper arm and went out the hatch.

Miles was walking back toward his stateroom with the intention of opening, finally, the package from Mrs. Banquette, when Robin in her T-shirt and shorts turned the corner and came straight up to him as though expecting him all along. "You," she said. Her eyes were sharp with purpose. "I need to talk to you."

"Of course." The willingness in his voice, where was it coming from?

She looked at his shoulders, as though appraising them. "Can we go to my room?"

"Of course." There it was again. Following her shifting ass down the P-way, he was wondering how much else he would agree to. *Help me shave around my panty crotch?* Of course. *Run with me naked through the tank deck?* Of course. *Tie up and gag the captain and fuck my brains out in front of him on top of the wardroom mess table?* Why, certainly.

He resolved to be wary. To put the brakes on as soon as he needed to. And yet he was following her eagerly into the room, was entering it with hands behind his back and eyes raised high, looking all about as though it were the Sistine Chapel, though it didn't differ from his own room: gray bulkheads, flap-down desk, a top rack and a bottom one—he was surprised at the lack of any feminine decor in the room. There were two chairs; she sat in one, crossing her naked thighs.

"Have a seat, Jim . . . you don't mind me calling you Jim . . ."

He sat, but he was nervous about her purpose, and he didn't know where to rest his eyes, which continued roaming the room. There was nothing of interest besides the woman sitting cross-legged in front of him. He realized that his old confidence with women, the dry humor and facile talk, was the dimmest history, as though all of it had come out of pill and liquor bottles, none of it from the true self sobriety had stranded him with.

He rubbed the swollen area on his head. It still hurt a bit. "Look," he said, showing her the top of his head. "I ran into a water gauge last night, during the storm."

"Why are you showing it to me? I'm not your mother. Take it to the doctor. Listen, you're the chaplain, I need you to do something for me."

"Of course." He looked her in the face. It was a corporate face, cast in seriousness, a face like that of a female vice president, Buick Division, who'd toured his father's factory—all of the bite was in the eyes, incisive intelligence ready to rip into facts; speech came in a jaw-forward way, not a tooth in sight—that was the way Robin looked at him and spoke to him now.

"That friend of yours, that fucking marine major, he had no right to make you talk to me the way you did. I've been thinking about it, and I've decided you men have a real double standard going. One of his marines has been sexually harassing me since we got under way, and I'd like to know what you're going to do about it."

"Me? Why don't you talk to the major about it?"

Her eyes reached for the ceiling, then landed their impatient focus back on him. "I don't know what's the matter with that little man, I think he must be bats, I went to his room to complain about this, and he started talking about some stupid island where he's going to drink coconut milk and forget what a pain in the ass it is to be alive. I think this guy is one tank short of an armored division."

Miles wanted to agree, but it would be unprofessional. He kept himself from smiling, and found himself apologizing for the major: "It's his wife, she's sick in the States, that's why he's acting this way."

"You're just defending him because he's a man, and because you're a man. If you were a woman you'd have the intuition to see how immature he is."

"It's not my place to say how immature I think—"

"Oh, but you *do* think it's your place to reveal confidences about his family, about his sick wife. I thought you chaplains had rules about that— I guess I won't be telling you any of *my* personal stuff."

"The only reason I mention his wife—"

"Was to blame his problems on a woman. Why don't you just admit that this guy is a scared little boy who can't handle being five thousand miles away from his wifey. And while you're at it, why don't you admit what a hypocrite he is, accusing me of going after his men, when he won't take action when I accuse one of them of sexual harassment, tells me to take it to the fucking chaplain."

Her eyes were black with anger.

A woman's shift in mood . . . he remembered what it had been like when he was young and it was eerie because it was so long ago. He hadn't had this experience in so many years, the way he'd meet a girl and decide she was remarkable and then learn about the things he didn't like and decide he distrusted her and learn even more of the good and have a deeper attraction—was it all going to happen like this again? In becoming somebody new, must he go through adolescence?

She touched him—briefly—on the knee. "It's not your fault," she said. "Not all of it."

Like a teenager, he was excited by this unexpected closeness, and he took advantage of it to say something that he thought would expand it: "At dinner last night, during the storm, did you really think we might sink?"

Her face drew back, becoming pinched with discerning intelligence, evaluating him. "You're the damnedest chaplain I've ever known. You don't talk like a chaplain at all."

Ordinarily, such a perception would've alarmed him, but he could see in her expression, which was becoming mild and curious, that the realization was one of favor, not suspicion. He said, "Were you afraid we were going to die?"

She laughed at him, a patronizing friendliness. "No, were you?"

"I was afraid."

"A minister afraid to die." She laughed again; she was enjoying him. He felt petulant, but the thrill of attention was the greater thing.

"A man did die," he said. "That sailor who was swept off the *Buchanan*."

"So what if a man dies?"

"Excuse me?"

"So what? He's only a man, it's not like a woman dying. Women don't make the trouble in the world that men do. I'm going to need your help."

"What—what would you like me to do?" Her breasts were pointed and her legs were crossed and smooth and tan and he feared he would agree to whatever she asked.

"I want you to find Private Tom Maxtutis of Squad Six, and I want you to tell him to stop bothering me, that I'm not going to sleep with him just because I—just because he thinks I slept with his corporal and his sergeant. I want you to tell him that I choose the people I sleep with, not the other way around, and I don't want to sleep with him. His ears are too big, and his eyes are too small, and he looks like a big bald rat—you don't have to tell him that, but let him know that he'll be in a whole lot of trouble if he doesn't stop bothering me." She paused. "If you do this for me"—her tongue appeared between her teeth for a moment—"I'll owe you one."

This was the time to stop. He didn't want to stop, but he had to stop; he couldn't take the risk. "I'm starting to change my mind about this."

"Explain what you mean."

"I'm not sure I can."

"I like to be straightforward and honest with people," she said, "and I expect the same in return."

He tried to be honest: "The problem is, I'm afraid I might do just about anything you ask."

"So what's wrong with that?" She laughed encouragingly.

He remained serious: "I can't do it—I'd better go." He stood up. She did too.

"You're not going to talk to this man?" Resentment had settled quickly on her face.

"I don't think I should. The only reason I'm mixed up in this is because the major—"

"First you say you'll help me, now you say you won't. I don't like people whose moods change that quickly."

"Fine," he said, "you don't like me."

"You don't like me either."

"I didn't say that."

"You don't," she insisted.

"There are things about you I like and things I don't."

"Such as?"

"I think you must have a pretty low opinion of yourself to sleep with all these squids."

"I have my standards. I won't fuck a chief, those fat old CPOs. Anyway, what is it to you? And why should I care what a chaplain thinks of me? If the admiral himself came in here and told me how to live my life I'd say, 'Listen, C.J., you're not so important-looking out of that uniform,' and that would be that."

Miles said, "You're the angriest woman I've ever met."

"Good. There should be more angry women in the world, and you should have to listen to all of them. We have every reason to be angry—at society, at the military, and at churches, Reverend."

He smiled, with tremendous effort. "Well, good-bye." He turned for the door.

She held his arm, a steady grip, like his father's. He'd never been touched like this by a woman, and something collapsed in him.

"Maybe," she said, "maybe the problem is that you find me sexually attractive, and you can't deal with it because you feel guilty—guilty because you're the chaplain."

The weakest part of him answered: "Maybe I just don't want any trouble."

"Maybe you're just afraid."

"I am."

She let go. "Get out of here, Reverend. I'll find someone else to talk to the marine. And don't ever come back here scared—it's the first thing I haven't liked about you."

He was grateful to be out of there and back in his room. He'd recognized the energy between them—he'd felt it with many women. It was the negative charge of sullen fighting, a compulsive activity, the positive charge of which was sex—it was the same energy. It was there if he wanted it, and it had him scared not only because of the trouble it could lead to, but because Robin was a kind of woman he'd never known before, a woman confident enough to fuck her way through a ship, to take men by the arm and demand answers, to push them down on the rack maybe and take them, a most unusual woman, an interesting and repulsive woman, indeed the only kind of woman who could live among six hundred boys and men.

He would be another conquest to her, of perverse value because he was a chaplain. He was offended. He felt silly for being offended, but he was offended all the same. To take his mind off these thoughts, which were more disturbing than the actual fight, he found the package from Mrs. Banquette, with the scissors still in it, and sat down to open it.

He was expecting homemade cookies, oatmeal or chocolate-chip, and he was hoping they weren't peanut butter, because his father owned stock in a peanut butter company and had decreed for thirty years that peanut butter be the only "dessert" allowed in the house, and so Miles had developed into the only person in the world who didn't like peanut butter. The item that began to emerge from the ripping of tape and cardboard and tissue paper was baffling—at first because he couldn't see it wholly and then because he could—it was a stuffed animal, a pink cat, very worn, with frayed ears and a single button eye and an oversized floppy mouth that opened all the way in—he looked inside but it was empty. So. Well . . . He tossed it on the desk, picked up the package, rummaged in the tissue, and found a letter folded once, folded twice, the second time crookedly, as though in afterthought.

Dear Jim,

Everything is so confusing between you and me, and I cry a lot. Sometimes it feels like you don't even know or care who I am anymore. I feel like such a fool having to tell you how hurt I am, how disappointed I am, how betrayed I feel. I try to find pride in myself, so I can hold things together, so I can be strong for Teddy and Laura, and you don't even seem to notice or care.

I'm sending you the toy kitten you sent me from your last deployment. I'm still not entirely sure why you sent it to me. I've tried to believe you sent it out of a kind of love. Maybe you will think back on the time when you gave me this toy out of affection, and you will think of me with sweetness again. It is my greatest hope that you will be led back in that direction, Jim.

That is all I'm going to say for now. Except for one thing. Please think of the man you are supposed to be. Not the man you are, but the man you are SUPPOSED to be. And then ask yourself why you would volunteer for a WESTPAC when you don't have to go, why you run halfway around the world from me and your kids.

Still loving you,

Michelle

P.S. It happened again, Mrs. Harrison found Teddy "playing doctor" in her basement with those bad ones from the neighborhood. I don't know where he gets that from.

The woman was desperate, and he felt for her, so he went to the computer to create a response. In twenty minutes he had this:

Dear Michelle,

What can I say to reassure you? I guess I'm not the man you married.

I have wanted this time apart so that I could think and pray about us, and about what kind of man I am supposed to be. Michelle, I want to change. I want to be a better husband and father than the one you've known. I know that the problems I've caused in our marriage have hurt you and the kids. I HAVE noticed how hurt you are, and I am very sorry about that and want to stop hurting you. I also know how strong you are in trying to hold things together by yourself, and I have secretly admired you for that for a long time. I just haven't known how to tell you any of these things.

Thank you for sending me the pussy. Yes, having it reminds me of the way it used to be between us, of the way it can be again.
I love you,
Jim
P.S. Tell Teddy his dad says to keep his trousers up.

He read it and reread it. He tried to imagine himself in her position, and he hoped the things he'd written would make her happy. It was odd, trying to make a stranger happy, but in a way she wasn't a stranger, she'd revealed herself to him, and part of being the chaplain was being the husband, and so it was his job to make her happy.

He hit the print command and went to the yeomanry to pick up the letter, and while he was there he got an envelope and sat in front of a typewriter and typed her name and address on the envelope so his handwriting wouldn't be a problem. Then he got a stamp and put it on and sealed the letter in the envelope and took it down to the PO and mailed it. He was as nervous as though she were behind the mail slot, and he hoped that he had done a good thing.

7

During the next six days, his fear of the gay priest waiting for him on Okinawa kept him irrationally in his room—lying in his rack, or sitting at the computer game—as though he might run into Father Tuttleman if he went out the door, no matter that the man was two thousand—one thousand—five hundred miles away, and so Miles didn't participate in the euphoria that was gathering as Okinawa grew closer. He worried instead about hiding on the ship for the one-day call, or wandering as far afield on the island as he could without knowing a syllable of Japanese, to avoid the priest, and then finding his way back before the ARG was under way. Then he learned that all the men, including officers, would be in civvies for the twenty-one-hour leave, and this relieved him greatly, if not completely: with no uniform, no stranger could identify him, though he still might be pointed out to Tuttleman, who would know at once this wasn't the chaplain he'd buggered in D.C., and Miles would have to threaten him with the letter he had in fact burned.

His worries rose and fell as the ship moved up and down and the Japanese island grew larger on the posted charts. He ate and slept and paced, Robin ignoring him in the P-way and mess, Lebedeen also. The major, if he spoke at all, spoke acronymically and distractedly to his JOs, and his face, whether speaking or silent, was tightly pained, the eyebrows even more archly slanted in their ever-questioning self-doubt, as though the news of his wife's cancer were revolving in his head with such thorough destructiveness that he could not only think of nothing else, but was becoming ill himself. The few times Miles asked him if he felt like talking, the major had looked at him warily and shook his head, which was fine for now since Miles had his own worries. He was able, despite them, to give a convincing performance the following Sunday, in front of half a dozen men for each service, including Kruger, who found nothing troubling in a sermon that Banquette, or whomever he'd borrowed it from, had entitled "Why Jesus Wants Us to Prey for the Pore." Between services, Miles was bold enough to ask Ogleby, the priest who heloed from ship to ship, if he knew a Father Tuttleman on Okinawa, but the priest, his breath still as bad as spoiled milk, told him, "Don't know any Catholics there, but I like to go bar-hopping with the air force Unitarians. Lots more fun than Catholics."

Liberty morning had him standing on the weather deck as the ship crawled along the jungly shore. He was overwhelmed by a sky so blue and a sun so bright and a bay so turquoise and flat that it all looked unreal. They were no longer on the ocean: the modest bay was forming itself out of the green shoreline, just a couple of buildings bright white in the tropic sun, a gravel parking lot, and a road leading into jungle, no dock, no people. No one! He was afraid to feel good about this, and sure enough, as the *Harding* and the four other ships crept into the bay, a white car appeared in the parking lot, and then a copy of it, and then three more. He was just close enough to make out the same Japanese characters on the doors, and he guessed the identity of the cars from the orange taxi domes on the roofs. Was Tuttleman in one of those cabs?

Miles guessed the only men as troubled as he was were the ones who wouldn't be allowed off till 1800, and those who'd pulled night duty, required to come back early. Everyone else was whistling, humming, swearing, slapping the bulkheads as he walked, snapping his fingers, the vapors of six hundred colognes rising through the decks, commingling in the heat into a stinky-sweetness that was even more annoying to Miles, who might soon be facing his unraveling in Tuttleman, than the festive attitude of the crew. It reminded him of being in high school and getting drunk before a football or basketball game and waiting in line for his ticket, worrying about which girls in the bleachers he could party with and seduce, which boyfriends might find out and come after him, that mobile excitement of fear, it was in his belly and chest, and everyone else smelling of aftershave and cologne, just looking forward to a good time, same then as now.

He went to the wardroom mess; there were few other breakfasters, no Lebedeen, no captain, no XO, no Robin either. As he sat there eating in sullen anxiety, Miles knew that most everyone else was too excited with liberty preparations to eat. He was ranking and the other men said, "Permission to leave," and he nodded as absently as a twenty-year alumnus of Annapolis. When he was done, he wiped his mouth and got up and all the officers and enlisted and sailors and marines that he passed in the P-way were wearing shorts and Hawaiian shirts or printed T-shirts. A couple of the marine JOs had on matching green T-shirts black-stenciled:

THE UNITED STATES MARINE CORPS
WE LIKE ASS THE WAY WE LIKE HAIRCUTS
HIGH AND TIGHT!

In his metal closet, he found Banquette's single Hawaiian shirt—flowers and coconuts and birds-of-paradise mixed incongruously—and a white pair of shorts, and he took off his uniform with its identifying collar crosses and put on the anonymous civvies. Somebody might still point him out to Tuttleman, but he hoped to be in a taxi racing somewhere—anywhere—before that could happen.

He had another look outside, and all five ships were anchored a thousand yards from each other, a couple of thousand from the long indentation of undeveloped shoreline that formed the harbor. Hundreds of men stood at the lifelines of the ships in their colorful shirts and shorts, and the men on the weather decks of the *Harding* were talking loudly and excitedly, like the boys he remembered lining up before the high-school games, boys who would fight other boys if their team lost and they'd had any alcohol, and he realized that most of these sailors and marines had been standing in such lines a year ago, and wondered what destruction they would do on the island.

He sat in the chair in his room with the POD in his hand and waited for the social-security-number endings to begin crackling out of the 1MC—it would be an orderly invasion. There was no place to dock, so the amphibious assault vehicles of the marines would be used for transport, throughout the day, ship-to-shore. As he waited he memorized the deadman's SSI number and skimmed the POD:

PLAN OF THE DAY
USS WARREN HARDING (LST–2282)
CO – Capt. John W. Shepard, USN
XO – Comm. Steven B. Jarvis, USNR
Monday, 24 June, 1991

LIBERTY OKINAWA!!!

will commence 0930 hours Time-Zone Gamma 24 June 1991 for all non-duty staff and crew and will expire 0630 hours said time-zone 25 June 1991. By order of the XO the following ADMONITIONS, WARNINGS, and ADVICE are to be published and posted for the crew:

1. Do not attempt to rent or operate any vehicle unless you hold a valid Class Zebra Japanese driver's license and are adept at leftside driving and/or want to wake up in a Japanese hospital with your balls up around your neck.

2. If you are unfamiliar with the physical characteristics of the Asian female, this is NOT the place to go for that particular merit badge. In other words, scout, if she looks twelve, she probably is. When in doubt, reel both inches back in and zip it up.

3. If you find yourself under arrest for any reason, please note: THERE IS ABSOLUTELY NOTHING THE USN OR USMC CAN DO FOR YOUR SORRY ASS. However, a State Department official will be happy to meet with you sometime within the next six to nine months. We thank you for your patience.

4. The following bars/nightclubs are off-limits to all personnel due to reported homosexual activity, and/or failure to comply with hostess-girl venereal health-check regulations of Okinawa Prefecture: The Yankee Diddle Club, 62 Shuritaki Avenue; Banzai Boys Town, 185 Kobe Street; Suzie Wong's Fried Chicken A-Go-Go Massage Parlor, 55 Jutaku Blvd.; The Butt Hole, 207 Ishimini Place. ADDRESSES ARE PUBLISHED ONLY SO THAT PERSONNEL WILL BE AWARE OF WHICH BARS/NIGHTCLUBS TO AVOID.

5. Will the person(s) who "borrowed" the doctor's enema kit please bring it back from town tonight IN ITS ORIGINAL CONDITION.

6. Observe the following late communique from Admiral Cornelius W. Jiggerston, USN, CO, 57th Amphibious Ready Group, as adapted from the San Diego Zoo's animal policies: "Please do not annoy, torment, pester, plague, molest, worry, badger, harry, harass, heckle, persecute, irk, bullyrag, vex, disquiet, grate, beset, bother, tease, nettle, bugger, tantalize, or ruffle the natives."

7. Finally, allow me to remind you of the farewell message to the crew from the wife of the Governor of Okinawa Prefecture the last time

we were here: "Americaneru, anatawa bakades, ka?" Translation: Why are you Americans such fucking dumb-asses?

8. Please have a pleasant stay.

Following was the list, by department, of the unfortunates who'd pulled the duty. As Miles was reading it, grateful to be free of schedules for six days out of seven, the 1MC announced, "Personnel whose social security numbers end in five may now proceed to the tank deck," and that meant that the navy was finally acknowledging what had been true since Jim Banquette had died of a heart attack with his cock in a man's mouth: the chaplain was on liberty. So Miles got up and went down to the tank deck to line up, with other wildly shirted men, for freedom. On the back end of the deck the gates, each thirty feet wide and fifteen high, were open to the sides, creating a large picture of sky and water bisected by a chalk-colored beach and green mountains. The line of men progressed between the cable-secured jeeps and trucks and tanks until they reached a clear area aft, where a row of card tables had been set up with letterboards reading NATIONAL BANK OF TOKYO—RATE OF EXCHANGE: ¥143.62. Two young Japanese women were sitting in pinstripe gray in the airless humidity, one of them wearing her black hair straight down her back, the other cropped short, and both of them sweatless and banker-eyed as the men announced their dollar amounts. No matter how flirtatiously the men tried to say "fifty" or "one hundred" or "two hundred," the women's hands were their only animated features, counting the dollars first, then the yen, "Fifty dora . . . seven tousen one huna eighty-one yen," and as Miles stood over the table with the chaplain's wallet in his hand, pulling out forty dollars— lunch, dinner, nothing else—he wondered why women like these had never been of interest to him. Then he knew: he could've made his father very happy any day of the week by bringing home a bank teller, a shy girl with good manners, perhaps even intelligent, in any case a modest person—but no, never, it had always been the wild ones for him. The closest he'd come to stability had been with Mary Lou, but the pregnancy had driven it fast off the rails. He was still crazy for the crazy ones, and putting the yen into his pocket, he was thinking of Robin, thinking of her in that dreamy lusty way that the humidity only augmented, and he was still thinking of her as he lined up for the amphibious-assault vehicle, even though he hadn't spoken to her all week—yes, he thought of her now, knowing he should be worrying about Tuttleman, he was escaping into the fantasy that was Robin's eyes and mouth and flirtatious talk and legs and breasts and shifting-walking ass.

As he stepped into the sunshine at the open end of the deck, he saw that the AAV that was filling with men was a kind of big rectangular speed-boat painted marine green, with a landing gate in front and the driver in the rear. A couple of seamen took the chaplain by the elbows and helped him drop five feet down into it, and it continued to fill with men, and the air was heavy with their colognes and the light was dancing all over the ripples of the water and the peacock colors of their shirts.

The next fifteen minutes were unlike anything in his life. For a while his mind became like that of simpler men, thinking only of what he saw. As the engine rattled into forward gear and the AAV went bouncing over the foam it was creating, it threw the men against each other, the square prow rising against the blueness of sky, the water spraying again and again in the men's faces, the wind running in quick patterns through their porcupine hair. When Miles started thinking again, the connections he made were with photographs in the high-school history book he'd opened two or three times between pot sessions—yes, this was the way men had arrived at Normandy, at Guadalcanal, here at Okinawa. This was a war machine, and the beach they were charging had probably been a war beach, though the boys around him were no warriors, ready to storm onto the island only for beer and pussy. He looked back toward the sea, and in the fierce light the shimmering water looked surreal, as though the only true things were the five anchored ships, bulky and ugly, and the AAVs roaring away from them. All of these ships and equipment had cost billions of dollars, and for a reason that had never been disclosed, if indeed there were a reason, these men had been brought here to drink and fuck and fight, here to this island that had been a place of horrible realities in 1945, but that now, spreading before them in layers of beach and jungle and mountain, was as tantalizing and pristine as the island Major Lebedeen carried around in his head.

The craft broke through the surf and the landing-gate crashed down and the men went whooping ankle-deep through the water and up over the sand and through the palm trees. He followed them with his dread scissoring up from his stomach—fear of Tuttleman. It ran up his back and neck and slackened his mouth, and he wondered if it was anything like the fear that the men who'd landed here in '45 had carried, for it was his death that might be waiting for him here in the form of the priest, it was the death of a persona that meant more to him than any other persona—the drunk or the cock-hound or the outsider—he'd ever devised for himself, this chaplain whom he could not allow to die.

His sneakers and socks were wet in the morning heat as he went with the swarm toward the taxis that were quickly filling and leaving the gravel lot. People were shouting in English and Japanese and there were fewer and fewer taxis. Whenever a new one arrived, it was surrounded and attacked and invaded and it lurched away, weighted with six or seven men. Miles moved with the crowd in grateful anonymity, testing his sea legs against the gravel of the lot—the earth was odd for not moving up or down or sideways or forward. He'd been in motion every moment for more than two weeks and now, back on land, he felt that if he stopped walking he would fall over.

One of the cabs drew his attention. There was a group of men around it, rocking it and yelling, real hatred knotting up red in their faces. One of the boys was slamming the windshield with his forearm and screaming for the frightened driver to open up. The sole passenger was sitting grimly in the backseat. It was Major Lebedeen.

Miles thought only a moment before deciding to help him. And himself, before Tuttleman might appear. He pushed his way toward the cab and grumble-shouted, as he'd been hearing chiefs grumble-shouting all the way from San Diego: "All right, you men, listen up! I'm Commander Jim Banquette and that man is Major Frank Lebedeen and you men are asking for an ass-whipping! Now clear the hell out of here!" The men's expressions went flat with repressed anger, and whatever obscene arguments they were composing were forced to remain locked in their minds until the officers were far away. Miles rapped on the window but the major, eyebrows slanting upwards in painful questioning, wouldn't move.

"Let me in, Major!"

The major leaned over and cracked the window just thinly enough to be heard: "Thanks—hey, I would've—you know, ordered them, but I thought if I opened the window they'd get their stinking fingers in—animals."

"Where you going?"

"I have to call my wife right away, she's sick back home, I have to call—"

"Okay, let me in, I'll go with you."

The major looked unhappy about it, but he unlocked the door and Miles got in, and the major said, "I gave him twenty bucks to drive me to the nearest pay phone and not to let anyone else in the car."

"That is correct," said the driver, a young man with glasses and a sallow academic look. "When I am perceiving a breaking in the crowding of vehicles before us, we shall be bound on the Highway Nashimuru." He edged the car forward, stopped, edged it forward again.

Miles searched for the black clerical clothes and squared-out collar of a Roman Catholic priest, though he supposed Tuttleman would be in tropical civvies like the rest. Lebedeen was looking out the other window, chewing his thumbnail.

The driver insinuated the car into the gravelly bottleneck where taxis were attempting to turn onto the road. Then a set of knuckles was rapping on the window and Miles looked up; it was the DISBO from the *Harding,* and he was smiling with his pipe in his teeth. He had a flask in one hand and he passed it to the man with him, a black officer, the radio officer, whose name was Smitty. They were both wearing sunglasses and Hawaiian shirts.

"Don't stop for them!" Lebedeen punched the back of the driver's seat.

"I am unable but to be stopping due to the conglomerating of traffics before us, sir."

Miles rolled the window down about an inch. "Can we help you, DISBO?"

"Hey Chaplain, how about letting us in this cab. You're a Christian."

"No way!" said Lebedeen.

"No way he's a Christian," said Smitty, "or no way we get the cab?" He and the DISBO were already drunk; their boozy stink came through the window.

"The major needs to call his wife," said Miles.

"Yeah?" said Smitty. "What's her name? Maybe DISBO has her fucking number tattooed on his skinny white ass."

"I'll check it later," said the DISBO as his pipe turned upside down and the tobacco fell out over his shirt. "How about it, Reverend? Do we get the cab? We're on our way to a highly important party."

"No!" said Lebedeen.

"You white boys being carjacked," said Smitty. "You white boys best be getting your white-moon asses out of the fucking car, you know what I'm saying?"

"Shut up," said the DISBO. "I'm white, you know."

"You about as white as my dick," said Smitty. "You really a nigger, DISBO. You just too stupid and lazy to know it."

"No," said the DISBO, "it's a tan."

"You white on the outside, black on the inside. Your mama must've fucked niggers so hard they turned inside out."

"You're wasting my time!" said Lebedeen.

"May I be suggesting a diplomacy?" said the driver. "Perhaps you white men and—and nigger—all can be riding togethers, in same vehicle."

"You listening to this motherfucking shit?" said Smitty to the DISBO. "You hear what this racist Jap just called me, in front of a minister and all?"

"I say we pound his Jap ass," said the DISBO, fiddling with his empty pipe in drunken perplexity. "And then fuck his Jap-ass sister."

"Uh-uh," said Smitty, "not this boy. I be waiting for the white pussy at that party, you know what I'm saying?"

"Get away from this car!" said Lebedeen.

Miles said, "You'd better let the major go, you'd better catch the next cab."

Smitty put the pinkish palms of his large black hands far apart on the window, then his round smiling face appeared between them, his sunglasses reflecting the occupants of the car, and he was starting to say something when a white hand fell on his shoulder and pulled him away, and he was replaced in the window by a boy wearing dress whites with black SP armbands.

"Thank God," said Lebedeen.

"Shore Patrol," said the DISBO. "Oh me, oh my, looks like our fucking asses are busted. Better hide this hootch. Oh me oh my." He drank.

"Gentlemen," said the kid, hooking his thumbs into his pants, spreading his shoulders and standing on his toes, "could I please ask you to roll your window all the way down, please?" Miles did so. "Thank you, gentlemen," said the kid, blinking with his mouth open as he formulated the next words. "Gentlemen, it would be a good idea if you let these other gentlemen into your vehicle and continue your—continue your conversation on your way to—your way to the destination you're on your way to, gentlemen."

"That's it, my man," said Smitty, "now you be talking Scripture, and to a motherfucking preacher too, you know what I'm saying? You want a drink?"

"I don't have to listen to you," the major told the SP. "I'm a major, and my wife is ill in the States, and—and I'm a major, so roll that window back up so we can get the hell out of here."

The kid, with his red face and buzzed blond hair, looking fourteen, rose on his toes again and said, "Gentlemen—sir—Section four-five-one point nine-three of the Uniform Code of Military Justice gives Shore Patrol authority over all liberty traffic, even when officers—even when officers are *willfully* obstructing the flow of that traffic—sir."

"That's good enough for me," said the DISBO, reaching in and unlocking the door, and then he was shoving in next to Miles and Lebedeen was saying "No no no!" and Smitty was getting into the front seat, and then a skinny sailor wearing jeans and a white T-shirt and a USS BUCHANAN ballcap came from nowhere and got into the front seat next to Smitty, and the car moved forward and Lebedeen was still yelling, he shook the seat of the driver, then his shoulders, and he was putting his hands around the driver's neck when the driver slapped them off and turned around and said vehemently, "I am perceiving you are making to me with violences! If you do not make stopping of it, I must transport you to the building of polices."

Lebedeen fell back into his seat. "There's such a thing as international, humanitarian law."

"That's right," said the DISBO to the driver. "You want a fucking drink?"

"I am student. I cannot be doing drinkings before morning of examinations."

"Student of what?"

"I am student of the engineerings of roadways—intercrosses and bridges."

"Intercourse and bitches?" said Smitty. "Those be my studies too."

It was tight in the backseat with Miles between Lebedeen and the DISBO, and there were three men in front too, and the DISBO said to the chaplain, "Maybe you'd better get out, Reverend, before we get on the highway. No offense, but it would be the Christian thing to do."

"Me? What for?" Tuttleman could be out there . . .

The DISBO turned to face him, hitting him in the nose with the pipe, and he spoke to Miles through his teeth: "You see, Reverend, Smitty and I are rather drunk, and we're going to be getting drunker—we still have thirteen minutes on this flask—and when I get drunk I like to talk about penises and vaginas and tits—I mean breasts—and all that sort of thing. And Smitty here—well, I don't even want to tell you what Smitty likes to talk about."

"Don't tell him," said Smitty. "I'm, like, embarrassed."

"Seriously," said the DISBO. "I could start talking about my cock at any minute."

Smitty turned around and said, "You fucking shitting me? You gonna be talking about that little white pud again?"

"Yes," said the DISBO. "First I'll be talking about it, then later tonight I'll be using it."

"On what? A fucking hamster?"

Lebedeen, calmer now that the cab was moving onto the road, said to the driver "Telephone? Nearest telephone, right?"

"I will be making attemptings to be transporting you to destinations of the telephonic, sir."

Smitty said, "Shit, this stupid Jap don't even speak no good god-damn English."

"How about it, Reverend?" said the DISBO. "How about finding another cab?"

"You can say whatever you like around me."

"Are you absolutely sure? I can say whatever I want around you and it won't be a sin or anything?"

"Say whatever you like."

"Damn it, Reverend, are you fucking sure I can motherfucking say whatever the fucking hell I want to fucking say around you?"

"Yes."

"Well then, you're one hell of a motherfucker, Reverend. One hell of a fucking sailor. Here, have a goddamn drink."

"I don't drink."

"Of course you don't fucking drink. Have one just for the holy hell of it."

"No thanks."

The cab was speeding along a highway now. "Telephone?" Lebedeen said again.

The DISBO leaned forward and said to the driver, "Take us to the motherfucking officers' club at Kadena Motherfucking Air Force Base. We're gonna fuck the living shit out of these motherfucking whores I know, gonna fuck 'em till they can't fucking walk. Comprende? Spokon spokon!" The DISBO hit the skinny sailor, sitting next to Smitty in the front seat, on the back of the head. "You know what that means, squid? It means 'fucky-fucky.' Remember that for tonight."

"Don't do that again," said the sailor.

"Shut up. You want a fucking drink? You going into town to fuck sluts or what? What's your fucking name, anyway?"

"John Swallow."

Smitty and the DISBO laughed very hard at this and the DISBO's pipe fell out of his mouth and he and Smitty high-fived each other and Smitty said, "I don't know about this fucking shit, man," and he was shaking his head and trying to stop laughing. "You know what I'm saying? I don't want to be sitting butt-to-butt with no fucking Seaman Swallow."

"Tell me you're not going to a butt-fuck bar," said the DISBO to Seaman Swallow. "Tell me you're not going to—what the fuck is the name of that fucking place in this morning's POD?"

Smitty said, "The Butt Hole."

"Yeah," said the DISBO, "tell me you're not going to the motherfucking Butt Hole tonight. Why don't we promote you to Admiral Swallow, so you don't have to be Seaman Swallow anymore, and we can take you up to the O Club at Kadena Motherfucking Air Force Base and you can help us fuck the shit out of these white whores from California we've got waiting."

"Leave that boy alone," said Lebedeen, elbowing Miles.

"Yes," said Miles, "by all means leave that boy alone."

"I don't fool around," said Seaman Swallow. "I have a girlfriend in New Jersey. Her name's Ronette."

"You be fucking black girls?" said Smitty. "Now, Seaman Swallow, you not be fucking any black pussy tonight, even if they was any, 'cause you scared of me, ain't you, Seaman Swallow? You scared of big drunk niggers like me. You be sticking to the Jap pussy tonight, motherfucker, you know what I'm saying?"

Seaman Swallow said, "My girlfriend and me are Church of the Nazarene, and we don't believe in premarital sex."

"Hell," said the DISBO, "neither do I. That's why I never fucking got married. It would be against my most deeply held values. By fucking definition, premarital sex can only lead to one thing—marriage—and nobody fucking likes *that*. Now get out your wallet and let's see a picture of the fat pig you're saving yourself for."

"That's enough!" said Major Lebedeen. "Stop this drunken talk, and stop abusing this man. I have to call my wife right away. Do you understand? My wife is—"

"Shit fuck beans!" said Smitty. "Man, don't be calling your motherfucking *wife*. You want to know what the bitch is doing right fucking now? It's three in the fucking morning where you live, man, you know what I'm saying, and this bitch be entertaining all the niggers in the fucking hood, all the big-dick niggers who been waiting for you to leave the fucking country, dude, so they can get theyselves a little piece of that raspberry-pink white-woman pussy, mmm, mmmm, mmmmmmm, you see what's happening here? Now you gonna be fucking calling and interrupting those mother-fuckers, and ain't no nigger likes being interrupted when he's fucking some white bitch, them niggers gonna be mad, maybe they rough her up a bit, and then all of them be taking a big black dump on your motherfucking whitey-white expensive carpeting when they through."

"Goddamn you," said Lebedeen. "I happen to love my wife, you lousy—"

"Bullcrap," said the DISBO, "you're just calling 'cause you want to see who the fuck answers the fucking phone at your house at three in the fucking morning. You want some good advice? Never trust anything that bleeds for seven days and doesn't die."

"Tell them," said the major, jostling Miles. "You're the chaplain, tell them about my—"

"Oh no you don't," said the DISBO. "Don't be dragging Banquette into this. Jim Banquette is cool, Jim Banquette's the only guy in this fucking car who's not a fucking phony. Can you imagine if we had some phony-ass preacher in here with us? Do you suppose he'd be letting Smitty and me talk the straight fucking shit to fuckers like you and Seaman Swallow? Hell no. I know what these fucking preachers are like, they're all a bunch of motherfucking phonies, but not Jim here, he's the real thing, in a world of phony-ass hypocrites. Look at this fucking cabdriver, posing as a student of intercourse, when he looks like he couldn't find the pussy with a big nautical computerized fish detector. And look at smutty Smitty here, posing as a bad-ass nigger motherfucker who'll drag your fucking sister by the hair out behind the fucking crack house and bugger her fucking eyeballs out, when actually he's as queer as Arnold Schwarzenegger, buffing himself up in the weight room all day with those other faggots, then taking white squid penis up the fucking ass in the fucking radio shack every night. And look at Seaman Swallow here, posing as a motherfucking human being. And then take a look at yourself, Major, you sniveling whining crying motherfucking little pussy-fuck, posing as an officer of the United States Fucking Marine Corps, can't even fight your fucking way to a pay phone.

And then take a look at me, I'm the biggest fucking phony in this car. You want to know what I'm supposed to be doing right now, the fucking DISBO? I'm drunk off my fucking ass, I can't find my fucking pipe, I'm on my fucking way to fuck some fucking whore, and right now I'm supposed to be in my fucking office, back on the fucking ship, disbursement officer, making sure everybody who's cashing their fucking checks isn't trying to cheat the fucking navy—my first real day of work since we got under fucking way—I'll probably have twelve grand in fucking cash going out of the fucking safe today, and I'm not even there to fucking supervise it—here I sit, too fucking drunk to get it up and I'm not even out of the fucking cab yet, but Jim Banquette here forgives me, he doesn't fucking judge, I can sense it, he's not like these other fucking chaplains, he's a real fucking Christian, and that's why he's the only fucking one of you lousy motherfuckers who's not a fucking phony, he's got the fucking tolerance and love and acceptance of Jesus McFucking Christ in his soul."

No one said anything for a moment.

Then Smitty said, "Fuck you, man. You be fucked up, man. Just shut the fuck up."

The DISBO's love, for being as profanely and drunkenly sincere as it was, gave Miles a strange and uncomfortable satisfaction at being esteemed as One of the Guys.

They rode in a liquor-stinking silence, through a jungle, on the left side of the highway, over which hung, on long curved aluminum poles, green signs with white Japanese characters on them. To Miles it was like being in a muggy science-fiction world where the familiarity of cars and freeways was dream-mixed with inverted flow and alien hieroglyphs. Then they took an off-ramp down to the left into a little valley and the jungle cleared just widely enough for a big red sign to announce over a chain-link gate:

CAMP CADMAN
USMC
GATE 3-B

And then Smitty was saying, "This ain't the fucking place, man," and the DISBO was saying, "This guy's fucking jacking us, what's the fucking meter reading?" and Smitty was saying, "Eighty-seven hundred motherfucking dollars!" and the DISBO was saying, "That's fuck-ass Jap money, you fucking fuck-ass," and Seaman Swallow was saying, "They got pinball here?" and the DISBO was saying, "We're gonna fight with this fucker, he's taken us all over this fucking island, we're gonna have to fucking kill him and dig a rat-hole for his corpse, then take this fucking car and drive all over this Jap-fucking place looking for that fucking air base," and Smitty was saying to the driver, "This be the wrong fucking place, Poindexter," and the driver was saying, "There are many military encampments in the Prefecture of the Okinawans," and Lebedeen was saying, "They'll have a phone here," and he was getting out, and the DISBO was saying, "You owe us whatever one fifth of eighty-seven hundred twenty-nine fucking yen is," and Lebedeen was walking away saying, "I gave him twenty before you car-jacked us," and Miles was trying to decide whether to go with Major Lebedeen, and Smitty was saying, "If there wasn't a reverend motherfucker sitting right here, we be dragging this Samoan out by his mouse ears and hammering his mango ass," and Miles was deciding he'd better stick around, and Major Lebedeen was walking away and through the gate and into the camp, and the DISBO, who'd found his pipe, was jabbing the stem into the driver's neck and saying, "Kadena, you ugly little gerbil, Kadena Air Force Base? The biggest motherfucking air base this side of San Antone? Comprende? Back this fucking pillbox the fuck out of here, and don't take us through the fucking papaya fields this time," and the driver turned his bespectacled face around and said, "Very well, mister sir, but please stop to be making the threatenings of violences," and the DISBO let out a rat-tat-taaatting of extremely potent farts that had everyone rolling the windows down, and then the cab was turning around and going back through the jungle and onto the Nashimuru Freeway.

In the next hour they stopped at Camp Kempton, Camp Kaiser, Camp Kennedy, and Camp Keaton, the driver giving them each time an inquisitive glare to see if this were the place they wanted, and the meter was reading over 16,000, and Smitty was saying, "Man, they got more ass-fucking jarhead camps in this butt-fucking place than motherfucking Burger King's got bung-hole-fucking drive-thrus," and the DISBO was saying, "Think of all these thousands of jarhead fuckers greasing-up their fucking pricks and then going out to fuck several tons of little Japanese pussy-fish, and the dumb-ass taxpayers paying for it all, fucking think of that," and Smitty was saying, "Thank God for the dumb-ass taxpayers, you know? I thank those lame-ass motherfuckers in white-corn Nebraska every night, I thank 'em from the uncut tip of my black-and-tan boner all the way nine inches down to my big hairy nigger baseball-balls going up and down in stink-ass whorehouses all over the donkey-fucking Far East," and in another fifteen minutes they were at a tiny, minor gate of Kadena Air Force Base and excitedly talking about the California prostitutes they'd arranged to meet, through the largess of the U.S. taxpayer, at the bar of the Kadena O Club.

The meter stood at 19,837. "This motherfuck," said Smitty, "be at twenty thousand motherfucking dollars. Jesus! I ain't paying this fucking shit, you know what I'm saying?"

"I told you, you fucking wet-brain," said the DISBO, "that's fucking Jap-money," and drunk as he was, with his accountant-brain-for-numbers the DISBO was able to do the calculations: "That's—uh—carry the fucking six, carry the fucking four—a fucking hundred and uh, a fucking hundred and forty-two and some fucking nickels—uh—divided by the four of us fuckers—uh—that's thirty-five-and-a-half fucking each."

"That's still too fucking much," said Smitty. "Man, this fucking squirrel drove us all over the motherfucking Congo, you know what I'm saying, and I ain't gonna pay this fucking shit, I ain't gonna pay it."

"Who the fuck said anything about paying it?" said the DISBO, popping open the door and stepping out. "I just thought the fucking math was interesting."

"Shit fuck beans!" said Smitty. "If you think the motherfucking math is so fucking interesting, why don't you do some fucking subtraction and measure the size of your miniature fucking dick, asshole," and they were all getting out of the cab, and Miles, thinking he'd probably eluded Tuttleman, was putting most of his yen through the window and the driver was taking it, and Seaman Swallow was digging around in his pockets, and when the driver saw that Smitty and the DISBO were leaving without paying, he got out of the cab and said, "You are making departures without making the payings of the owings which you have made," and he went up behind Smitty and touched him on the shoulder, and Smitty said, "Don't be fucking with me, Jap-ass!" and turned around, landing a brick of a fist so hard into the taxi driver's stomach that the gasping-out of air was like the distant sound of a tire exploding, which Miles had heard when he worked at a gas station across the road from Dayton Tire in Rapid City—ridiculously, it was all he could think about, that huge distant wind-popping sound, as the driver doubled up and fell to the ground and the DISBO with his pipe upside down under his cockeyed sunglasses raised his foot and with the heel of his sandal kicked the driver on the side of the head as hard as he could, then slammed him three more times with the bottom of his foot in the face, and as Seaman Swallow leaned over the driver trying to pay him, Smitty and the DISBO were moving quickly across the empty parking lot toward the chain-link maze leading to the checkpoint cabin. Miles turned in a circle and saw nothing but the parking lot surrounded by palm trees. He told Seaman Swallow, "Shit, we're the only witnesses." Then the driver pushed himself up off the asphalt and threw his elbow so hard against Seaman Swallow's face that Miles could hear the snapping of bone and there was a fan of blood in the air, and Seaman Swallow was screaming with his hands over his face as he went down on his side and his ballcap rolled off and the driver started kicking him desperately in the head saying, "*Anatawa bakades, ka! Anatawa bakades, ka!* Fokeru you! Foke you!"

Miles was shaking as he hurried to the checkpoint cabin for help. Of course, in his roadhouse days he'd seen more fights than a dozen ordinary people could expect in their lifetimes, but this was the first time in sobriety that he'd encountered alcoholic violence. The shrieking of Seaman Swallow was opening the memories of what that world was like, and he was just as amazed that he'd been a part of it as he was that it had continued to exist without him. Reality was composed of a thousand sick and dying worlds, he knew, none of which you could protect yourself from, not for very long.

When he reached the checkpoint cabin there were a couple of air force boys in blue uniforms sitting in it, and they were listening to the rebroadcast of a baseball game. "Hey!" he said and one of them got up and came over to the window. "There's a sailor getting the shit beat out of him, and you'd better get somebody to stop it right away." By vocalizing it, he'd made it possible for the boys to hear the screams through the baseball game, and they both looked out the window and one of them said, "Oh shit, come on," as they went running out a side door.

Miles was alone. He saw that the bloody-faced driver, with the running approach of the air force boys, was getting into his cab and starting away. They knelt over Seaman Swallow. Miles wanted to go back and make sure the sailor was all right and to let the air force boys know what had happened, but Tuttleman was on this island—perhaps even on this base or en route to it—and Miles didn't want to risk attention. He decided to look for Smitty and the DISBO and threaten to turn them in if they didn't take responsibility. Wasn't that what a chaplain would do? He went through the checkpoint without having shown any ID and was conscious of breaking the rules but, compared to everything else, it didn't seem so bad.

He was walking through a park-green area along a golf course that he could see through an iron-rod fence and then he passed a McDonald's, and over its door the big yellow arches were blurring in his eyes from the heat, and he wiped the sweat out of his eyes and wondered if he were hallucinating because a concrete American city was appearing, a boulevard with civilian vehicles and dark blue air force buses, and there was a theater and a library and a lot of apartment complexes, and he could've been in humid Miami. He asked a man where the O Club was, and after another twenty minutes of walking through the military city, he arrived at a ranch-style, hedge-and-lawn-landscaped building marked, in standout metal letters over the door, KADENA OFFICERS CLUB.

The band was loud enough for him to hear the music distinctly—Led Zeppelin's "Whole Lotta Love"—as he crossed the grass to the entry patio.

Opening the door, he was blasted by the air-conditioning and music. Behind a podium there was a man in a blue air force uniform with sergeant's chevrons. "Do you have a reservation, sir?"

"A reservation?"

"This is a reserved party for officers of the USS *Warren Harding* and their guests."

Miles got out the dead man's ID and handed it over and he fingered his mustache as the card was inspected, and the sergeant gave it back and said, "They invited the chaplain? That's pretty sick."

"I'm just looking for a couple of guys."

"Tracking them down, trying to keep them out of trouble? You a Mormon, sir?"

"No, I—"

"You know that Mormon Tabernacle Choir? Ever hear their version of 'Ninety-Nine Bottles of Beer'?"

"No—I'm a Methodist."

"Go on in, sir. If you don't see the guys you're looking for, just check under the tables."

"Will do."

It was his first time in a bar in four years of sobriety. He saw at once that it wasn't the somber kind of place he would've wanted to drink in. On a stage with neon lights moving pink and blue around its base, an all-woman band, wearing cowgirl miniskirts and halters, was performing "Whole Lotta Love" in as loud and sloppy a fashion as possible, while on the dance floor the officers of the *Harding*, including Smitty and the DISBO, were gyrating drunkenly, each by himself, their faces contorted as they concentrated closed-eyed to the beat, their arms doing the Hawaiian sway as their knees bent and their asses moved back-and-forth. If they had any individuality it must've been in their singing—their mouths were all giving different shapes to the words.

The areas beyond the stage and the dance floor were dark, but in the shadows, around a long table, he could make out men who, drink in hand, were standing or sitting, and some of the ones who were sitting had their heads on their crossed arms. Then he saw that three others were crawling on the floor near the table, and he realized with twinges of horror and dismay that one of them was the captain.

Miles went uncertainly toward the table, knowing only that he must tell about the cabdriver and Seaman Swallow, and when he got close enough he could hear the captain yelling from beneath the table, "Found it? Found it or what? That was a good American comb . . . I'm going to order every man who's still standing to come under this table and look for it," and when the captain looked up and saw Miles he came out from under the table and got up, his face so red with alcohol that his standing hair looked very white, and he lifted his tropical shirt and reached beneath his white belly and into his enormous shorts and scratched and adjusted things and said, "Who the hell sent for you?"

"Sir, I have some bad news to report."

"How stupid you think I look? You think I expect good news from chaplains?" The captain's breath was a sour blast of Jack Daniel's.

"Sir, I have to report that two of my fellow officers roughed up a taxi driver about twenty minutes ago, and there's a seaman pretty hurt too."

"All right, what's the bad news?"

"Sir, I—I just thought you should know about it."

"If I exercised my bowels every time some guy tried to beat a little honesty into one of these crooked Japs, I'd be flopping around on a stinking mountain of shit bigger than Mount Fuji. Now get down on the goddamn floor and don't get up till you find my fucking comb."

"Sir?"

"Get down and look!"

"Yes sir." Miles got down and crawled beneath the table and started feeling around for the captain's comb. Doing so, he analyzed the CO's management style. Only things of immediate pertinence were important: a meeting with the admiral, a storm, a lost comb. Whatever his officers or mistresses did out of sight was apparently their business. The captain's emotions were consumed by the practical. He would deal with Smitty and the DISBO only when—if—he had to.

And where was Robin? He was intrigued and turned on by the possibility that she might enter the bar at any moment and start dominating everyone, using her aggressive intelligence, mobile eyes, skimpy attire.

Feeling around for the comb as the cowgirl band segued into Lynyrd Skynyrd's "Free Bird" and the air-conditioning drafted up his shorts and under his shirt, he knew this place was hell if you didn't drink, but since it was a private party he thought it a good idea to hang around. Tuttleman couldn't get in. And then one of the officers crawling alongside him found the comb and they stood up and the CO said, "That's not my goddamn comb, you idiot," but before Miles could be reordered to the floor the DISBO had him by the arm, was pulling him away, into a corner. He had his pipe burning again; he was still wearing his sunglasses. He shouted over the music into the chaplain's ear, "What the fuck you telling the CO? You still a cool fool or what?"

"We were talking about his comb."

"Do I look like I'm from fucking Iowa? Why would you fuckers be talking about that?"

"That cabdriver's bloodied up, and that seaman's in pretty sad shape too, DISBO."

"Did he mention my fucking balance sheets?"

"Who, the cabdriver?"

"The CO! They say I knocked up some fucking whore in the fucking Philippines on last year's WESTPAC and embezzled three fucking thousand dollars to buy her off but it's all a fucking lie, Jim, it was just one of those clerical errors that grow in the books like an ingrown butt hair, that was all. Was the motherfucker asking about it? Does he think I confide in anyone, or tell the fucking truth to chaplains?"

"I doubt it."

The DISBO put his arm around the chaplain's shoulders and squeezed hard and shouted, "You're a fucking friend, Jim, you're one hell of a decent motherfucker," and Miles was sure if he pulled away the DISBO would stumble over drunk, and the DISBO motioned with his pipe across the room and said, "You see those beautiful fucking girls up there? The ones playing this beautiful fucking music? The ones in those beautiful fucking western outfits?"

"You mean, the only girls in the room?"

"Those are the ones! These girls play music all fucking day, Jim, and then they fuck officers all fucking night. We flew them in from fucking Los Angeles, man, paid for them out of the fucking entertainment fund—and I mean fucking entertainment. It's all fucking paid for, Jimmy, charged to the fucking taxpayers, deducted from the payroll in creative little ways by your friendly neighborhood DISBO, so just pick out the one you like and I'll fucking arrange it."

"No way—I'm the chaplain."

"They don't fucking care about that, Jim, they're not fucking prejudiced. One of them's even going to fuck that crazy nigger Smitty, you know, on account of we don't stand for any fucking prejudice of any kind around here. These girls are open-minded as all fucking get-out—they'll fuck niggers, drunks, women, dogs, chaplains, zucchinis, whatever the fuck we throw at them. Don't fucking put yourself down, Jimbo. You're just as fucking good as any of the assholes in this room."

"Thank you."

"Now come on over here with me, I'm going to fucking introduce you to these—"

"No," said Miles, trying to throw off the DISBO's arm, "I can't do that—"

"You can't fucking do what?"

"I can't sleep with a prostitute, DISBO."

"Goddamn it, Jim, I'm not asking you to sleep with some fucking prostitute. All I'm suggesting is that you insert your erect penis into her vagina and go in and out a couple of times until something squirts out the front end of it and into her gorgeous fucking body, that's all. Who said anything about sleeping with a prostitute? Your fucking wife's the one you go to sleep with, man. Jesus, you religious guys are confused."

"I'm the chaplain, I can't—"

"So what? So fucking what? Suppose the fucking whore finds out you're a fucking chaplain? Probably won't make you wear a fucking rubber, is all. They generally charge fucking extra for that, you know, you'll be getting a fucking bargain when you're fucking."

"I can't do it!"

"Okay! Okay! Look—why don't you just fucking pretend you're *not* a chaplain? Can't you fucking pretend for one fucking night? Don't you have any fucking imagination? Just pretend you're a normal fucking guy. You know, like the rest of us. Just pretend you're the supply officer. Okay, so you're not fat enough to be a fucking SUPPO, pretend you're a fucking JAG or a fucking CHENG—anybody can look like a self-satisfied prick lawyer or chief engineer, especially when he's fucking a gorgeous fucking girl like that, you know? You can be whatever you fucking want, Jim. This is America."

"No it's not."

"Of course it is. Every fucking place we go becomes America. We take it with us."

The band concluded "Free Bird" with a torturous twittering of guitars and then the DISBO was sprinting away from Miles, across the dance floor, toward the stage, and the DISBO tumbled off his feet and fell, and he got up and staggered onto the stage and took the microphone out of the blond singer's hand and said, "Let's get it up—let's get the clap—aw shit—let's get our hands up and clap for these beautiful fucking girls!" The men were hooting and applauding. "And now I'd like to bring up our NIPPO—that is, our Japanese Cultural Affairs Officer—with the fucking emphasis on affairs—Jim Banquette!" Hearty laughter all around. "Come on up, Jim, have a dance with the pretty lady." There was an explosion of applause, and the anger shooting up inside him surprised him with its force, and then as his fellow officers took him by the arms and laughingly pulled him toward the stage he knew for the first time since adolescence, since his father's parties on yachts and in ski resorts, what it felt like to be thoroughly abused by drunks, and his anger had him squirming in their grip.

The woman had come down off the stage, microphone in hand, a small person, older up close, with thin blond hair and a narrow face, and she offered her hand and despite himself Miles shook it and she said, with a jaunty professional friendliness, "Hi, I'm Carolyn," and then the band went bomp-bomp-bomping into "Satisfaction," and Carolyn was singing, she was dancing, and the DISBO was saying, "Her fucking butt is tighter than Mick Jagger's," and they were pushing Miles to dance with her.

He felt he had no choice. Angry as he was, the chaplain could not tell these men to fuck themselves; the chaplain had to be a sport. And so he started dancing. The buckskin tassels were bouncing off the woman's cowgirl top and cowgirl miniskirt, and Miles was dancing with her, and the officers were hooting and laughing in a circle around them.

When was the last time he'd danced? It was hard to do, foot here, foot there, knees bending, elbows in the air—had he ever danced sober? Each time the woman completed the word "Satisfaction," she licked the air obscenely at him, but as debauched a life as he'd once led, he'd never had sex with a prostitute, and he certainly wasn't starting tonight. My God, it was hard to dance! And all the men were laughing at him. No, he'd never danced sober in his life, there was none of the fluidity of his drunken-boogie days, he felt like an awkward bird with extended wings and backward knees.

At last they were done and she hugged him and kissed his neck and said, "Thank you," and the officers were chortling and somebody said, "We made the chaplain dance with a whore!" Miles took her hand, and feeling very much like a chaplain, he told her, "You don't have to do this, you know, you can be whatever you want," and he was more surprised than any real chaplain would've been when she said, "I'm making five thousand dollars tonight, Wilbur, why don't you mind your own fucking business," and turned smartly away from him.

That was when he saw Lebedeen. The major, his eyebrows angled upward in shock, was standing on the periphery of men, and when he saw that the chaplain had spotted him he put on a neutral face and started toward Miles, who was ashamed at what the major had seen him doing, and surprised at his shame. He was startled to realize how much he cared what Major Lebedeen thought of him. Miles cared nothing for the opinion of the drunken officers who were shaking his shoulders and punching his back and pumping his hands and telling him he was the best fucking chaplain the ship had ever had. But he cared what the sensitive Lebedeen thought.

"You're a regular fucking human being," the DISBO was saying. "You're fucking incredible, Jim. The last chaplain motherfucker we had wouldn't let me play my Madonna tape in my own fucking stateroom."

Miles shrugged. "Jesus kept company with prostitutes."

The DISBO took a swaying backward step. He was apparently—and it was hard to believe—offended. His pipe came out of his mouth and he fumbled with both hands to catch it. "You shouldn't tell a lie like that, Jim. I mean, I don't fucking believe in Jesus or anything, but a motherfucker like you is *supposed* to."

Lebedeen had finally worked his way through the admirers. He took Miles by the sleeve and said, "I gotta talk to you, I came here right away in a cab, you probably can't tell but I'm going crazy."

The band erupted into "Sympathy for the Devil" as Miles led the major to the other end of the room, as far from the amplifiers as possible.

"The only reason I'm here is to talk to you," the major made clear right away. "I wouldn't hang around these kind of people ordinarily—I just thought I'd come in and ask these morons if they knew where you were. I tried the chapel first—I didn't expect—I guess you must have some good reason."

"Jesus kept company with prostitutes," Miles tried again.

The major gave him a dubious look and said, "Wouldn't make up things like that, I were you. I mean, once a rumor like that gets started . . . Look, you're the chaplain, you got to help me, I called my wife from that other base and she's real sick, she's got breast cancer, and they have to decide whether to remove the entire—breast—or, or just a part of it, and I radioed Brigadier General McMinn back on the *Natchez* about hardship leave, so I could go home—I mean, who am I kidding, anyway, I'm not a leader of men—and the general looked it up and said I need a letter from the ship's doctor and the chaplain, so I'm asking would you do it, I know it's like asking you to lie, to say that I'm undergoing disabling stress, you know, to say I'm kind of nuts, when we both know how sane I am, but it's lying for a good cause, so would you write a letter saying I'm nuts except don't make it sound like I'm *too* nuts, just nuts enough, would you write that letter?"

The DISBO came stumble-dancing over to them and was dancing in place, shaking his behind and pumping his arms, his pipe upside down, and he said through the clench of his teeth, "What the fuck, Jim? Gone over to the fucking jarheads? Those pussies aren't even allowed in here. This party is fucking private, USN only. No ass-licking, cum-tasting, weight-lifting, marine faggots are allowed."

The major told the DISBO, "Stop that dancing! You listen to me, because I have a few things to say to you, DISBO." The major's anger gave an organization to his face that Miles had never seen: there was nothing doubtful about his eyebrows, which were straight with purpose, as were his mouth and his crossed arms. The DISBO stopped dancing and stood there disheveled and swaying and listening. "I don't like you," Lebedeen told him. "I think you are a nasty guy. You like to say bad words, and I don't think that's right. When I hear you using bad words I know you are a mean man. And I don't like the gross ways you talk about women, either. If my wife was here, she wouldn't like it. She would agree with me that you are a mean guy, and I think she would probably knock you on your butt. I know I'm not talking like an officer or a gentleman, but somebody had to be man enough to say these things to you."

"Oh yeah?" said the DISBO. "You fag-assed little pussy-fuck—"

Tooting whistles punctuated the music as five air force men entered the club—blue uniforms, blue helmets, black armbands with MP in white—and they were bringing with them the thin academic-looking cabdriver with his bruised-up sullen face and the DISBO said, "Look at that poor Jap, somebody beat up that poor motherfucker."

Two of the MPs guarded the entryway, so that no one could escape, and another went into the kitchen to guard that exit. This left two MPs to escort the driver up onto the stage where the women had just started crunching into "Purple Haze." One of the MPs waved with both hands for them to stop, and they did, the music unraveling into random snarls of guitar and a diminishing progression of bass, and there were a lot of boos. The MP who'd waved his arms took the microphone from Carolyn, and the women and all the officers stood waiting resentfully to hear what he would say. His blue helmet looked too big for his head and his glasses reflected the bar-light in two big ovals.

"I'm Chief Master Sergeant F. X. Wetherall of the Eleven-eighty-second Fighter Wing Military Police. These airmen and I are here to do an investigation of what amounts to some pretty serious charges." He paused, licked his lips, looked at the cabdriver and around the room, continued: "What we have on our hands here, gentlemen, is a situational—that is—a situation on our hands. A set of situational problematics. As we say in the air force."

"Fuck the air force!" said the captain. "Let the lady sing!"

"The lady may resume singing after the resolution of this delicate—ah—our positional delicacy—that is, delicate position in terms of our—that is, your—apparent violation of our Status of Forces Agreement with the Government of—with our Japanese, that is to say, our Okinawan hosts. This cabdriver here in particular. I mean to say specifically. Mr. Obe here. I will now ask him to please identify which individual or individuals caused his particular rights under—that is—under the Agreement between our two governments to go into a state of—to be precise—violation. Can one of the airmen do a rough translation for him?"

But the Okinawan was already pointing at Smitty and saying "This dark man in which the Americans are calling him 'nigger' is a man who is having made to me with actions of violences."

"You racist Jap-fuck," said Smitty. "Can you believe this fucking shit, I mean can you fucking believe it, just on account I'm the only black man in the fucking place, this motherfucker be calling me out, you know what I'm saying? This Jap bastard be saying I done some shit to him, I ain't done no shit to this fucker, man, no fucking way, I ain't guilty, he just be calling me out on account of I'm black, this is prejudice, I'm the only black mother-fucker here . . . "

Miles turned to look at the DISBO, but the DISBO was gone; so was Lebedeen, presumably in search of the doctor, from whom he needed the second hardship letter.

Two of the MPs, one coming from the front door and the other off the stage, approached Smitty and began to escort him—he continued to shout, but he did not resist—up onto the stage to be confronted by the helmeted MP with the microphone and the cross-armed, smug-smiling cabdriver. The one with the microphone said to Smitty—it was amplified throughout the room—"Would you please furnish us—that is—as part of any prear-raignment statement or—to be exact—confession, the names and ranks of those other individuals who involved themselves in the—that is, the distur-bance and/or specific violation, along with the current whereabouts of such individuals if not now present, and—as well—whatever ancillary chronologies relevant to the situational—that is, the case, the problem, with Mr. Obe—"

"Say what the fuck? You want what? Just what pre-cise-ly is your moth-erfucking problem, jack? Somebody slam they dick too hard up your bung-hole this morning? You want me to fucking give you the whos and the whys and the whences and the herebys and the what-alls? You want onion rings with that, you pink-assed racist? Can't you see what's going down, motherfucker, this is a total racist fuck-over, you know what I'm saying, I'm about as guilty as your virgin prick. Just on account some nigger messed up this yellow-faced Jap-fuck, and he come in here looking for a nigger, and I be the only fucking nigger in the room, on account the whole fucking navy's racist, ain't got but one black officer out of a hundred, you know what I'm saying, even the goddamn army's got generals who's black, but you know well as I do there ain't no black admirals, hardly no black officers, and me being the only black man in the motherfucking room you going to haul my ass off to some Jap motherfucking jail—"

"Please provide the names and/or ranks or rates of the other person-nel," said the MP.

A buzz of disapproval rose from the men, and some of them shifted their feet, and some of them stared at Smitty with contempt, and then somebody said, "Only ingrates turn in shipmates!" and somebody repeated it more loudly and then everybody but Miles was saying it, chanting it, *Only ingrates turn in shipmates,* and some of the men were stomping, and some were giving the finger. Smitty looked down on their faces, which were white except where they were red with alcohol and anger, and his eyes widened and his mouth opened with the fearful recognition that he was disliked far more than even his cynicism had allowed him to believe, and then his expression collapsed into a look of desperate horror. He limply allowed one of the MPs to lead him off the stage, and Smitty's mouth was making words that nobody could hear. The chief master sergeant said to the other MPs, "Before you—ah—execute him in terms of—that is, execute the arrest—please ask Mr. Obe, in his native tongue, I mean dialect of course, to identify the other—that is, the perpetrating individuals—ah— the ones other than Seaman Swanson—"

"It's Swallow, sir," said one of the other MPs.

"Excuse me?"

"Swallow."

The MP with the microphone swallowed visibly, appeared less agitated, then continued: "I mean besides that seaman in the—under arrest in the hospital-medical unit. Please inquire of Mr. Obe as to the identities of the other perpetrating—oh hell, just ask him who the other guys in the car were. But do it with procedural correctness."

"I am not needing the translationings," said the driver, "as my knowledges of the English language it is the superior of my studies. However but, I cannot to make selections of Americans because Americans always having same hair of shortness, same face of pinkness. It is in the scientific knowledges, the biologicalness, the inferiority of race of white peoples, making everyone look too much like everyone."

Everyone stared at him a moment, and then all the MPs were leaving, hustling Smitty out, and Miles was looking for the captain.

The CO was no longer watching the proceedings; his drunken focus was now aimed, as he walked with stooped petulance, at something in the far corner, and Miles jogged up alongside him and said, "I saw it, sir, it's the DISBO, that's the other one they want. That's what I was trying to tell you before."

The CO continued across the room, in a sway-path toward whatever it was that was reeling him toward itself, as though he were a wobbly thing on wheels, pulled by a wire. "Can't you see I'm in the piddle—middle of a problem? This goddamn lesbo thing. I'm going to go over there and punch out the good eye she has left."

"Sir—the DISBO—"

"Can't spare my fucking DISBO, only fucker we got who can count, do a goddamn payroll without more than two or three grand turning up missing at a time. Just about the only motherfucker we got who can add two and two and come up with . . . come up with the answer. Except for this lesbo of mine, and all she is is a goddamn civilian. Smitty, radio man, no fucking loss. Pick one up in Subic faster than you can pick up the drip. Same as we can replace *you* with some virgin-hole Presbyterian who likes to jerk off in the shower and wears his wife's panties in his stateroom and otherwise minds his own fucking business. Now are you going to make me order you to pull out your left nut and make you bite it off yourself, or are you getting out of my way?"

The women on stage concluded a frenzy of whispered conversation and started blasting the room with "Purple Haze." The CO continued toward the far corner of the bar, and Miles was following him saying, "Captain? Can I get you to listen to one more thing? That seaman, Swallow, under arrest in the hospital? He's innocent," and the CO was saying, "Who!" and Miles was saying, "Swallow, the seaman, sir," and the CO was saying, "Watch your fucking mouth, you drunk idiot," and as they were approaching the CO's destination Miles saw that it was a long table recently occupied, probably during the arrest crisis, by five short-haired women in blue air force uniforms and one woman in a red-sky blouse with purple palm trees on it, and this woman was Robin. A quarter of her face was raccoon-marked with the swelling where somebody had punched her in the eye. And some naval officers standing nearby were saying, "Military women, they're just dickless men, you know?" and "Can't allow gays in the military, that'll destroy our moral standards," and "What's *she* doing with *them*? I thought she liked bones in her fish." And the CO, instead of saying, "What happened to you?" said, "Who invited these fucking dykes?"

"They're my guests," said Robin. "We're allowed to bring guests, right? When they're the only people on the island who'll talk to you? I waited for you all morning in that restaurant."

"Couldn't let down the staff," said the CO, adjusting his crotch.

"You couldn't let down your whores," said Robin, and the word appeared to mobilize the air force women, now unclasping their hands or sitting up straighter or looking up defiantly, each with a distinctive face, boot-jawed or pickle-nosed or wattle-necked or possum-eyed or freckle-chinned, but the haircuts were the same, pageboy blond, pageboy red, pageboy brown, pageboy gray.

Miles asked Robin, "What happened?"

"I smacked her," said the air force woman with the red hair.

"What for?"

"For being a self-sabotaging, man-pleasing, oppressed fool!"

The one with gray hair said, "For waiting all morning to have breakfast with a certain CO who never showed up because he couldn't wait to fuck his whores." She said it directly to the captain.

"Knocked some sense into her," said one of the dark-haired ones.

"I were you," the CO told Robin, "I'd charge charges with the officer in charge. Charges charging assault charges against this lesbo. I mean this lesbo against you. Or something."

"I would file charges against a man," said Robin, "but I would never file charges against another woman. Women don't resolve things that way, we're not competitive. Daisy hit me out of emotion, not because she was trying to dominate and control me, the way a man would."

"Get the hell up," said the captain. "Let's dance."

"She doesn't have to do what you say," said Daisy. "Robin, I refuse to let you do anything he says. You don't need him. You are a person of gender."

"That's right," said the blond one to the CO. "You treat her like less of a person just because she doesn't have a penis between her legs."

"She'll have one later tonight," said the captain. "Now get the hell up and dance, girl."

"She's not your little girl," Daisy said. As she stood up, stumbling into her drunken balance, Miles saw that she was a big woman, tall, her large breasts and stomach stuffed into her bulging uniform, and her size made the monkish red hair look even shorter.

The CO said, "This party is private, Private, private, Private. I mean, it's a private party, Private. No privates allowed."

"Corporal," said Daisy.

"So salute me and shut the fuck up, Corporal. Get the hell out of here, go to some goddamn corporal private party."

"You don't talk to me like that," said Daisy, coming around the table. "No officer talks to me that way, and no man should treat women the way you treat Robin."

"No captain owns me," said Robin. "I'll even kiss a chaplain if I want to," but Daisy and the CO were yelling into each other's faces, not watching her as she approached Miles, the black and purple of her eye injury looking more zany than painful, and the swampy odor of beer was on her as she locked her hand around the back of his neck and forced her mouth onto his, shoving her tongue into his mouth and giving him his first taste of alcohol in four years. As he twisted his head out of her grip, Robin laughed and said, "Men don't dominate me. On the ship, guys clean my toilet."

Daisy and the CO were shoving each other, shouting over "Purple Haze," and the other air force women were rising from the table and circling them. Robin said to Miles, "We're going to have a riot! You gonna fight for your ship?"

"I don't see you fighting for it."

"I'm a feminist," she said. "I have all the rights of a man, without any of the responsibilities."

"Well, I'm a chaplain. I'm committed to peace."

She reached up and pinched his cheek and he shook his face away and she said, "You're a coward. Defend your CO, beat up somebody."

"Ministers don't beat up people."

"They do if they want to sleep in *my* rack."

"I don't want to sleep in your rack."

"I like a challenge," she said. "You're the only one who's a challenge."

"Leave me alone."

"Yeah? You too good for me? You think you're different from other men because you wear a plastic collar one day out of seven? Fuck you."

"Fuck you too," he said.

"A chaplain isn't supposed to talk that way."

"Neither is a lady."

"I'm no lady."

"Well I'm no—never mind."

Some of the officers had stopped dancing, were surrounding the air force women, the men's fists on their hips, ready for confrontation, while others were shouting as they attempted to separate Daisy and the CO. Meanwhile the DISBO, having eluded the MPs, pulled Miles, by the elbow, away from Robin and said, "You're sucking face with the captain's woman, Jim? Fucking wake up, man. She's just a fucking sexual predator. Females can be sexual predators too, you know. Is that all you fucking want to be, sexual prey? Doesn't your fucking pecker have a mind of its own? Like a real man's? No way I'd ever bone a fucking wacko like her. You fucking ask *me,* I think your thing with her is pretty fucking sick, dude."

He was trying to formulate a response when a lanky redheaded fellow with a pear-shaped, freckled face approached him, tall and pale in salmon-colored shorts and a green T-shirt with the yellow word ECUMENICALISM! across the chest, and he said, "Excuse me, which one is your chaplain?"

"I'm the chaplain."

"Well, that's what those other fellows said, but I'm looking for the chaplain from the *Harding.*"

"That's me."

"Are there two chaplains on the *Harding*?"

A sheet of ice crystallized in his chest and wrapped down over his stomach as he realized who this tall, shuffling, goofy-mannered guy—whom everyone in tenth grade no doubt had called Stretch or Red, when he was around, and other things when he wasn't—must be. Miles felt icicle needles go up his back and neck and under his scalp.

"Father Tuttleman?" he squeaked.

"Chaplain talk," said the DISBO. "Well, this is going to be fucking boring. Think I'll join the riot." And he departed, with an anticipatory smile, toward the mass of people who were shoving each other and shouting over the music.

The tall man who was Father Tuttleman laughed, winging out his elbows and his knees, nodding, vibrating with laughter, one of those people who are just big kids and think, for whatever nervous reason, that the smallest social interactions are funny. "Yes, I'm Tuttleman," he said, and laughed again, as though at his own name. "I sneaked in during the racial arrest," he said, laughing. "Who are you? Friend of Jim's?"

Miles was terrified, and his fright was making him feel very short and compact before the tall chaplain, as though there were nothing about Miles anymore except what was essential, and out of this tiny cornered essence came the only possible words of survival, and his throat was so dry that his voice had a scratchy kind of depth, which couldn't have been better calculated to cut open the fear in his opponent:

"We have that letter you wrote, Father Tuttleman."

Frozen grin, and standing straight as a pole: "What?"

"I think you know what."

Tuttleman's face collapsed, and it drained so completely that the paleness made his freckles look like a sudden disease. "Oh my God," he said.

Miles felt sorry for the man but there was no other way. "We can have that letter in your CO's hands by four o'clock."

Tuttleman stepped back. "Dear Christ in heaven."

"Stay away from Reverend Banquette. Stay the hell away from the *Harding*."

"Oh my God—are you—are you NIS?"

Miles didn't know what this meant. Then he thought he remembered from the DICNAVAB, Naval Investigative Service, and decided he'd better not impersonate one of *those* guys. Better to keep it ambiguous, as the NIS undoubtedly would. "Stay away from Banquette and the ship, Tuttleman. Otherwise your CO gets the letter."

Tuttleman took another half-step back. His eyes were getting wet. "Oh sweet Jesus—"

"Do you understand?"

"Am I under arrest? Oh please don't say I'm under arrest, oh sweet Jesus—"

"Just stay away from—"

"I'm going to shit myself, I've never been arrested in my life, not even that time in Phoenix," said Tuttleman, still pale, eyes red and wet, and Miles felt pity for the suffering priest, shaking in his off-duty shorts, but Miles knew he had to be as thorough as possible:

"Your whole career is going to be destroyed if you don't stay away from—"

"Oh no, Jesus no, please—"

"If you ever write another—"

"I'm just going to die . . ."

"Now listen," said Miles, afraid he'd overplayed it, "nobody's going to—"

"I'm just going to shit myself . . ."

"Father, listen to me."

Tuttleman had his hands in his pockets and he was a little bent over with his knees together, and his eyes squeezed shut, more like he was going to pee himself. His voice broke: "No jail, please, no jail, oh I'm just going to shit myself . . ."

"You're not under arrest, Tuttleman, you're not under arrest, this is just a warning, do you understand, just a warning."

"You're NIS, I knew it . . ."

"Just stop writing those letters, and stay away from the ship, and leave Reverend Banquette alone . . ."

It took another ten minutes to calm Tuttleman, and they even shook hands, and Tuttleman was knuckle-wiping his eyes and said, "I was just going to ask him out for a drink, that was all, friendly-like, you know."

"Okay, Tuttleman. That's fine, Tuttleman, that's all right, you get ahold of yourself now."

"I don't suppose—"

"Tuttle—"

"I don't suppose—well—that *you* would like to have a drink? Have a drink with me?"

"What?" said Miles.

"Have a drink with me. You know."

"That won't be necessary, Tuttleman. Be on your way. Now get going. Remember what I said."

Tuttleman finally left, and Miles was *ready* for a drink, and the bar was right there, but there was a riot evolving, everyone was shoving and punching, the cowgirl musicians had ceased playing, and the MPs were running back in with their piercing little whistles, and Miles decided to look for a late lunch or an early dinner.

Within, he was trembling as badly as Tuttleman, and as he found the dining room of the O Club, he was relieved to see it was empty and quiet—all at once he felt that he hadn't been alone in weeks, and solitude was an oasis, incredible but real. He took a seat at a mahogany table that was round and large, and the backs of the chairs rose up all around him in hand-carved, Arthurian splendor. A flyboy, white napkin over arm, took his order—salad, filet mignon, baked potato, butter, sour cream, chives, coffee—and the flyboy asked if he were with the *Harding* party, and he charged it to the ship's officers' rec fund, and he ate. He had seven-layer chocolate cake for dessert.

Then Miles was outside, wandering the base, squinting against the tropic sun, and when he went into the movie house, it was only because it was air-conditioned. The movie was a terrible one called *The Hunt for Red October*, a slow predictable thing in which the uncharacterized hero and bland-faced navy men saved the world from nuclear incineration, laboring in a highly professional and ethical heterosexual atmosphere of easy racial harmony in which not a single sailor, despite the world-threatening tension, uttered as much as a *damn*. Miles was at first bored by the lies, then baffled, and finally offended. He left the theater with the distinct feeling that the filmmakers were banking on his gullibility and ignorance, and the more he thought about it, the angrier he got. Of course every civilian who saw the film would think the military was overflowing with heroes.

When the movie let out, it was night, and he ran into some officers from the ship who were too drunk to fight or fuck or drink or walk. He got into a cab with them and it took them—everyone but Miles hooting like a high-schooler—back to the landing beach, which was littered with passed-out men lying in the same places and positions as the war dead of '45.

In about ten minutes the next AAV for the *Harding* bobbed up in the surf. Getting on was easy, wading through the tide in the moonlight and stepping onto the lowered landing gate while the drunks behind him staggered and fell and crawled, a legion of the dead in the gray light. When the gate went up they were shoulder-to-shoulder and it was hell, men stinking and swearing and falling against one another and vomiting on their neighbors as the craft backed up and turned, humping up and down over the waves, each time with a blast of spray in their faces.

The tank deck was weirdly illuminated, red, and the men were stumbling all over each other to reboard, thinking, if they were thinking at all, only of their racks. The drunks had to be helped up out of the craft, which was moving up three feet and down three feet relative to the ship. Any drunk-dazed man falling between vessels would've dropped to the dark bottom like a bomb. The handlers, resentful as they might have been for pulling the duty, helped each man up with careful if rough efficiency.

Back in his stateroom, he was startled to find Kruger in the chair, reading a paperback Bible, his glasses shining with reflected light. Standing quickly: "Um—excuse me, sir—wardroom CPO said I could wait for you—I stayed in, sir! I stayed on the ship all day, I didn't go on liberty, and I didn't get in any trouble, praise Jesus, and thank you, Chaplain. You told me to focus on the Bible-study group, and that's good advice, that's just common knowledge, and I stayed right here, which was the right thing to do. I stayed right here and I did nothing to offend the Lord, and I'm not in any trouble at all."

"That's good, Kruger. That's real good."

8

Chief Ditchfield rapped on his door the third day out of Okinawa. Miles, who didn't even hide being on the computer game anymore, reached over to open the door, keeping his eyes on the screen, and the old man said, "The major wants to know if you got his hardship letter ready, couldn't come up himself, staff meeting, whining he couldn't get out of it, so he sends *me*, never mind the PHILCOM chits I gotta see about before thirteen-fifty, he's whining whining whining, hardship my dimpled ass, we didn't have any whining marines in Harry Truman's navy, you could bet your nut-sack on it, they all had to be men. Now every joe with a hair growing the wrong way on his butthole is a certified victim." As the chief was talking, Miles was clicking into the dead man's letter file, finding the generic Hardship/Sick Wife letter whose blanks he'd filled in with the appropriate information, then he clicked on Print and told Ditchfield to fetch it from the yeomanry for his signature, in fact Banquette's signature, which he'd been practicing for two days, a script so loopy-perfect and unmanly that it looked as if it had been ruler-slapped into the young Banquette by German nuns between toilet trainings—but he was Methodist so there must be some other explanation. The old man started away saying, "Aye-aye, Commander." And then, down the P-way: "It's a chief's navy, no other man jack does any work, never did, not even in Roosevelt's navy."

The ship was heave-rocking on the South China Sea, along the coast of the main island of the Philippine archipelago, Luzon, whose greener-than-green steaming jungle hills Miles had seen this morning through one of the

"Big Eyes," high-powered telescopes mounted tall as men on the deck of the signal bridge. The crew had recovered from the fights and hangovers of liberty, even the officers, whose facial cuts and black eyes had passed their aesthetic nadirs and were now so familiar that nobody noticed their gradual improvement. It had taken the ARG Command until last night to calculate the "casualties" for all five ships, and the full inventory had only just appeared in this morning's POD:

AWOL: 12

ARRESTS (BY SP, MP, AND JAPANESE ENFORCEMENT AGENCIES):

I. THEFT—
    A. of taxis: 11
    B. of motorcycles: 2
    C. of handbags: 3
    D. of sushi chef aprons: 1

II. ASSAULT—
    A. on cabdrivers: 17
    B. on bartenders: 5
    C. on prostitutes (licensed): 2
    D. on prostitutes (unlicensed): 5
    E. on fellow personnel: 391
    F. on sushi chefs: 1

III. RAPE—
    A. of females (adult): 6
    B. of females (juvenile): 2
    C. of fellow personnel: 3
    D. of sushi chefs: 1

IV. DRUG VIOLATIONS—
    A. marijuana: 43
    B. cocaine: 43
    C. heroin: 43
    D. LSD: 43
    E. whipped cream canisters: 1

Miles sat back in his chair and thought. Okinawa, more than seventy-two hours in the past, already felt like it had never happened, less real now than the sucking sound of dirty slush under his galoshes in Illinois—Okinawa was still real only for the people who'd been robbed, assaulted, and/or raped, only for the sailors and marines sitting in Japanese jails or U.S. camp-brigs. Ditchfield came back with the letter and Miles signed it—J-a-m-e-s J. B-a-n-q-u-e-t-t-e, C-d-r, C-h-a-p C-o-r-p-s, U-S-N, loopy-loop, it wasn't hard—and then the chief was gone.

Miles sat back once more and everything felt distant again. Even Robin's kiss. Especially Robin's kiss. Her slippery tongue . . . the moldy taste of beer. It was as otherworldly a memory as though he himself had been drunk. Aside from a mild revulsion, he had no emotions about it. He'd avoided talking to her since. Whenever she passed in the P-way or the wardroom mess, she raised her eyebrows at him in acknowledgment of their shared secret, and her left eye was still black as an eight ball, and he just looked away, wishing she weren't the only woman he knew in the Far East.

Outside the rocking box of a ship, across the water, beyond the shoreline, beyond the nearest mountains, there was the cough and rumble of a volcano.

Through the loudspeakers a metallic reverberating voice announced that the gunnery exercise would begin in thirty minutes, and Miles checked his watch, because it was something new to see and would split up the tedium of a chaplain's day. He was on the firing deck ten minutes early. The sun was baking-bright against the gray steel of the deck, and he brought the dead man's sunglasses out of his breast pocket and slipped them on. Across the shining surface of the gulf, two miles at most, the island of Luzon rose in a jungle wall that ended so abruptly against the water that there was no room for a beach. Higher up, the foothills became mountains and the mountains went from green to blue-green to blue as they soared into the heat-hazed atmosphere before dissolving into clouds of steam—and like the longest greenest dragon in the world, the jungle coast bent inward and outward for miles before tapering away in a blurry outline of serpent tail.

Including Miles, there were seven officers standing on the broiling deck in their black-polished shoes and thick white socks and starched and pressed khaki uniforms, with the undershirt necks showing as required by regulation, and then the hair-cooking hats. There were many more enlisted men, in denim, also with undershirts and thick shoes, but wearing lighter white caps, and with their obscure work to do—hustling here and there with clipboards and headphones—at least they had something to think about besides the heat.

The gun rose twenty feet, blue-gray, at an angle just a degree from straight up, the sunlight glinting off its shaft in a blinding streak, the phallic god impossible to look at longer than a glance, and at its base, in the metal cubicle that was its balls, sat an enlisted man with headphones, his hands, orange-gloved, moving over a console of switches and buttons and dials with a routine studiedness, as though death in the shape of a 203-mm shell would be the outcome only of professionalism and logic.

A clipboard-wielding seaman wearing the ubiquitous navy-issue black-framed glasses approached the chaplain and said, "Welcome to exercise four-eight-two-delta-charlie-five, sequence seventeen, Commander. Observing today?"

"If it's all right."

The seaman looked directly at Miles's crotch. "Sir, you aren't prepared."

"I'm not?" Miles looked down at his crotch. Then he looked at the other men's crotches. They were all wearing little plastic tubes hanging on rubber cords from their belt buckles.

"Earplugs for the chaplain!" the seaman yelled so sharply that Miles wished he was already wearing them. "Earplugs now!" A passing seaman pressed one of the little plastic container tubes into the chaplain's hand and Miles saw that it contained two spongy-yellow earplugs exactly like the ones worn at Zincville Electroplate.

"Of course," Miles said. "My earplugs."

"Wouldn't want to blow out your drums, sir. We'll clear your sinuses too," the man with the glasses said with a cockeyed smile. He had freckles, and Miles decided he wasn't yet twenty-one. The boy was earnest and happy and the navy was his career and he was exactly the kind of kid Miles knew his father would love to get hold of for thirty years and work him till he collapsed into a bath of nickel solution.

"We're very proud of what we do, sir. Observation is always welcome. Gunnery staff, as you probably know, is made up of the most professional and responsible and career-minded segment of rates in the command. We've had no arrests in the past twenty-one liberties, you'll be pleased to know, Reverend."

"I am pleased to know that," said Miles.

"We're the only rate that never makes errors of any kind. You might say we're pretty damn perfect." He pushed his black-framed glasses up the sweaty bridge of his nose with a precise jab of his index finger. "Do you have any questions, sir?"

"Are those the hippest glasses they let you have?"

"Excuse me, sir?"

"Nothing."

"Well, enjoy the show. If you have any other questions, please wait till after the exercise. I cannot be disturbed while I'm plotting stereoscopic range calibrations, sir." The seaman strode away.

It was very hot on the firing deck. He thought he could feel the end of his nose starting to blister, and a ball bearing of sweat went rolling down his back. He took the spongy yellow earplugs out of their container, scrunched them up tightly, and inserted them into his ears, muffling the technical talk around him. Looking out to sea he found that there was no horizon, the heat-mist curtaining off the place where the horizon should be, enclosing this sector of the world like a big private steambath, a hazy blue lagoon for the ARG. Farthest to port was the helocarrier called the *Natchez,* flagship of the group, the surface of its long deck mottled in the mist with the dragonfly shapes of its helos; closer in, the *Buchanan,* tub-nosed, its two turrets aiming landward; far off the stern, the single-turret-ted and jumble-masted outline of the *Felton;* out to starboard, the short fantail and tall superstructure of the *Lompico,* whose two guns were in slow rotation.

More waiting, more heat, more muffled talk mixing with the electronic talk from a speaker planted high up outside the plotting room, and the occasional, unrelated staccato of a 1MC announcement . . .

The *Felton* fired. A yellow streak in the mist, skip a pulse, then the boom. Two streaks from the *Lompico,* a second later the compounded blast. Miles was watching the ships and had forgotten about his own when the explosion from the gun ten feet from him shook the deck and thick-ened the air with a metallic odor and the sound was cracking and echoing and ringing in his head despite the plugs and he could feel it in his nose and in his forehead—the explosion with its air-pressure change and its invisible shock wave made his nostrils and forehead feel as though they were splitting apart down a center line of pain. His sinuses and brain cav-ity felt horribly open, sucked clean, and his eyes were watering. He looked around and noticed one of the corpsmen wiping two lines of blood from beneath his nose.

Then he felt absolutely normal, as though a fever had melted to nothing, and everyone was talking again and they were looking with the Big Eyes and with field glasses and with both hands shielding eyes into the near jungle, at a rising finger of white smoke . . .

He was finishing dinner, sinking the side of his fork into a quivering triangle of key lime pie, when Ditchfield was at his elbow saying, in a tone that was insulting for its forced formality, "Commander, the admiral has requested your presence ashore."

"Ashore? What?"

"A smallboat will be arriving under K-level section seventeen at eighteen-forty hours, sir."

"Ashore?"

Miles looked upranks for help. The CO's chair was empty but the XO was there, lighting a cigarette with an expression of forced blankness, and everyone was quiet as the XO said, without looking at Miles, "Better take your last rites with you. Or whatever it is in your denomination."

"Sir?"

"Better go now."

Miles stood, leaving his dessert, and went out of the mess feeling more insecure, if not yet more frightened, than he had with Tuttleman, and neither could his rational side comfort him, for the only thing he knew was that no matter what was happening, or had happened, he was wholly unqualified to deal with it. Stopping at his stateroom to pick up the prayer book, which contained the chapter "Services of Death and Resurrection," he found that the book, which had become a comfortable weight in his hand on his way to and from Sunday services, now felt like what it was, somebody else's heavy and mysterious book of incantation.

At K-level section 17 he stood with one hand on the lifeline and the other gripping the book, and he looked down at the metal ladder that had been hooked sideways for him on the hull. He asked the seaman standing there what it was all about, but he didn't know, saying only that the smallboat would be there soon. The sun was beating at their backs, poised brightly over the water as it considered whether finally to go down; the ships were blockish outlines in the hazy distance; the mountains of Luzon were a montage of jungle backdrops, one behind the other, each one higher and less green, the tallest range losing itself in steam, a landscape revealing nothing. To port, far below, bobbing on the golden-rippled water, was the gray open box of the smallboat with three sets of heads and shoulders huddling over its benches.

As the boat came nearer, almost directly below him now, he saw that one of the men was Bernard Ogleby, the Catholic priest from the *Natchez*. Miles started down the spindly ladder, one hand tightly on the single railing and the other just as tightly on the prayer book, and when he got to the bottom, the boat was rising and dropping three feet, four feet. He watched it twice, waiting for the next crest, and then he jumped. As the helmsman backed it away with a high grinding of the ferocious little engine, Miles fell into a seated position next to one of the men, across from the two others, including Ogleby, who greeted him with, "We're not getting hazardous-duty pay for this. I was just saying to Jerry and Tom we should all write letters." Ogleby's breath was spoiled milk, even in the salt air.

"It's not an issue for me," said the man sitting next to the priest. "Jerry Wachtel," he said, offering Miles his hand. It was the rabbi; he had metal Magen Davids on his collars. The rabbi had blond hair and a square chin and his eyes were as green as the jungle. "It's about time we met."

Miles said, "Jim Banquette, Methodist," and the man sitting next to him offered his hand and said, "Doctor Thomas Asher, Episcopal." The Reverend Asher was a small man with pudgy kangaroo arms covered in black hair, and there were sprigs of the same hair coming out of his undershirt at the neck.

"So what is it all about?" said Miles.

"It's a secret," said Father Ogleby. "They're keeping it a secret from us, at least until we're ashore, and even then it'll stay a secret to all other hands. But we have a reliable rumor."

"So what is it?" he asked the rabbi this time, hoping he would answer and not Ogleby, the man's breath was that potent.

Father Ogleby said, "It was the boom-boom boys. They put the boom-boom in the wrong place. Which happens. Only this time there was a Filipino village in the way. Which also happens. To tell you the truth, men, I'm glad we're all together on this one. I don't think I could manage it on my own."

Miles saw that they were all holding black books of one kind or another.

"Casualties?" he said. "Deaths?"

Ogleby fingered his khaki-covered belly and gave a jowly nod. Miles felt something shift in his own stomach, like a brick tumbling from one side to the other. He was sure it wasn't the boat's fault, though it was pitching more miserably than anything he'd experienced, and he had to hold on to the bench with both hands, prayer book between his knees.

Father Ogleby said, in an obviously false burst of good humor, "Doesn't this remind anyone of a joke? Seems to me it should . . . a Catholic, a Jew, two Protestants . . . in a boat . . . anyone?"

Nothing was said. The engine ground away and the smallboat dropped and was scooped up again.

"Please?" said the priest. "I don't want to tell mine first."

"All right," the Reverend Asher gave in, and his tone convinced Miles that he wasn't doing so out of pity for Ogleby, or even their situation, but just to keep the priest from telling a certain kind of joke. "Okay, all right. Just to pass the time. . . . I suppose it can be adapted to a boat." He cleared his throat. "Okay, all right. Four chaplains—no, make it three—three U.S. Navy chaplains in an open boat, on their way to—well, actually—on their way to hell—"

"Can't you come up," said the rabbi, "with something more hypothetical?"

"No—it's—it's just a joke. All right, okay, three chaplains, a Catholic, a Jew, and an Episcopalian, on their way to hell. They—let's see—they each ask each other what they're in for, you see. And the Catholic one goes, 'I once ate a hamburger on Good Friday.' And the Jewish one goes, 'I once ate pork on Yom Kippur.' And then they turn to the Episcopalian one, and they ask him why he's on his way to hell, and the Episcopalian one goes, 'Well, it shames me to have to admit it, boys, but I once ate an entire meal with my salad fork.'"

Ogleby was the only one who laughed, slapping his big thighs. The rabbi crossed his arms; he was looking with concern toward shore. Miles was looking too, deeply worried, but he couldn't see anyone, just the green wall of jungle rising straight up from the sea. The smallboat was falling and rising and Miles, with enormous concentration, was trying to keep his stomach in one place. The red-orange sun was beginning to go from mostly orange to mostly red on its way down and the humid wind was picking up and with every hump-and-slam of the boat there was an unpredictable amount of spray across their knees. They were heading for the great rounded hull of the *Felton* to pick up the fifth and final chaplain, Miles figured; he wasn't sure but he thought it was a Lutheran.

"All right, I have one," said Father Ogleby, as though he'd just thought of it and hadn't been aching all along to tell it. "Five navy chaplains—no, wait, better make it *six air force* chaplains—are riding in a plane and it gets hit by enemy fire, loses an engine, starts going down. The pilot says he's got too much weight on board, they can stay aloft only if one of the chaplains jumps out of the plane. They all look at each other, a Baptist, a Catholic, a Muslim, a Jew, a Hindu, a Mormon—"

"A Hindu chaplain?" said the Reverend Asher.

Ogleby waved it away, impatient to go on. "It could happen, we're more inclusive now. So it's a Mormon, a Catholic, a Baptist, a Jew, a Muslim, and a Hindu. The Catholic volunteers to jump out of the plane, he makes the sign of the cross and jumps out, yelling, 'For the Holy Virgin!' But they're still going down, so the pilot tells them another one has to go. The Baptist pinches his nose and jumps out, shouting, 'For Jesus Christ, my personal Lord and Savior!' The pilot says the plane is still going down, so the Mormon shakes hands good-bye with the others and jumps out of the plane shouting, 'For Brigham Young and Joseph Smith!' They're still losing altitude, so the Hindu says, 'For the Lord Vishnu!' and he jumps out too. Still the plane is going down, and there are only two of them left, the Muslim and the Jew. They look at one another, and the Jew says, 'It's up to us to decide according to the conscience of our individual faiths,' so the Muslim faces toward Mecca and says 'For Allah, the one true God, and for Mohammed who is his prophet!'—and he pushes the Jew out of the plane."

At his own joke, as at the previous, Father Ogleby was alone in laughing, slapping again at his big and tightly khakied thighs. The rabbi, arms crossed, gave him a grim sideways look, and Miles was embarrassed for the Jewish chaplain.

"Now you tell one," the priest erupted at Miles. "Your turn, what stories do the Methodists tell?"

The boat fell forward and Miles retreated on the bench, in fear of everything: Ogleby, the ocean, whatever was waiting on shore. The only story he knew about a chaplain took place at the Little Pink Bookstore and Miles's own presence was the punch line. He was feeling as desperately insecure as he had on his first day aboard the *Harding*—he couldn't minister to the dead, he couldn't ride this boat without holding on with both hands, he couldn't tell a Methodist joke. Finally he said, "I don't know any. Methodists don't tell jokes."

To his bewilderment, all three of them blew up laughing. "Dry humor, dry humor," the Reverend Asher managed to gag out after a short while. "Pithiness, blackness, satire, it's the best."

"It is," Ogleby wheezed.

"I'm envious," said the rabbi. "I envy a natural wit."

Miles felt fraudulently triumphant.

They were alongside the *Felton* now, in its shadow, its gray hull rising forty feet over their heads and the superstructure continuing after that like a shifting skyscraper, the steel side of the ship looking as though *it* were the permanent feature, not the ocean, whose water in the ship's shadow was crystal black and turned frothy white as it rode up the hull and down, revealing, as it made its sucking retreat below the waterline, the barnacled and red-rusted secrets of the hull, a hidden disease, and yet no matter how violently the water went crashing back up the side of the *Felton,* the ship was able to persist in its lie that it was hardier than the pliable sea. Hooked sideways to the hull was a spindly diagonal staircase like the one Miles had used, and coming down the staircase quickly, without even touching the rail, one hand on top of his hat and the other holding a black book, his khaki uniform turning pumpkin-colored as he passed through a shaft of light coming down between two segments of superstructure, was the fifth chaplain.

"You can't come aboard," Ogleby called up, "unless you tell a joke about chaplains in a boat."

"You're the joke, Ogleby," the Lutheran called back. "You just don't know the punch line yet."

At the end of the stairs the Lutheran waited for the smallboat to rise and he jumped the four feet down, his arms out. His hat flew into Ogleby's lap, where the priest covered it with his chubby hand, keeping it hostage as he said, "Give us a joke. Give us a joke or we'll toss you out."

The Lutheran shrugged, seating himself behind the rabbi, and reached into his black book for a shiny blue bumper sticker that he handed to Father Ogleby. "Some clown gave me this on Sunday. Maybe this is the punch line you're looking for."

Ogleby held it up:

JESUS IS COMING
LOOK BUSY

The priest said, "Let's stick it to the stern of the *Natchez,*" but the small-boat took a pitching turn and the bumper sticker blew out of his hand and went spiraling up the side of the ship, glinting sunlight with every turn, and then it was as gone as Jesus, leaving Miles and the chaplains to their pitching fates.

The jungle wall of the Luzon shore rose closer. Miles couldn't tell how much of the tossing in his stomach was fear and how much was the sea, but he was enough of a sailor, after five weeks on the *Harding,* after a storm, after the worrisome ride in the AAV to the beach at Okinawa, to know that fear and the sea were often the same thing. They were quite close now, the jungle an improbably massive presence here in the middle of an ocean, and yet it was indisputably here, tall as a city, bunched and green, a place whose mysteries were not for sailors. That was why the marines were here, their camouflage-painted trucks and jeeps parked on the ribbon of sand that was finally making itself apparent as the smallboat approached.

None of the chaplains spoke, none had spoken for a while, not even Ogleby, and the silence continued as the boat rose and fell in the storming sound of the final waves that were driving it toward the beach.

Miles desperately wished he had time, even two minutes, to look up the death rites in the dead man's book, but all he could do was hold on to the bench in the roller-coastering boat.

"Jarheads are in force," Father Ogleby shouted over the surf.

"They're from the *Buchanan,*" the rabbi shouted back. "It pulled up about two hours ago and they rolled out the causeway. It was really something watching them drive over it in a long line. This is the only stretch of beach for miles. They drove right up through the sand, into that clearing. First amphibious operation I've ever seen—I was on sub tenders before this."

"I still say we should be getting hazardous-duty pay," Ogleby shouted back. "I still say we should all write letters."

But there was no more time for talk because the boat was sliding quickly into the surf on the final wave. The helmsman gave the word and they were all scrambling over the sides, into the crashing foam, steadying themselves against the boat before wading through. Ogleby fell, got up. His uniform was darkly wet and clinging burstingly to his bulbous form and his hat was gone. "Look at me," he said miserably. "I'm General Douglas MacArthur."

"Except," said the Lutheran, "that Douglas MacArthur would never let his trousers ride up into his butt crack like that."

"He had a lieutenant to pull them out," said the Reverend Asher.

A camouflage tent, its entrance flapping in the humid air of the sea, was centrally staked among the jeeps and trucks, and marines in cammie uniforms and helmets were walking around with clipboards and headsets, their faces blackened. One of them approached the chaplains who were walking up from the beach, saluting them, and they all saluted back, Miles snapping his hand the most sharply, having practiced at odd hours in his head-mirror. The marine said, "I'm Captain Palethorpe." On his hip he had a green walkie-talkie that was cackling incomprehensibly until he thumbed down a dial on it. "Have you gentlemen been briefed?"

The waves landed softly behind them and the sun was on the chaplains' backs and a seagull tittered and it could've been a holiday at the beach until the rabbi inquired, "We understand you have casualties."

In his blackened face the marine's eyes, surrounded by ovals of unpainted pink, made a squint that was defensive or angry or both, returning to normal as he said, "It was a coordinate problem within the flagship DATCOM condenser-chip calibrations—a *navy* problem." He smiled. "Of course, it could've happened to the army or the air boys, too."

"Where are the"—Asher paused—"fatalities?"

"At Coordinate Bravo Zebra Niner Alpha Delta Twenty."

"Aha," said the Reverend.

The marine put his hands behind his back and set his jaw with a satisfied nod. "We're lucky the command was able to come up with five Roman Catholics. Your mission shouldn't exceed an hour."

"Roman Catholics?" said the Lutheran in a relieved tone only slightly disguised as confusion. "I'm not a Roman Catholic."

"Neither am I," said the Episcopal.

The marine opened his mouth, his eyes squinting again, as though he were trying very hard to divide integers in his head, and he looked down and toed the sand. When he looked up his mouth was still open and he said, accusingly, "But we need Catholics. This is the P.I., the Philippine Islands, gentlemen. We need Roman Catholics here. What have I got on my hands here, what have they—you're not Mormons, are you? We have no Mormon corpses. They're burnt up like my wife's bacon, but they're definitely Catholics, that village is entirely Catholic. This is the goddamn Philippines. Jesus, what are you guys trying to do, create an international incident here?"

"It would appear," said the rabbi, "that an incident has already been created."

"That was a *naval* incident," said the marine. "I'm responsible for *these* perimeters. Oh holy Jesus, they've sent me five Baptists here, five podium-pounders, five snake-handling—"

"We have a Catholic," said the Lutheran.

"Yes?"

"He's a Catholic." The Lutheran indicated, with a straight finger, Father Ogleby, who was standing behind them all.

"He is?" said the marine, peering at the rear of the group, as though afraid of being fooled, trying to make out which man the Lutheran had pointed at. "A Catholic? Bona fide?"

"Yes," said the Reverend Asher, "he certainly is."

"Prove it," said the marine. "Let's hear him say something in Catholic. I want to hear some Latin stuff, Sominex Nabisco, along those lines."

"Go ahead, Bernard," said the Episcopal. "You heard the man. 'Sominex Nabisco'—those little crackers that put you to sleep."

"Leave him alone," said the rabbi. "The man is obviously terrified."

"Oh, I'm not scared," Ogleby warbled in a voice hollowed out by fear. His uniform, still wet, was clinging to every fold of his belly like soggy newspaper. He ran a hand shakily over his baldness, the horseshoe of gray hair, and he held up his prayer book. "I'll simply go in there—it won't bother me—I'll simply go in—I will give them—I really don't mind going alone—I will give them, all of them—extreme unction, yes, I certainly will. Extreme unction."

"Unction?" said the marine. "*Unction?* You've got to be kidding me, sir. Either that or you really are a Catholic. All right, give them just as much unctioning as they need. Only, don't make it too extreme. We already have an incident here."

"Don't make him go alone," said the rabbi.

"Any other Catholics?" said the marine. He looked directly at Miles. "You're not a Catholic, you look like a hard-headed Christian Scientist, the people that raised *me*." He returned to Ogleby. "Okay, Reverend—Cardinal—Monsignor—I'll call up the jeep for you."

"I volunteer," said the rabbi, the setting sun coloring his hair a blond fire, "to go with this man."

The marine squinted at the rabbi's collar. "Jew a Jew? The parameters for this mission make a specification for a Catholic, it's black and white, Lieutenant Bent has the orders, I can have him here in two minutes. It says Catholic, not Hebrew, not Bantu, not anything else."

"Then I want to make a formal protest," said the rabbi. "Under no circumstances should this man be forced to go alone. I know this man, and he will not be able to withstand—I want to protest formally, I want to speak to Brigadier General McMinn or to Admiral Jiggerston."

The marine clucked his tongue. "That's your prerogative, sir, our COMCOMM unit is over there in the F-COT." He gestured with his eyes toward the tent. "But right now this Catholic is going to be transported to Coordinate Bravo Zebra Niner Alpha Delta Twenty for a—for an *unctioning mission*—and when he has completed his activity-specs for the unctioning action—moderate, not extreme—he will be returned to you gentlemen."

"Very well," said the rabbi, and started resolutely for the tent as Father Ogleby, running his hand compulsively over the hairless top of his head, palming into place something that wasn't there, went along with the marine toward a group of jeeps. Miles went down the beach a ways, not worried for himself anymore, but for the people in the unseen village, and for the priest. The rabbi remained in the tent and the other two chaplains, the Episcopal and the Lutheran, borrowed from the marines what appeared to be a camouflage Frisbee and sent it boomeranging over and over up against the sea wind, idly, not running to catch it, letting it fall into the waves and come tumble-floating back to them on the beach as they discussed whatnot. The top dome of the sun was burning red through the horizon mist, scorching the farther reaches of it orange, sending long licks of yellow up against a turquoise sky, which darkened to purple where the easternmost coastline of Luzon disappeared into the vaporous horizon of impending tropical night. For the first time without prodding, Miles thought of Peacock Island. Lebedeen was right. An island empty of people, walked by peacocks and shadowed, in both sun and moon, by the sea-bent arches of palm trees, with a sugaring of beach ringing the lip of a lagoon, was the only escape from the steel mind and the iron reaching fingers of the military. As he walked and daydreamed, the sun went lower, igniting the sweep of sky silver and purple and gold as the higher clouds glowed like liquid rubies over the slate expanses and mirrored corners of the sea. This sunset was occurring on Peacock Island, too, he thought, but as the fire grew across the sky, he forgot the place he'd been imagining and in its stead there was only conflagration, flames, a fireball, the myth of the Little Pink Bookstore, except that it wasn't a myth, because he'd been there, he'd burned it out of existence. It was a truth, a terrible one, a distorted recollection, like the sins that writhed just over the horizon of his drinking memories. He wouldn't think of the bookstore, he refused, he wouldn't wouldn't would not, and then he all but tripped over a marine on his haunches in the dusky light of the beach, and the surf and the fish air broke through his musings with a kind of violence.

The marine, cammied and black-painted, getting to his feet, M-16 held as a cane: "Sorry, sir, thought you saw me."

"Excuse me."

"I'm the north sentry."

"Of course," said Miles. "I wasn't going any further."

"If it was just me . . . but orders. You a . . . chaplain?"

"Yeah."

They both got on their haunches looking out to the darkening sea, at the sky without a sun, just streaks of bile and blood, the remnants of a crime.

"You been up to Paraíso?" said the marine. He was a black boy wearing the black cammie gunk on his face.

"Paraíso? That the village?"

"That be it."

"No. A priest went, they didn't want me. Methodist."

Silence.

Then, Miles: "This is a hell of a thing."

"I've seen worse. Or anyway just as bad," said the marine, who was only a boy of about twenty.

"You have? Where?"

"Iraq. In the desert, sir, the Gulf War." The boy shifted on his haunches, his gaze attaching itself, like the chaplain's, to the band of blood that hung in the sky like the spoor of the sun, and he continued, in the slow, instantly confidential way of military downtime: "There was this naval bombardment, just south of Basra, and we marines were amphibbed up the beach, like today. We were supposed to fight whatever Iraqis were left from the bombardment. Except there weren't more than ten or twelve that were left, out of a couple hundred. Just a few shaking wounded guys with dirty white shirts on the end of their rifles to surrender, and the rest were corpses, *burnt* corpses. Laying around everywhere, couple hundred of them, a stink like you wouldn't believe, some of them still smoking. Their uniforms burnt off, just the charred human bodies in all kinds of twisted death positions. I'll never get that smell out of my nose, no matter how long I live, human flesh that's been cooked. Tanks and trucks still on fire all around us. We'd never seen anything like it. It was hard to handle—none of us had

ever been in combat before, even the officers, they'd just been paper push-
ers. Well, a couple of the guys went kind of catatonic on us. Just wandering
around the camp with their hands in their pockets and these nothing
expressions on their faces. They were written up, they told them they had
bad morale, it went on their service records. The general said they were
missing out on a learning experience. Thing was, there were a couple officers acting the same way, couldn't handle it, just mooning around
depressed, and they got special counseling. They flew in military psycholo-
gists from an aircraft carrier, a couple of chaplains too, carrying black
books like that one you got there. The officers got pulled from the mission,
the doctors and chaplains wrote letters for them, they got special medical
leaves and got to go home. Meanwhile, me and my buddies had to stay
there burying the burnt-up corpses. They said we were there to hold the
position, hold the line, but there wasn't any line to hold 'cause what was
left of the Iraqi army was running back to Baghdad. They just wanted us to
get out our shovels and clean up the mess, in case the news media ever
came. They said there was no way the news media should be allowed to
show what we'd done, 'cause if people saw it, there'd never be another war.
I've got four hundred and twenty-seven days left in the Corps, sir."

"Jesus," Miles said. "I mean, I'm sorry." He realized that even a qualified
chaplain might find it hard to respond to this. Finally he said, "I don't
blame you for being bitter."

"I'm not bitter, sir. I'm not anything. Not anymore. I'm just a guy with
four hundred and twenty-seven days. That's all." There was more silence,
less awkward. Then the boy took an under-wristed look at his watch and
unhooked a green walkie-talkie from his belt and spoke acronymically and
numerically into it and it garbled back some scrambled language. The
marine told Miles, "Well, you heard them, I have to pull back the north
perimeter two hundred meters in the next five minutes."

"Yes, of course." Nightfall was complete, and Miles looked back toward
the marine encampment—spooky shapes, vehicle rectangles and tent tri-
angles, poking up into the blue military light. He didn't want to go there,
but he would.

There was no moon yet, and the tropical mist that hung over the night
like a magic veil, both invisible and concealing, was hiding all but a few
stars, whose pin lights were blunted, smaller than usual, unwilling to
sparkle, as though aware of their own irrelevance tonight. The soft and
freakishly blue lighting of the camp was all that mattered in the blackened

world, even though the camp was an aberrant growth planted between the lathering of surf and the silent massiveness of jungle. Miles walked into the blueness of the artificial light, the tents and trucks and jeeps and helmeted men blue-washed into components made of the same malignant steel. When Miles looked down at his arms and hands the blueness was on them and there was a sickness of fear in his stomach and the color of this feeling was the same washed-out blue, and the dread was creeping up inside him. It wasn't at all like the dead man tumbling out of the door with a hard-on, there was nothing absurd in this new feeling. There was the tailgate of a blue truck backing toward him and it was open with three pallets stacked inside and the sheets over the bodies made them look like blue loaves, and they were cooked, there was a smell like burning skunk or burning tar or burning cabbages but it was worse than all those things put together, gagging-worse, and Miles turned away with his hand over his nose. He was shaking, he was sick with the blueness and the smell of it. And then he looked back, even though he was telling himself not to; he just couldn't help looking, as though unable to control himself in a nightmare, and a marine was lifting the sheet by a corner and it was a head, a human head, round, blackened, the only thing left in the world that hadn't turned blue, it was cooked black, it was round and black and bald with the hair burnt off and smelling like a fire into which people had thrown skunks and tar and cabbages, and Miles knew, in a kind of hypnosis of horror, that he would keep this with him for the rest of his life, knew it was weightier than the bookstore fire, he knew this as he turned aside and resolved with all his will not to look back again.

A jeep pulled up, kicking up blue sand, and in the passenger seat was the blue staring thing that had been Ogleby. He didn't move. Even after the driver had gotten out and come around and opened the door for him, Father Ogleby just sat there, gazing ahead, as though the jeep were still moving. When the driver spoke, the priest looked up at him distractedly, then, with a kind of lazy resignation, pulled himself out of the jeep with both hands trembling on the door. He stood in the blue light, dazed, without out his prayer book. If it was still in the jeep, he didn't reach in for it, just ambled away, his hand palming back the hair that he didn't have at the top of his head.

The rest of it happened with a military efficiency that was both unusual and terrible for its speed and its mechanical choreography and its silence. The five chaplains were standing in an AAV this time, cutting through the

water too quickly for the waves to raise or drop them, they just went gliding through. Nobody was talking, though the one most noticeably not talking was Ogleby, who stood gripping the starboard lip of the AAV. He was
looking into the ocean night where you couldn't even see the ships, lights
out. His face was hanging like a wrinkly jowly mass of meat, disconnected
from the underlying muscles and nerves that might make it speak or react.
His face, sketched out by the yellow light attached to the helm, was con-
toured with the heaviness of rock. His eyes were dead. They were like those
of a sculpture, just two carvings in marble, open, but lacking any glints or
movement. The rabbi stepped up next to him and the rabbi's mouth was
making sounds and no one could hear the words, not anyone, not Ogleby,
alone with the pictures in his mind.

Even in the salt wind Miles could smell the cooked flesh; the tarry
skunkiness of it was lodged way up in his nose where nothing could reach
to pull it out, and as he gagged again, he knew he didn't want to return to
the ship, and knew also, to his misery, to his shock even, that what he
wanted no longer mattered, because this AAV, like it or not, was indeed
taking him back to the *Harding*, and he had no other clothes but his naval-
officer uniforms and no other name but Banquette and no other billet but
that of the chaplain.

And it was just as clear that Ogleby, who'd been a real naval officer and
chaplain, was no longer either, standing there like a gigantic toddler at the
side of the AAV, his hands placed up high on the hull edge, chin-level, as
though he were a supplicant . . .

The Lutheran was returned first and then it was Miles. As he lifted
himself onto the ladder and looked back a last time, the yellow light of the
AAV made it look like a stage as it floated in the blackness of water, and the
helmsman was efficiently backing it away as though he were on any cargo
run, and Ogleby was still standing there dead-faced as the rabbi consoled
him uselessly.

Miles went as quickly up the steps as he could go with care, and then he
was on the weather deck, and the AAV was a firefly in the night, and then
he was through a hatch and back in the diesel-smelling humidity of the
ship. The P-ways he went through and the ladders he climbed were the
same gray as before, but everything inside him felt different, jumbled and
tossing, though the sea was relatively even. He remembered the story of an
older man he used to drink with, Skeeter Toomey, ten years ago, in
Zincville. The story was that when Skeeter Toomey had gotten home from

Vietnam, he landed in Seattle at two in the morning, no one to welcome him but the floor-waxing guys in the blazing-bright airport terminal, and he had to wait fifteen hours for his connection to Chicago, arriving at O'Hare at three the next morning, alone in the terminal this time with the window guys with their big yellow squeegees five feet wide squeaking on the windows, and he had to wait eight more hours for a bus and then it was another eternity bouncing down the road. Throughout all these thirty-six hours back in America, trying to get to his parents' house in Zincville, there wasn't much to think about but every single damn thing that had happened in Nam. And there hadn't been much of anything since.

Finally one night Miles, drunk, said to Skeeter Toomey, "You told that story a hundred times. Where's the details? How many people you kill over there?"

And Skeeter Toomey had said, "Fuck you, Derry," and gone to the other end of the bar, and he never drank with or spoke to Miles again.

The story of Skeeter Toomey's homecoming, told so long ago, had never meant anything to Miles until now: it was like a familiar hieroglyph suddenly given pronunciation and meaning. Walking the empty, red-lit P-ways of the *Harding,* Miles was in those airports in Seattle and Chicago, and there was nothing left in his mind but the head shining like black marble in the blue light of the marine camp, all the hair seared away, and the burning skunk-and-turpentine odor, and the ever-twitching eyelids and frozen gaze of that crazy guy Toomey from the bar. And the catatonic glare of Father Ogleby. There was a twitch beginning in his own left eye as he emerged from the final ladder onto the first deck of Officers' Country.

At that moment he was sure that nobody on sea or land cared the smallest bit about him, and this notion set loose a flock of fluttering desperations in him.

He was working his key in the lock when the door to the stateroom next to his opened and the person standing there in pink pajamas was Robin. There was a circle of makeup carefully layered over her black eye.

"What happened?" she said. Her hair was ponytailed over her right breast and her eyes were on him, straight on.

"Nothing," he said.

"No, what happened?"

"Not a thing."

"You have to tell me," she said. Then, "We all know about it. Or think we know. But you've seen it. And . . . well."

"And well what?"

"And," she said, "you'd better tell me about it right away. In here."

He didn't say anything. She looked at him inquisitively, encouragingly, widening her eyes and giving a small shrug. He still had his hand on his key in the lock, and then he felt himself falling for it, but he didn't care, anything was preferable to being alone with the fresh memories and smells of the camp. He took his key out and he was sliding past her into her room as she brought the door soundlessly shut behind them.

She said, "You look like you've seen something gross," and without waiting for him to answer she put her arms around him and snuggled the side of her face into his shoulder. His embrace was reactive and his nose went into her hair, which was slightly damp, a chemical strawberry from a shampoo, and he willed away the smell from the marine camp and let himself be subsumed in this other smell, in her embrace, his arms tightening around her, she tightening hers, it was such a good thing to get lost in her, the feel of her body rigid against him with the intensity of holding him. He knew what he was doing was a mistake, but he needed it for its oblivion that same way he'd always needed a drink. The three years since he'd held anyone—Mary Lou—conspired with the marine camp he was running from—with the burning bodies—with the burning bookstore—with everything he'd been and become—all the things he wished to flee—all of it made him give in to Robin now and he was holding her head in both hands and finding her mouth with his and yes it was like his drinking days, odd how you could still sometimes act 100 percent like a drunk, even when drinking had nothing to do with a thing, and it was exactly like going wild with a girl after a long night of buying her drink after drink and slamming down just as many himself—their tongues were doing the sloppy fight and their front teeth hit each other—you could chip a tooth kissing a woman that madly—and his hand was snaking its way between them, it was doing the button-fumble, two buttons, slipping in for a breast and putting thumb and forefinger hard on that nipple and she was writhing against him, but he still felt the gloom of the camp.

He knew how much he was going to regret this, and tried to tilt, with a mental pinky, the enormous consequences off the cliffs of responsibility—more important things—the clothes were coming off—the hopeless attempts at disrobing each other ending in open shirts but no way to get them off each other's shoulders so damn it, give up, chuck off your own clothes, so the frenzy was solely on themselves, pants down, her bra was off, he was hopping around trying to extricate his shoes from the ankle-tangle of his trousers feeling like a fool because he knew none of this would erase the camp but he couldn't stop—

She had something out of a cubbyhole in her fold-down desk and it was a shiny pink-and-white square of plastic with a dark ring in it . . . she was holding it up . . .

She said, "You're just going to have to wear one of these, bud."

Numb, wishing he weren't doing this even as he undid, from one foot, the knot of shoe-and-bunched-up-trouser-leg and the shoe went flying across the room, thudding unseen, he said, "All right."

"Stop arguing with me, you're just going to have to wear it."

And then it was all happening so quickly that his dazed awareness could absorb each event only as the subsequent one was occurring— Robin in her panties and he in his shorts with one shoe still on and his pants tangled around it and she pressing against him with her cool naked skin and kissing him assertively, shoving him toward the rack—he stumbled but she kept pushing and along the way she slapped at the light switch—in the dark he was landing on his back against the thin mattress with steel underneath—she was on top, heavier than expected, mouth on mouth, exhaling her quick breath into his mouth as she wriggled out of her panties and then she was yanking down his shorts—he couldn't move, woman on top of him, waistband tight about his knees, feet knotted in the twisted trousers, the room black. His prick, straight up against her belly, was the only part of him having a good time, as though it were a separate being, then her hands were working down there and it felt too weird, he realized she'd opened and unrolled the rubber and forced it down around his cock as though she were wringing an orange-half down onto the phallus of an orange squeezer, and by the time he realized what had happened she was already engulfing him and he couldn't feel anything except for the circular grinding of her groin against his pubic bone and her breath was quick and persistent in his ear. He lay there helpless in the dark, getting fucked.

It wasn't fun, it went on, it went on, he couldn't see or feel anything, was it twenty minutes?—he thought it would keep up all night, he thought it would never be finished, he couldn't even touch her breasts because she was right on top of him. He began to worry how long he could remain hard under these conditions, and to his horror he felt himself becoming only semirigid, quivering on the periphery of absolute limpness, and his apprehension did him in. To his terror, he had no erection at all, but it didn't matter, because now everything was changing again, she was making faster broader circles on him and her head was turning back and forth with a whipping sound next to his on the pillow, and he got the impression she'd be shouting if they were alone on the ship and he thought, *Oh, that's the way you come.* Every woman had been different, all the many styles . . . the sweaty epileptic, the screaming twister, the silent shudderer, the single-spasm gasper, the deadly scratcher, the pillow-biting kicker, now this, which he might describe as the rotating flailer—all of it was good, he had always enjoyed it when a woman came, though this time he didn't feel crucial to the event. As Robin lay on top of him breathing wetly into his ear, her hair all over his face, he reached up and stroked the back of her head, moved his thumb over her cheek, kissed her forehead. Having her close, touching her this way, brought him a sweet tactile memory of being with Mary Lou.

At the caress, Robin rolled off him, up on one elbow, on his chest, and when she threw back her ponytail it made a slapping sound in the dark. "I have to be up early," she said. "I have to teach navigational trig at eight o'clock."

He said, "Let's just lie here a while."

"You can't hang around here," she said. "What if the wardroom CPO comes? Huh? What about that? What if the captain comes?"

"*I* haven't come," he said. Even though he knew he didn't want to.

"Well, I did," she said. "You had your chance, much chance as you guys usually give us anyway."

He heard footsteps in the P-way. "This was a mistake," he said.

"Don't be a little boy. You screwed around, you'll probably pay for it. You think you're the first chaplain in this situation?"

"Why did I do this?"

"All I know," she said, "is it took you long enough to get around to it."

"Why'd *you* do it?"

"That's my mission on this ship, to make men feel the way you make women feel. To make you know what it's like to be used."

"That's all it is to you?"

"You're a chaplain, you wouldn't understand about sex. It's like drugs, like any drug you take into your body. Booze, pot, coke, dick—it's all good, you take it in and you get to forget about all the bullshit for a while."

"So sex is just a drug to you?"

"You wouldn't understand anything about the other ways of making love. You're a man, so you don't know anything about the tenderness and the closeness. That's something women can only get from each other, that's what I'm learning. That's what I like about sleeping with someone like Daisy. Also, she stood up for me against the CO."

"You slept with her?"

"On Okinawa. She was so sweet."

"That air force dyke who gave you that black eye?"

"If that's the way you want to see her. You Christians are all homophobes anyway. And biphobes. The CO doesn't get it either and this is the last cruise I'm taking with that pig. I can get a billet onshore, someplace with a woman CO."

Aside from her elbow propped on his chest, he had no sense of her physical presence in the dark, just a voice, and into this vacuum the stench of burning skunk returned, and he felt he had to get out of the room right away.

"I have to go," he said.

"How're you going to handle it?"

"Handle what?"

"How're you going to handle it? Now you can't talk so proud. At least not to yourself, not now, because you did a sin. The worst one. That's what religion says, right? That sex is worse than even murder? So now it all comes crashing down on you, and I was just wondering how you were going to handle it. Your whole male-oriented, bullshit, patriarchal, Christian, hypocritical thing, it's destroyed, it's over, because of what you just did with me. And you don't want to talk about it, do you? Why is it men never want to have serious discussions in bed? Why do you find it so impossible to express your feelings ever? It's all over for you—you'd better face it, bud, you're not who you thought you were."

"I've got to get out of here," he said. Pushing her elbow off his chest, he sat up in the dark, his feet still knotted in the jumble of trousers, and he stood up but he was afraid to go farther. "Turn on the light."

It was her rack light, soft and green, and in it she was green marble carved in angles, a knee up, head on her fist, propped on an elbow, ponytail straight down to one side, eyes set on him with more precision than the gunnerymen could've hoped for. One look at her was enough, just as a single glance back at the burnt top of the corpse's head had been enough, and he busied himself with the pulling-up of trousers and the collecting of shirt and hat and prayer book and stray shoe, wondering why this room had the burning odor of the hateful camp.

"Your uniform's all wrinkled, Commander."

He said, with his back to her, "It has to go to the laundry anyway. Smells bad." And then he was standing there fully dressed in the green light—too much unnatural lighting tonight, blue camp, red P-ways, green room—he found himself longing for the skull-cracking brightness of the tropical day—and without any more words between them he was out the door, in the P-way, back in his own room.

Not two minutes later there was a knock and with a sickness in his heart he knew it was her.

But when he opened the door, it was Ditchfield. The old man: hands and face red-gray in the light of the P-way, as were his uniform and chief's brimless cap, which he was wearing jauntily back, as though he were a merry cook, forehead lining itself mirthfully as the eyes examined Miles with the shining daring of a sixteen-year-old boy's. The old man said, "CO wants to see you, Chaplain. Got me looking all kinds of places for you. AAV dropped you off forty minutes ago, I says to him. Well, I'm glad you finally made it back to your own room. Now please come along with me, sir, and we'll go see the captain."

9

On the endless climb to the captain's quarters Ditchfield said nothing and Miles was behind him, unable to decide if the slow, sure-plantedness of the old man's steps was due entirely to age or if there was something else to them, a teasing drama, an intentional prolonging of the trip— Ditchfield would be enjoying it even more, Miles thought, if he knew all the things that were swirling inside the condemned man trudging up the steps behind him—fires on fires, ashes on ashes, the unseen and therefore less real charred corpse in the bookstore, the absolutely real ones of tonight, whose fried odors were rising out of this uniform he hadn't had the time to change, as though it contained ash and were letting smoke out of the sleeves and collar, that was the size of the odor he wanted to reach for with both hands up his nose and pull out, impossible, and he wasn't even a chaplain anymore, he was sure he'd given that up in Robin's arms, and now the CO wanted to see him, why did The First Time in Four Years have to be like this? It had been as wrong, worse even, than he'd known it would be.

As he followed the old man up the last two ladders, into an altitude of Officers' Country that Miles had never been invited to, he rebelled at the idea that he had ever been with Robin. That was the kind of thing he'd done only when he drank; the loving had been there only with Mary Lou. He wasn't the man who'd been with Robin, he was the man who'd been with Mary Lou, at the beginning, before it flew apart, that was the man he was, not this ragtag "Banquette" going up the ladders of humiliation in a wrinkled uniform smelling of burnt human flesh, no, he was the man who'd walked out of that treatment center four years ago without shaking, without a blur in his vision or even a tic over an eye, he was the man who'd worked with serenity and hope on his father's loading dock in the winter, his senses open to colors and touches and sounds and tastes and smells seemingly for the first time—there was nothing fresher than January air!—and he was the man sitting on his couch in his apartment with Mary Lou in the candlelight and he was sitting up and she was gathered up against his chest with her hands on his shoulders and they were necking like teenagers, stopping just to touch each other's face, trace each other's mouth and eyebrows, and he was stroking her hair, he was that man, that was the only man he'd ever been.

"You're the chaplain," the old chief said as they were approaching the top of the final ladder. "I reckon maybe you know what he's wanting to talk to you about. You ain't asked me, anyhow."

"I don't intend to ask you." He wasn't going to help Ditchfield enjoy this.

He was enjoying it anyway: "That's why you're an officer, sir. Always on top of matters."

Miles was resigned, afraid but resigned to it, he was beyond panic, he was willing to give it all up, he wasn't the person in these foul clothes.

Ditchfield knocked three times quickly. There was a faraway growl of assent, and Ditchfield opened the door and they went through. The CO's quarters were as large as the wardroom mess and the galley combined, directly over which they stood, separated by several decks. The large space was green-carpeted and darkly paneled and the doorknobs were brass, while the captain's rack was brass-trimmed and double-sized. There was a desk the size of Miles's stateroom, with an indentation into which fit a high-backed leather chair, and the surface of the desk was inlaid glass, bare except for a black rotary phone, 1950s vintage, the sole example of naval nerdishness in the room, which was softly lit with an amber, civilian light. Miles followed Ditchfield through the quarters, out a hatch onto the weather deck, and Ditchfield said, "I found what you was looking for, Captain."

"You found a single-malt? Glenlivet?" A yellow hammock was strung from post to bulkhead and weighted down in the mesh like a load of cargo dangling off a helo was the CO, in a lavender robe, his white hair lying straight back like a peroxide pompadour.

"I ain't got nothing but the chaplain, Captain."

"Well, leave the son-of-a-bitch here and don't come back without a bottle. Try the SUPPO. Try the fucking DISBO."

"Aye-aye, sir." Ditchfield started away.

"The old pencil-dick," the captain said to himself, the only man on board who spoke to himself, Miles thought, the only man with the authority for informal asides. He was holding, on his lavender-robed chest, a white plastic cup with a blue anchor on it surrounded by blue lettering: COURAGE INTEGRITY STRENGTH—WARREN G. HARDING.

"Sit down!" he said. "You want a goddamn drink or what?"

There were two stools, children's furniture, about a foot high; one of them was bare and the other had a stack of the *Warren Harding* cups and a bottle whose label Miles recognized as that of a cheap blended Scotch whiskey that probably no captain in the U.S. Navy would be proud to drink, quite apart from the breach of regulation.

"Sir, I don't drink," Miles said, still standing.

"Don't give me that phony holy-joe line, you want a fucking drink or not?"

"No thank you, Captain." Miles read the inscription over the CO's robe pocket—probably everything he owned was someway inscribed—SAMURAI MASSAGE PARLOR, OLONGAPO CITY, SUBIC BAY.

"You don't want a drink? For Christ sake sit down!"

Miles sat down on the bare stool, his knees propping his chin. He could no longer see the captain's face; the man was a kind of ambiguous and lavender-wrapped mammal in the deeply hanging mesh of the hammock, something waiting to be airlifted to the zoo, and as the voice came again, Miles calibrated the CO's drunkenness at half the Okinawa level, which would probably make for a combination of cunning and ruthlessness that would be terrible, and Miles was more afraid now.

"You wrote a letter for that faggot Lebedeen?"

"Uh—yes sir."

"Without asking me about it first?"

"No sir—yes sir."

"I'm going to nominate your lame ass for the motherfucking Congressional Medal of Honor. Initiative. First time a chaplain's done me any damn good since that pissy-faced Mormon sliced up his arm with a letter opener in a swell and had to be heloed the hell out of here, forever, all the fucking way back to Utah. We don't need faggots like Lebedeen on this ship, going around whining like a woman all the time. He's shoving off in three days. They're flying his replacement into Subic to meet us, and I'm going to have his goddamn skivvies checked for testicles before we allow him on board. You have the official appreciation of the command of LST-2282."

"Thank you, Captain." Miles waited, anxious, huddled on the little stool, looking up at the faceless mass of hammock-man. The CO did not shift or speak, just hung there as though waiting for the next cargo helo to clip him up. Finally Miles said, "Is that in the form of a—of a certificate or something, sir?"

"Certificate! What the hell do you want, Banquette, a fucking blow job? That's not what I called you here to talk about, anyway, you fucking idiot." The plastic cup moved off the captain's stomach, disappearing behind the robed mountain of belly, slurp, reappearing. "I want to talk to you about— how shall I phrase it for your sensitive churchly ears?—*this un-for-tu-nate oc-cur-rence.*"

Miles couldn't take it any longer—sitting with his knees up under his face, the cooked-flesh odors of the uniform directly under his nose. He started quick-talking: "I know it was a mistake, Captain, I wish I hadn't done it, I didn't want to, it just happened. You can do whatever you want to me—you can send me back home—I don't care anymore—you can punish me any—"

"In other words"—the hammock shifted hugely—"you already told about it?"

"Told, sir? You mean, *bragged* about it? I'm ashamed of it, it's not something I would brag about, Captain."

"Who'd you tell about it? Your superiors in the fucking Chaplain Corps? You radioed them right after it happened, or what?"

"You mean, like a confession? Like the Catholics do? No sir, I haven't told anyone, not a single soul, Captain, I swear it."

"That's good, you had me fucking concerned, that's exactly what I need to prevent, this is top fucking secret, this is an order, you're not to tell *anybody* what you saw on that beach today. You're not to tell anybody about the people that got fried, is that understood, Chaplain?"

"Sir?"

"This whole mess is going to be handled in Washington, we're not to say a damn word about it. Right this minute, deep in the bowels of the motherfucking Pentagon, in some little office between a janitor's closet and a rest room, some geek-faced yeoman is rolling a little card into a fucking 1933 typewriter—Form nine-twenty-seven-slash-J, Naval Ops, Apology to a Foreign Government. That and another half-million in foreign aid ought to make the Flips happy. But I have to make sure you're not going to be a bleeding-puss Christian about it and tell the whole goddamn world. You're not a fucking idealist, are you?"

"Well—I don't know what you—"

"All the trouble in this lousy world is caused by idealists. Me, I'm a realist. You take your Stalin, you take your Hitler, you take every troublemaker in between, they're all idealists, don't have any fucking realism to them. That Marxist crap, just a lot of bullshit idealism, starving and butchering hundreds of millions. Nazis—master race—just a bunch of idealistic bullcrap, a lot of faggots who liked to dress up and march around and worship the blond male body and try to change the world. And Christians are the worst ones—you lousy fuckers have caused almost all the trouble in the history of the Western world. I'm a better-read man than any of you goddamn Bible browsers. The Roman Empire fell *after* the fucking Christians took it over, after they made Christianity the state cult, started spreading all that goddamn idealism around. Rome was doing just fine under the pagans, fuck you very much. Your whole setup is bogus—the idea that the universe is gonna cut you a break just because some kike got nailed to a plank of wood two thousand years ago. Now don't argue with me on this, you got to admit it's just a lot of idealistic bullshit. I'll bet you thought I was just an old fart barnacle, not a thinking man. Well, you're wrong. There's a little concept called Manifelt Destiny. Manifold Destiny. It's the idea that God wants us white Americans to rule this lousy rotten world, on account of our superior technologicalness—and ideas—and minds—God created this Maniford Destiny for us—hell, I don't have to explain this to *you,* you're a fucking minister. But look at the goddamn history. You think it's an accident? Well? Do you think it's a motherfucking accident or what?"

The hammock shifted but the captain's face did not appear. "No sir," said Miles. "No accident, sir." What accident? Today's? He was uncomfortable on the little stool with his knees almost to his chin and his arms with nowhere to go but around the knees. Was it his penance to have to humor a drunk, for all the years he himself had required humoring in bars?

"Hell, it ain't no accident," said the CO. "White men came to North America from Europe, fought their way all the way to the California coast, didn't stop there, sent the navy to take Hawaii in 1898, then your

Spanish-American war, same year, the navy took the whole goddamn Philippines in about twelve hours—Manifelt Destiny—keep moving west, don't even let the oceans stop you—we've been in these islands ever since, teaching these little brown fuckers how to live, how to scrape and paint our fucking ships. We're shoving off in the morning, gonna be there tomorrow afternoon, and that's what they'll be doing, like they've been doing for almost a hundred years, scraping and painting our fucking ships for twenty-five cents an hour, small fortune to them, more than they're worth anyhow. You been to Subic? If you have, you know what I'm fucking talking about, and if you know your Manifeld Destiny you know we just kept going west, out past California, Hawaii, Philippines, World War II, Japan—boom-boom with big fucking nukes if you want to see some *real* bacon bodies—Korea, Viet Fucking Nam. Someday we'll swarm across China and Siberia and take eastern fucking Europe from behind, then France and England, and by that time we'll have to build new Columbus ships and go across the Atlantic and rediscover America and take it back from the bleeding-puss, wussy-wristed idealists who're fucking ruining the joint. You following me at all, you raisin-balled son-of-a-bitch?"

"Yes sir, Captain, I am following you, sir." His legs were aching and he wanted very much to stand, but of course wouldn't till ordered.

"So you're going to keep those gums glued? About that mess ashore?"

"I think there are rumors throughout the ARG, sir. The other chaplains knew about it before we landed."

"I don't give a chicken dropping about all that, I'm talking about your goddamn goody-do-good chaplain pals back home. The kind who think Jesus wants them to call up the *Washington Post* every fifteen minutes. You're not going to tell anyone in the States, right?"

Who? Mary Lou? *Sir, I don't know anyone in the States.* He said, "No sir."

"All right. Now get your droopy pimpled ass out of here. If you see the SUPPO tell him I need a goddamn bottle of Glenlivet."

"Yes sir. Good night, sir." Miles was relieved to stand and was walking toward the hatch when the CO stopped him with:

"Oh, by the way. The next time you fuck the math teacher, don't lay there in her rack for half an hour talking to the goddamn bitch."

It was like a kick to the stomach, punching all the air out, and he could feel the blood draining from his face and his skin icing over and he couldn't believe what the captain had just said. *"Sir?"* Miles was standing behind him; the man in the hammock took another drink, making no effort to look up at the chaplain or say anything more. *"Captain?"*

"Ditchfield heard everything you said in there. Bulkheads are damn thin in Officers' Country. If I wasn't through with the bitch—and if I was a fucking jealous idealist instead of a pragmatalist—practicalist—I'd have a couple of hull techs hold you down on the doc's table and order him to slice your nutbag off. What the fuck, the cunt is a psychopath. I'm going to order her off the boat soon as we hit Subic. I tell you I'm through. Next thing, she'll be fucking the goddamn mast poles. So you don't tell what you saw today, Banquette, and I don't tell what I know. Now get the fucking hell out of here before I start being an idealist about the whole thing and have you shot."

"Yes sir, Captain." Shaking, he went through the hatch feeling had, and back through the CO's quarters feeling supremely had, and cherished more closely the fact of his imposture—if possession of secrets were the only thing of value in this game, then his imposture was the ultimate trump on the other players . . .

He returned to his stateroom feeling as though the events of the day had been a forced patrol through the steamy heat of a rain forest, and though there'd been dangers ahead and to either side and he'd been marching all day, he had safely and finally arrived at the place from which he'd begun: he was still the chaplain, a role at which he felt dismally inadequate. The legacies of the day were a total distrust of Robin and the CO, a burning stench in his uniform, a memory from the beach that he would repress now as he stood before his rack stripping off the wretched khakis . . .

He was walking up the beach with the cymbaling surf on his left and the monstrosity of silent unseen jungle on his right, present only like the shadow memory of pain, and ahead lay the marine camp in its oval of blue, washing him blue as he entered the perimeter, and the blue men and blue jeeps were moving around him as he approached the truck that was parked with its tailgate down, the scene mesmerizing and frightening not only because of the stack of blue-sheeted pallets in the truck, but because Robin and the captain were sitting next to it on folding chairs. Blue and naked, they were laughing at him, and Robin was holding against her breasts a blue bundle. It was one of those dreams that required his approach to the center of horror. He dragged his feet through the blue quicksand with the blood beating in his ears louder than the surf and the fear hollowing out his chest, and all he wanted to do was run the other way, but he was walking toward them—Robin held out the bundle to him—she and the CO sat there naked and blue and laughing—Miles looked—the face of the child was the burnt but undeniable face of Kari.

He struggled against the straitjacket of his rack and couldn't wake up, couldn't scream, Robin and the CO laughing at him, and then he was alone in the absolute darkness of the room, listening to his explosions of exhaled breath.

He would call Mary Lou right away. He would do it from Subic. He wouldn't have to say where he was. He hadn't seen his daughter in too long, and how could he know she was all right? The time and distance separating them were suddenly huge to him.

In the morning they were under way, rocking moderately, the green coast sliding by in the humidity as he passed an open hatch when he went to breakfast. Opening the door to the wardroom mess, he saw that the captain and Robin were seated at their opposite ends of the table, so he shut the door and went back to his room, read an article entitled "Submarine Warfare: A Hypothesis in Tactics" in the magazine *USN Proceedings,* unable to concentrate on a word of it, and then he went to the next seating, which put him elbow-to-elbow with Lebedeen.

The major got out half a syllable to him before he was interrupted by the DISBO, who, sitting across from them, having remained from the previous seating, now lighting a pipe, told Miles, "I like you. I think you're the most competent man on this whole fucking ship."

"This A-hole fucking ship," said a JO.

"Uh—thanks."

"What's your secret?" said the DISBO.

"My secret?"

"How are you able to keep your fucking head when lesser chaplains are losing theirs?"

"They are?"

"What'd you see ashore?"

"I don't think I'm supposed to talk about it." He had the electric sense that everyone, even the men moving bins behind the galley counter, had an ear discreetly cocked to the conversation. No one else spoke.

"The DISBO from the *Natchez,*" continued the DISBO, "told me on the radio this morning that their chaplain went fucking insane from what he saw. Soon as we hit Subic, they're flying him all the way to fucking Guam for observation and treatment. Can you imagine sending a guy to motherfucking *Guam*—for his mental health! Do you know what GUAM stands for? Look it up in your fucking DICNAVABs: 'Giving Up And Masturbating.'"

Someone added, "Gooks Under American Management."

Someone else, "Girls Ugly As Mangoes."

Someone more, "So what did that chaplain see to make him so fucking Guamable?"

"Well," said the DISBO, "since Jim here is too much of a straight-up-and-down professional navy man to tell us, I'll just report what the DISBO from the *Natchez* heard from their SUPPO who got it from their CHENG who heard it from the JAG who was told it by the ward CPO who was listening at the door of the MEDTECHCOMP when the fat bastard was spilling it to one of the docs. That village looked like a fucking barbecue pit. Black toothpicks sticking up that used to be fucking palm trees, piles of smoldering shit that used to be huts, dead Flips lying around in every fucking direction naked and black as niggers with their guts exploded out and being picked at by birds. Women and babies lying around wounded and screaming. Must've fucking smelled good, too. One of the marine docs said there was no one they could save—by the time they got there anyone wounded—anyone not fucking fried outright—was already meat. Only survivors were a few lucky ones outside the target zone, except for those women and babies who were too far gone to be saved but taking too fucking long to die."

"Hell of a thing," said a JO.

"We got blueberry pancakes this morning?" said another.

Nothing more was said about it, save a final comment from the DISBO, departing with his pipe in hand, to the chaplain:

"You must have blood like fucking ice water, Jim. Able to sit here contemplating your breakfast after seeing those women and babies bleeding to death and bawling and those other Flips lying around all burnt up with their smoldering guts hanging out."

Actually, the odors of flapjacks and frying eggs and grease-spitting bacon were nauseating, bringing back the cooked flesh, and he wanted to get up and slink back to his room and be miserable there, but Lebedeen, his eyebrows scissoring upward in humble gratitude, was hot to talk to him.

"I thank you. My wife thanks you. My son thanks you. We all thank you, Chaplain. Thank you for writing that letter getting me off this crummy ship. The only bad thing is I won't get to go to Peacock Island."

"Uh—don't worry about it." Miles was aware again that every man in the mess and galley was listening.

"I'm real glad to be going home. And I'm sure glad me and my marines didn't have to go ashore and see all that yucko stuff."

Miles saw that everyone was staring at him and the major with tight-mouthed contempt. Lebedeen wouldn't shut up:

"I'm flying out of Subic two days from now, just as soon as my replacement steps onto the quarterdeck. I thank you, my family thanks you . . . "

Miles couldn't leave now, not with every man watching him; he would have to swallow his shame and nausea and stuff a breakfast on top of them.

He spooned unconvincingly at some oatmeal until a plausible length of time had elapsed for him to ask the CHENG, who was ranking, to be excused, and then he lay in his rack with his hands behind his head for the rest of the morning, paralyzed by his memories of the burnt people and sex with Robin and the talk with the CO and the talks this morning with the DISBO and Lebedeen. Well, he'd helped Lebedeen; that was good. He realized he was jealous that the major was going home—he was jealous that the major *had* a home. He resolved to call Mary Lou as soon as they got into port. Maybe she'd put Kari on the phone.

The ship was proceeding smoothly over the coastal waters, and at noon he was standing in the shade of a hanging smallboat, at the lifelines, watching in his melancholia as the green and alien coast, the inscrutable and bunched-up jungle, identical to yesterday's, slipped past in its protrusions of carpeted rock filigreed with bow-necked palm trees angling out over the water—indentations of muddy beach—sudden islands that rose in every possible madcap shape, overgrown in hanging gardens that were emerald-green in the ferocious sun, vines like knotted telephone poles, leaves the size of bedspreads, and red, up-pointing, trash-can-sized, tooth-lipped, man-eating flowers. The ship cruised along, a gray, small, engine-whirring and diesel-stinking thing that could not say it was any less odd than the shoreline. At least the jungle had its ancient reasons for being here. Watching it unroll past him like an infinite embroidered drapery, Miles was reminded that he would be entering a world larger and more obscene than his own sordid past, and he was afraid that yesterday's events were only prelude, that these islands called the Philippines were a wilderness of frights and horrors, the urban manifestations of which he would be forced to experience the minute he stepped off the ship to call Mary Lou.

In the afternoon, he was standing on the signal bridge in the humidity,

which was like a slick layer of lamination against his skin, and there across
the green-black water was the torn-up place in the jungle where human
beings had erected the ugliness of a town. It was dirty-colored and garbage-
smoking. There was a warehouse row of blue naval buildings: a waterfront
heap of tangled and rusted industrial junk that shone like metallic measles
in the sun and that was in fact the maze of docks, in whose slips were
parked the identical twins and wide-assed grandmothers and whale-faced
fathers and uncles of the little gray ship that was his home.

The *Harding* sat there waiting as the *Natchez* and *Buchanan* took the
creeping lead into port, and he went across the hot deck of the signal
bridge to one of the Big Eyes, pulled the telescope to his face, and aimed it
at the town. In the circle of magnification appeared a skyline that was a
child's collection of piled and tumbled blocks, ashen white even in the
tropic sun. The sky was yellow in the heat haze, divided by the black funnels rising from unseen garbage fires. Between the sky and the town, in the
hills cleared of jungle, were the uneven rows of shanty hovels, their roofs of
rusted tin and aluminum throwing off red sparks of sun here and there
between the tortured streets of mud. He moved the Big Eyes down along
the waterfront and, looking up just beyond it, found the flat green
expanses of the Subic Bay Naval Base, its primly landscaped lawns and golf
courses shining almost blue in the heat, and he studied the many struc-
tures—perhaps a theater, a library, O clubs, chiefs' clubs, mess halls, E
housing, O housing, all of the buildings white with blue trim and blue
roofs—the largest American military base outside the United States, he'd
heard. He passed the telescope over the gray menagerie of ships with their
combined manes of mast poles and lines and antennas and deck cranes. He
alighted upon the airfield, on the long concrete landing strip and green
parked cargo planes and helos, the silver-colored hangar with the black
print over its enormous doors—UNITED STATES NAVAL AIR STATION CUBI
POINT—and he thought jealously of Lebedeen flying out of there in a few
days, flying home, back to the people who loved him.

There was a low quaking sound, harsher than a rumble, from many
miles away, the cracking voice of a volcano.

Going down a P-way toward Officers' Country, he ran into Kruger
coming the other way, and the enlisted man with his cockeyed black-
framed glasses enlarging his eyes to the size of Ping-Pong balls appeared to
Miles ready to jump out of his denim uniform with hopping nervousness.
The sweat was strung across the tops of Kruger's eyebrows like disorga-

nized pearls of various sizes, several of them skirting down his face as he moved its muscles to say, "It's common knowledge, it's just common knowledge, it's common knowledge."

Miles was instantly defensive. "*What* is?"

"It's just common knowledge what kind of place this is, Reverend."

"Yes?"

"We're going to be here for a whole week, it's not even safe to go to dinner."

"I don't understand."

Kruger spoke in a fevered whisper. "The girls, Reverend, the girls. You know I can't leave the base without sinning."

"So don't leave the base."

"Ever? Not even for lumpias?"

"Lumpias?"

"They're real good-tasting—Kong's Cafe on Magsaysay—I can't go there alone, can't go to dinner or anything, sir."

"So eat on board."

"The whole week? Can't you go with me, sir? Make sure I don't get into trouble? Please? It's common knowledge that Proverbs, chapter twenty-eight, verse thirteen, states, 'He who covereth his sins shall not prosper: but whoso confesseth and forsaketh them shall have mercy.' That's all I'm asking for, Reverend, just a chance. I'm big enough to admit how small I am. I need your help so I can forsaketh my sins and sin no more. No man can take that walk alone, that's just common knowledge."

"All right, okay, I'll have dinner with you in town. But I have to make a phone call first."

"The States, sir?"

"Yeah." He tried counting how many time zones it was to Illinois.

"Long distance, I know where you can do that real cheap," said Kruger. "National Philippine Telephone Company, end of Magsaysay. I can take you there, Reverend. Meet me on the quarterdeck eighteen-hundred hours?"

"All right." Miles went past him toward the stateroom, becoming aware of motion and sound compressing upward from belowdecks—not the vibration or grinding of diesel engines, but the shouted conversation and frenetic hatch-slamming preparation of six hundred men:

. . . "seven bucks!" . . . "poontang!" . . . "pussy!" . . . "fifteen all night!" . . . "hoooooooo!" . . .

10

He supposed there'd still be a dinner seating at 1700, despite the commotion of liberty preparations on every deck, despite the fact that every office he passed on his way to the wardroom mess had been abandoned. Just as he arrived at the mess door, he heard the choked-off sob of a man trying to control himself. Miles paused only a moment before opening the door to see about it, and it was Major Lebedeen, which didn't surprise him, sitting alone, at the end of the table, in his green uniform with his arms crossed and his face down in them. As his head snapped up, his eyes were a pair of swelling brown horrors surrounded by a growing shock-whiteness ringed in red. His face was puffy and pink. His humiliation at being discovered like this must've been acute, for he rose so quickly that the chair toppled behind him, and he assumed the rock-rigid stance of the Corps and said, "Sir!"

"Sit down," said Miles.

It was the first time either of them had acknowledged that Miles, as a commander, was a rank above the major. The major obeyed, and Miles himself sat down.

"All right, Leb, I guess you'd better tell me what it is."

"I'm screwed." His face, though red and wet, assumed its usual configuration, the mouth a line and the eyebrows slanting into their questioning attitude. "We got a communiqué, if I was getting ready to go out and be a pig like everybody else I wouldn't even know about it yet, came in over the wires about five minutes ago. Damn it. Excuse me, but damn it anyway."

"Is it about your leave?"

"There isn't going to be any. I have to lead men, I have to lead them, and I don't have the experience, I can't—"

"Should I write to Admiral Jiggerston?"

"You'd be wasting your time." The major released from his fist a balled-up piece of paper, and it rolled toward the chaplain. Miles uncrumpled it, flattened it out, tried to read it, but it was entirely DICNAVABic, full of IMSACOs and PACSUPDEPs and NAVPHILCOMs and DROITWAPs—he thought he did comprehend one word—BURMA.

Just to be sure he asked, "What does BURMA stand for?"

"What the hell do you mean what does BURMA stand for? BURMA stands for Burma! We are going to freaking Burma, Jim. We're shoving off tomorrow at nineteen-hundred hours. Can you believe it, can you believe my lousy luck?" His voice cracked on the word *luck,* and with tightening lips he made himself stop.

"What do you mean, Burma? We just got here, we're supposed to stay a week."

"Well, you read the communiqué," the major said hotly. "The government in Rangoon's been overthrown by a bunch of generals, they're killing students and Marxists in the streets, it's chaos, there's a hundred and ninety-two Americans barricaded in the embassy, and we got to get them out, that's our mission, how am I supposed to be a leader to anyone?"

"The whole ARG is going?"

"The whole ARG." The major shook his head unhappily. "You squids will stay on the ship—it'll just be us jarheads going ashore."

"You mean—like a war?"

"Like a little war, but big enough to be bad. Look, you can't tell anybody about this, this is classified until oh-five-hundred tomorrow morning. Only a few top officers know, they're afraid what would happen if those five thousand guys going on liberty found out tonight—it's best to tell them in the morning, keep them on board." Lebedeen shook his head, looking down and biting his lower lip. "I've never led men into battle, I can't do it, I pushed a pencil in San Diego all through the Gulf War. If I were on an AAV headed for the invasion beach in Burma, I think I would just climb up on the lip of the thing and fall off. On purpose. Just fall off and let myself drown."

"But you don't have to go, Leb. I wrote that letter for you, and they granted you hardship-leave."

"HARDELDISC."

"What?"

"Hardship Leave, *Discretionary*. If we're in the middle of a mission and my replacement isn't here, I've got to go. He's not going to be here for another two days, and we're leaving at nineteen-hundred tomorrow night, so I'm screwed, I'm screwed right into the deck this time. My wife—"

"I'll talk to Admiral Jiggerston, I'll call him right away, I'll say it's an emergency."

"That's no good, only General Washington could fix this one."

"There's no need for sarcasm, Leb."

"I'm talking about General Rusty Washington. He's in charge of REEPERBLAT."

"REEPERBLAT?"

"REEPERBLAT, do I have to explain everything to you tonight? General Rusty Washington, he's in charge of the Re-Encoding Eligibility for Personnel Early-Reassignment Billet Location Allocation Transfers."

"Oh," said Miles, "of course, *REEPERBLAT*."

"He handles it for the entire northern DITMARCLOIN, and he's the only one who can order a last-minute billet change."

"All right, I'll call him. Where do I reach General Washington?"

"He'd never talk to you, marines don't care what sailors have to say. Besides, it's seventeen-hundred, he's probably just leaving the office for the day. Even if you called him first thing in the morning and actually got through to him, there's no way he could fill a billet like mine by nineteen-hundred, not without pulling every string between here and Pearl Harbor. It's over, I'm going to die on the streets of Rangoon, and my wife—"

"I'll call him right now. I'll say it's an emergency, and I'll have them patch me through to wherever he is. I'll explain the whole thing."

Miles waited for a lift of hope in the major's face, or at least a nod of gratitude, but the major stared ahead in an unfocused way, the way Father Ogleby had been staring after he'd returned from the village.

Miles slapped his palms on the table—"I'll do my best, you'll see, it'll be all right"—and he got up determined to be a good chaplain, to extricate the major from the mission, so that the unnerved Lebedeen would never be allowed to endanger men's lives by leading them into battle.

In less than a minute, he was on a deserted deck, at the radio-shack door, hoping there was still a man on duty. He rapped on the door and opened it and heard "Shit" and saw the flesh-colored pages of a porno magazine flapping through the air as the radio man, sitting in a swivel chair with his pants around his ankles and his erection in his hand, spun the chair and kicked his legs trying to get his pants back up. "Help you sir!"

"Oh, sorry—I need to reach Rusty Washington."

"That near Seattle?"

"No, not the state—"

"D.C.?"

"No, it's General—"

"The Pentagon, aye-aye sir!"

"No, no, it's General Rusty Washington, he's a marine. He's in charge of—of REEPERBLAT. For this entire zone."

"What's his NUTCOC router?"

"I don't know. I need to be patched through right away, though, I don't care where he is or what he's doing, it's urgent."

"Aye-aye, I'll look it up in the ROUTSNART."

The radioman slipped the headphones over his USS WARREN HARD-ING ballcap and threw a pair of switches on the console and began turning a dial and soon he was speaking with acronymic urgency. There was a pause, more urgent talk, then he moved the earpiece away and looked around at the chaplain and said, "He's got a FARTRECOONY but the orders are INTERPERSNOT."

"Uh—radio lingo isn't really my—"

"He's about five miles from here, and his exec has a Field-Artillery Reception Unit, but the orders are Interruptions from Personnel—Not."

"Say it's an emergency."

"Well, unless we're under attack he's probably not going to accept a Code Roger Red—how about a Betty Blue, or maybe a Jell-O Yellow?"

"Uh—I'll try a Betty Blue."

"Code Betty Blue, aye-aye sir."

There was more talk, then the radio man took off the headset and offered it to Miles. When he put it on there was a little wraparound mike for him to speak into: "General Washington, sir?"

"No, goddamn it, this—is the exec—Colonel Reno. What the—hell's going—on?" The colonel sounded out of breath.

"I need to speak to General Washington."

"Just tell me your Betty Blue—Blue—quickly and I'll reroute you to Major—" The colonel stopped, as though his battle for simultaneous speech and breath had been lost.

"Thank you, sir, but I must speak with the general right away, it's an emer—it's a really big Betty Blue, sir."

"The general is quite—bu-bu-busy—why don't you let me—shit I'd better—concentrate, I'll lose—oh God—"

"Is the general there, sir?"

"Ruster-Luster—you better take this Betty—Betty Blue—Jesus, I can't even hold—catch!"

There was a knocking-skidding sound, as though the receiver had landed on the floor, and Miles heard music, Jim Morrison singing "Alabama Drinking Song," men laughing; one of them said, "That's his wife it's your ass," then a voice came on saying, "Colin? This a joke? What the hell time is it in Fairfax?"

"Sir, this is Commander James Banquette, Chaplain Corps, USS *Warren Harding*."

"Not this stupid—chaplain prank—again." The general sounded even more out-of-breath than his XO had.

"Sir, this is not a joke, I am calling about tomorrow's mission to Burma—"

"That's it, oh, that's the way, just like that . . . now listen, you want me to lose my . . . concentration and lose . . . hundred bucks . . . you goddamn fat . . . head . . . head . . . yeah that's the way . . . that mission is classified and this line is unsuc . . . unsuc . . . unsecured . . . I could have you . . . have you anytime oh Jesus . . . and calling in a false Betty . . . Betty Blue . . . oh Betty Betty Blue . . . carries a stiff, a stiff . . . penalty . . . that's the way, that's it . . . shit I'm going to lose . . . and I've never . . . never heard of any . . . ship called . . . the *Hard* . . . *Hard* . . . *Harding* . . . oh my sweet beautiful darling, that's exactly it, just like that, just like that, oh shit oh shit oh shit oh shit—"

—nothing but static—

Returning to the wardroom he found Lebedeen sitting as before, despondently composed, dead-faced, hands finger-laced on the table.

"Couldn't get through, I'll fax him in the morning for you. He was in a—sounded like a—round-table discussion."

Nothing.

"Major?"

"Mm."

He squeezed the major's shoulder and went into the galley and found fried chicken from yesterday in the square refrigerator and took a few pieces back to his stateroom to eat. At 1800, just as the liberty whistles were blowing on all five ships of the ARG, Miles was on the quarterdeck to meet Kruger and they watched as hundreds of men went running and whooping down the five enlisted gangways and then he and Kruger went down and were in the crowd.

It was military marching, not the way he'd ever expected; it was a colorful swarm, pastels, lima greens and pimento reds and wine-grape purples for the five thousand shirts; all of the pants were shorts and they were all white; the sun, which was still baking the world in the late afternoon, made the buzzed heads appear bald to the skull, cooking the commingled smells of five thousand colognes into a revelation of their common origin in the extract of skunk, and this brought back the burning corpses, which he tried to shake from memory as he marched in the dead chaplain's guava-colored shirt and immaculate white shorts in the throng of men, Kruger at his side in a yellow shirt and flowered shorts, the only man in five thousand with his shirt tucked into his shorts, the only one reciting Scripture to himself: "And Jesus said unto them, 'Ye are of thine father the Devil, and the lusts of thine father ye will do . . . '" The excited bluster-talking crowds pushed Miles and Kruger shoulder-to-shoulder through the heat, across the lawns of the Subic Bay Naval Station, through the arcing spray of a dozen sprinklers, blankets of mist everyone was glad to have on his face and arms in the bright humidity, which was like a transparent marmalade to walk through. They went past the white-walled, blue-roofed buildings he'd seen through the Big Eyes, and then the men were being funneled into handrail-divided pedestrian lanes under a roof of corrugated metal, which would've made it cool if not for the sweat and the pressing-together of hundreds of men, the skunkiness of their commingled colognes, the burnt corpses of yesterday. Kruger, still at his side: "But put ye on the Lord Jesus Christ, and make not provision for the flesh, to fulfill the lusts thereof." Miles wondered what these five thousand men would do if they knew what he knew, that they were leaving for Burma tomorrow. He waited with them in the humidity and sweat, in the unbreathable air, to be checked through by marine MPs, everyone around him willing to suffer for the whoring-drinking night to come—even Kruger was happy, muttering to himself—Miles alone was worried, burdened by the knowledge of war, and he had no purpose in this alien place unless it was to keep Kruger out of trouble and to call Zincville, talk to Mary Lou, perhaps Kari.

There was a dull ache in his pubic bone from Robin's grinding assault, and he couldn't imagine ever wanting sex again as he and the men around him approached the cammied marine guards with their M-16s shoulder-strapped . . . a mass fluttering of upheld wallets and IDs . . . and he and Kruger had theirs out as the perpetually saluting guards dart-glanced at them. The soreness of his groin was worsened by the disjointed punch lines around him—"So then I give the old one a ten-cent tip for cab fare, on account of her tits were hanging so low she couldn't hardly walk for tripping on 'em"—"She goes to Ron, she goes, 'Feels like you got a whole roll of dimes in your pocket'—we all bent over laughing, a thin little fucking roll of dimes, not even fucking quarters!"—"So then Davey yells up to the window, 'You know what you is? You's just the life-support system to keep a pussy alive.'" To himself Kruger was saying, "There hath no temptation taken ye but such as is common to man," but Miles stopped listening because all at once it looked like back home, a parking lot full of American cars shining all colors in the sun, a strip mall transplanted from Any Suburbia, a Wendy's and a Burger King and a McDonald's—though no one was stopping there: they were still on the base.

There was a pungency of sewage so strong that it was more like an industrial stink, and he thought it was an unregulated factory but there were no smokestacks in the sky.

"Which way?" he asked Kruger.

"Don't follow these fools to the money changers, everybody here takes American, that's just common knowledge, they think they need pesos for the girls." Kruger led him across the parking lot. "I don't think you've ever seen hell, Reverend, but I'm going to show it to you, it's exactly the way it's described in the Scripture. You've never seen it but it's right here on Earth, in Subic Bay, right here in Olongapo City." There was a jumpiness to Kruger that differed from the nervousness Miles had seen before: there was a boyish showoffiness in the tonguing of the upper lip, in the wide-open magnified eyes. But he was glad to have Kruger guiding him to the telephone office.

The air was heavy with the vapors of sewage cooking nearby in the sun, a stench like all the rotting eggs in the world, and there was a porten-tous din from beyond the chain-linked perimeter and blue-roofed guard-house and heat-withered droop of the American flag—Eric Burdon shout-singing "Sky Pilot" on top of Jim Morrison talk-singing "Waiting for the Sun" on top of Jimi Hendrix garble-singing "Wild Thing" on top of a lot of honking on top of the steady cacophony of hundreds of nineteen-year-old boys talking sex. They went through the next checkpoint in their endless collage of pastel shirts, which Miles now realized had never been innocently colorful but had always promised to be a mockery of decency.

"Hell," Kruger said as they were going past the final guardhouse with their IDs held out, "this is hell. It looks like hell, it sounds like hell, it's hot and sticky just like hell, it even smells like hell. Everybody knows it's hell, that's just common knowledge."

They followed the swarm around the corner of a barbed-wired concrete barrier and then they were on a bridge walled on the sides with metal slats, and some of the slats were missing, and looking through them he could see the black river, Kruger explaining, "That's Shit River, that's the real name, Shit River, American sailors named it back in 1898, that's the smell you smell, disgusting, isn't it?" When Miles opened his mouth to agree, he had to close it right away, without saying anything, because it was bad enough to have the excremental vapors up his nose without feeling their heated-shit taste in his mouth. Holding his breath, he looked down through the missing slats at the blackened hump of a junked car, at a tire stuck in the tar-goo of the unmoving surface, at a pinball machine, new and shining in the sun, dropped there in the night, no doubt, by crazed sailors. And then he and Kruger were across the bridge. And the grimy blaring town was before them with its muddy main drag getting churned up by rainbow-colored, chrome-dazzling, golden-tasseled jitneys honking in each direction, and the music was on top of the music on top of the music, and the sidewalks were thick on both sides with the buzz-cut men-of-pastel. The big concrete building immediately on the left was FANTASIA DISCO—scaffolded letters on the roof lit up red even in daylight—the one on the right was CONCUBUS CLUB, and down the Strip he could see the signs for the TEXAS BAR, the SAMURAI MASSAGE, the BASKET ROOM, the MAMASAN, the TIGER PIT, the PUSSYCLUB, the QUIM OF HEARTS. The row of whorehouse-bars was so long on either side that he couldn't read all the names.

There was a rectangular sign, pitted metal, hoisted high on a pole in the middle of the street, and as his eyes found it he heard Kruger reading it as though reading Miles's mind:

WELCOMING TO OLONGAPO CITY,
REPUBLIC OF THE PHILIPPINES
STATUS OF FORCES AGREEDMENT ARE NOT INFORSE
BEYOND THIS POINT
ALL LAW OF PHILIPPINE REPUBLIC ARE STRECTLY INFORSED
BIOLATE AT OWN RISKS

Kruger said, "All of this junk is left over from World War Two and Vietnam, this place is the white man's creation, that's just common knowledge, it wouldn't be here except for us." He swept his hand over the traffic rows of jitneys, multicolored and bus-long, with jeep fronts—"Those are jeepneys, they're made out of jeeps left by MacArthur. And that music is old forty-fives, the USO shipped them out of Saigon when we got our butts kicked out of there. I praise the Lord we don't have wars too often. These undisciplined lechers wouldn't hold up too well in combat, don't you think, that's just common knowledge."

Miles had the sensation of walking through the exotic overlays of history . . . at the corner, the unpainted walls of the stone-block buildings bore metal plaques with Spanish street names on them, VIA SAN RAMON, VIA SAN ANGEL, bringing back the study units of high-school history class, scrambled by his bombed-out teenage mind and forgotten till now, something about Magellan—he was a seafarer, right?—and three hundred years of Spanish occupation (wherever the Spaniards went they always seemed to stay three hundred years for some reason), and then the Americans were here, something about Teddy Roosevelt and San Juan Hill—or was that Mexico? Cuba?—and then Pearl Harbor and the Japanese—had the Japanese been here too? The Baton Death March, why had the Japanese carried batons? To hit the Americans with? Or wait, was it Bataan? And what about MacArthur? He shall return? From where, and why? The jitneys, their World War II jeep faces painted red or yellow or blue, and the blasting overlapping pop sounds of America 1968, preserved in South Vietnam and then shipped here in crates of old forty-fives, combined to give him a nostalgia for the wars and upheavals that had shaped this place and that were beyond his understanding.

"This is a Disneyland," Kruger said proudly. "A sexual Disneyland, or a kind of sex hell, depends how you look at it."

Miles went alongside him on the sidewalk crowded with pastel men and stepped around groups of them, into the muddy gutter, back onto the sidewalk, and he saw his first pair of Filipina prostitutes before he realized what they were. Two girls, cinnamon-skinned, their impossibly young faces—fourteen?—molded into professional boredom, stood bare-legged in buttoned lab coats in the entryway of a building, talking under an arrangement of neon bulbs, the current running through them to spell, one letter at a time, BABYGIRL MASAGE.

"Those are what you call your whores," Kruger said. His tongue paused between his lips. "The Devil's workers, the temptresses. Remember John three nineteen, 'And this is the condemnation, that light is come into the world, and men love darkness rather than light, because their deeds are evil.' Young girls, see how young and lovely. They tempt sailors away from the light. Young girls," Kruger said again, making an adjustment with his hand near his belt buckle.

Miles looked away from the distended front of Kruger's flowered shorts, finding, just up the street, the bony face and simian eyes of a woman crouching on a doorstoop, probably in her fifties, thin, making a number ten at him with her bone fingers, the 1 of the one hand going in and out of the 0 of the other. Her tongue flicked out dark and spearlike at him.

"Mamasan rike you," Kruger told him in a bad accent. "Mamasan want make sex-sex with you. Mamasan see you make dick-dick eye at her. Mamasan take upstair for seben dolla," and Kruger laughed—a girlish unexpected sound—as, sure enough, the old mamasan, as Miles and Kruger continued up the Strip, came off the doorstep like a spring toy, all wiry and Brillo-haired and coming directly for Miles with crimson-boozy eyes, one hand held up in an opening fist and the other a claw, and when she came up to him the fist went around his cock through his shorts and the claw was up under his balls, hard, her face swaying before him as she stretched her mouth open over the yellow bones that were her teeth and said, "Sucky-fucky. Me sucky-fucky you."

Kruger was laughing his laugh of an adolescent girl.

Miles was disgusted and frightened and angry and he lurched away, the insult to his balls spiraling into his abdomen as a sharp ache, accentuating the soreness of his pubic bone from last night, and the idea of sex nauseated him. A sea breeze sent the odor of sewage over them again, and as he and Kruger walked away from the cackling woman, Kruger said, "You want some common knowledge? Try Romans thirteen fourteen, 'But put ye on the Lord Jesus Christ, and maketh not provision for the flesh, to fulfill the lusts thereof.' That's my advice to any man," said Kruger.

"Amen," said Miles, rubbing his crotch.

There was only one thing to hearten him and that was the certainty that at the end of this street, the Magsaysay Strip, sat the National Philippine Telephone Company and—very soon!—he would be talking to Mary Lou and possibly Kari. He'd done the time-zone mathematics in his head; he figured it was six A.M. in Zincville and they would be home.

"I want to show you something," said Kruger. "This is the kind of place I won't be patronizing anymore, on account of the grace of the Lord Jesus Christ, and with my own personal reverend escorting me through town and keeping me out of trouble. But you've never seen it, right? The shows? Razor blade? Banana? Basket-effing?"

Before Miles could answer that he didn't care to see such things, that all he wanted was to call home, Kruger was leading him down the steps of an entryway, parting with both hands the twin flaps of red leather that were a door, and they were in the place, at a kind of promontory at the top of a stairway from which they could see, in the center of a darkness of seated men, a white square of light that was a stage with a mirrored bottom and mirrored sides. On it was a girl. She was young, not possibly eighteen, endlessly reflected by the mirrors, sitting naked with her knees up and spread, ebony hair straight down her back. The sitar music coming pop-and-crackle in its lazy loudness was colder than the jets of recycled air-conditioning as the girl, slowly and with great concentration, pulled a string of razor blades out from between her legs and Miles saw with a horror of fascination that they were coming—plop, twirl, one by one—out of her widely exposed and completely shaved pussy.

"How they do that?" Kruger insisted. "How they do it? They got something fitted up there a special way? Or they just blunt those razors down supersmooth? Or what?" Again he adjusted his crotch. "I'm glad I'm not watching stuff like this anymore. Praise the Lord." In the blue light his face was a cement shape of hardened jaw and invisible lips and flat cheeks, and his black-framed glasses had little blue mirrors where his eyes used to be.

"Let's go," said Miles. "We're out of here." He turned, but Kruger didn't follow, so Miles went back, took Kruger's arm, and said again, "Let's get the hell out of here," and this time Kruger followed, but with shuffling feet, his head rotating back toward the girl.

Outside it was the heat and the sewage and the crowds and the jeepneys and the ghost voices of Hendrix and Morrison and Presley. Then he was again smelling the burning corpses, but this time really smelling them—it was sickening beyond any memory or delusion. He and Kruger were going past a steaming cart overhung with horizontal poles of dangling black meat.

"My God, what is that?"

Kruger looked bored and dejected, watching his feet as he walked, hands in pockets. "Monkey-meat sandwiches. Two for a buck. They're not so bad."

Miles hurried along, only to be stopped by the wares of the next stand, the up-pointed weaponry of a row of dildoes, pinkly artificial in the sun, and the hanging contraptions of bondage with their straps of studded leather, reminding him of that old and brief profession that had slingshot him across the ocean, and that now felt as foreign to him as the town he was standing in. He stared at the dildoes as though he'd never faced an army of them before. The salesgirls, who looked twelve or thirteen, were, to his relief, too busy talking to notice or care about him. Then Kruger was alongside, taking from the display what looked like a limp hammock. "You know about these? They're these baskets, they're part of the common knowledge of the Mysterious East, it's called basket-effing. Lots of the, uh . . . clubs . . . have them in the . . . in the upstairs. They hang them from this big hook in the ceiling and they put the girl in the basket, see, with her knees up under her chin and her bottom at the bottom, and you lie on this table underneath, and they take this gunk and grease up your hubert, and then you put it through here, and these other two girls turn the basket around and round, and that feels pretty interesting, and then the line on that hook starts to getting real taut, and they can't hardly turn it no more—so they let it go. She starts to turning faster and faster, and her pee-you-ess-ess-why is going faster and faster around your gizmo, and there ain't nothing else like it, that's usually when I—that's usually when you can't stand it anymore and you kay-you-double-emm. Now what do you think of a Satan machine like that, Reverend?"

But Miles wasn't entirely listening. He had found a row of items more arresting than the basket netting and curiously more familiar than the dildoes, and he was holding a toy, a stuffed kitten almost exactly like the one Mrs. Banquette had sent him, except that this one was furry-new and had, implanted in its wide mouth, the pink convolution of a rubber vagina.

Why had Banquette given his wife a male jack-off toy? Where'd he gotten it? Banquette had been on the Atlantic only—had someone sent it to him? Apparently he'd removed the fake vagina before giving the toy to Michelle. Miles wondered at the twisted guilt behind such a gift.

He set it down and they were walking again and Kruger was saying, "All of this is from original sin, that's just common knowledge. You're born in the fire of hell, the minute you take your new name you're in the fire, original sin gives you your name and your destiny and your own personal hell . . . "

From beyond the jungle mountains the abrupt cough of the volcano came low and lingering.

A jeepney stopped in front of them; two white men in safari outfits, gray hair, banker faces, stepped out, followed by two little Filipino boys wearing nothing but matching green shorts, and one of the men spoke briefly to the other in what sounded like German or Dutch, and the four of them crossed the sidewalk in front of Miles and Kruger and went into a peeling yellow building. "See?" was all Kruger said. It appeared he would say nothing more as they continued walking, and then: "Romans one twenty-seven, somebody ought to read it to those perverted Krauts. Don't think there aren't a lot of business-Krauts making big devil money on it, flying them right over the North Pole, straight into Manila. They call it a sex vacation, it's the most common knowledge in the world."

They continued up Magsaysay, past the music and air-conditioning exploding from neon-bordered doorways, past the corners where girls stood in short black dresses, bored, arms crossed, weight shifted onto one leg. As they went, Kruger described, and Miles apprehended, with a passive dreary feeling, every bizarre practice of the evil town: A) It was just common knowledge, didn't the reverend know, that men sat around tables in whorehouses playing the Smile Game, ten or twelve of them sitting there and just as many girls down on their knees beneath the table, the huberts in their mouths, moving one man to the right every sixty seconds, and the first man to smile would have to pay for the drinks, and the first to ejaculate would have to pay for the girls; B) How about this, Chaplain, the girls squat-walking on the bar tops in front of the drinking sailors, playing the Peso Game, the men stacking their coins on the tops of beer bottles, the girls squatting over the bottles, effing the bottles, knees around the men's heads, and when the girls stood up the coins were gone, kept as tips, and then there'd be a girl squatting center stage and asking for a number and when it was called she concentrated real hard and shot out exactly that number of coins, and more coins would be thrown at her, and there'd be times when a sailor would decide to heat his coins with a lighter before putting them on the beer bottle, and then there'd be screaming and kicking and brawling and many arrests and missed deployments—there were "banana shows" and "broom-handle shows" and "papaya shows"—what did the reverend think of *that;* C) And the funny thing about so many of the whorehouses was that they had in a corner, like many Filipino businesses and homes, a flowered shrine to the Virgin Mary, a statue in painted plaster, the girls saw no contradiction between the necessity of their livelihoods and the religion left by Spain, it was the kind of thing you'd never see in a decent Protestant country, that was just common knowledge, but it was quite usual here to walk into a massage parlor and find behind the counter a sixteen-year-old girl in a negligee, standing beneath a poster of the bearded red-haloed sad-eyed Jesus, his hands raised in blessing, and believe-you-me a lot of the Catholic boys had trouble with the paintings and statues and shrines they found in the lobbies of ef-houses, a lot of them wouldn't even go in, a lot of them couldn't get it up if they did, but the worst part about it was an incident three years ago, there was this JO off the *Buchanan,* an RC on his first WESTPAC, drunk as a maniac, got pissed when he saw those statues of the saints of his boyhood in a whorehouse, started yelling at the whores and kicking them and before you could say hail-Mary-full-of-grace he was beating a fifteen-year-old girl to death with a statue of the Virgin Mary . . . well, that was Roman Popery for you, the whore of Babylon, the Bible forbids graven images, that's just common knowledge.

And then they came up against a group they couldn't get around, a lot of prickly-haired American boys, rosy-cheeked and gangly in the sun, looking like pink salamanders plucked from beneath their cool rocks and stretched out tall in the overheated Filipino day. They were laughing at and teasing the boy who, standing in their circle, blond with a raspberry rash of pimples on his chin, was relating, with the prancing animation of the drunken adolescent, the most important event of his life:

". . . So then we run upstairs"—he jogged in place, pumping his arms—"and we roll around on the goddamn bed for a while"—he hugged his shoulders and stumbled around quickly in a circle—"and she ain't wearing no panties, no damn panties at all!"—he put his hands to the side of his head and enlarged his eyes in mock horror—"so I drop my skivvies"—he did a worm dance—"and I don't even take off the bitch's dress or nothing, I just roll it up over her face, and she doesn't hardly have no titties nor nothing, hardly no pubes nor nothing, and I put my dick in her, I put it in!"—he started humping the air with his hands on his hips and the shouting and laughing of the boys around him rose to such a racket that he had to yell out the rest of it—"and all through it she's say- ing how much she loves me loves me loves me, and she wants me to marry her and take her to San Diego, she's telling me what a fucking stud I am and she's taking my cherry, I'm losing my goddamn cherry, I'm fucking her in and out and I'm getting off, I'm getting off right inside her tight lit- tle pussy!"—and then his friends were on him, shouting, shoving, laugh- ing, punching him on the arms and back and chest, and Miles couldn't decide whether the frenzy was anger or approval or drunkenness or horniness or all of it. The boy was now One of the Guys. Miles and Kruger finally had room to step around them, and as they did so, Miles thought it impossible that he'd ever been as young or as drunk or as licentious as that blubbering sailor, yet he certainly had been, at one time he'd possibly been even worse. It was strange to think about: it had never made him feel like One of the Guys. Being the chaplain was the closest thing to that feel- ing, a feeling confirmed when Kruger addressed him: "Reverend: by the grace of the Lord Jesus Christ that is finally the telephone office right across the street."

Leading him across in well-timed pauses-and-runs in front of the speeding jeepneys, Kruger was saying, "One walk down the Magsaysay Strip, it's worth ten years of college, it's worth a master's and a pee-aitch- dee. No one's got anything on you now, Commander—seven-dollar hook- ers?—a month of rice for a family of twelve, these girls are feeding all the villages in that jungle, that's just common knowledge, the Lord is working his mysteries. Look out, Chaplain, two of them are behind you now."

Miles turned, stepping onto the curb, and yes, there were two young women in blue-glitter dresses doing the dance-and-run across traffic, after them.

"Quick," said Miles, "let's go inside."

"Don't know what makes you think you're safe inside." They pushed through the wooden swing doors in the middle of the concrete wall, which had been painted green many years ago but was now green only in its crevices and dimples. Miles followed Kruger into the weak air-condition- ing, which nevertheless felt good, and they found themselves in a high- ceilinged room layered in cigarette smoke and filled with alleys of wooden telephone booths that were loud with the discord of sailors calling home.

Kruger took him to a counter where a fat toothless woman who was too old to be a bar girl pushed a pad and pencil at each of them.

"I guess I'll call Papa Whitehead," Kruger said.

"Who's that?"

"He's my pastor in Fresno."

Miles filled out the top sheet on the pad with his name and Mary Lou's name and the words Zincville, Illinois, and the area code and number, pushed the pad back at the woman, and she tore off the top sheet and the carbon, slammed them both with a rubber stamp as big as each square of paper, and said "Boot dirty-tree."

He nodded at Kruger and went down the aisles looking for the number, found it, went in, shut the door with its rectangle of glass at face level, sat down, looked at the black pay-phone-shaped thing on the wall, picked up the ancient gummy receiver, heard nothing, waited. The floor of the booth was sticky and it smelled beery—he thought ruefully that if his imposture were ever discovered he could get a job here mopping. He was surrounded by the warblings of drunken speech. Waiting with the sticky receiver a half-inch from his ear, he followed one of the voices from a neighboring booth:

"What ya mean? You can't do that . . . What ya mean? *Dave's my best friend* . . . What ya mean? You got the seashells I sent, or what? You can't do that . . . *He's my best friend,* Rhonda. What the hell ya mean, anyhow? . . . So I can't leave Sheboygan-fucking-Wisconsin for five months without you fucking my best friend? What is this shit anyhow? . . . What ya mean? I ain't touched nobody, we're in the middle of the fucking jungle here, nothing but monkeys and coconuts between here and the Chinky-land . . ."

The line came alive with a sea of hiss and there was a ringing behind the surf like a telephone at the bottom of the ocean and Miles was happy and nervous and excited.

From the sea floor, a man: "Hello?"

"Uh—hello? Is this 309-555-9096?"

"What? I can't hear you."

"My name is Miles Derry!" Was it? It didn't feel true. It wasn't his name and he had the wrong number.

"Miles, huh. What're you, calling from jail someplace? Mary Lou ain't here, she left for work."

"Wha—who is this?"

"This is Doug."

"Doug?"

"Doug Suveg. Ka-hee-a-hee-a, pal!"

The name and familiar expression rolled in his mind like big black dice before coming up yellow snake eyes. The lines had crossed between here and Illinois, between here and fifteen years ago, he'd rung up a telephone from long ago. He felt as though the floor were moving, and it wasn't just sea legs on land, because he was sitting down. "Jesus," he said. "This is Doug Suveg? For real? What goddamn year is it, anyway?"

"Drunk, huh. Of course. Well she ain't gonna send you any money, fella, not dime one."

"Did she get the money I sent? The thousand dollars for Kari's college fund? Jesus, this is really Doug Suveg?"

"Yeah, we got it, and no, you ain't getting none of it back, neither. We don't know who you killed to get it, but we're keeping it for the kid."

"We?"

"Ka-hee-a-hee-a, buddy."

"Stop saying that! Where's Kari? She there?"

"Who wants to know?"

"I just want to know if my daughter is there with you, Suveg."

"She's got the cartoons on. Ain't you outa quarters yet? I have to drop her off at the day care and get to work myself. Good-bye, Derry."

"Wait!"

"I'll give Mary Lou your message. I'll let her know you called from the drunk tank out in Texas or California or wherever the hell you're locked up. I'll tell her how you tried to get that thousand dollars back. But I'll let you know right now, pal, she ain't gonna send you dime one."

"Suveg—"

"Ka-hee-a-hee-a!"

Sitting there with the dead line in his ear Miles stayed in the booth a long while, remembering and fretting, and he continued to sit there even after he'd numbly rehanged the receiver. He sat there in a growing nimbus of pain that silenced all of the sailor voices around him and withered his vision to a telescopic blur until he wasn't in that booth at all anymore.

He was in Vail, Colorado. There was snow all around, with a cold, sun-burning quality to the light. He was sixteen. It was his father's annual ski trip for the top sales reps at the plant, and as usual Miles was there, at five dollars a day, to carry the bags and set out the cold cuts and mix the drinks (and sneak a few) at the rented lodge. Both of his brothers, Purvis and Lamar, were there as guests, sales reps, and his father's thundering voice was in every room, and among the reps there was a guy who was only a twenty-year-old trainee but who'd broken the incredible figure of forty contracts that year, and this plump blue-eyed kid with the blond crew cut was named Doug Suveg. Doug Suveg thought it was uproarious that the old man never called Miles anything but Smiles, and he started doing it too: "Smiles, get me a razor . . . no, not that lady's leg-shaver you use, a twin-blade, you know, for a *beard*." "Smiles, there isn't any hot mustard, I can't eat this puke." "Smiles, you put a faggot green cherry in my vodka and I asked for it straight up." "Smiles, here's a penny tip, I'm gonna stick it in your mouth and see if a gumball rolls out of your ass." His father and brothers thought Doug Suveg was a damned funny guy all right, gut-laughing with their sandwiches and drinks in their hands, and if Miles hadn't been zonking himself every hour on screwdrivers and reds, he would've . . . would've . . . aw, fuck them all anyway.

Besides getting high, there wasn't much to do when the older guys were out skiing, so on the third day he joined them, just a little addled by his morning gin. When the ski lift arrived at the disembarkation point, he tried to get off as he'd watched the others do, but he was too drunk. After a tumble so quick its mechanics were beyond him, his face ended up so deep in snow that his ears were buried. Laughter boomed all around him. Doug Suveg helped him up, hard-patting the snow off his back, and said, "Man, if you fuck the way you ski, some poor bitch is gonna end up with four elbows up her ass." The laughter—his father's, his brothers', the sales reps'—echoed off the mountainsides.

Miles staggered down the slope with a ski under each arm, and had to wait five alcoholic years, till he was twenty-one, for his revenge, but when it came he took it with both hands. Suveg was up in Detroit, attending the GM school, and Miles found Doug's fiancée, Terry, drunk and alone at the Union Bar & Grill, and they ended up at his place. He enjoyed himself: holding her breasts in his hands he said, "Don't get me wrong, I've always been a great admirer of dugs—uh, Doug." She blew him. Minutes later, shaking the semen off her engagement ring, she looked up at him with a simpering expression and said, "Ka-hee-a-hee-a." He asked her and she explained that she was an anthro major and there was this tribe in the South Pacific run by women and they shared all the men once a year in an orgiastic ceremony which was known as Ka-hee-a-hee-a.

Over the next few years, whenever he passed Doug Suveg on Broad Boulevard, Miles would greet him "Ka-hee-a-hee-a!" and Suveg, returning a lofty stupid look, never knew what it meant until Terry told him years later after the divorce, and by then it was too late to be punching mad about it.

Now Miles was punching mad, but only at himself, he could've punched himself for the way his life always turned out . . . Doug Suveg and Mary Lou, the kind of life-skewing coincidence that could occur only in a small town . . . punching mad, but also woefully depressed, as though something irreplaceable had just fallen out of him . . . *Kari* . . .

Punching mad—somebody was punching—it was the kid in the next booth, the one who'd been fighting with his girlfriend in Sheboygan, Wisconsin. He wasn't talking anymore, he was crying and punching the wall between the booths so hard that Miles could no longer rest his head against it. At least there was somebody nearby who felt just as bad. Miles made himself stand up. He left the booth and opened the one next door and said, to the red-faced, sweaty, pastel-clothed boy splintering the wall with his fists, "Hey, why don't you stop that, seaman. You want to talk or something? I'm a chaplain, if you want—"

Turning at him, the boy raised his red fists in front of his red wet face and said, "I'll fucking kill you, man!"

"Or if you don't want to, that's okay too."

Walking away, wishing *he* had someone to talk to, Miles knew it wasn't really the karmic turnaround of Doug Suveg being with Mary Lou, that wasn't the awful part, it was the truths and lies his daughter would grow up hearing about him. She would know nothing of the crap jobs he'd taken over the years, anywhere he could, just to support her, she'd never hear anything good about him at all, and Miles wanted to drink, he wanted it more powerfully than he had in four years of sobriety. There was nothing now. He wanted to go next door to whatever bar was there and toss back endless shots of whiskey. There was a widening abyss where his little hill of Kari-hope had stood. Okay, he was no father at all, not as bad as his own father, but still no father at all, Miles Derry's life had rung up zero, as usual, and yet . . . there was still this man walking around in a chaplain's vacation shirt and shorts . . . at least he was keeping Kruger out of trouble. As he heard the kid from Wisconsin tearing the phone out of the wall and throwing it to pieces over and over in the booth, Miles tried to be thankful for his new life. He wasn't the best chaplain in the United States Navy but he wasn't the worst, and everyone believed he was a chaplain. He hadn't been discovered yet, and he should be grateful.

So he wasn't going to drink right now. The boy breaking the phone behind him would drink and fuck with real violence tonight—which was what the kid might've done anyway, but now he had his reasons. Miles wouldn't allow himself to consider a reason. Drinking over Kari wouldn't help Kari or anyone else.

Going up and down the aisles, he looked for Kruger and found the booth with him in it. Through the rectangle of window he could see Kruger's head, his face in a kind of religious ecstasy as he spoke to his pastor in Fresno, the eyes almost completely closed and the chin lifted and the lips moving with a trembling kind of joy. Miles experienced a pang of jealousy at the depth of Kruger's religious belief, the exuberance of it: it was an intensity of faith that a chaplain should surely have.

Then Miles became aware of a fact that appeared to be supernatural, as though he'd just caught himself admiring a table that he now realized was aloft without any legs. Kruger wasn't holding a receiver, it must be a speaker-phone. Stepping closer, Miles looked through the rectangle of window and down into the booth. Kruger's shorts were down around his ankles, and kneeling between his legs was one of the girls who'd followed them across the street. As she held back all of her black hair with one hand, she was with quick efficiency and sucked-in cheeks swallowing and unswallowing the fat short thing that was Kruger's cock.

Miles's shadow was in the booth, and when Kruger turned and their eyes connected, Kruger's pupils, already magnified by the black-framed glasses, swelled brownly into the whites, which were also swelling, and then Kruger's whole face was swelling and coloring into a melon of paralyzed shock.

And then Miles had finally experienced too much, and he was walking with numb speed toward the turnstile with the telephone carbon slip pulled out of his pocket and extended toward the man behind the counter. The old man with an angled gold tooth poking over his lower lip took the sheet from Miles, studied for a moment an old-fashioned alarm clock, the round kind, standing on the counter on four stick legs, and the old man said "Foety-two."

"How much is that in dollars?"

"That is dolla my man."

Miles didn't even care. He got out two twenties and two ones and crumple-tossed them on the counter as the old man click-released the turnstile, and then he was out, he was on the sidewalk, he was alone in the honking-crowded-neon-in-daylight swirl of Olongapo City with its rotten-egg odor of sewage.

Two yellow motorcycles with sidecars came up onto the sidewalk behind him, pipey little honks, and the drivers were just boys but one of them was saying, "Joosy poosy! We take you! We take you house of girls!" and the other one was saying, "Hey, joosy poosy! Come on! We take! Two mile, twenty-fibe cent, we take you to see beautiful joosy-poosy girl!" They meant anyone, and roaring past him they meant Miles, and then they meant the men walking in front of him. Twenty-five cents. Miles couldn't feel too sorry for himself. A quarter was rice money to these boys, though not as much as the women could make. His self-pity was made ridiculous here, and it gave him a bit of shame.

He walked back to the ship, ignoring the calls from the prostitutes in the doorways.

On the quarterdeck the OOD saluted him with "Back kinda early aren't—oh, the chaplain," and crossing the quarterdeck toward the hatch he realized to his gathering astonishment that he was acting—had been for how long?—just like a chaplain without being conscious of it. Of course he should be the only man returning at this hour.

He walked in the silence of the parked ship with only a compressor humming somewhere belowdecks and the deck unmoving—it wasn't a ship anymore, just an iron extension of the world to which it was tethered, with hookups for electricity and water and telephones and computers. He was lying in his rack, unable to stop thinking about Suveg and Mary Lou and Kari . . . there was a pounding on the door.

He got up and felt his way toward it in the dark wearing nothing but his briefs, opened the door, and it was Robin standing in the red light of the P-way in a pink bathrobe. Her arms were crossed and her eyes and mouth were thinly horizontal with anger. In one hand she held a small black camera.

"Oh no," he said. "This is all I need."

"You're ranking tonight," she said as though accusing him.

"I can't be with you again," he said. He felt very naked, then looked down and saw that it was because he was.

"You think I'm here for a session? I swear to God, is that all you men think about?"

"No, I—"

"What makes you think I'd want another session with a bum lay like you? Most chaplains are pretty good, but—anyway, that's not what I want. Everyone's gone tonight, you're ranking, and I want you to open the captain's quarters for me."

"What for?" said Miles.

"You're ranking. Order them to open up his quarters. If you don't do it I'm calling AFUCT."

"A-what?"

"AFUCT, the Armed Forces Union of Civilian Teachers. I'm filing sex-harassment charges against the CO. You too if you don't order his quarters opened *right fucking now.*"

"I don't understand."

"It's bad enough," she said, "being stuck in this white-slavery—*brown-slavery* sexist dump of a port where nobody pays any attention to you—without that pig trying to get me thrown off here. He says I'm a slut, he says I'm an immoral woman. It's all right for all of you pigs to be fucking everything between here and Arabia, but he's going to call in my district supervisor from Manila the day after tomorrow for a special hearing and try to get me thrown off in this dump, and I don't even have any money to fly home. We'll see about this shit. He has *Playboy* magazines up in his quarters, I know where he keeps them hidden, and I'm going to go up there and take pictures of them"—she held up the little camera—"and claim hostile work environment, because pornography is a form of female enslavement, and he shouldn't be allowed to have it, it's harassment in the workplace, and then I'm going to file sex-harassment charges against the entire Seventh Fleet for putting him in a position of authority. He tries to throw me off this piss-bucket I'm going to sue for ninety fucktillion dollars—"

"Whoa," said Miles. "None of that is going to happen."

"Just watch. "

"We're shoving off for Burma at nineteen-hundred hours tomorrow. This ship won't be here for any special hearings. You'll be all right."

"How come Burma?"

He told her about the government in Rangoon being overthrown and the 192 Americans holed up at the embassy and the marines being deployed on a mission of rescue.

"Men are going to die," she said. "Ha! Anyway, someday soon I'm going to do something to really embarrass that pig. He's out with his whores tonight, but someday I'm going to get him, you'll see." And she went door-slamming back into her room.

Miles shook his head and went back to his rack.

In the morning, before breakfast, he typed out and printed another letter for Major Lebedeen, explaining the special circumstances, and gave it to the fax yeoman for immediate transmission to General Rusty Washington. Miles was on his way to the wardroom mess, wondering if there'd be breakfast, when the XO, his no-sleep frog face leering at him with heavily pouched eyes and a web of broken blood vessels over his wide nose, stopped him by the arm and said in a booze breath, "You read my POD? You know about Burma? We've gotta do seventeen DIMWEDNUPs before we shove off. I've got it down from thirty-one in the past two hours but that looks like the best I can do. They're waiting in the crew's lounge, how fast do you think we can get it over with?"

"Sir, I don't understand."

"I tell you seventeen's the lowest I can go. Everyone's of age, they've all got their licenses directly from a Flip court, the girls have their birth certificates and all that jazz, you know how they carry them in their fuck boxes with all their rubbers and K-Y and everything else just in case. Well, they're getting lucky as usual and I can't stop them, I stopped fourteen of the couples though—some of those poor guys were so drunk they thought they were just stopping off to shower and eat before going out bar hopping again, they didn't know they were getting married, these girls bringing them back will tell them anything. Well, you know all about that."

"You want me to perform seventeen weddings?"

"Not one by one, of course. On this boat we just do them together, a mass wedding, quick like that. I'll go down to the crew's lounge and see if I can't knock that number down a bit more, but I'm not promising anything, they're all within their legal rights. Meet you there in fifteen? Can you put on your robes or whatever and get your book and be ready? Look, I apologize for the short notice. While I'm at it I've got to find the yeoman of record for DIMWEDNUP, these girls don't miss a move, they want to see him right away after the services to get signed up for all the FAMPER-NAVBENnies."

"FAMPERNAVBENnies?"

"I know, right off the bat, it stinks, but what can we do? These whores have the right to be flown immediately to home port San Diego, get put up in naval housing, full dental-medical and living allowance, access to the dweeb's car if he's got one in storage—in a few weeks they'll be sending for the whole goddamn family too, no wonder all of Southern California's starting to look like Manila. But what can we do? Sometimes I think I'd like to dress up one of the JOs in a preacher suit and have *him* do the ceremony so it wouldn't be legal, but I don't suppose I could get you to go along with a thing like that, if I had someone impersonate you. Still it's a goddamn shame, isn't it? The U.S. taxpayer having to support all these immigrant whores in California, all of them bringing their families over, pooping out half-breed kids every nine months, all these whores driving around San Diego without licenses and turning every goddamn shopping-center into a demolition derby—well, I don't have to tell you, I'm sure you've seen it all. These guys do it because they think they're getting a subservient wife, but after six months in the States, she either disappears or she's running his life. Whoever said a whore is a docile creature? It's a terrible shame, and there's not a goddamn thing we can do about it, it's the price we pay for maintaining a first-rate pussy paradise like this—oh, sorry. Well—I'll meet you down there in fifteen, right?"

In the stateroom, after changing into the black clericals, the white plastic collar tight about his throat, he sat at his desk and flipped the prayer book open to the section "Additional General Services & Formats of Worship," and then to the chapter "A Service of Christian Marriage," which looked, at a glance, simpler than the Sunday services, which were routine to him now, and he felt confident. Who knew, maybe he'd even be doing some good, helping these women out of prostitution and their families out of poverty.

Descending through the decks on his way to the crew's lounge he could hear the protests of hungover men hearing the news for the first time; they'd been promised seven nights in a sexual Disneyland but would have to leave after one day, the muttered epithets culminating always in a stressed grumble—

"... *sucks.*"

"... *sucks.*"

"... *mutiny.*"

"... *sucks.*"

"... *sabotage.*"

"... *sucks.*"

"... *fucking sucks.*"

He entered the crew's lounge and the XO was standing at the podium saying, "If you want to ruin your lives," and then he saw the chaplain and said, "this is the guy who'll help you." He continued, "If you want to ruin your lives and marry all these whores, that's your business. The Department of the Navy can't stop you. If you wanted to put engagement rings in your nostrils we could rip them out. If you wanted to have the names of these whores tattooed on your foreheads, we could have your heads peeled, we have the authority to do that. But we can't stop any of you fools from getting married. The power of the Department of the Navy to protect anyone from his own stupidity exists in direct opposite proportion to the greatness of that stupidity. I'm giving you one more chance: any man here considered what it would mean to his dear old mother when she finds out you married a whore?"

The seventeen boys were invariably slumped back in their folding chairs, white boys and black boys, their naked legs spread out way in front, the once-white shorts and once-pastel shirts soiled into khaki hues, arms crossed or dangling, a few of the grooms slumping so severely that their knuckles were on the deck, and all of the faces were like red apples rolled in dirt and variously bruised. Their eyes were open, except those that had swollen shut, but none of the open ones was capable of more than a droop-stare, none of them moving except to squint at the world. The eyes of the women, by contrast, were awake and alert, fixated on Miles (to his prayer-book-clutching unease) and their postures were forward-leaning in opposed symmetry to their grooms'. Most of the women's faces were wrinkled brown apples accented with gold teeth, though some of the faces were young, full of catlike adolescence—Miles wondered at the age of consent, didn't doubt a desperate parental approval. The brides were still wearing the glitter dresses or the suspendered shorts and tight blouses or the lab coats or the miniskirts of their profession, and at their feet they all had their wicker-looking sex boxes, purse-sized and full of condoms and jellies, soon to be flung overboard.

No man was awake enough to answer the XO's question, so he rephrased it: "Pay attention, damn it, which man here is ready to inform his dear-forgotten little old mother back in Missouri that he has gone and married a goddamned whore?"

One of the boys stirred himself to the point of punching a buddy on the arm and said, "Joe here says his mother *is* a whore."

A titter.

"That's my second mother, dick-hole."

"Come on, let's all get fucking married."

"Seeing's we got to leave tonight we may as well get married and shit."

"We got six hours to go chase more squawk, let's get it over with."

"Club Boom-Boom, have a nine-some."

"Let that chaplain say his shit so we can get the fuck outa here."

The XO turned to Miles with a look of froggish resignation. "I guess it's all yours, Reverend. We're not meant to understand it, just do our duty before God and country. Oh well, I've got a quick tennis with the boys from WITNIT. Luck, no one'll miss me for an hour." And across the room and out a hatch he went.

Miles took the podium, feeling the women's eyes move with him as though magnetized. He nodded at the yeoman at his desk in the corner, ready with a stack of fat folders, the dependents' paperwork.

Miles opened the prayer book to the ribbon marker he'd placed in front of the marriage rites, tried to center himself with a look at the congregation, found, among the bombed-out sailor faces and young and old bar-girl faces, the face of the boy who'd just lost his virginity, the boy who'd been entertaining his circle of friends with the story on the Strip yesterday, the blond boy whose raspberry rash of pimples was now the most vibrant feature of his hungover half-sleeping face. It was too much to look at, it was too much to think about, but the XO had said he had to do it, so he dropped his gaze to the text, raised his arms and began, "Brethren, we are come together in the sight of the Lord, and under the jurisdiction of the Undersecretary of the Navy for Dependent Affairs, to sanctify and witness the joining together, in the Holy Covenant of Christian Matrimony, insert name of bride and name of—" He looked out at them, feeling his face heat up. "Well, there's a lot of you—seventeen times—ah—that's thirty—thirty-four names I guess—well, I'll just skip this part, you all know each other's names."

One of the women said, "No, I must know name of sailor. Must know name before marry. Not legal without knowing name."

"My name's Rudolf the Red-Nosed Reindeer. Now let him finish."

"My name Rosita Camanguay. Become Mrs. Rudolf."

"Whatever. Let the fucker finish, we got brewskis to kill."

No matter how destructive it might be for all these people to marry, no matter the greatness of his unease, no matter how strongly he felt that a chaplain should counsel these men, Miles understood this ceremony as an order from the XO, and so he again attempted the text: "The Lord our Father, having created us male and female for one another, and having instituted the Covenant of Christian Marriage—"

"No, I don't think so," said a man with a nasalized hangover. "I want Jewish Reformed."

"Well, okay," said Miles, "but I don't know if the rabbi—"

"This Jew be getting a rabbi? He be getting Jew church, I be wanting Muslim. Who do Muslim? I be entitled to everything this Jew boy gets, you know what I'm saying? How come there ain't no Muslim chaplains in this racist navy? Ain't no himey-ass fool got any more rights than I do."

"Who you calling himey-ass, you Congo-bongo."

"I be calling you out a pickle-nose vanilla-face Jew who be wanting all the special treatment, I be Muslim, I be Muslim and proud, motherfucker."

"Leave Rosen the fuck alone, he's a STERTECH, you fuck with him you fuck with the whole department."

"Fuck your department, Stevens, what you be getting married for any-how, you got married last time, asshole."

"Yeah, but when I got back to Oceanside I couldn't find the bitch, got a better one now."

"I still insist on Jewish Reformed."

"I re-form your ass, you Zionizing dick-nose Jew bloodsucker."

"Least I don't put pig bones through my nose like your sister."

"Kike."

"Nigger."

And then the folding chairs were flying and seventeen women were screaming and Miles, who'd been uttering useless interjections like "uh" and "ah" and "gentlemen" and "please" throughout the exchange, fell behind the podium as chairs shot over his head and rang against the bulk-head and the women screeched and the fists and feet made their rapid muffled landings on flesh and bone as men shouted that the men they were beating were faggots and queers and jarheads and squids and Nilla wafers and pussies and coons.

It went on and on. Whenever the shrieking-swearing-fisting-kicking mélange of sound grew scattered and paltry, it revived itself with a den-sity even more ferocious, like a train blowing past that was composed of alternating segments of lighter and heavier cars. Miles kept close to the floor, in a tight ball, as though he were huddled between the rails and the freight cars were screaming overhead—the chairs were still flying and crashing and getting snatched back up and flying and crashing all around him . . .

Order, when it finally evolved from the melee, did so grudgingly, as though the train were braking, rolling free, braking and rolling and, at last, stopping. There was nothing organized about the process—men passing in the P-way would leap into the room yelling, "Hey, hey, hey, stop this shit"—man after man, a couple of dozen eventually restraining the fighters. There were no sounds now but swearing and the moaning sobs of the women. Miles, able to crawl out of the compartment, didn't stand up till he was halfway down the P-way.

The XO rushing back to the scene was going too fast to avoid smacking chest-to-chest with him, grabbing the chaplain's shoulders, shaking them. "What happened? They're fighting? Stopped me on the gangway, they radioed the OOD. It's true? A fucking riot?"

"I'm afraid so. Uh—I'm real sorry about it, but—"

"There's a fucking riot and you're not stopping it?"

"Well, I really couldn't—"

"That's great! That's great! No weddings at all? Banquette, you're a fucking genius, and I'm gonna nominate you for a Distinguished Service Cross. Those seventeen guys are going to the brig, and those seventeen whores are going back to short time. Banquette, I could fucking kiss you."

Miles believed it, and was relieved when instead the XO gave him a frog smile, shook him again, and ran for the crew's lounge.

On his way back up to Officers' Country, he could feel the ship's mood souring into something more acid than before—

". . . the fuck, we just get here and now we gotta leave."

". . . the fuck is Burma anyway?"

". . . fucking Africa, man."

". . . dumb fuck, it be in South America."

". . . all the fuck I know is the Annual Pussy-Eating Finals at the Babysan Club start tomorrow night and we won't fucking be here."

". . . the fuck you say."

". . . yeah, it's hard to believe another year's gone by."

". . . it be better than Christmas and we be missing it."

". . . the fuck, they had a pussy-eating contest in Tijuana that one time, I got first prize, no shit, we had to eat guacamole outa their twats."

". . . least you hope it was guacamole."

". . . the fuck, I ain't gonna miss these fucking roaches. They's all over this ship, and we ain't even been here but one day."

". . . the fuck you mean? It good pot or what?"

". . . not fucking *roaches*, you dumb-ass, fucking *roaches*."

". . . the fuck, on account the Flip government gives them two cents for each thousand roaches they bring in, they figured it's gonna eradicate them, so now the Flips are just farming the little shits, millions of them, got more fucking roaches here than anyplace on the fucking globe."

". . . we be taking the fuckers with us."

". . . the fuck, you hope that's all you're taking."

". . . fuck it, I don't wanna go!"

". . . fuck this shit!"

". . . fuck this boat!"

". . . the fuck!"

He went out a starboard hatch, stood on the weather deck looking at the ship docked alongside, which had been here when they pulled in. All over its superstructure, standing on decks and walkways and ladders and scaffolding in the morning heat, which was already a choking-humid ninety-five degrees, were dozens of Filipino men, all of them in green T-shirts and shorts, raising a metallic beehive sound as they scraped and scraped at the gray paint, taking off acres of it one curl at a time, endless labor in the sun, and Miles remembered the CO saying they did it for twenty-five cents an hour. What else could they do? Probably nothing in the town paid half that. They weren't women or young boys—they couldn't be whores. There was nothing for them but this slavery to the armed forces of another country.

He wondered at the difference between him and them—he was leaving today, they would remain, working, their misery unchangeable—never mind fairness, where was the logic of it? Why could possibility and willfulness never intersect for them? The lowest sailor had a thousand times their status, and the marines also—

Of course, some of the marines could be dead in the next few days. Where was the fairness or logic in *that*?

He didn't know. He didn't suppose any chaplain knew. He was still thinking on these matters at 1900 when four of the five ships of the 57th Amphibious Ready Group, including his own, with Major Lebedeen still aboard, dropped the last of their lines and began nudging away from the piers inches at a time and then feet at a time and then yards at a time, slowly turning, picking up speed across the bay, and on the open sea accelerating to twenty-five knots. It was a long way across the South China Sea and around the island of Singapore and up the far side of the Malay Peninsula, and they wouldn't stop moving until they'd gone two thousand nautical miles and come within assault range of the beaches of Burma.

11

Sunday services were well attended, two dozen men at each hour, mostly marines, since no sailors would be going into combat. The marines came into the room with glum faces tomato-colored from PTing on the fantail, released for sixty minutes between training sessions by Major Lebedeen, the glummest marine of them all, who showed up himself at the second service, sitting empty-eyed in the farthest row. Miles had chosen, off Banquette's every-occasion homily disc, a sermon that Banquette had probably never had to deliver, "So Now You're in Combat: How the Power of Prayer Can Help You to See a Command Mission in the Bigger Context of the Mission of Christ," and the marines filing out looked just as glum as when they'd filed in. Miles was painfully sorry that there'd been nothing on the computer disc or, more importantly, in his past that he could share to lighten their souls. He wondered if there was anything anyone could say.

For the first time, Kruger didn't attend services, and the only time Miles saw him during the transit to Burma was in the middle of dinner one night when Kruger came into the wardroom to have one of the JOs sign papers on a clipboard. The whole time that he was holding the clipboard for the JO to sign, Kruger wouldn't look once at the chaplain, though the chaplain was sitting across from the JO. Miles said nothing, and Kruger said, "Thank you, Lieutenant," and turned so abruptly he dropped the clipboard and went fumbling down on one knee to pick it up and stood up and the roll of the ship carried him—he must've been relieved—toward the swung-open door and then out as it closed behind him.

This noninteraction with Kruger was the only awkwardness to echo from the recent past: Miles didn't mind sitting now at the dinner table with the CO at one end and Robin at the other, because the negative energy of sex-and-discovery had been discharged, along with most other previous energies, by the overwhelming current now running through everybody, the electric impulse of The Mission, the topic that everyone talked and breathed and dreamt and ate: How many go ashore in the first wave?—Burmese units on the beach or not till Rangoon?—Helos from the start or just armored vehicles at first?—and onward like this throughout each meal. If Major Lebedeen was present, he was asked a hundred other questions, his drooping dead-eyed face generally viewed as the mark of daily exertion rather than the near-catatonic despair that Miles knew it to be. The poor major had to give so many answers about the last-minute training that he could barely get a forkful into his mouth before he had to mush out acronyms and logistics and coordinates through his food.

The marine JOs, growing grimmer with the approach of combat, said less and less during meals. Their depression, their unworded fears, their resistance to questions, soon produced a short circuit in the electrical excitement the naval officers had for the mission, a deadening compounded by the rumor, easily confirmed by a stroll on the weather deck, that there were only four ships going to Burma. The *Buchanan* had stayed in the Philippines. In a couple of days the facts, which lowered everyone's mission morale into a dark sexual jealousy, appeared in the POD: somebody, or a group of somebodies, who hadn't wanted to leave sexual Disneyland, had poured forty pounds of sandy Filipino mud into the rudder-steering gears of the *Buchanan,* disabling the ship, and the Naval Investigative Service had become involved. Sabotage was a felony punishable by life imprisonment, and the admiral had ordered any sailor or marine with information to come forward. But it was more than sabotage, for the ARG was now going into action without its full complement, and that made the crime treason, punishable by death. "All for a few more nights of scrogging," wrote the XO in his POD, "not that they can, all liberties secured." The fact that the ARG was going to Burma undermanned brought a gloom over the ship that even the tropic sun couldn't penetrate.

The *Buchanan* was being repaired, and there was debate at meals over whether she'd be able to rejoin the group on time. Some of the JOs said no, not at twenty knots, and the XO called them ignorant wogs, pointing out that the *Harding* was, the last time he checked, doing 25.97 knots, and while the rated speed of an amphibious-landing vessel might be twenty, everyone knew the classified maximum to be higher, and Robin interrupted to say that the assertion was easy enough to prove mathematically, "Because the optimum efficiency is 2x over x plus y where x is speed and y is sternward propeller thrust relative to the ship, so if we call the quantity x minus y the propulsion quotient and divide it by x we arrive at r, the propulsion ratio, and it follows that the theoretical efficiency can be expressed by one minus r over one minus one-half r."

The men looked at her a moment, then returned to their conversation. Miles felt for her, because no matter what she knew, she would never be one of them; she was less at home here than even he was. Her expression as she rose virtually unnoticed and went for the door was one part hurt to one part anger, and there was a cloudy lack of focus to her eyes over the tight bitterness of her mouth.

When Miles was alone, when there were no combat discussions to follow, and he was in his stateroom playing computer games or lying in his rack with his hands behind his head, his thoughts returned to Zincville, to Mary Lou and Kari and Doug Suveg. The more he worked the thing in his mind, the more he writhed beneath the deadweight of certainty that he would never again be in their lives—it had been over a long time ago, it was an old thing, a fantasy, nothing. He was a man with the wrong pictures in his wallet. No matter what he felt about it, he was married to Michelle Banquette and they had two children, Teddy and Laura, and he couldn't even see what these people looked like because he'd dropped their pictures over the side on the first day aboard. Now he was curious. He had a wife, Michelle; he'd seen her picture once; he couldn't recall her face. He might write to her and ask for another photo—but God knew when the next mail would go out. At Subic there'd been a warehouse glitch with the mail, and it hadn't been located in time to be loaded before they got under way. The lost mail hadn't helped morale, especially among the marines, who needed to hear from girlfriends and wives and families to be reassured of faithfulness and love before they went into battle. Miles, like the other men, now found that he'd like to hear from his wife. He wondered what she'd thought of his response to her last letter. He wanted—needed—her love and support, even though it could exist only as a fantasy, for she wouldn't know she was writing to a man named Miles Derry who needed his morale lifted because of Mary Lou and Kari and Doug Suveg.

The captain, in between helo flights to the *Natchez* for strategy sessions with the admiral, was working hard on the problem of morale, putting a suggestion box in the wardroom, unfolding the slips at dinnertime and sarcastically disposing of the ideas—"*Chess tournament.* Which of you faggots is kidding us? . . . *Scavenger hunt, look for helmets and boots and old porno magazines, etc.* Now how hard would that be? You wet-brains are really thinking. . . . *Pin the tail on the SUPPO.* Yeah, that might be all right—except, even with your eyes gouged-out you couldn't miss walking right into his fat ass . . ." and then the CO came upon a suggestion written by the DISBO: *Since we're embarking on this mission in order to save the butts of women and children, let's do something that appeals to family values and true togetherness. Let's have a contest throughout the ship where you tell your best getting-laid story. First prize: Free short time upstairs at the club of your choice when we get back to Subic. Hey, a seven-dollar value!* "This is a great fucking idea!" said the captain. "Get everybody's minds off this morbid killing and dying shit we've got coming up, let's have a few laughs before you jarheads hit the beaches."

And so the DISBO was commissioned to spend the following day going keel to mast and bow to stern with a camcorder taping the entries, and by dinnertime he had his winner. He popped it into the wardroom VCR just as they were starting their salads. A sailor stood in the sun before one of the weather deck bulkheads. He reached for the brim of his USS WARREN HARDING ballcap in a perfunctory hat-tipping gesture and said, "I am SN-3 Santos Rodriguez, and this is my best story of the getting laid. Okay, me and my friends, they are Julio and Chuy, we drinking in Pancho's, it is bar in North Hollywood, and we meet the old rich white lady, very old, maybe she is forty, forty-five years. She have the nice big round booty on the barstool. The four of us we are drinking and talking, and she is inviting us to go to her apartment to play the game of the quarter flip. So I go with her in her old Chevy and Julio and Chuy they are following in the truck. In the car she is always with her hand in the between of my legs, rubbing my *vergota,* that is a Mexican word. In her apartment we are sitting on the floor playing the quarter game which is the game when you take two quarters and you use one to flip the other one to the ashtray. We are drinking the vodka and playing. Soon we are playing for strip. This woman she is without shirt, her big *cheechotas* they are hanging there. Everyone trying very hard to lose to become naked. First she take Julio in bedroom. Julio very drunk, he lasting one minute, come back out and fall drunk on floor. Then Chuy go in, he is much macho, lasting two minute maybe. Then is my turn. I am more experience with the womens, I have eight childrens in Mexico by time I am twenty-five—maybe I am counting wrong but it is many kids—so I am lasting one hour with the woman and she is very happy. She fall asleep with her big booty shining in light from street. When I go back to living room all furniture is gone, Julio and Chuy carrying coffee table through door. They have everything in truck—stereo, TV, sofa, lamp, Mr. Coffee. We driving away, we drunk and very happy. Then I am thinking something trouble, I say 'Oh, chingado!' I do not have my wallet. Is no money in it, but inside is my green card, with name and address. I very much afraid, go back to empty apartment. Still she is sleeping in bedroom. I see wallet on floor and pick up but then I see something also too. Her booty it is very big and round and shining in light from street and on one of the butt cheek is something stuck on it, it is a quarter from the flip game. So I am thinking about it, I am shrugging the shoulders. I take quarter off butt. Flip in air and catch and put in pocket. Go home with big smiling, and that is my best story of the getting laid!" Rodriguez smiled hugely in the sun, nodding maniacally.

Everyone in the wardroom was laughing, the battle gloom forgotten, and the men nearest the DISBO were punching him appreciatively in the shoulders. That evening the tape was played over the 1MC while the video ran on the TV in the crew's lounge. The bulkheads, all the way from the engine room to the signal bridge, reverberated with laughter. The air was full of happy talk: "This Rodriguez knows his shit," "What you wanna bet he can get laid on all nineteen continents," "My buds and me be trying that shit when I get back to Baltimore." The tape was so popular that it was repeated the following evening, and possibly the only people whose morale was not lifted by the experience were the chaplain, whose sense of ministerial decorum was becoming internalized, and Robin, who, just after dinner when Rodriguez's voice took over the ship, got out of her chair and said across the table to the CO, "I'll get your sexist ass for this, remember that," and left the room. The DISBO pulled his sunglasses out of his shirt pocket and put them on and turned his head to one side and smiled like a Hollywood producer.

The captain ordered copies made and had them heloed throughout the ARG, and the XOs of the other ships, after playing their Rodriguez tapes for their crews, each radioed a note of thanks to the captain for helping them build up morale, and the captain read the transmissions over the 1MC, to the hooting applause of the ship, and then announced that he was awarding the DISBO a special commendation and appointing him the new morale officer—the MORALO. The DISBO told everyone at the next lunch seating that he was going to develop and market a series of tapes, a home-study course that people could listen to in their cars, describing his philosophy of life, which would become a worldwide movement when everyone saw his infomercial, in which he'd be shown on a yacht with a dozen bikini babes or standing in front of his mansion in Olongapo with a couple of hundred prostitutes. When one of the JOs asked him what the course would be called, the DISBO put on his sunglasses and turned his head to one side and held his pipe aloft and gave his Hollywood smile and said, "How to Stop Being a Mortgage-Paying Boss-Blowing Pussy-Whipped Loser and Take Control of Your Half-Assed Middle-Class Life and Make the Big Bucks Speculating in the Stock Market and Quit Your Shit-Eating Job and Go Out and Ball All the Firm-Assed Big-Titted Babes in the World."

Morale in the wardroom was pretty good after that. Nobody thought about anyone dying.

Until lunch the next day. After the coffee and dessert, Major Lebedeen pulled a white board out of the corner (it was slat-footed to keep it from tipping at sea), and he got out a black grease marker for the daily strategy briefing he gave his JOs. Miles and a few of the other naval officers stayed around with their coffee cups to watch. The major, like all the marines now, was wearing cammies, and they fit him loosely, like pajamas, giving him an overgrown childish look which was augmented by the slant of his ever-questioning eyebrows. His eyes were morose as a dog's. His manner as he stood before the white board with both hands clasping the grease marker behind his back was listless, and his voice trembled:

"I want to begin with some . . . good news. They have a gunny, he's on the *Lompico*. He was a guard at the . . . embassy . . . Rangoon . . . 'bout three years ago. He's heloing over. Around fifteen-hundred. Brief us on the compound . . . the configuration . . . three floors . . . and which of course he knows so well. Now." He uncapped the marker, dropped the cap, it rolled away with the down-angling of the deck, he watched it race away, then looked up as though he didn't know where he was. Then a moment in which he apparently remembered. "Today's briefing. Latest . . . mission plan . . ." He began drawing, tentatively, as he spoke, beachheads and roads and rivers, taking a clipboard up from the table every few moments to study it, study it long, too long, and the men looked at each other, embarrassed. When the major finally had everything awkwardly illustrated on the white board, he stood there looking at it for a long while, as though it were a Picasso hung upside down, as though he wasn't quite sure he would understand it even if it were right-side-up—and then, with a marshaling of vigor and concentration that Miles sensed was going to mentally exhaust the major for the day, Lebedeen took a square look at the white board and said, with his finger moving from place to place, "This is where Second Battalion is, this is where Division is, this is where Reconnaissance is, this is where the Bangwa Bridge is, this is where First Phase HQ is, this is where Second Phase will be . . . this is where . . . uh, where . . ." The major was pointing at a Y formed by the forking of roads, he didn't understand what he was looking at, he dropped his finger and raised it again and said, "This is where . . . where . . ." and he sat in the nearest chair and stared at the white board helplessly and said, "This is where . . ."

The DISBO got up and walked over to the white board and picked up the grease marker and began filling the crotch of the Y with a lot of loopy squiggles and said, "This is where the pussy is!"

The room detonated with laughter. The men slammed the table, they whooped, they screamed, they cackled, they wailed, they shook, they screeched, they leaned to one side, they wheezed, they yowled, they had laughing-coughing fits, they choked, they wept, they hoo-hooed, they laughed so hard, some of them, that they farted explosively. Major Lebedeen was sitting at the end of the table with his face in his hands. On the white board, the furry triangle was proportionally positioned below the regiments that the major had indicated with small circles, which now looked very much like nipples. The men laughed and laughed. Miles sat there repressing a smile, shaking his head, the proper chaplain, unhappy for Lebedeen, but happy for the major's young lieutenants because, since leaving for Burma, they'd been wearing expressions of professional seriousness that had to be false, had to be hiding their inexperience, their combat nerves, their fear of following the major into battle—they needed this explosive release.

Plates crashed. Ditchfield had been clearing the table when the DISBO had gone to the white board—the old man had been laughing along with the others—now he was dropping plates and snorting and the room-size laughter began to subside as the men became aware of him. He was saying, "I can't—I can't—" and he was stepping across the shards of broken plates, cracking them, his hands gripping his left breast, his face grayer than usual as he snorted and said, "I can't—" and moved across the room like a man walking a wire but beginning to sway off his balance, and he said "—breathe!" and did a brief jig, and then he was down out of sight on the floor with the rattle-scuff of bones hitting the steel plate.

Everyone was standing and shouting and gathering around the fallen chief, the nearest of them kneeling. Ditchfield was quiet now and the doctor was yelling for them to shut up and get out of the way, and he dropped from view, and he said, "Hey Ditch! Can you hear me!" and a couple of moments passed, and the doctor said, "I'm not getting a pulse, he's in ventrical fucking tachycardia! Call a code blue stat to the wardroom!" Nobody knew what he was talking about, so he ordered one of the JOs to run down to sick bay and bring back the medics and a stretcher and a cardiac defibrillator, and the men were crowding in too closely again and the doctor said, "Stand back!" and they stepped away and he said, "I need someone to help with mouth-to-mouth"—they all stepped back even farther. There was the thump-thump of the doctor pounding Ditchfield's chest and then the doctor said, "I can't do mouth-to-mouth and chest compressions at the same time, I need—" and two medics came running in with the equipment in large gray bags. "I'm giving him precardial thumps without results," the doctor said desperately. "We need to start CPR, get him on the monitor, get a line in him, get that mask on him, attach the wires and hand me those paddles, we need to defibrillate at two hundred joules"—scuffling sounds as the medics followed the orders, then the thudding of Ditchfield's lifeless body as it bounced on the deck from the electric jolt—"He's still in V-tach, give me three hundred joules . . ."

Miles was sitting now, grimly hoping the doctor wasn't going to find it necessary to order him to get his prayer book. Lebedeen came over and sat next to Miles.

"Rotten luck," said Miles.

"Thanks," said the major.

"For what?"

"For caring."

"Well, I meant—"

"I know you've been wanting to see these." The major's face, as he lifted his left buttock and reached behind for his wallet, bore a look of crazed happiness, the little fat smile of a cherub, eyebrows arching over a child's Christmas eyes. He opened the wallet on the table, pulled out photographs, showing Miles the Asian woman, large, short-haired, in the red muumuu, and the light-skinned boy with Asiatic eyes in the yellow shirt with the black Charlie Brown stripe zagging across it. "That's my wife and boy." The major aligned the photographs on the table with a trembling hand. "Boopsy and Pogo, that's what I call them, and they call me Cookie." Abruptly he jammed the photos one by one back into the plastic sleeves of his wallet and returned it to the rear of his cammie pants, his face stiffening in anger. "Everybody thinks my wife was a bar whore, just because she's a Filipina."

"I know she wasn't," Miles said, gently.

"You've been asking me about a hundred times a day to see them, so you finally got to."

"I've been asking to see them?"

"Not with words."

"Leb—you showed me those pictures the day I met you."

Lebedeen looked at him suspiciously, lower lip curling inward and eyes unblinking. "Stop talking about my family. Stop using your religious ESP on them." He got up and went to sit in the chair farthest from everyone, in the TV corner, across from the dead screen, sitting with marine rigidity with his arms on the rests and his face vacant.

Miles was thinking of going after the major to ask him carefully what he meant when he heard the doctor say, "All right, I think he's coming around," and in a minute the stretcher with Ditchfield on it was being carried toward the door. The old chief, his face as gray as the soft cap he was still wearing, his eyes hollowed out and his mouth outlined in spittle, was still alive, and as the stretcher went past he fumbled for the DISBO's hand. They held the stretcher in place long enough for Ditchfield to say, in his cigarette-thinned voice, "You're the best ... goddamn ... MORALO ... ever had. Korea ... I remember ... we had a MORALO ... the admiral's cook ... made tit cookies, raisin nipples ... damn funny ... but you're the best."

"All right, old fellow," said the doctor, "let's go," and they carried him out.

Miles followed the XO into the P-way and stood in front of him to stop him. "Listen, XO, Leb isn't psychologically fit to command, anyone can see that. He should be relieved. He's not fit to lead men into a situation where they might be killed."

"If he were fit for *that,* there *would* be something wrong with him. No sane man is fit for it." The XO went around the chaplain and continued after the medics.

In his stateroom, at the computer, Miles began composing a memo to the marine CO on the *Natchez*, General McMinn, citing his concern for the emotional stability of Major Lebedeen, detailing the background and as many incidents as he could recall. Then he sat there reading it over. He wondered if he should send it. He didn't know what else a chaplain could do.

He had it sent.

After he got back, he was lying in his rack reading a month-old issue of the Pacific edition of *Stars & Stripes* when there was a rap at his door. When he opened it, two of the marine lieutenants were standing there with one of their enlisted men, and they were all in cammies.

"Yes?"

"May we come in sir?" said the JO whose name was Reynolds.

"Of course, Brian. What can I do for you?"

"Major Lebedeen told us to bring you Private Brown, sir."

"He did?"

"Yes sir. He ordered us. He said we should make use of your . . . well . . ."

"My well?"

"He said," said the other JO, whose name was Hawes, "that we should make use of your . . . well . . . what he said was your psychic abilities. It was an order, sir," he added.

"I see," said Miles.

"Sir," said Lieutenant Reynolds, "could you please talk to Private Brown anyway? It might do us some good."

"What is the problem with Private Brown?" Miles looked closely for the first time at the young marine, who had a narrow dull-eyed face, John Lennon glasses, and a mouth worried-small.

Lieutenant Hawes answered, "Chaplain, we've been attempting to determine the location of Private Brown's M-16 clip for some time without success."

"We've turned three decks inside out," said Reynolds.

"Well, I don't know if it'll do any good, but I guess I can talk to him."

"Thank you, sir. We'll be waiting outside."

The officers left, shutting the door. Miles sat in his chair, crossing his legs; the enlisted man remained at attention, looking straight ahead.

"So how's Private Brown?" he asked Private Brown.

"Fine, sir!"

"Everything all right back home?"

"Excellent, sir!"

"Worried about tomorrow?"

"No sir!"

"No concerns at all about the mission?"

"No concerns, sir!"

"Was lunch satisfactory today?"

"Satisfactory, sir!"

"Where the hell is your M-16 clip?"

Private Brown looked down at the chaplain for the first time, as though checking the man's collar to make sure it was a chaplain who'd addressed him like this. The private licked his upper lip and stared ahead again. "I don't know where it is, sir."

"Did it walk away?"

"I don't think so, sir."

"Would somebody steal it? Not very likely."

"Wouldn't know about that, sir."

"Well, you can't go on tomorrow's mission without it, can you? That's too bad."

The marine said nothing.

"You got a girl stateside, Private Brown?"

"Yes sir. No sir."

"We haven't had any mail. Call her from Subic?"

Nothing.

"Call her from Subic, marine?"

Private Brown's face was moving as though he were trying to twitch off a bug crawling on it as he stood at attention.

"Your ammo clip, Private Brown, is at the bottom of the South China Sea, isn't it? Tell me that isn't so."

The boy continued to chase the invisible bug across his face with a twitch of his cheek and nose.

"Don't lie to a minister. Your ammo clip's at the bottom—"

"Yes sir—I mean, my girl—"

Miles felt strongly for the boy and hadn't enjoyed having to be an officer with him, nor did he enjoy opening the door and asking the lieutenants back in to tell them, "Private Brown finds it impossible to go into battle without the love and support of the woman he loves, so he threw his ammo clip over the side."

"Brown, your ass ain't worth the pink hairs covering it."

"He was honest with me, so I hope you won't be too harsh with him." Miles looked at the JOs: they were in their mid-twenties, kids themselves, they hadn't had the life experience that would've helped them guess, and then elicit, the motives of Private Brown. When the JOs had pushed the marine out of the room, Miles sat in his chair, sorry for the boy but knowing that he was getting better at doing a chaplain's job—odd that succeeding at it was as problematic as failing. He wondered how it would feel if he himself were going ashore tomorrow, without the love and support of Mary Lou and Kari—knowing what he knew about Doug Suveg. Then he went back to his rack and was reading *Stars & Stripes* when the 1MC started hissing but nobody was talking, just a lot of hiss and a person breathing into the mike.

Miles lifted his head; six hundred ears must've been similarly inclined.

"Attention all hands. This is the doctor. I am sorry to have to announce that Master Chief Petty Officer Dennis Ditchfield, chief of wardroom crew, expired of a myocardial infarct—that's a heart attack— about an hour ago in the med unit of the USS *Natchez,* where he was heloed after experiencing a ventrical tachycardia at his duty station. He is the first casualty of Mission Burma. Ditch had a long career, and he will be missed. His service stretched from the Second World War through Korea through Vietnam through the Gulf War through the present day. Some of the many, many commendations he earned throughout his years of service to the Seventh Fleet included Best Waitress—no, excuse me, that's wrong—I'm reading off an old mimeograph of his service record— his commendations include Best Waterglass Placement for 1944, Best Wardroom Vacuuming for 1953, Special Mention for Porthole Windexing for 1962, All-Fleet Bird-Napkin Citation for 1971, Best Deck Mopping Crew for 1980, and Fastest Head Detail for 1989. I think that that last accomplishment is a very significant one for a man well into his sixties. The remains will remain in the walk-in freezer for remains on the *Natchez* until any remaining relatives can be informed of the remains. The most recent family information we have on file is a Philadelphia street address from 1942, so if he had any friends—I mean, it would be helpful if one of his many friends would come forward with a more recent address so that we can ship him—so we'll know where to forward the remains. Now, let's have a moment of silence for this proud sailor who has given his life for his country."

The hiss continued. Miles was lying in his rack feeling pity for the loneliness of Ditchfield's life when he became aware of a pair of voices, thinking they must be down the P-way, then realized they were near the doctor, were being picked up by the mike and broadcast, just audibly, beneath the hiss, throughout the ship.

". . . was giving it to them three at a time at the Puss-in-Boots Club on Magsaysay."

"The old fucker. Wonder he didn't bust his ticker then."

"They say he had all kinds of little brown bastards. Little aboriginals down in Aussie Land, little Flips and Malaysians, little Japs and Vietnamesers, little Koreans, even little Eskimos, up in the Aleutians."

"That shit true?"

"The oldest ones are in their forties now, lots of them in their thirties and twenties and teens, all the way down to this year's bambinis. And next year's."

"He did all that scrogging? A dude that old?"

"Man, what ya think he stayed in the fucking navy for?"

"What a life. It's all right, though. He served his country, he brought his kids into the world, he kept all the heads clean—he was the best at it, they say. There are guys don't do that shit by half."

"Yeah. It's not a wasted life."

"Want the rest of these Fritos?"

"You left the moldy ones."

The doctor ended the moment of silence with "Dennis Ditchfield, United States Navy, Master Chief Petty Officer. That is all."

Miles was grateful to the doctor for eulogizing Ditchfield, that the chaplain hadn't been required to try it.

A knock, as though the person in the P-way had been waiting for the doctor to sign-off. Miles said from his rack, "Come in." The XO, with a clipboard under each arm and another in his hand, was standing there holding the knob, a besieged look pulling down the froggish cast of his eyes and nose and mouth.

"Got a minute, looks like you do, orders from DETNAVNATA, they're putting you on the AAVLOR-7, you want a copy?" Awkwardly he exchanged the clipboard in his hand for the one in his left armpit and thumb-flipped the sheets, then scrunched one up by bunching his fingers on it and tore it off and dropped it on the desk. "All right? Got questions, Lebedeen can answer them."

The XO was retreating but Miles didn't understand so he said, "What you mean?"

"Don't ask me, command wants chaplains, you know, civilians involved, hundred ninety-two, hysterical, I don't know, you're trained to deal with upset people, right?"

"You mean—I'm going with the marines?"

"Stop making small talk, Banquette, I haven't got the time, Lebedeen can fill you in." The XO backed into the P-way. The ship roll threw the door fully open and then slammed it shut behind him.

Frost came down on his skin like the feeling of stepping into the Illinois night in February in shirtsleeves to set out the garbage and having the ice drizzle on his face as the wind got through his shirt like frozen hands running all over his skin. He was going with the marines in the morning. He was scared. He had no way of thinking about it, there was only the crystallization of frost across his skin, and he was lying straight as a dead man on the tomb slab of his rack. Ditchfield. The old man was dead, and it was only the start of things. There would be many more deaths, and Miles would witness a number of them. The skunked-up cabbage smell of the burning corpses came back to him so powerfully that his stomach rose with nausea through the ice that encased it. Men would die. They would die and the corpses would burn. He also might die, and if he didn't die, he would watch others suffer and burn, and he didn't want to see it, he didn't want to go. This was happening because of his original sin, his willfulness acting on the possibilities posed by the death in the video arcade, the fire that he'd thought would hide everything, but it couldn't hide anything from him, because now he knew he would be punished. He couldn't breathe. The ice of fear on his skin enclosed him tightly and made the humid air of the ship even more indigestible to his lungs. He stood up and tried turning the vent control on the overhead air shaft, but it was already all the way open, the weak current of air-conditioning covering an area on his palm the size of a quarter. He would go outside—no, it would be even hotter and more humid out there—he was trapped in a tossing can. His life had been a series of escapes and he'd run out of them. He was going with the marines in the morning.

What if he were killed? No woman, no child to mourn him. Jim Banquette would be mourned—at last—but not Miles Derry. He would be targeted, mortared, misidentified as a part of this absurd navy and killed.

But he was part of it, he'd made himself so, he even had the feelings of a sailor: having no one at home to support him as he faced what was probably the most fateful morning of his life was a painfully hollow feeling, and he thought again of Michelle Banquette, irrationally craving her faith and love.

Dinner was solemn. The demise of Ditchfield, for being unremarked, was all the more oppressive, and sat atop the men's battle tensions like an arsenic icing on a cake of hemlock. Nobody spoke at all, eating with lethargic gloom in the heat. They were only four degrees north of the equator; the air-conditioning panted in the humidity, which made all the machinery sluggish; pearls of sweat formed at the tips of men's noses and dropped onto their plates as they ate. The CO's seat was empty, his presence required tonight on the flagship, while at the other end Robin's chair was also vacant. Miles wouldn't allow himself to speculate on her whereabouts. The tortured dinner—whose last would it be, Reynolds? Hawes? Lebedeen?—dragged on in the heat. The DISBO was present, his face assuming, from time to time, an enthusiastic openness, as though he'd just thought of something hilariously vulgar to entertain them with, but his expression invariably fell back into doubt, and he was silent. The food was quiche and noodles and Brussels sprouts. No matter what sequence Miles combined them in, they formed an unswallowable paste in his throat, undissolvable by the hottest coffee. One of them would have to say a word about tomorrow, anything at all about it, or Miles and the others, especially the marines, would choke on their gummy food and repressed fear. Miles was the chaplain, he would act.

He turned to Lebedeen, who, with head bent toward his plate, was making a game of wrapping noodles around his Brussels sprouts. "I'm in your AAV tomorrow," Miles told the major.

"Mm."

The men, forks paused, were watching the chaplain, who was immediately sorry he'd broken their unspoken code of silence. Having started, however, he had to continue, and said miserably, "I'll borrow some cammies. Anything else I'll need?"

The major, head down, played with his food.

"Leb? Is there anything else I'll need for the mission?"

The major turned and gave him an angry-annoyed look, eyebrows straight and eyes momentarily focusing, and he said, "What mission?"

"Tomorrow's mission?" Miles felt stupid. "You know, Burma?"

Lebedeen thought a moment, as though considering the mission for the first time. He said dryly, "Bring a damned helmet."

The major went back to his food, but he was the only one. The other men, first the marines, then the navy, one by one asked the XO's permission to leave and pushed back their chairs and wandered out of the wardroom mess. The DISBO-MORALO sat there with his elbows on the table and his hands propped in a single finger-laced fist on which sat his chin. He had an upside-down quarter-moon for a mouth, with a pipe stuck in it, and his eyes were the blank ones of a man with nothing to say. Soon he too was mumbling for permission to leave and was pushing back his chair and striding away with his hands balled up in his pockets.

The stateroom again. In his rack, as throughout the ship, the minutes moved like tombstones or fault lines or continents, shifting imperceptibly into the decades yet never filling an hour. He couldn't bear to read, he couldn't bear to play on the computer, he couldn't bear to think. The cammie uniform and helmet, which he'd borrowed from one of the marine JOs, stood waiting in the closet—shirt and pants on the same hanger, helmet sitting above them on the shelf—empty of a man. He got up, pacing before the closed cabinet. Kari, Mary Lou, Suveg. The Little Pink. The ocean. War. And who was he? What was he? He'd been Miles Derry the Drunk and Miles Derry the Recovered and Jim Banquette the Fraud and Jim Banquette the Chaplain, and now there was nothing but an empty uniform and helmet waiting for a man who didn't exist, whom he hadn't had the time or talent to create. There'd been any number and variety of panics in his life, but this one was growing so terrible he was actually beginning to feel calm, like the feeling they said you got just before freezing to death, as though he knew he was going to die and wanted only for it to be done. The blankness of tomorrow—the blankness of himself—nothing meant anything. The marines were afraid, yes, any man would be afraid, but they had their training. All he had was his acting. It wasn't going to fill the uniform and helmet waiting in the closet. At dawn, he'd fill them only with his body and go into the AAV with the scrambled Lebedeen. If Miles had the vaguest hope of reprieve, it was in a response to his fax to General McMinn about the major's state of mind, but the long minutes slid into one another and no yeoman came to his door with a message. Nothing changed at all in the dead-aired dead time of the stateroom, there was nothing but the regular dropping and upslanting of the deck as the ship tore through the night in its straight line toward the beaches of Burma.

At last, the heat had him pulling off his shirt and reclining in his rack, still in his pants, one foot on the deck. He knew he would not sleep. He lay there in the torpor, wondering for a long time if he should rise to turn off the fluorescent tube on the ceiling—darkness might cool the room—but he didn't move.

His dark fantasies:

. . . being shot in the chest or stomach or face as he ran through the surf with the marines . . . or riding the road to Rangoon in an armored vehicle as it exploded going over a mine . . . or Lebedeen allowing his unit to be overrun by the Burmese army on the streets of the capital and all of them being captured and shipped up-country to a POW camp . . . they'd be chained down together in bamboo huts with mud floors and he'd be shoulder-to-shoulder with the major, unable to swat the flies off their faces, squatting there together, shitting their pants and dying of dysentery and thirst, and Lebedeen going on madly about finding a pay phone to call his wife . . .

There was a fist landing again and again on his door, and it fired up a panic in him as he jumped bare-chested out of the rack and went for the door with the terrified knowledge that it was the XO coming to tell him he was going ashore in the first wave up the beach and oh—but it could be good news—the XO was coming to tell him he didn't have to go at all, it was a mistake, but why was the punching of his door so demanding? And when he opened it it wasn't the XO at all, but Kruger, the dark eyes enlarged behind the lenses of the black-framed glasses and the mouth already talking as he openhandedly shoved the chaplain in the chest back into the room:

"What you been saying? What you been saying? You been saying something, got to have been, no other way, that's just common knowledge, answer me, you fraud."

"What?" said Miles, walking backwards to keep his balance. "What?"

"You're just a fraud and a hypocrite telling stories about me, when you fornicated, you told me that in this very room, you fornicated once, and now you're going around telling—"

"What are you—"

"I heard them talking!" Kruger had him backed up against the bulkhead and was close enough that a fine spittle landed on Miles's face with the words: "I was going down niner deck when I heard some guys around the corner talking about me and one of them said I was 'abnormal,' what's that supposed to mean, he said, 'That Kruger, he's always fucking abnormal'—how does *he* know whether my fucking's normal or abnormal? Huh? Unless somebody *told* him, and that somebody could only be you, because you were the only one at the telephone place who—you've been telling people I'm a *sodomite*, that's the only way they'd know, just common knowledge—"

"This is Officers' Country, sailor!" Miles was too perplexed and uncomfortable to try anything but rank. "If you don't have official—"

"I ought to pound in your hypocrite face, I ought to follow the Scripture's injunction against the heretic . . ." and as Kruger began quoting, ferociously, the King James, Miles saw Robin in her bathrobe in the P-way, come to investigate the racket, and then she was gone.

"I didn't say anything to anyone," Miles tried.

"Then how'd they know that! How'd they know it! I'm going to kill you!"

"They didn't mean that, they just meant that you're kind of a freak—I mean—weird—"

"Anybody might sin! Especially with girls like that! You don't have to be a weirdo—"

"That's not what they—" And then Miles said, "No!" because Robin was coming into the room hoisting a toilet-plunger and she said, "Fuck this place, the toilets don't work right, can't get any sleep, you're assaulting an officer, squid," and to Miles's astonishment she was pummeling Kruger over the head with the plunger, and there were little bursts of toilet water as Kruger yelled and tried to cover his head with his hands and his glasses fell off and then there were men in the room, marine JOs in their khaki skivvies, taking Miles and Kruger and Robin to different corners of the room and taking the plunger away from her, and everybody was shouting. Miles thought it would wake the whole ship, if indeed anyone had been sleeping on the eve of battle. They asked Miles if he was okay, and he said yes, and they were taking Kruger away to the brig, and Robin was exiting the room saying, "*Men,*" and then the XO was there, wearing only his trousers and asking if Miles wanted Kruger to go before the CO for punishment, and Miles said no, he didn't want to pursue it, they should let Kruger go, and as quickly as it had happened he was alone again in his room. He picked up Kruger's glasses. They were intact but twisted out of shape, as though by somebody's shoe. He dropped them in the trash.

Miles was sure the only thing that had changed in the aftermath of this strange incident, and in the news of it as it traveled downdecks, was that every marine was lying awake in his rack even more tightly nerved than before. Nobody would sleep. There was nothing to do but lie there in the pitching darkness and sweat out the long approach of dawn.

In his own rack, in the stillness, time again lost its shape, slackening to nothing. He lay there in the unlit shifting room as though he were already dead and floating in that humid place, nameless and endless, where there was no height or breadth or sound or light to give dimension to a nonsequence of being that had replaced time. If this place did have a name, he didn't want to admit what it was, though he would heartily admit, had always admitted, even when he boozed and pilled—*especially* when he boozed and pilled—that he belonged here. And it wasn't possible just now to return from the metaphysical to the real because he was in fact nowhere, no place with a name, a blankness of ocean on any map, perhaps broadly marked *Andaman Sea,* but still just a blankness of water. If one went up to the plotting room one might find a red digital readout on the console of the computerized compass, 96.3364°E for longitude and 11.9011°N for latitude, but it didn't denote a place, it was just an abstraction describing a point on a grid existing nowhere but men's minds.

The places and people of his life were formless, he could call on none of them for company in the dark. They dissolved into one another as soon as he summoned them, Mary Lou becoming his mother becoming his father becoming his brothers becoming Doug Suveg becoming the DISBO becoming Major Lebedeen becoming the captain becoming Robin becoming a girl he was drunkenly driving back to his apartment who had no face or name becoming the high-school girls who could be any of the college girls becoming the girl who'd been blowing Kruger in the phone booth and Kruger becoming Ogleby becoming Smitty becoming a corpse burnt black and bald and here came the smell, the only smell, tar, burnt cabbages, and rotting skunks. The marine encampment rose in the blue light, the only memory that could thrive in this place where he was, the details accumulating like objects in a photograph being relentlessly developed in its tray; here were the blue tents, the blue jeeps, the cammied marines with their blue washed-out faces; here was the kicking-up of blue sand by spinning jeep tires and in the passenger seat the blue staring thing that had been Ogleby; here was the blue truck with the tailgate down, the blue sheet thrown back, the singed tops of heads, the surrounding details of more tents and trucks and palm trees filling themselves in, the picture tightening with details and growing darker, those burnt evil-smelling corpses lying there in the truck and the rest of the world filling in darkly, going blue to black, black as this encased night, nothing now but darkness and the smell, a sickening blackness like a bile moving within him as he lay there paralyzed with terror. He was sick, he was very sick, and who could say how many shapeless and sleepless hours had gone by before there was the rap on his door that said this day had begun?

12

Standing naked in the dark with the door open an inch, he saw, in the red light of the P-way, that it was Reynolds, his face blackened with the gunk the marines wore for night maneuvers, his eyes set in pink ovals, and he told the marine, "Thank God it's dawn—finally." Reynolds looked up and to the side, as though to point out the red lighting, that it wasn't the white they turned on at daybreak, and said, "Oh-three-thirty, Chaplain, sunrise in a hundred and twenty-eight minutes, we're in the advance party, sir, as you know"—the lieutenant glanced doubtfully at the chaplain's naked-ness—"remember?" and Miles said, "Right," though he didn't remember, hadn't studied the DICNAVABic orders in their entirety, and the marine said, "Tank deck? Fifteen minutes, sir? If you would?" and Miles said, "Right." When Reynolds was gone, Miles had the light on and was looking on the desk for the orders but couldn't find them, looked all around, they were under the desk, he picked them up and in the confusion of acronymic sentences there it was—0400—and he realized the deck wasn't moving, they must be near the invasion beaches. And so he got into the cammies, which were a bit tight. He already had his crosses and commander bars on the collars, and the name of the donating marine had been torn off from over the pocket. He put on the helmet, an unfamiliar heaviness on his head, and despite the war dress, or indeed because of it, he felt insubstan-tial, unsure, with none of the identity or authority that came with his usual uniform or with the preacher suit. He was a timorous fraud. As he started for the tank deck, it was as though he wasn't even walking, just letting his feet drop rung-to-rung on the ladders, the clumsy weight of the helmet pushing him down. He saw no one, but the sounds coming up from the innards of the ship were frantically metallic, as though platoons of monkeys in steel cages were throwing knives and spoons and toasters into metal suitcases but missing sometimes and hitting the steel bars or the metal floor and then again croink! hitting a suitcase in the monkey mania to pack as much metal as possible before leaving on an all-metal hejira to hell. A couple of levels above the tank deck he came upon marines running in the P-way in both directions, wearing only their khaki boxers, or boxers with helmets, or underwear with cammie shirts, or cammie pants with nothing else, some of them running with M-16s held bayonet-up, the red light of the P-way flashing everywhere on metal and flesh in motion. He continued down the ladder and there were more of them on the next deck and then he was on the tank-level P-way dodging the marines on his way to the iron cavern housing the bestiary of tanks and jeeps and trucks. Entering through one of the many hatches, he found a yellow-lit world stirring from hibernation, marines climbing vehicles, running from one to the next, canvas coverings thrown back and flaps flung open, some of the headlights already burning, engines being intermittently tested and shut off, and the agitated talk between men who ran and met and ran again. The seaward end had been opened at the stern gate, creating an immense square of night. Figuring that that was where he'd find Lebedeen and the AAV, Miles began his nervous approach toward the blackness, forcing his steps, a mechanical man, knowing he must step into the square of night and accept, despite the bile of fear moving within him, all of the things the blackness held.

When he was halfway there, he was approached by Lieutenant Reynolds, who regarded the chaplain's shoes. "Sir, you're not wearing boots."

"I didn't know that. I mean, about needing them."

"Sir, there's no time. You'd better put this on right away." It was a black round tin and Miles took it and the marine was gone and when Miles opened it it was more of the black facial gunk. It smelled like fresh asphalt and it made everything more unnerving to him: the clanking metallic mysterious preparations, the sick-yellow lighting, the green metal trucks and jeeps rising all around him, and, farther back, the high-nozzled block-on-block hulkishness of tanks that looked capable of crushing villages beneath their obscenely segmented treads, and he imagined the torpedo shells and lashings of fire that could explode from the tank cannons and destroy any number of human beings in a moment. Blackening his face with his fingertips, he felt again the biles of sickness and gloom moving within him and perceived that he was blotting himself out with every finger-layering of the gunk on his face.

At the open end of the tank deck stood Reynolds and Lebedeen, their faces too black and far away to be read, and Miles was afraid anyway of what might've been legible in their faces as he started toward the two marines, who were outlined in the yellow perimeter of light just before it terminated against the square of blackness into which he'd have to follow the major. Miles didn't want to go, but his desires didn't matter. They'd become irrelevant at a moment that had slipped his attention, and he wondered when it had been and realized with a shock of certainty that it was the moment when he'd first stepped aboard the ship. There was nothing left of him; he was an empty man walking toward the square-edged night; he felt the awful sagging illness within him; he walked toward the blackness only because it was the only thing ahead of him.

Reynolds lowered a clipboard he'd been studying and said, "Major, the chaplain is here," unnecessarily unless Lebedeen had fully lost his mind by now, which Miles thought possible. "Shall we?" said the lieutenant as though they were friends without ranks, as though they were simply going someplace together. Well, they were, and that made it all the more awful; they would simply step into the blackness as if it were a mundane affair. Miles realized that the final moment of a man's life was not an extraordinary one, just the last in a series, a thought, a movement, the end. Terrible knowledge he'd never wanted. Reynolds, his back to the night, was stepping beneath the lip of the deck and descending the ladder to the AAV and disappearing. Miles turned to Lebedeen. "Leb? After you?" The painted face was without eyebrows or mouth, just the pink ovals around the red enlarged eyes. It was a face that had been trained to speak matter-of-factly and confidently and knowledgeably, and when it spoke now it did so in all those ways, if not about the mission:

"We passed Peacock Island in the night."

Miles, accustomed to the madness, didn't hesitate. "We'll hit it on the way back."

"There is no way back." And then the major was stepping beneath the lip of the deck as the lieutenant had done, green binoculars swinging side to side around his neck, and then he was gone. Miles thought desperately

of turning around and running through the yellow headlights of the waiting vehicles shouting that he wasn't James Banquette at all, that he'd never
been, but in the most insane of circumstances only the insane could speak
sanely and the major had done so—*There is no way back.* So Miles, his soul
feeling as though it were sinking and draining and evaporating into a hollow within him, lowered a foot beneath the lip of the deck. And climbed
down toward the waters of the night.

There were no lights burning in the AAV, and he went down the ladder
with the pessimistic faith that the hated craft was there. At the end of the
ladder, he let go and fell the last four feet, landing on hands and knees with
his helmet bang-bouncing on his head.

"Watch your step, sir," said the lieutenant.

"Are you going to say that throughout the mission?"

"Sir? I don't get your meaning."

"Sorry. I'm just—never mind."

"He's a psychic," said Major Lebedeen fearfully in the dark, apparently
meaning Miles. "If he says you're going to say 'Watch your step,' that's what
you're going to say. Somehow he knew I was going to show him pictures of
my family. He knew where that M-16 clip was. Don't ask him the future.
Things we don't want to know."

The invisible helmsman throttled the AAV forward with a jolt, and the
chaplain and the major and the lieutenant sidestepped into their balance.
Lebedeen's shadow climbed up onto the outline of the railing as though
that were the best place from which to monitor things with the binoculars,
though he wasn't using them yet.

They were quiet, and Miles tried to contain the illness of fear by thinking about the mission only as a mechanism of delivery: two AAVs would
constitute the LST's advance party, this one and the other just now revving
away from the yellow-lit stern. Miles figured he was attached to Lebedeen's
because it must be the command craft, the one for officers, and the other
must be for the enlisted who were bringing the equipment and supplies
that Lebedeen would need for his command post at the beachhead, which
wouldn't be formed until after the AAVs from the other ships and the
copters from the *Natchez* and the armored vehicles from the *Harding* had
succeeded in the initial assault. It was the major's job, Miles understood
from lunchtime conversations, to direct, while using binoculars and radio,
the armored-vehicle embarkation: the *Harding,* the only ARG unit with a
flat bottom (since the sabotage of the *Buchanan*), would pull up to the

beach, the bow doors would open, and the causeway, supported by the cable system suspended from the twin derrick arms that rose over the prow, would slide out, and the trucks and jeeps and tanks would come rolling forth, over the waves and through the surf and onto the beach. Then Lebedeen's AAV would land and the major would take field command of his troops. Miles understood also that the guns of the *Harding* and the choppers from the *Natchez*—none of the helos were in the air yet, lest too much noise spoil the surprise of attack—were the only protection for the craft he was riding in, and should a Burmese battery spot them . . . This was where he stopped thinking.

The outline of Reynolds was speaking into the outline of the radio handset held up to his mouth, numbers and logisticalese. Miles wondered: would this garbage be the last thing he ever heard? They'd raced far from the ship, the square of yellow from the open stern was small, shrinking, the only light in the night, the fantail pointing away from the unseen shore to conceal the ship's position. When the AAV turned for its coordinates, the light from the *Harding* disappeared. Miles examined the night, but it was too dark for him to locate the forms of the other ships, though he knew they must be there. The lieutenant was still conversing with the handset, speaking numbers and acronyms and listening to more of the same cackled back. Then the lieutenant turned to the shape of Lebedeen, who was still sitting on the lip of the AAV, spray at his back, legs dangling, balancing there as the craft sped over the smoothness of the bay, and Reynolds said, "Major, Coordinate Gamma Bravo Seventy-Niner confirmed," but Lebedeen didn't reply, he didn't move, he was just sitting up there balancing on the railing, nothing but darkness where his face should be, as though it were made of the same metal as the rounded outline of the helmet, and Reynolds repeated the coordinates and said, "Sir, we'll overshoot, the bridge is waiting for your acknowledgment," but the outline of Lebedeen remained silent, unmoving, and Miles could imagine an indifferent look of paralysis beneath the major's helmet, the zoned-out eyes and angling eyebrows and slightly parted mouth, the inertness of *I'm not here.*

Lieutenant Reynolds said, "Sir, we'll overshoot the pattern!" and the major gave a small motion, it was a tiny rise of the shoulders, barely signifying a shrug, as though he hadn't the energy for anything more. This gesture was enough, seemingly, to tilt his balance—or was the gesture merely the first nudge of his intention?—or was it an imperceptible nod of the AAV?—or was it a simple loss of balance? The major fell backward. His shoulders and head fell away from the men watching him and his arms never reacted and his knees remained bent as they rose and then his boots were showing the shapes of their soles as he rolled backward and out of sight without any sound to challenge the spray or the engine. The major was gone! The lieutenant looked at Miles, and Miles looked at the lieutenant, and they looked back at the outline of the railing to affirm its vacant reality, and the lieutenant was saying, "Holy shit! Holy shit! What do we do! Do something! Fucking do something! Holy fuck!" Time and identity and danger were meaningless as Miles acted—his legs were transporting him from one void to another, no willfulness or possibilities here, perhaps because he no longer thought of himself as anyone—he was an outline in a set of relations—he didn't even have to think of himself as ranking, the lieutenant's hysteria took care of that—and with nothing to lose or gain, the chaplain/nonchaplain who no longer had any idea of himself and who had no time to be afraid was running without being aware of his legs moving and he had his hands on the lip of the iron wall—up, presto, straddle, a fluid movement without thinking over the side and whomp-crashing into the water—like falling on exploding glass—and down into the sightless soundless airless world of tropical warmth, and then kicking back up, breaking the surface with an eruption of sight and sound and quick-inhaling, and then it was time to look for the major. The direction he chose was instinctual, the opposite of the craft's direction as he heard it churning by in the distance, and only now, as he swam in the dark, did a formal thought occur to him: he might never find the major and swim in a straight line to nowhere. But he heard something. It was a gurgle-shriek, a screaming over an intaking of water, and Miles turned toward it, his arms cycling fast and his legs kicking and his face emerging side to side to gulp at the air, the screaming closer, interrupted by hacks and gurgles but coming back each time in a madness of pain that Miles took no time to speculate about, and then his head was blomping against something hard-and-soft, he imagined it was the major's back or shoulders, the screaming was coming from here, pitched so highly it was going raw, and Miles brought up his head to say "Leb!" He got his arms around the marine's waist but Lebedeen knee-kicked him away and Miles kept trying to grab the flailing elbows and all the while the screaming was hollowing itself into increasing hoarseness, losing itself in hacked-out gargles, then coming back loud and raw. A light passed over them. The AAV had come circling back and it churned the water as Miles locked his arms around the major's arms and held them behind the major's back, and as the major kicked and twisted his screams were louder than the engine of the approaching craft. The light, beaming in contradiction of standing order, passed over them once more and then returned and stayed, too bright for Miles to keep his eyes open against it. The lieutenant was yelling orders at the helmsman but the shrieking and the engine hid most of them from Miles. With the light on him and his eyes shut, he could see all the webbing of the veins in his retinae, and the lieutenant kept yelling and the engine kept roaring and the major kept screaming as he tried to twist and kick his way free, and the roar of the AAV came closer as it churned them up and down in the water and then there were hands on Miles. He bumped against the hull and felt the hands sliding off him toward the major. Then the lieutenant was saying, "We got him, up, grab him, we got him, that's it, up," and the major was gliding up and away from Miles and gave him a final tremendous kick, knocking Miles back, and he tried looking. Opening his eyes changed nothing, in the spotlight it was a world of blood, he was swimming in it. As his vision adjusted he could see the gray hull of the AAV but the water was still red. They had the landing-gate down, they had Lebedeen up on it, the lieutenant and the helmsman were dragging the screaming coughing flopping Lebedeen into the vehicle. An object bobbed against Miles's head. Grabbing at it more out of instinct than thought he saw that it was a boot and he brought it with him like an absurd prize of war as he swam through the water, which still looked like blood in the white light, toward the craft.

"Oh my Christ!" said Lieutenant Reynolds as Miles pulled himself onto the landing gate. Miles could see only the two shadow men leaning over the third, who was thrashing and coughing and screaming on the deck. It was hard climbing onto the gate with the boot in his hand so he threw it into the AAV and its flying shadow hit one of the shadow heads and he heard the other shadow head, Reynolds, say again, "Oh my Christ!"

Then Miles was standing, ape-walking toward them on the slippery deck, and he fell on one knee and both hands, thinking it was water, but when he stood up his hands came up sticky with blood and the lieutenant and the helmsman were both yelling and the major was rolling on the deck and hoarsely shrieking with an insane pitch to suggest there was nothing left of his mind.

It took a moment of watching Lebedeen for Miles to see that the major

was still wearing one boot and the other leg of course had no boot, but neither was there a foot where it should be.

Miles was capable of just enough thought to coincide with action: he
pulled his shirt open, popping buttons off, ordering "Hold him down!
Hold him!" The lieutenant sat on the major's chest and the helmsman sat
on the major's legs and Miles knelt next to the footless appendage that was
shooting spurts of blood and he ripped his shirt for the tourniquet. He felt,
for the first time in the act-now-think-later intensity of the crisis, an emotion concentrated enough to condense itself into small words in his mind:
Leb, you dumb-ass. Then Miles was busy wrapping the shirt strip about
halfway down from the major's knee, not knowing as he tightened it
whether he were applying it in the right spot, but having no time to question himself, he was kneeling in blood, he tore the remainder of his shirt
into strips and worked fast to wrap and tighten and tie them farther down
on the leg and the major was still screaming and hacking and trying to
twist free and the engine was whirring without taking them anywhere, and
Miles's next thoughts came out immediately as orders to the helmsman:
"All right, get that gate up and let's get the hell out of here, I'll sit on his
legs, radio, tell 'em what happened, tell 'em we're coming back, lieutenant
you stay on his chest like that, all right let's move *now!*" and the helmsman
yelled, "Aye-aye sir," leaping up to do as told, and the major shrieked and
twisted as Miles and Reynolds held him down. The AAV pitched and
turned and roared forward. On the way back all he had to do was sit on the
major's legs; he could rest; he was soaking, bare-chested, it felt good in the
humidity, but the fatigue came on. He realized he'd been wearing the chin-
strapped helmet the whole time, it was heavy, but he was too tired to take it
off, his shoulders and arms and legs aching with weakness, his weight the
only power keeping the major's legs down, weariness taking the place of
crisis to contain thought. Except: as his eyes roamed the shadows of the
deck and stopped at the boot shape, he was aware dimly and morbidly of
what it contained, and there was a creaky mechanism of logic in his mind
that concluded that the only possible cause was the prop.

The square of yellow light at the end of the *Harding* enlarged steadily as
Miles watched it in a hypnosis of exhaustion. The square grew in the dark
into a television screen, an odd offering, black figures of men moving with
mysterious purpose among the black shapes of trucks and tanks; there was
the occasional, distant, metal-clanking sound. The AAV skim-raced over
the flat water and the major screamed and struggled and the face of

Reynolds, which was toward Miles as they sat on Lebedeen, displayed, despite the darkness and the cammie gunk, pure horror, delineated by a longness of features and round panicked eyes that Miles refused to take on, so searchingly did they implore his own. He focused instead on the yellow TV screen formed by the open stern of the *Harding*, where, in the foreground, a clutch of men stood with elbows highly splayed as they followed with binoculars the trailing spotlight of the AAV. Miles, who'd assembled them by the words he'd given, and who, at one time, would've enjoyed his power to assemble men through orders, thought of his authority in an egoless way, a power as natural and essential as being able to move one's arm or leg.

He became aware, as though floating closer toward reality from the realm of his dazed exhaustion, that the major was no longer screaming or moving. How long since he'd stopped? Was he dead? In shock? It was as much as his mind could ask; he was still heaving-exhaling from his efforts, and he heard his own breathing for the first time; the formal part of his mind was still not fully operative; he couldn't begin to say if Lebedeen was dead or alive; he couldn't say if they'd been in the water an hour ago or five minutes ago.

The open stern of the tank deck, no longer a TV screen, was close enough to have become a stage lined with players in costumes of cammie or khaki, standing bent over with hands on knees, shouting and watching from the very edge of the deck. Their faces, some blackened, some not, were character-sketched into looks of puzzlement, or dread, or shock, or confusion, or chagrin, or fascination, or disbelief.

"Jesus!" "What in hell happened?" "Christ he look dead don't he?" "This mean the rest of us ain't going?" "Look at all that blood." "Shot through the head." "Through the gut." "Look at it, that's disgusting." "Gross, dude."

At last Miles saw that a vital mission component had been irreparably fucked up. The entire deployment of armored vehicles would be delayed.

They were directly beneath the ladder, the point they'd started from, and down the ladder came the doctor and the medics and a lot of other men filling the AAV, and they handed down a stretcher. They pushed Miles and the lieutenant out of the way and tied the limp cammied footless Lebedeen to the stretcher and upright-up he went. There was so much fast and speculative talk, among those in the AAV and those watching from above, that it sounded like a party full of excited drunks, and Miles knew there wouldn't be a fact among them because in the crush they were all ignoring the lieutenant and the helmsman and him. They were the last three out, and the other two had already climbed the ladder, but before he did he had a last look around, surveying the deck, incredibly painted hull-to-hull with blood, and then he saw the boot in the corner and, with a quiver of revulsion, turned away from it. And then he thought the major might need its contents. So Miles swallowed his disgust and reached down to pick the heavy thing up by its bloody laces. He climbed onto the lip of the AAV, which was now tethered to the ship, and took hold of the ladder with his free hand and pulled himself up.

It was clumsy, climbing with the boot swinging from one hand, and by the time he was at last emerging onto the deck Reynolds and the helmsman had begun to relate, each to a gathering group of men, the story. But when these men, first one by one, and the rest of them all at once, noticed Miles climbing out of the night and onto the deck, they gave their attention solely to him. Reynolds and the helmsman stopped talking and nobody else spoke and everyone's faces, painted and unpainted, were as long-jawed and frightened-eyed as though Miles were a disfigured walking corpse. Self-consciousness paralyzed him; he stood there; he looked down at himself. The cammie pattern of his pants had a new mottling to it, shiny with jigsaw splotches of blood, and his naked stomach and chest had large caking areas of the red-brown stuff, and dangling from the laces twined in his fingers was the tilted boot whose contents, suspected by every man, were pit-patting a stream of blood onto the deck. Looking back at the sailors and marines from beneath his helmet and through his face-black, Miles knew he must appear to them as though he were a monstrous warrior climbing up from the trenches of blood-and-hell battle.

He had his first complex thought since diving after the major: how strange that he should look like he was coming straight up from hell, when the only place he'd come from was the water, and all the many times in his life when he'd been to hell and back he'd never looked this bad. He walked through the silent congregation of men, who opened a way for him, some of them saluting. He didn't return it: he had the thing they feared hanging from that hand. To none of them and all of them he said, "I better get this up to sick bay."

He was running up a ladder and turning for the next one when he saw the DISBO talking to two sailors. "Well, if you can't afford it you shouldn't fucking play. It's my own damn fault anyway for taking IOUs. If poker wasn't against the fucking UCMJ I'd have you—what?" The DISBO turned to see what had distracted and enlarged the sailors' eyes, and when he saw the chaplain he had to mouth-juggle his pipe to keep it from tumbling out. "Jesus, Jim! What in fuck happened to *you*?"

Miles was on the first rung going up and eager to keep ascending but he stopped to say, "Leb fell out of the AAV and I had to go in after him. They can maybe reattach this," and he raised the boot, and was turning to run up the ladder but the DISBO was right behind him saying, "Way to go, Jimbo, you're a fucking war hero!" and he gave him a pounding on the shoulder that threw Miles against the ladder, both hands opening, one catching himself on a rung and the other releasing the boot, which fell soundlessly until there was a climp and a clomp, and looking down he saw, around the ladder, the oval space that was replicated on every deck below, all the way down to the engine level, a dizzy blur telescoping to nothing, and then he heard a series of clips and clonks and thumper-thumps and katonka-tonkas and there was finally the distant skiddle and thud repre-senting the unknown resting place.

"Goddamn you!"

"Jim—"

"DISBO, you idiot!"

"Now Jimbo—"

"You've lost his foot, I'll kill you!"

"Jim, you've got battle fatigue or some—"

Miles grunted dismissively, and running down the ladders he knew he *could've* killed the DISBO, not for Lebedeen or even out of the outraged propriety of a chaplain carrying a disattached appendage back to its owner, but simply because the DISBO was such a hard-assing kid-smiling pipe-smoking shallow-japing ego-posturing asshole. Miles went down a few decks before beginning his frenzied inquiry. "See that foot go by? That boot? See it or what?" and down to the next deck, and the next, asking sailors' backs, their faces turning, shock-hanging expressions at the look of him, no one understanding, no time to clarify, they'd know it if they'd seen it, the next deck, the next. Along the way he was tangentially aware of the rapid air-sucking thwacks of a helo coming close, staying, staying, lifting away, and only later would he learn it had taken Lebedeen to the *Natchez*. Running, squatting, asking without explaining, he searched the ladder vicinities of every deck for the boot—"That boot fly by? Go bouncing? Seen it?"—and the sailors stared at the helmeted black-faced bare-chested bloody-cammied boot-talking chaplain as though he were from a country they'd only heard about—War—as though he were speaking a language they should've understood but could only be transfixed by, as though, if they'd known where he'd been and what he meant, they might well wish not to understand. Nobody asked. He kept running down the ladders, inquiring, looking in corners, finding nothing, it could've been three minutes or thirty before the 1MC ordered, "Will the chaplain please report to the wardroom," and he ignored it, still looking, despairing of finding it, time passing, again the 1MC ordering, "Will the chaplain please report to the wardroom at once," and he started up, not from obedience, but because it occurred to him that he could give orders for a 1MC announcement of his own: "All hands be on the lookout for a USMC boot, shoe size unknown, left foot—if found please return to Major Lebedeen in sick bay." He'd get the XO's approval; where was the XO, in the wardroom? In Officers' Country he passed an open hatch and the milky illness look of dawn was bisected into a lighter illness that was the sky and a darker one that was the sea. If there was nothing to love above or below that horizon, at least it was only daybreak, too early for the heat and the lung-clogging humidity, and he had no ability or desire to guess the meaning of this new day. So the wardroom was a surprise. He opened the door and the men sitting around the table for breakfast—none of them marines—pushed back nineteen chairs, leaping to attention, a trickle of applause and then a waterfall of it, keeping him in the doorway, as though the sound were a force he couldn't press against. It was confusing: he couldn't see why he should be applauded: he'd lost the boot. One of the JOs yelled over the applause, "Speech."

"I lost the foot. All hands have to look."

But no one heard. It was an ovation. The men regarded him with several varieties of awe, with startled eyes or unhinged mouths or faces respectfully set. It was as though they'd all heard that a warrior was walking their decks and they hadn't believed it, but now they did, his bloody bare-chested black-faced helmeted presence going beyond any notion of heroism they'd been able to fantasize in a peacetime navy. Miles thought their praise extravagant—the way he looked was an accident, making it appear he'd been through more—he felt as out of place and uncertain as on the first day he'd come into this room, when he hadn't known a single DICNAVABic word or the seating arrangement or whether he should've brought his hat.

The captain, coming around the table toward him with his white hair combed entirely back and his red face smiling and his hand extended, said, "I'm making a recommendation, I've already got them looking for the paperwork. Banquette, you're a goddamn hero and the rest of us haven't even had breakfast yet."

The others went from clapping to laughing.

"Captain, we've got to get on the 1MC so the major can get his boot. The DISBO slapped me and I dropped it."

"Don't worry, he's gotten the boot all right, I just heloed him over to the flagship, he's going to the hospital in Singapore, we'll never have to look at his sorry puss again. And if the DISBO slaps you around, just slap him back. That's an order. Who the hell's he think he is, Patton? You're the war hero, you do the slapping. The son-of-a-bitch is just jealous. Now I'm gonna sit down and you stand at the other end of the table there and tell us all about it."

"Sir?"

"Tell us what happened out there. In your own words."

"Captain, are you sure Major Lebedeen's going to be—"

"Tell us all about it, I'm ordering you, Chaplain."

"Well sir—he fell in—I went in after him. That's all, really."

"How can that be all?"

"Damned modesty," said the XO. "You know how these religious guys are. Probably thinks he'll go to hell if he starts to look too good."

"Goddamn it," said the CO. "I want to hear about it. Tell us what you were thinking when that damned coward jumped overboard."

"Captain, he didn't jump—he kind of just—fell."

"What were your thoughts," said the XO, "as you went in after him?"

"Sir, I had no thoughts. I was just reacting."

"Weren't you afraid of sharks?"

"I really wasn't thinking, sir."

"You must've been doing a lot of thinking," said the XO. "Quick thinking."

"I know what he was thinking," said the CO. "He was thinking, 'This goddamn coward's jumping overboard, and it's up to me to save the mission—from cowardly jarheads—for the honor of the United States Navy.'"

They were all explaining it now, even the JOs—how Banquette had been thinking about his family, and all of their families, how it would imperil every man's life and reputation if the coward Lebedeen were permitted to swim back to the ship, how Banquette had known that only an extraordinary act of courage could kick up everyone's morale, how Banquette feared sharks but had gone in anyway, how Lebedeen had begged him to let him drown rather than force him to go into battle, how they'd wrestled in the water even as they debated tankpower versus airpower versus seapower, how the major started raving about the marine corps being superior to the navy, how he started ranting that the mission was flawed, that they were all going to die, how Banquette, making exception to his ministerial vows, knowing that God would understand, punched Lebedeen in the mouth rather than hear the mission disparaged, how he pulled the major onto the craft and arrested him for treason and took the helm himself and returned the AAV to the stern of the tank deck, where he'd been applauded by three hundred men as a naval hero.

"Man," said the XO, "that's one hell of a story."

"It's one hell of a *navy* story," said the CO. "The navy is always saving the lives of those marine pussies, that's military history. I think we have a real strong basis for a recommendation here."

Again everyone was applauding, some were whistling, a man shouted, "Guts and glory," another "Dude dude dude," and another "Big navy balls."

When the applause waned the captain said, "Seen the doctor yet?"

"Sir, I don't need a doctor."

Said a JO, "What a testicular gent."

"Aren't you in pain? How many times were you shot?"

"Sir, I'm fine."

"Christ, you're the toughest chaplain I've ever seen. Usually they have to wear a goddamn jock to play shuffleboard."

"Well, I'd better go now, sir." He wanted to get a shower. He thought even if they found the boot it would be too late to help the major, who, though apparently still alive, had been disattached from it too long and was now on a different ship. "If you'll excuse me, sir," he said, but:

"Stay put, Chaplain." Then the CO said to the XO, "Look at this stud cock, he's all hot for Rangoon."

"One medal before breakfast isn't enough for him."

The CO told Miles, "Lieutenant Reynolds has relieved Lebedeen and already deployed out. Your eagerness to engage the enemy is duly noted, Chaplain, as is the enormous size of your nutsack, and I'll reference your hunger for battle in my recommendation. But for now you're staying right on this goddamn ship. This command isn't going to lose its first hero just because you're feeling cocky and reckless and need to go out and kick all the Burmese tail you can find. I've got the one thing no other CO in this WESTPAC has, maybe the world: a chaplain with balls the size of church bells, these others just have rosary beads, and the size of your huevos reflects extremely favorably on this command. Now you go back to your stateroom and pray for little starving Africans or whatever else you do and stay there doing it till I'm ready to show you off."

"Okay, sir."

"Excuse me?"

"I mean aye-aye, sir."

"All right. Now get your holy-joe big-balled crotch out of here before you make these JOs feel like they have even smaller dicks than they do."

He was standing in the shower cubicle thinking he was entirely naked when he heard rain on the roof but felt nothing and realized he was still wearing the helmet. Undoing the chin strap, he knew he wasn't entirely back in the world yet. He threw the helmet into the sink with a *thump-croik!* and took an illegally continuous shower, leaning his face into the warm spray, and it was glorious and soothing to let the water stream down and over him, and soaping away the cakes of blood he felt his aversion to them, especially as they reconstituted themselves into liquid blood around his feet. And then he thought of the major's foot. God. And the odd way everyone had been. As though he'd actually thought everything out before acting, as though he'd understood every implication of the major's fall. He'd only done what was necessary, perhaps wouldn't've been able to function at all had he been thinking; in any case there'd been no opportunity for thought, it had happened and then it was over, fast, either a very long five minutes or a very short hour. He'd gone in and found him and restrained him, nothing else. He couldn't see why everybody wanted to pump it up into something larger than it was.

Stepping out of the shower and toweling himself he was more tired than he'd realized. There was a slackness from his shoulders down his back over his hips and down his legs to his feet. He had only enough energy to cross to his rack and stretch into it, as though his body had known to reserve this much terminal power and nothing more. On his stomach with his face to the bulkhead and his arms angled out beyond his head on the cool sheet. Out.

There were no dreams, no passage of time, not even the vaguest sleeping sense of its passing. When he awoke, it was as though it were morning, any morning, except he'd left the light on, there were no thoughts or memories, only a contentment that the alarm on his ten-dollar watch hadn't made its cheepy-beepies because their absence meant that this again wasn't Sunday, there was no reason to get up, he could even sleep again if he wanted. They were still ambling toward Burma, an automatic dread . . . wait a minute . . . and it broke into consciousness in a clean, complete way, lacking the pain of a hangover but retaining that initial disbelief, *No, that couldn't've*—but it was true, he'd already gone on the mission, *I've already done it*, a wash of relief, then an aching in his arms and thighs accompanied the memories of swimming and the boot and the applauding men of the wardroom. It was incredible. "Smiles doesn't have any sense," his father had once said, "except to save his own sacred ass." But he had saved Lebedeen, doing the necessary thing without awareness, except it hadn't been for his own sacred ass, his father's voice was wrong. Perhaps the men in the wardroom, despite their exaggerations, had been right to applaud him. Did the CO actually like him now? Was it because he was a hero, or because he'd kept his mouth shut about the burnt bodies, or both? Would a real hero have kept his mouth shut about that? And yet it hadn't been a real issue—whom would he have told? Burning bodies. He'd burned Commander Banquette, thrown porno novels on him and lit a match and burned him more unrecognizably than any corpse on any target beach. What hero would have done that? His father was right, it was absurd to think of himself as a hero. He wondered if other heroes felt this way. Maybe you weren't really a hero *until* you felt this way.

And Lebedeen. Falling. Intentionally? Accidentally? Likely the military would never learn and likely it didn't matter and likely everything was for the best for Lebedeen. He thought of Leb together with his wife again; he didn't have a foot, she didn't have a breast. But they both had navy psychiatrists, likely he'd get a big disability award and detachment—ha—from the Corps, likely he and the wife would never work again, likely it would be nice for them, even without a foot and a breast.

Miles thought about things a long while and didn't get up to put on his trousers until there was a knock. It was a kid in enlisted blue with a clipboard. Salutes traded. "Commander, it's so exciting to meet a HONEY like you."

"A what like me?"

"A Hero of Naval Engagement, Y-Class."

"Oh, a HONEY. Well . . . I just hope the mission works out."

"Sir, you haven't heard?"

"We succeeded?" *We:* at what stage had he invested himself?

"Mission canceled, politicians talked it out, you know, all that diplomacy crap. Ask me, sir, we shoulda gone in there and set their asses on fire."

"You mean—it was all for nothing?"

"I'm sure it was the sound of our AAV motors got them talking, sir."

"You figure they heard them all the way in Rangoon?"

"Sir"—the seaman shifted foot to foot—"I got this message for you." He tore a square off the clipboard and handed it to Miles. "It's been a pleasure talking to a real HONEY like you."

Hero of Naval Engagement, Y-Class, Miles repeated in his mind, liking the ring of it.

The kid left and Miles read the message, which the route-script header showed had been sent late last night:

```
NAVNATCOM OPB275LGCO67 071291 23:58 USSNATCH[LPH665]xUSSWARHARD
[LST-2282] BANQUETTE CDR WARD

CDR BANQUETTE: UNDER ADVISEMENT YOUR CONCERNS RE MJR LEBEDEEN
[CO USMC 1381ST COMP] TO BE CONSIDERED DURING OCTOBER FITNESS
REPORT. BUT FRANKLY NO IDEA WHY NAVY CHAPLAIN SHOULD SET SELF UP
AS EXPERT ON MARINE READINESS.

BRIG.GEN. J.M.MCMINN CO 1033RD BATT
```

He crumpled it. McMinn had wanted to wait till October? The major was even less fit now than last night.

Going into the wardroom mess for lunch, he heard the conversations halting in sequence as he passed, the gazes following him to his seat, next to Lebedeen's empty one. As Miles sat down the captain raised his water glass and said, "We may as well toast the son-of-a-bitch, he's the only hero in the whole goddamn Ready Group, and he's ours. Makes us all look like a bunch of slack-weenies that it has to be the chaplain. Oh well, least it wasn't the DISBO, we'd all feel like clit-dicks." Gentle laughter. The DISBO smiled tensely around the stem of his pipe, out-MORALOed. The CO, still with his glass up, said, "To the chaplain," and everyone raised glasses and drank as the captain drank, and then he said, "It's only water, Banquette, regulation, but seeing as how you're not only the bravest fart in the room but the holiest, you shouldn't mind too much."

"Thank you, sir."

"Don't thank me yet. I'm recommending your ass for the Navy Cross. Now you can thank me."

"Sir?"

"Thank me. I'm ordering you to thank me."

"Thank you, sir."

"Don't thank me, Banquette. I'm doing this for my own feather. Looks good to have a genuine war hero in my wardroom. So don't waste your time thanking me."

"Aye-aye, sir, I won't, sir."

"You ungrateful son-of-a-bitch. Won't even thank me."

"Captain? I—"

"You may be a hero, but I'm still the CO, and I'll fuck with you any way I want to."

"Thank you, sir."

The men laughed, and the CO folded his hands on the table, grinning his authority. The food was brought out, and they began eating. Swallowing, his throat hurt as though it were a cold coming on, which was annoying and strange, he hadn't been sick since the gas-station winter of Cheyenne, then he wondered how long he'd gone around drenched on his boot search. If his heroism was costing him only a cold, how much of a hero was he? Even the CO, behind his forced disdain, thought him more of a hero than he was. As they ate, the officers were passing around a blue book open at a certain page and he had the idea it was something to do with him. When it got around the table the XO passed it to him, saying, "Seen this?" It was a color plate of a bronze cross hanging from a blue ribbon that had a white stripe down the middle. Looking more closely at the cross, he saw that its dark bronze ends were rounded, that between the crossbars there were bronze clusters of berried laurels, that in the center, in a raised circle of bronze, there was the relief of a schooner riding six great waves, her sails in full billow as she arched into her course. "'The Navy Cross,'" said the XO, reading from the text on the opposite page, "'is awarded to any person serving in any capacity with the naval service of the United States of America who distinguishes himself by extraordinary heroism in connection with military operations against an armed enemy.' That's you, Chaplain. There were armed Burmese on that beach waiting for those AAVs. You could've been shot out of the water at any time if they'd known you were there. Once it gets through channels, this is going to be your medal." Miles studied again the blue-and-white ribbon, the bronze cross hanging from it with its rounded ends and laurel clusters and full-sailed schooner. Next to seeing his daughter at twenty minutes old, the medal was the most beautiful thing he'd ever beheld, and in the scratchiness of his sore throat he felt a child's excitement that it was going to be his.

He was conscious of looking at it too long and lovingly, so he turned to pass it to the next man, but Lebedeen wasn't there.

At 1530 hours, investigators arrived from the *Natchez*, two senior-grade navy lieutenants and two marine captains, saluting him in the wardroom mess evacuated for the interview, and politely and routinely, as the five of them sat at the table for coffee, they asked him thirty or more questions about the morning. He gave the facts as simply as if he were unspooling the memory of a movie. There was only one difficult exchange, it had to do with the major falling into the water, and they didn't ask about it till the near-conclusion of the interview: they wanted to know if Lebedeen had been a coward. They'd already told Miles that the major was going to live, that he'd already denied falling off the AAV on purpose, that he'd be flown by way of hospitals in Singapore and Seoul to San Diego, where he'd be given a medical discharge—the only question being whether the discharge would be honorable or dishonorable. Miles decided that their interest in the issue went beyond a question of honor, and was afraid that a matter as important as the major's lifelong disability payments might turn on these responses, so they were the only ones he contrived, elaborating on the major's dedication to duty. . . .

One of the marines pulled from a folder a sheet of paper which he placed before the chaplain. "Sir, I don't mean to contradict you, but didn't you send this communiqué to General McMinn just last night?"

Miles touched it and glanced at it without bothering to reread it and said, "The major was despondent over his wife, that was my only concern, there's a difference between being despondent and being a coward." His cold had reached his nose; it was running. He got his handkerchief out of his back pocket and sniffed into it.

The investigators looked at one another.

"Chaplain," said one of the green-uniformed, buzz-scalped marines, folding his hands on the table and leaning toward him, "isn't it your professional opinion, as a man trained to counsel soldiers, that the mental state you ascribe to Major Lebedeen in your memo—the overly sensitive reactions to his wife's illness—doesn't it signify a kind of—a kind of womanish imbalance, a kind of cowardice in a man who should be a leader?"

"Well, I didn't say he—"

"It's the feminization of the military," said the other marine. "When women act like men and men act like women, it isn't good for men *or* women. By the time it's over they'll have us all in skirts sitting in sensitivity classes."

One of the navy lieutenants said, "Eric, you would enjoy that way too much." But nobody laughed.

"Chaplain," said the other marine, after a sour look at the lieutenant, "don't you think that your psychological profile of Major Lebedeen indicates that he was no longer a true marine, and that therefore his actions do not adequately represent the unusually high standards and training of the United States Marine Corps?"

"Well, I didn't—"

"The chaplain," said one of the navy investigators, "with all due respect"—nodding to Miles—"is not as qualified as you gentlemen to say who is and who is not a true marine. Let's not stray from the purpose of this interview. The point isn't 'Who's a true marine?' but 'Who's a true navy man?' The man sitting before you is a true navy man. Obviously, the superior training he has received from the United States Navy has led directly to his becoming a naval combat hero. He deserves the Navy Cross."

The interview was soon concluded; they had to go interview Reynolds and the helmsman, who were up for commendations.

As the investigators and Miles were going out the door, the XO, who'd been waiting outside, showed him a radio message: the admiral was requesting the honor of the presence of Commander James J. Banquette at dinner tonight in his private mess aboard the USS *Natchez*. Miles was uncertain about meeting the admiral but experienced a boy's anticipation of his first helo flight. At 1830 hours, in a clean, pressed uniform, he was standing where men in headphones were indicating for him to stand on the fantail at twenty paces outside a white-painted circle quad-sected by an X that marked the landing spot. The sun was as hat-baking hot as though it were noon, and the visor of his cap wasn't long enough, and even with the dead man's sunglasses on, he was squinting against the sea, a blue mirror flinging light in his face. From far off came the air-sucking throb of a helo. It came closer, a chop-whipping sound, and then the shadow of the thing was growing over him, sparing him the sun but creating a deafening wind that blew his clothes tightly about him and made him put both hands on his cap as the gray navy helo, a long cabin with two sets of blades, fore and aft, descended before him like a mechanical god. The headset men waved him toward the opening hatch with its down-folding steps. Miles ran. In the cabin he strapped himself into a window seat, the only passenger in the space of a bus. The pilot, acknowledging him with a miked "Good afternoon, Commander," nodded the back of his head at him and pulled the copter immediately off the deck, and the down-drag held Miles at a tilt against the seat. Out the window the horizon whirled into a diagonal of blue-bright sky on one side and sun-reflecting sea on the other—or were they transposed? No, the horizon rotated into his expectation for it, and they flew as straight and as smoothly as though they were gliding on glass. The whirring of the engines and the chopping of the blades were softened by the painful plugging of his ears, which was a result of the air-pressure differential working on his cold—the running in his nose dried up and contracted into a painful hardening snot, and his eyes felt hotly sucked into his head, and his ears were congesting so completely that he was afraid some inner convolution would rupture. Indeed, he was suffering more than he had during his heroism. Out the window, the ships were anvils cast against the blue-steel surface of the sea. They were under way again for the Philippines, and at the edge of his window the green Malay coast drifted by. He shut his eyes and stuck his pinkies into his ears in a careful and useless attempt to work something loose. Then there was an up-drag on his body, and his left ear popped relievingly with an influx of helo racket. When he looked out the window it was filled with an anvil shaped like the *Natchez*, its flat top decorated with helo shapes and divided by a single tall superstructure. Then the carrier disappeared beneath them, and there was nothing but sea and sky and horizon. They were going down fast, the up-drag was increasing, and the other ear popped. The landing was as gentle as accommodating oneself into an easy chair.

The hatch opened, the steps folded down, he was stepping onto the deck in the noisy wind of the blades with his hand on his hat. There were enlisted men in headsets and an ensign in navy khaki and a lieutenant in marine green and they were all saluting. He switched hands on his hat and returned the formality quickly. Handshakes, the officers. Hand motions, saying come-with. They weren't able to speak until they were across the deck and through a hatch, and then the talk was of the greatness of the honor, a man like him, they related to him exaggerated versions of his exploit, and if they'd given him a chance to talk he wouldn't've known how to correct them. He was learning again, in the fact of his fame, how unprepared and confused he was. He was nervous to be soon meeting the admiral, and not only the admiral but, according to the marine JO, General McMinn and members of both COs' staffs.

Up many ladders, through decks busy with purposefully walking men, he followed the ensign and lieutenant through a floating metropolis, twelve times as large as the *Harding*, solid as a city, too mammoth and deeply keeled to register any lurch of the sea. Fifteen ladders and his knees were aching. "This way, Commander," and a door was opened into a low-lit paneled room, the admiral's private mess, with a round table at the center, white-covered and laid out with symmetrical placements of glittering goblets and silverware and various dimensions of china. The table was surrounded by high-backed green-cushioned wooden armchairs—around these stood officers in khaki or green who stopped talking and turned to look as the war hero was led into the room.

No salutes, informality, a couple of handshakes and shoulder-clappings and pleased-to-meet-yous. Admiral Jiggerston was a reedy, red-skinned man whose ancient head was dusted around the top with white hair. His head was a red podlike thing culminating from a red, webby neck, which expanded craggily into what was visible of his chest in the V of his shirt. His small green eyes clashed with the red flesh, but were crinkle-friendly as he shook hands and said, "I've met some heroes, but I've never met a chaplain who had what it takes to be a hero. Well done, Reverend."

"Marine chaplains," said the large-shaved-head-on-a-squat-green-uniform who was General McMinn, "win medals all the time. See a lot more combat duty. Your typical navy chaplain is usually just a custodian of morality."

"Custodian!" said the admiral. "Don't talk about him like that. He's not a janitor."

The admiral insisted that Miles sit to his immediate right. Everyone sat down. "We have Torrance Bulgorky tonight," the Admiral told Miles, looking at him with expectant pride.

Miles smiled back, unsure.

"Did you hear me? Torrance Bulgorky."

"Is that European food, sir?"

"It is not. It is my aide-de-camp. Don't you read your bulletin board? Ensign Torrance Bulgorky, first in his class, Annapolis, just graduated, do you see, has an IQ of one eighty-nine. I had to pull a string all the way up the skirt of the Navy Secretary's wife to get him assigned to us. We picked him up in Subic last week, and he's been keeping us on our toes ever since. Another example of superior naval manpower, like yourself. Torry, this is Reverend James Banquette."

A pale hand came across the table toward Miles and he shook the girl-ish thing, which was attached to a wrist so small that the end of a watch-band stuck out about an inch and a half, and the wrist became an arm without widening much, and the arm was attached to a shoulder joint that looked only slightly larger than a golf ball, and there wasn't much distance between it and the golf ball on the other side, and in the space between them sat a creamy white purple-acned face whose sharp nose supported black-framed glasses that matched the moist-looking hair that was combed straight across the top of the head, with the part just over one ear. "Sir," said Ensign Torrance Bulgorky, mouth turning up on one side. Admiral Jiggerston, the wrinkles on his red pod face coiling up happily into some-thing approaching a huge thumbprint, looked haughtily with his little green eyes at the marine general as if to say *Gotcha*. What the admiral did say was:

"Two of the most extraordinary men in the western Pacific are now sit-ting at this table, do you see. And they're navy. The reverend's CO was dying to come to dinner this evening, to show off his chaplain, but we don't want to listen to that windbag all night. Besides, I'd rather show off this hero myself." The admiral then introduced Chaplain Banquette to the other men, even though he'd shaken hands with most of them before sit-ting down—the admiral introduced him each time as "Commander James J. Banquette, naval war hero." In addition to Ensign Bulgorky and General McMinn there were a navy doctor, a navy lawyer, a navy engineer, three members of McMinn's command staff, and a couple of other naval officers whose names and positions Miles would never remember. Then, as serving boys in white jackets brought salads, the admiral, his red thumbprint of a face whorled up in pride and pleasure, told everyone The Story:

"So a chaplain of the United States Navy finds himself on an amphibi-ous-assault vehicle, do you see, it is the morning of the mission and the Burmese are threatening to land fifty-caliber shells at three hundred sixty degrees—imagine these shells exploding all around an AAV, throwing up columns of water, you can picture it, and he is with a marine who is going perfectly berserk, do you see, this marine is not so high up the evolutionary ladder, he is jittery and scratching himself in semblance of a baboon, drooling, and urinating on himself, talking, do you see, uncomprehending talk, a commander who has lost command of his command, de-nerved by battle, and in the thick of it he jumps overboard, do you see, he takes a standing dive and down he goes. That is when Chaplain Banquette, a highly trained and disciplined officer of the United States Navy, announces that he is going to go in and save that marine so that he may stand court-martial as a coward and a deserter. The others plead with him not to go, because the waters are full of sharks, do you see, but Chaplain Banquette makes an insistence that it is his duty as a naval officer, and he goes in after dictating a brief farewell to his wife and children. He does not know that the AAV propellers are chopping the AWOL marine into macaroni. In fact, as Chaplain Banquette swims by, he is dangerously near the propellers, do you see, and they actually take off a small piece of his elbow, and then a piece of his knee, and also a small piece off the back of his scalp and a bit of bone from the bump we all have on the backs of our heads, so Chaplain Banquette is bleeding and in pain, but he continues swimming along. He is swimming in pure blood, his own and the cowardly marine's, and when he finds the wounded man, he throws him over his shoulder and carries him in this fashion, do you see, swimming back to the amphibious-assault vehi-cle, where he flings the marine onto the deck. Then Chaplain Banquette removes all of his own clothing, tearing his shirt and trousers and under-wear into tourniquets which he expertly applies to that chopped-up marine from head to foot, or from head to stumps, do you see, for the man has lost both of his feet—it was both, wasn't it?—I wouldn't want to exag-gerate—and in so doing Chaplain Banquette saves the life of that particu-lar coward."

General McMinn turned his big shaved head to Miles with scowl-twisted lips and then back to the admiral, and the general said, "Has all of this been confirmed by NIS, Cornelius?"

"You are the bureaucrat *sine qua non,* Jeffrey. It is the story everyone knows by now, do you see, and the crew never knows more than half the story of a combat hero."

The general looked back at Miles with grim skepticism, and the admi-ral looked at Miles with red-wrinkled love, and the others looked at Miles with marine detachment and naval awe.

The fluids of his cold were loose again—his head had had time to decongest from the altitude of the helo ride—and he'd been holding back the mucus as manfully as he could during the admiral's story—but now, to his embarrassment, with the men studying him, he felt the snot about to flow out of his nostrils. He got out the handkerchief and blew his nose—too loudly, though nose-blowing of any kind would've been loud here and now—and he despaired that they would think him emotionally overcome.

Nobody spoke for some seconds. Then Ensign Torrance Bulgorky asked, almost soothingly, "What is your denomination, Chaplain?"

"Methodist."

"Sir, you must know John Wesley very well."

"Who?"

"The Reverend John Wesley."

"I'm sorry, but I've never met the man."

Ensign Bulgorky let his mouth turn up on one side, shifting the purple pattern of acne on his creamy face. "I should think not, sir, as he died in 1791. I'm referring to John Wesley, the founder of Methodism."

"Torrance Bulgorky doesn't make mistakes," said the admiral. "That's why he was number one at Annapolis, do you see, and that's why he is my aide-de-camp."

"I was wondering, Chaplain," said Ensign Bulgorky, "where you stood on Wesley's abridgment of the Articles of Faith."

"Abridgment?" From necessity and a desire to stall he blew his nose again.

"I did some reading on this point," said Torrance Bulgorky, "for a Survey of World Religions course in my plebe year. What we need to realize as we deploy to the Far East is that the various cultures we interface with are deceptively monolithic—as is our own. Hinduism is as much a fragmented and self-contradictory system of belief as is Christianity. You have to agree, don't you, Chaplain, that John Wesley's abridgment of the thirty-nine Articles of Faith of the Church of England to the twenty-five accepted by Methodists poses as much of a barrier to ecumenicalism today as it did in 1738?"

They all looked from the aide-de-camp to the chaplain for the answer.

"Well—uh, that may be so—actually, I'm more of a—more of a minister, really, than a scholar." His face was on fire and his eyes and nose were running and he felt frightened and stupid and ill. Had he come all this way from the Little Pink Bookstore to be unmasked by a kid-freak of a genius?

"Therefore," said Ensign Bulgorky, "we can postulate, sir, that you, as a minister rather than a scholar—as you put it in your somewhat disingenuously dichotomous way—would ally yourself with the more pastoral and social-activist elements of modern Methodism, rather than with those original pietist and perfectionist ideals as they are so tersely expressed in the major theological writings of John Wesley."

"I guess so," said Miles. "I mean, if that was a question."

Everybody laughed. He hoped they were laughing at Bulgorky but he saw with a sick-sinking feeling as he glanced around the table that they were all laughing at him—except for the admiral, whose tiny green eyes were set coldly on him.

"Are you sure you're a Methodist?" said General McMinn, and they laughed some more at Miles. He wanted to lean down with the top of his head at table level and slide his salad plate on top of it.

"He's forgotten his religion," said McMinn. "Must be the blow to the back of the head he took from the AAV prop," and they laughed all over again. The admiral was looking redder than ever and glancing with impatience from the general to Miles.

When they were done laughing, the doctor, a jolly-jowled man with black hair combed forward in bangs over a frontal baldness, apparently feeling at last the need to defend the navy, said, "A blow to the parietal bone—that's the bone in the back of your head—clearly isn't enough to affect the combat performance of a naval hero."

Torrance Bulgorky turned to the doctor. "Occipital, sir."

"Excuse me?"

"That bone in the back of your head is the occipital, not the parietal, sir. The little bump we all have back there is called the occipital protuberance."

"I always thought that was called the parietal protuberance," said the doctor with a paralyzed look.

"No sir," said Bulgorky, "you're thinking of the occipital protuberance."

"That little bump on the back of your head?" The doctor felt the back of his head with both hands. "But what about the parietal bone? Isn't that in the back of my head?"

"Sir, not quite," said Bulgorky. "There are two parietal bones, left and right, and they form the left and right sections of the skull, directly above the temporal bone and the mastoid process. I did a little anatomical extra credit during my CPR competencies."

"I thought the mastoid process," said the doctor, "occurred just before menstruation."

"Not process in the functional sense, sir, but in the appendant sense."

"What?"

"Bill's not really a doctor at all," said the lawyer. "He's a cribbage player."

Again laughter, again everyone but the admiral. Miles was happy to laugh along.

"I'm a urologist," said the doctor.

"Truth is," said General McMinn, "most of you navy docs are urologists. Ninety-nine percent of all naval medicine is just giving out clap pills. Now you take the marine docs, a lot of them have been combat heroes. There was a famous case on Saipan, when it was being liberated during World War Two, the Philippine campaign, 1943. The Japs dropped this marine doctor's CO and he had to lead a platoon through the jungle for five—"

"Saipan," said Torrance Bulgorky, "is one of the Northern Marianas, General, not the Philippines. Wrong archipelago. And Saipan wasn't liberated until July 1944. It's probably been a while since you studied military history, sir."

This time the admiral alone laughed. His laughter was squeaky and prolonged. He said, "Are you sure you're a general, Jeffrey? What could you really be? I don't think you'd make a good travel agent, do you see."

The large gray eyes in the general's shaved head were directed at Torrance Bulgorky with a contemplative malevolence. The ensign was eating his salad, momentarily oblivious, as though he were without social intellect.

The admiral, having regained his dominance of the table, turned happily to the chaplain. "You no doubt appreciate being able to discuss religion intelligently for a change. It makes a tremendous difference. Another reason I didn't invite your CO, do you see, is the fact that—for some reason—he doesn't seem to like Torry. I find it surprising, since I've always known your captain to be a deep and powerful thinker, if something of a prattle-mouth."

Ensign Bulgorky glanced up from his salad long enough to shrug, then he looked down to fork a cucumber slice and said, "The captain of the *Harding?* We were discussing lawn furniture, it was his idea. But for some reason he kept saying 'chaise lounge' instead of 'chaise longue.' I couldn't get him to stop. It was almost as though he wanted to argue with me about it."

"He probably wanted to put a shoe up your ass."

It was the general. His gray eyes had never left the ensign, and now the general's mouth was turned down pitilessly at the sides.

"Excuse me, sir?" The ensign looked at the general with an expression as simple as mild confusion, as though anyone's outraged arrogance were beyond his understanding—surely the general must've misspoken.

The general didn't answer, staring with grim superiority at the ensign, who stared back in wonder. Men looked into their laps, made alignment adjustments to their silverware, shifted in their seats. Miles would've felt as uneasy as the others, and perhaps even a little sorry for the ensign, but Miles was experiencing too much relief, at no longer being the focus, to feel much of anything else.

Even the admiral was wordless. The general was straight-eyeing Bulgorky, who was working bemusedly, slowly, at his salad.

A shoe up your ass. The words would live in the air until somebody spoke. It had to be the admiral, and at last he did:

"Shoes, that's what I want to talk about. While we were at Subic Bay, I took the opportunity to visit the duty-free, do you see. I have two nieces, fifteen and seventeen, and I went about shopping for sandals for them. For their—for their feet, do you see. I was able to acquire two pairs of delectable little flip-flops. All of the toes will be visible, as well as the arches and heels and the tops of their feet. Only the soles of the feet will remain hidden. But everything else will be fully in view, do you see. And when they paint their toenails—as they both do—the painted nails will be fully visible. All of the toes will be out in the open, because these are flip-flops, that's what they are." The admiral paused, licking his lower lip. Miles was certain the admiral had succeeded in skirting attention from Bulgorky. But then, in his effort to aid the inept ensign, the admiral overreached: "I showed them to you, didn't I, Torry, aren't they the most delectable flip-flops? That you've ever seen? Everything will be fully visible."

"They're espadrilles, Admiral."

"I'm sorry?"

"They're not flip-flops, sir, they're espadrilles. They have soles of rope and uppers of canvas, that's what makes them espadrilles. It makes no difference how many toes are showing. The word 'espadrille' has an interesting etymology, by the—"

"Ensign," said General McMinn, "I don't know what these desk commanders and female instructors at the Naval Academy have been letting you get away with, but you may still make a good naval officer someday if you can learn to pretend to be an idiot."

The ensign's mouth was open and his black-framed glasses were a bit crooked, and he looked for the moment rather dumb. It was a scene unfrozen finally by the admiral:

"That's not very fair, Jeffrey. Hiding one's intellect, do you see, is only a part of being a good officer, naval or otherwise. Certainly, in order to rise through the ranks and impress colleagues and superiors along the way, there will be many times when Torry will need to pretend to be stupid. It's so essential to getting along with the majority of people, do you see. But any ambitious young officer must rely on his own initiative and testosterone as much as he does on a feigned dullness of mind. What do you think, Reverend Banquette? You're an officer and a war hero."

Miles looked up from his plate: they were all waiting. Ensign Bulgorky was looking at him with cautious stupefaction, eyes widely prepared to widen even further in intellectual contempt, or to squint with perspicacity at the chaplain's wisdom.

"Well," Miles began, setting down his fork, "I guess it's true that you have to have—well, balls, that's what everybody calls it—in order to get anywhere in life—you know, to be accepted someday as One of the Guys. I guess you have to wait for your opportunities and take them. But the general is right too. A cagey guy can't let too many people know he's smart, it becomes self-defeating. I've never made an enemy in the wardroom, because from the minute I got there I just acted like I didn't know the first thing about the navy. Like an impostor, almost. I was never trying to show I was better than anyone. That's the only way to become One of the Guys—you can't let them think you know the truth, that everything is really just bullshit."

The ensign squinted at Miles, nodding, learning. Miles shrugged and went back to his salad.

"That's the dumbest thing I've ever heard," said the general.

Miles said, "Sir, you just proved my point."

Everyone was laughing. "Hear hear," said the admiral. "That's real intelligence, do you see."

The conversations that grew in the aftermath were two-manned, technical, quiet. Miles gave in to his cold, blowing his nose liberally, unable to taste the food but comfortable with the cocooning of his consciousness that the head cold provided. The lieutenant commander sitting to his right initiated conversation with Miles about the dearth of shipboard recreation, and Miles said there wasn't much beyond computer games, and the lieutenant commander said his favorite was a submarine game called Depth Charge, and Miles admitted that the counter on his computer showed he'd played that very game over thirteen hundred times, and the other man admitted to eighteen thousand games during the past year, and they had a pleasant talk for the next half-hour about their favorite strategies, and if anyone had overheard them, it would've sounded like two highly trained naval tacticians discussing real warfare that they'd assisted in planning.

Miles looked around the table. None of the men, uniformed and mildly natured, appeared any different from what he imagined he himself looked like. Miles Derry was One of the Guys—had been for longer than he'd known. It was extraordinary and ordinary and, finally, like any other fact of one's daily existence, remarkable only for being unremarkable. He was struck by this for a moment, then quickly forgot all about it.

Dinner ended with handshakes, and his flagship stay ended with a helo rise into the night, and the ride ended with another easy-chair landing, and his day ended with an hour of wide-wakefulness in his rack, Zincville, walking up the steps to his parents' door, dangling the Navy Cross, the beautiful medal from the book, before his father's face, the bronze disc shining at the end of its blue-and-white ribbon, the glint on metal daring his father to make sport of it—of him—and his mother was standing there just to the left and back of his father, the frightened pigeon woman too zoned-out on pills to fathom the meaning of the medal, but look now at the confused outrage on his father's face . . . Miles was succumbing to sleep, to a dream composed of these images. Then the 1MC rattled him awake with "Attention trusty shellbacks—Wog Day! Wog Day! USS *Warren Harding* will be arriving at zero degrees latitude tomorrow at twelve hundred hours and parking until oh-six-hundred next day. Shillelaghs can be signed out in the quartermaster-yeomanry on deck seventeen anytime before arrival at zero degrees. Pollywogs should consider themselves duly warned. That is all."

He didn't understand about Wog Day—he knew from the POD that they'd be crossing the equator tomorrow on their way into Indonesian waters to meet a carrier group, coming from Australia, whose tenders would UNREP the ARG—Underway Replenishment—but Wog Day he didn't begin to understand until he was at breakfast and half of them were talking about it with jocular animation, the others sitting in unhappy silence. The XO said to Miles, "You're a trusty shellback, aren't you, Jim?

Take an African cruise in the Atlantic? Just show me your card and I'll make sure you're issued the shillelagh with the razor studs. War hero ought to get the best one, don't you think?" Miles had been wondering what that particular card was about. He got out the dead man's wallet, opened it, went behind the credit cards he'd never had the temerity or opportunity to use, and slid out a white card depicting a green smiling turtle smoking a pipe and wearing a jauntily angled white cap and brandishing from a green paw an evilly studded shillelagh. In green lettering:

Certified United States Navy
SHELLBACK
Cdr. James J. Banquette

"I knew it," said the XO. "You can't be a war hero without being a trusty shellback. I just wish old Ditchfield was here for the ceremonies. He was a golden shellback."

"Golden?"

"The highest level. He once crossed the equator at the date line."

"That guy," said one of the JOs, "was a fucking stud-cock."

Wog Day: everyone who'd crossed the equator was a trusty shellback and everyone who'd never done it was a pollywog and at noon the ship would stop at zero degrees for eighteen hours and for that time these two distinctions would be the only recognized ranks. He was just leaving the early lunch seating when a whistle screamed over the 1MC and the announcement was made "Wog Day, Wog Day, Zero Latitude!" and around the corner came the DISBO with a shillelagh of yellow wood spotted brown with old blood. He swung it in the air and said, "We're going to beat those fucking wogs till they shoot blood out of their fucking eyeballs. Come on, Jim, let's start with those JOs. Show 'em what a war hero can do." Miles went to his stateroom instead. He didn't think it was proper for a chaplain or a war hero to participate in a blood hazing. He was sitting at his desk about to access the computer game when he heard the first clubbings and screaming and begging from the wardroom mess where the JOs had been ordered to report for a meal of last week's garbage. The JOs were pleading and crying against the thudding of the clubs—even a chaplain, an officer, a war hero had no authority to stop it, but he didn't have to listen to it, so he took an old *Stars & Stripes* downdecks toward the library. Two levels down he encountered a group of enlisted men who were holding down three squirming cursing wogs as two other men came waddle-running down the P-way with a bucket hanging from each hand. "Hey, Chaplain, we're gonna pour piss and shit down their throats, wanna watch?" It smelled true; he continued downdecks. Then he had to stop when he saw that the trusty shellbacks had a wog tied to the next ladder, stripped to his underpants, and they were taking turns punching him, a left-right from each man in line as the wog, windless, silent, jerked his agonized face to the side with every punch. "Kick him in the head, Chaplain!" Unable to help this wog or any other, sickened and piteous, Miles went up a deck and down a P-way and out a hatch to the weather deck, grateful for his head cold, that it muffled the thuds and cries coming from every deck. As he was going down an outside ladder, his eye became peripherally aware of a vast pinkness, and when he looked all the way left and down to the fantail there were about a hundred men, all of them naked in the sun, crawling on elbows and knees, butts in the air, across the burning deck. Occasionally one of their shellback enforcers, of whom there was a circle of about twenty, would say "Do the Wog Crawl!" and go over to kick a man off his hands, down onto his elbows. Miles had heard this ritual discussed at breakfast: The wogs had to crawl from hitch-hole to hitch-hole—hooked indentations in the deck for helo or cargo cables— and each hitch-hole had been filled with a bowl-sized sampling of last month's galley items: moldy macaroni and cheese, spoiled potato salad, brown Brussels sprouts aged in their own foul juices. There was also lemonade made freshly this morning with shellback piss. Wogs not eating lunch with vigorous enough appetites risked the pressure of a shellback boot on the back of the head. Miles turned from the spectacle, through a hatch and back inside, the deck housing the library. To get there he had to go past the crew's lounge, site of his weekly services, and he passed it quickly because he knew, from wardroom conversation, that the fattest chief on the ship was in the crew's lounge—King Neptune—holding a trident fashioned out of an old broom wrapped in tin-foil; the man was naked, coated with the moldy macaroni and cheese and rotted pork and beans that the wogs were forced to lick off his body. Miles ignored the laughter coming from within and continued toward the library, but as he approached it he heard laughter coming from there, too—then he remembered that this was the venue of the Pornolympics. Wogs were compelled to sit nude on the floor while shellbacks read them pornography, and whenever a wog's penis began to stir a shillelagh would land promptly upon it. Miles did a U-turn in the P-way and went out on the weather deck and found a rope spool to sit on and read his *Stars & Stripes* in the hundred-degree equatorial shadow of the superstructure. The shouting and clubbing and crying, filtering through his head cold, sounded as though they came from a distant shore. War hero—chaplain—what could he do for anyone?

There was a clinking sound up and to his right, coming from a suspended smallboat. He thought he saw it shift just perceptibly, thought he'd imagined it, and returned to his paper. Then he heard a sigh and looked up again. The canvas covering of the smallboat, though still on, was clearly unsnapped all the way down one side.

"That was so good," Robin said.

Miles closed the paper and looked at the deck in desperation. He wasn't going to be able to get away from anyone today.

"Wasn't that good?" she said, and the smallboat shifted with another clink. "You have to admit it's better this way, better than anything you ever paid for."

"That's just common knowledge," Kruger said.

Miles dropped the paper and put his face in his hands.

"This way you're not out exploiting those girls."

"It's the guy gets exploited and all, that's just common knowledge, all they want is your money."

"We like to argue," she said contentedly.

"I would like to quote to you from the Song of Solomon—"

"Cut out that Bible crap and put your hand back between there."

"You really like me? Ever since you hit me over the head with the plunger?"

"No, not that soon," she said. "It was when we were arguing on the weather deck, after the marines went back to their rooms. I thought you were really forceful. That you had a lot of exciting energy. It made me curious."

There was a happy silence.

"We're both shellbacks," said Kruger. "We could paddle each other."

"Mmm."

"I really like—I mean—this is going to sound like the most common knowledge—I really like"—it was as though he were struggling with a word he'd just learned—"I really like *fucking* you. If you don't mind me saying so."

"Mmm, then fuck me some more, right now."

Miles, who'd never been sick at sea, was certain that the next sounds to come from the smallboat would make him throw up, and he thought for a moment of snapping down the sides of the canvas covering to trap Robin and Kruger in there forever, but fortunately, before he could hear any more or throw up and snap them in, the 1MC rasped to life with:

"Will the shellback chaplain please report to the fantail. Will the trusty shellback chaplain please report to the fantail. Please bring your funeral book."

It was the first 1MC announcement since the start of the equatorial ceremonies. Had someone actually been killed? He hardly thought the funeral would be so soon. But he went anyway to his stateroom for the prayer book, on his way to the fantail.

A hundred naked wogs stood at attention in the heat, facing aft, squinting, displaying their heavily purpled buttocks, black eyes, blood-running noses. At the stern, the captain and other shellbacks (uniforms, sunglasses, shillelaghs) stood talking as they waited for the chaplain. Miles went through the columns of naked men, through the humidity of their sweat, and when he emerged from their numbers he saw that one of the shellbacks was wearing headphones with a bend-around mike and another had a megaphone and another was holding with both hands a fat item wrapped triangularly in an American flag.

"The hell you been?" said the captain to the chaplain, his white hair tangle-sweated down, looking like a load of cottage cheese. "Been waiting here in the sun a whole minute for your lazy heroic ass."

"Had to get this, Captain," he said, holding up the black book.

"Well, open it to the funeral services and read it into this damn thing. At them." The CO motioned to the man with the megaphone who passed it to Miles, who had to fumble through the book one-handedly three times till he found the chapter. He raised the heavy instrument, triggered it to raspy life, and having been in the navy too long to question orders, he lifted the book immediately and began broadcast-reading:

"Lord, we gather here in Your name and presence to consecrate the passage of this soul—"

A guffaw.

"Goddamn it," said the CO, taking the megaphone from Miles and speaking into it. "One of you degraded wogs thinks this is funny. S-O-U-L, you dumb-asses, the man's reading it the way it's fucking written. He's a shellback and a war hero and a minister of the Lord, so you'd better have some fucking respect. Do you wogs understand that I can make you eat the damned thing? Read it again, Banquette."

Miles snuffled through the preamble, thinking he must be the only man in history to have a cold on the equator. The sweat was dripping into his eyes, making it hard to read, and the next time he came to the word "soul" there was a titter and the CO shoved a shellback who went into the ranks with a shillelagh raised high, and no one laughed the next time Miles said "soul" as he sniffed-and-muffed through the funeral service. It was tiresome holding up the megaphone and the book and trying to read, with a cold, through his sweat-blurred vision. Whenever he looked up from the text to blink he was jarred by the reality that he was reading a religious service to a hundred men standing in naked formation with their cocks and balls hanging out of their pubic hair.

"How many more pages is this damn thing?" said the CO.

Miles thumb-flipped through the book. "Fifteen or twenty more minutes, Captain."

"You Presbyterians take that long to drop 'em in the hole? You ought to take after the black Baptists and get a drive-thru."

"I'm a Methodist, sir."

"Well, the talking part is over. Only reason I wanted it was to stop any rumors of cannibalism. I was gonna make these degraded wogs eat the damn thing, but the XO said you can't order cannibalism, not even on Wog Day. Between you and me, I doubt you can find it outlawed in Regulations, but I rescinded my cannibalism order anyway, just to be legally careful, and now I have a Christian witness. Still I'd like to see these degraded wogs pass it around and take a bite out of it. Back in '62 when I was a wog they made us eat Australian galoots; that's an ostrich egg that's been buried for six months. Wish we had some for *these* wogs. But a cannibal lunch woulda been even better, wish I could make them eat the damn thing."

"What damn thing is that, sir?"

"That foot, you idiot. The one that came off your deserter friend." The captain nodded toward the shellback holding the fat object wrapped triangularly in the American flag. "Some degraded wog was chasing rat droppings with his nose down in the engine room about half an hour ago when he bumped into it. Wish I could make these faggots eat it for lunch—not just the boot, the whole damn foot, the rotting, pus-filled, blood-soaking thing. XO said I'd get a nickname, 'Captain Cannibal.' Can't have that, not in today's limpy-wristed faggoty navy. Now there won't be any nicknames, no rumors, no doubts of what really happened here today, we've had a Christian service." The CO took and raised the megaphone. "Salute it, you pieces of shit." A hundred hands went up to a hundred glistening foreheads. The CO gave a thumbs-up to the man in the headphones and he spoke into the wraparound mike and above and fore the 203-mm gun went off with an ear-cracking sinus-sucking head-cold-clearing blast and the man with the foot in a flag dropped it over the stern.

"Wish I could've buried the whole jarhead at sea, not just the foot," the CO said when they could hear again. "At least made these wogs chow down on the fucking thing, pass it around, hold it by the ankle like a big fucking drumstick. Boys don't want to become men anymore, that's the problem with the world. It's evolving into a whimpering fag-assed humanity these days. Well—better clear the trash off this deck. I'm ordering up a helo, take me to the *Natchez*. Lot of smart-assed ensigns over there I'd like to paddle the piss out of."

"Bulgorky, sir?" said Miles.

"He's one of 'em. I figure to apply the broad end of my shillelagh so many vigorous times against his puny college-boy ass that his balls'll be hanging out of his mouth and his pecker'll be drooping out of his nose. That is, if he hasn't already been paddled so hard his guts aren't falling out of his ears. All right, time to clear the trash off."

The CO gave orders and Miles watched the naked wogs turn as one company and their bruised buttocks, white ones and black ones, began marching toward the superstructure, to experience the atrocities waiting within. Seaward he could make out the shapes of the other vessels, lined up distantly on the hot-purple water, on the imaginary line dividing the planet in two. He blew his nose and went across the fantail and down the weather deck on the other side of the superstructure from the mass of wogs but came upon more of them, about a dozen, naked on their elbows and knees as two shellbacks took paddles to their asses with the swings of home-run hitters.

The suffering of the wogs ended at precisely oh-six-hundred the next morning after a night of screaming and crying that Miles tried his best to sleep through with two pillows under one ear and two over the other. By breakfast they were under way for UNREP. The few JOs who showed up in the wardroom mess had black eyes and swollen blue faces and were limping and didn't have much to say, despite the DISBO's compliment: "Somehow you sorry-asses are motherfucking shellbacks now. I didn't think you'd fucking make it. In fact, I don't see how you fucking did it. Maybe we ought to beat your asses again when we cross the fucking line on the way back."

The paddlers were as tired as the paddled, and nobody had the energy to discuss Wog Day further, so the conversation, as the ship cruised more deeply into the southern hemisphere, turned to the UNREP goodies. The group they were meeting was a large one, flagged by the city-on-water *Eisenhower,* fourteen ships coming up from Australia with refrigerator compartments stuffed full of steak and lobster. Everyone on the *Harding* was a shellback now and everyone would feast.

That afternoon, following his after-lunch nap, he was putting on his shoes to go out to the weather deck and watch the approach of a tender when the knock that his father had always said would never come to Miles Derry's door—opportunity—came as literally as it could. He opened the door: unassuming enough: a thin young man, navy lieutenant, already a little bald, sideburns. He was Lieutenant Senior Grade Jerry Alpern and he'd just been DU for two weeks—Down Under—with the aircraft carrier *Ike,* writing human-interest stories for *Stars & Stripes.* He wanted to hear The Story, and if it was good enough, he wanted to send a photographer.

Miles told it through his diminishing head cold, the words echoing nasally in his inner ear. None of it sounded real as he told it, though he told only the truth; it certainly didn't feel real that he was telling it to a reporter who was shorthanding the whole thing into a small notebook.

"That's a wonderful story, Reverend. I've never met a man with a Navy Cross. It's an honor."

"I haven't got it yet."

"But you're a sure thing. Listen, I'll send the photographer over later today. What do you think, Reverend, you in a helmet and cammies, holding a Bible, 'The Fighting Chaplain.'"

"Well—I don't—"

"Or maybe in your robes—your vestments, whatever you call—"

"No, no thanks—I prefer no pictures."

"I'm sure this'll make all editions, sir, Far East, Middle East, Europe, every base in the States of course, could be page one. And when you get back to Subic I can have AFR and AFTV waiting there."

"AF-who?"

"Armed Forces Radio and Television, worldwide. With a thing like this, there's also a good chance the major wires and networks will pick it up, sir. You could be the lead-in to the last commercial break on *CNN Headline News.*"

"No, I don't think that would be a good—"

"And *Reader's Digest,* sir. They're always looking for true-life dramas like this. They'd pay a nice chunk of change to reprint your story. You could—you could give it all to charity if you preferred . . ."

"No—I don't want my picture—"

"Let me pitch it to *People* magazine, sir, I've always wanted to sell a big story like this to a major—"

"No photographs, I have to insist on that, really, I have to draw the line. I can't have my picture broadcast worldwide. I can't give permission for a thing like that. It's—it's a rule of my denomination."

Lieutenant Senior Grade Alpern frowned. Then he looked a little happier. "Modesty, okay, that's the pitch. Good. I'm looking at ten thousand words, worldwide, front-page *Stars & Stripes* and we'll see what the wires do with it. If it clicks we can condense it to a feature for *Reader's Digest* or *People.*"

Miles was sick with anxiety as he shook hands with the reporter. To have his face appear in newspapers and TV, over the name COMMANDER JAMES J. BANQUETTE, would be the disaster of his life. When they got back to Subic the SPs would be waiting to haul him away.

He heard the captain stop Lieutenant Senior Grade Jerry Alpern in the P-way: "Wait, you're that news grunt came aboard."

"Sir?"

"I'm the man you want to interview."

"Thank you, Captain, but I've interviewed my man."

"That chaplain? He doesn't know anything about heroism, all he did was save a guy's life once. I'm the one who's responsible for the *training* each man receives on the *Warren Harding*. With the proper training, you can save a man's life not just once, but every day. Without the proper training, there are no fucking heroes."

"I think Commander Banquette has given me all the—"

"Open that goddamn notebook and start writing, Lieutenant."

"Sir, I'm due back on the—"

"Do it!"

"Aye-aye, Captain."

The CO clucked his tongue, paused, began. "Aboard the LST USS *Warren Harding*—a ship named for one of our most accomplished presidential leaders, by the way—I have undertaken to personally train each and every goddamn officer—you can take out the 'goddamn' if you want—I have trained every goddamn officer in the same highly competent manner in which I myself was trained. I've been working closely with the chaplain in question ever since he was billeted aboard the *Harding,* and I have taught him everything he knows about being a man and a hero, which just goes to illustrate that a CO who has the balls and the goddamn intellectualness— you can take out 'intellectualness' if it's too big a word for your readers—a CO like me can make any man into a superior human specimen . . . "

Miles shut his door and retreated into what was left of his head cold. He waited for dinner. When he got to the wardroom mess there were Australian steak and lobster, and a galley chief from the *Eisenhower* to explain the food to them. The chief was bald and triple-chinned and rotundly covered in a white apron from neck to knees. He folded his pudgy hands on his belly as he spoke:

"What you have in front of you, gentlemen, is your finest steak to be found anywhere in the world, better than anything we can get in the States. Back home we don't even have butcher shops anymore—like everything else, there don't seem to be any standards now. What you are about to consume, gentlemen, perhaps for the very first time in your lives, is your classic well-marbled prime cut of beef, with real texture and taste. Your steak in American supermarkets isn't much different from cow manure, it's just your inferior cuts aged in wet plastic. Your Australian beef, on the other hand, is dry-aged. This makes your steak more juicy and flavorful and tender. Ninety percent of your Aussie beef can be graded as prime, as opposed to two percent in the States, where most of your steak is only choice or select. Your Australian cattle are superior, you've got all your original English breeds—your Shorthorns, your Herefords, your Aberdeen Anguses. Compare that to our American stock—just a lot of French and German and Belgian mongrels crossbred into the original English breeds. What you have in front of you, gentlemen, isn't just a mongrel steak cut by your untrained high-school kid in your typical supermarket meat department and then sealed up all wet and mushy in cryovac. This here is your prime Australian beef, butchered by professionals, carefully aged in cold lockers for exactly twenty-three days and nights and monitored every six hours for barometrics. You will taste the difference, gentlemen."

"If it isn't cold by now," said the DISBO.

"Please enjoy."

"What about these lobsters?" said the DISBO. "Are they superior to American mongrel lobsters? You know, those faggoty crossbred Maine lobsters with their pinchers all taped up?"

The chief from the *Eisenhower* looked at the DISBO as though the DISBO were both serious and an idiot. "Lobster is lobster," said the chief.

There were so many lobsters and steaks UNREPped onto the ship—twelve hundred pounds of shellfish and sixteen hundred pounds of beef—that steak and lobster was lunch and dinner for all hands for each of the three days it took to return to the Philippines. By lunchtime of the third day, the gourmet effect had worn to the point that the DISBO, not entirely joking, could stick his head over the counter and into the galley, take his pipe from his mouth, sniff audibly and say, "Aw, man, steak and lobster *again?* You expect us to eat this fucking slop? What ever happened to creamed weenies with those little blue lima beans? You call this the fucking navy? Lobster and prime beef just won't keep me regular like those pork-and-bean enchiladas do."

Except for the occasional love sighs of Robin and Kruger coming through the bulkhead, Miles's life was placidly comfortable during those three days; it was a time of continued congratulation, of medal-dreaming, of impressing his father and mother in his daydreams, of computer-gaming, of naps, of steak and lobster. He was glad the reporter had respected his feelings about not being photographed. These pleasures lasted until the hour before they were due to pull into Subic. As ever, news was preceded by a rap on his door.

It was Lieutenant Reynolds, and behind him were all the marine officers. They crowded into his stateroom with hands deferentially clasped in front of their belt buckles. Miles was in his chair looking up at the semicircle of men.

"How can I help you marines?"

Reynolds was the leader: "Sir, we were going to wait till after we pulled in, but everyone's going to be eager to go on liberty, so we decided to tell you now. Sir, all of us marines on the ship have taken up a collection. Just as a gesture for saving the life of a member of the Corps. We have a special gift for you."

"You didn't have to do anything like that."

"Yes sir, but we wanted to. We've reserved a suite for you, sir, four days at the Admiral Hotel. That happens to be a very fine hotel located in Manila, the jewel of the Philippines, Chaplain."

"Oh . . . well . . . thank you very much, Lieutenant."

"Tell him," said another.

"There's something else, sir."

"Yes?"

"Sir, we want you to know that we are so grateful for what you've done for the marines that you won't be alone in that suite. Somebody very special will be there waiting for you. Sir, your wife."

13

It was such a panic that his stateroom, once they were gone, wasn't big enough for him to pace around in, so he went outside, but the weather deck was too narrow for a pacing circle the size of his desperation, so he went to the fantail, pacing hands-in-pockets from port to stern to starboard to bulkheads and around again, and as he did so, glaring fearfully at the jungly hills opening to the north into Subic Bay, at the sky, which was an odd, ashy color, almost a brown, he was thinking madly that the only escape was to jump, and he wondered if this was the way Lebedeen had felt in the AAV. A hatch opened in the superstructure and distracted him with the emergence of a line of galley men in white aprons dragging out large, clear plastic bags red with beef and shellfish, and they went to the side and one by one, grunting, threw the bags into the sea. He asked one of the men, a galley chief he recognized, who explained that all of the uneaten steak and lobster had to be disposed of before they entered Subic Bay, because it was an agreement between the U.S. government and the U.S. cattle and fishing industries, only American beef and fish products were allowed to enter American bases, so the Australian stuff, the last eight hundred pounds of it, would have to go. "With all the people starving in the Philippines?" But the chief was too busy to answer, following his men back for the other bags as the cracking voice of the volcano sounded across the sea, sharpening Miles's panic, and then the voice was silent, and the silence heightened his panic even more. What was he going to do? He had to get off the *Harding* and run—there were no competing ideas, and he realized that even if he could think calmly he might never be able to produce an escape plan in the time available. His panic was too great for him to continue pacing the fantail, so swinging his arms he went as quickly as he could without running—would've run but didn't want the attention—back to his stateroom, where he yanked open the metal closet and grabbed the duffel bag and started stuffing all of Jim Banquette's belongings into it. He hadn't shut the stateroom door all the way, and with a slight lurch of the ship, it opened slowly, fully, and the XO coming down the P-way noted the chaplain's frantic packing by saying, "Man, you must be hot to see your wife. We got you a four-day leave, you figure that'll be sufficient, Reverend?"

Miles just kept packing.

"Chaplains, war heroes, doesn't matter," said the XO, "everybody needs a good rumble-tumble. Just don't let that volcano make you think you're the one moving the earth. Read my POD?"

Miles kept packing.

"Jesus," said the XO, as if the obvious were just occurring to him, "you haven't been laid since we left San Diego, have you? You poor shit. Get yourself packed and out of here."

When the XO had left, and Miles had most of the clothes—mainly the civilian things, portions of a couple of uniforms—shoved into the bag, he paused to pull out the wallet and count. $141. That might take him anywhere in the Philippines, but not off the islands. Credit cards, okay, but a digital trail. Could he get a cash advance from the DISBO? Did the disbursement office take credit cards? An advance against salary? Would the DISBO do it for a war hero, a friend? Was the DISBO a friend?

The volcano moaned doubtfully.

He opened the dead man's passport. The face looking back from the photo wasn't the one Miles would find in a mirror; Banquette's was a longer face and his jaw was a bit more square, but the gray eyes and the mustache were the same. Although the face in the passport wasn't the exact copy of Miles's, which the smudgy face in the USN ID might pass as, neither did the passport photo look entirely like the man Miles remembered—who'd been dead, after all—but when you thought about it, few photographs ever looked entirely like the subject, and so the passport photo might still pass for Miles. Would have to.

And then he couldn't think any further. His gaze strayed to his desk. The morning's POD was lying there and he saw the words, eighteen points high:

VOLCANIC ERUPTION!

So he picked it up and read:

According to the latest seismic report forwarded by NAVPHILCOM, there is substantial probability that volcanic activity on Mount Pinatubo might intensify over the next few days into an event of eruptive significance. Clark Airbase has been shut down since 2100 last night because of visibility problems associated with airborne ash. Official reports confirm up to half an inch of volcanic ash on the streets of Angeles City, just outside the airbase. Several hundred Filipinos living on the volcano's slopes have been made homeless by flowing lava and there are reports of many deaths. The implications for us are these: In the event of a major volcanic eruption, high levels of ash may reach as far south as the Subic Bay Naval Station and the adjoining town of Olongapo, making travel difficult or impossible. Personnel on liberties of less than 24 hours should limit their movements to the immediate area of Zambales Province. Travel to Clark Airbase or Angeles City is strictly prohibited, as the situation in the vicinity surrounding Mount Pinatubo is considered HIGHLY DANGEROUS.

He was pacing his room, hands behind his back, trying to determine the volcano's portent for him, when a radio yeoman coming down the P-way stopped just long enough to wordlessly hand him a message through the open door.

```
NAVMANCOM CCK26R WHE735 071791 10:41 DETNAVAPHIL xUSSWARHARD
[LST-2282] BANQUETTE CDR WARD

CDR BANQUETTE: HAVE ASSEMBLED AFR-AFTV TEAM MANILA AND WAITING
FOR WORD OF HARDING ARRIVAL SUBIC. UNOFFICIAL FROM NAVPHILCOM
YOUR ARRIVAL 1630 TODAY. SETTING FORTH TO MEET YOU BY SAID TIME.
ADVISE IF ARRIVAL SOONER. APPRECIATE YOU DELAY ANY LIBERTY TILL
AFR-AFTV CREWS HAVE CHANCE TO INTERVIEW. CONGRATULATIONS ON
CROSS RECOMMENDATION AND LOOKING FORWARD TO MEETING WITH YOU.
CDR COLE SCUDALCZYK, AFTVNAVPHIL

P.S. LT(SG) ALPERN, STARS N STRIPES, 30 MINUTES AGO BY RADIO
INFORMS HAS SOLD YOUR STORY READERS DIGEST TEN THOUSAND DOLLARS
CONGRATULATIONS AGAIN.
```

He would run, he was out of options, as soon as the ship docked he would throw the duffel bag over his shoulder and go running down the gangway as fast as he'd gone running out of the incinerating bookstore. No one would think it remarkable—they'd just laugh at how impatient the chaplain was to fuck his wife. But he needed money. He took the radio message down to the disbursement office.

The cage was still closed, but the door next to it was open, and sitting at his desk next to the safe was the DISBO. He was hunched over a large green-paged ledger book, his pipe smoldering aromatically. He looked up, then sat back, pipe in hand, his tan face smiling lewdly. "So, you holy-ass, holy-joe, war-hero motherfucker, XO says you're finally going to wet your pecker."

"DISBO, I need money."

"Don't throw me softballs, Jimbo, there's no fucking challenge."

"I need an advance against my pay or something, I'm going on a four-day liberty in Manila—with my wife. I'm good for an advance: look, I just sold my story to *Reader's Digest*."

The DISBO took the radio message; his eyes, when they arrived at the postscript, grew to the appropriate dimension. "Jesus Fucking God," he said. "Ten gees? If I'd known a jarhead was worth that much I woulda been out saving their fag asses a long time ago."

"So I can have the advance?"

"You need that much? Taking the wife shopping?"

"How much can you give me?"

"Christ, she must like to fucking *shop*. You married guys have it for hell. Ten grand? What're you gonna do, buy the fucking Philippine Islands and have them crated up and shipped home?"

"I just want—"

"I guess you want cash. Navy check wouldn't do any fucking good outside 'Po City." The DISBO turned to the green screen of a computer, typed for a few moments, then leaned back with his hands behind his head as a printer went spit-zapping on the next desk. He reached over to tear off the sheet. "Ten gees," he said. "That's fourteen hundred short times in Olongapo. The wife'll spend it faster than that. Jesus, you married guys have it for shit. Sign this. If a goddamn chaplain isn't good for it, who the hell is? War hero on top of it, but sign it anyway. If you don't pay it back out of that *Reader's Digest* money, I'll just garnish your fucking pay for the next twenty-two cycles." Miles signed; the DISBO said, "Now you can buy 'Po City and shut it the fuck down, if that suits your Mormon ass—and if the volcano doesn't fucking beat you to it." The DISBO swiveled his chair around to the safe, which he opened with an upward crank of the lever. Inside there was a great heaping of banded notes, the liberty monies they'd soon be lining up to cash checks for. The DISBO took two of the banded blocks and threw them on the desk in front of Miles. "Five, ten. You did all the ass-busting hero work, now she gets to do all the shopping. But I guess you religious guys *have* to fucking get married. I just hope there's a heaven up there for sweethearts like you, Jimbo."

Miles put five thousand into each of his front trouser pockets and went back to the stateroom to sit at his desk and try to think his way through his continuing panic. He had money, but where would he go? And where would Jim Banquette go? For the first time since he'd burnt the bookstore they were two separate questions. Miles Derry would have to go one way and Jim Banquette another. Which for which? His elbow was on the POD; he reread it. Okay, maybe . . . He turned to the computer and started tapping out an idea:

To Whom It May Concern—

I write this in the event I do not return. Although I appreciate the opportunity to spend four days of liberty in Manila with my dear beloved wife, I feel that the suffering of our Filipino brothers and sisters in the area destroyed by volcanic eruption must take precedence over my personal and selfish desires. Accordingly, I must first go to the aid of those who suffer and risk my life to help in any way I can, as that is the way of Christ's example. Should I not return, I want my wife and children to know how much I dearly love them. But I hope to return from the area of volcanic devastation and be with my wife in Manila when my work with the lava victims is done.

Yours in Christ,

CDR Rev. J. Banquette

He sat before the computer, fiddling with words, working against the implausibility of the tone, concentrating desperately. He had the door closed, but it was no protection: the rapping felt like it was driving his heart up his throat, and he jumped in his chair. Through the door: "Who is it?"

"Seaman Jennings, sir, radio shack. Sir, you have a telephone call."

"*A what?*"

"A telephone call, sir."

"*At sea?*"

"Radio-telephone, sir."

"Who's calling?"

"I don't know, sir—a woman, sir."

Mrs. Banquette! "Tell her I'm not here."

"Sir?"

"I—I don't want to speak to anyone, seaman."

"Sir, it's costing her five dollars a minute and it's holding up the channel for Admiral Jiggerston. She's insisting on talking to you at once, sir—she's screaming, sir."

This was it. What could he say to her? Pretend to be someone else? In front of the radio guys? Could he concoct a conversation ambiguous enough to satisfy them *and* Mrs. Banquette? He couldn't know till he was actually speaking to her. He rose shakily and opened the door and followed the seaman like a prisoner following his executioner. In the radio shack he was handed a headset with a wraparound mike.

"Hello?"

"Chaplain Banquette?"

"Yes?"

"This is Nalgona Lebedeen."

A second of confusion, then his panic subsided, replaced by a memory flash of the photo of Lebedeen's wife—a large, short-haired, bullet-headed Filipina in a red muumuu. "Mrs. Lebedeen—uh—how are you?"

"I'm calling long-distance from Pennsylvania, and I don't have time for a lot of chitchat, Chaplain. What I want to know is why didn't you save my husband's foot?" Her voice had self-amplified over the scratchy tenuousness of the connection.

"It was dropped overboard, ma'am."

"You people expect anyone to swallow that?"

"No, nobody's going to eat it, Mrs. Lebedeen. It's true that I lost it, but it was buried at sea." My God, what barbaric rumors had the woman heard?

"Are you drunk? I've met more drunken chaplains! Listen up, bud, I had to call all over the Pentagon to get your ship's movement and QSI numbers so I could call you before you hit Subic—and now I'm glad I did, because you're just going to go out and get drunk with your chaplain pals. I have to undergo a partial mastectomy the day after tomorrow, and my husband won't be here to help with anything because of *you*. He's lying in a hospital in Korea, without a foot. What good is he going to do me there? Who's going to make Pogo's lunch? Who's going to pick him up after school? Who's going to take Pogo to badminton?"

"Uh—"

"If you can save an entire marine, the foot shouldn't be that much of a challenge. I can't believe how they're making you out to be such a big war hero and everything, and him out to be just a cowardly wuss. Okay, maybe I can believe a part of that. But now we have to get lawyers and witnesses and everything and sue to get those disability payments. We're suing everybody, including you, you drunken irresponsible foot-losing—"

"I don't think you're being entirely fair, Mrs.—"

"You drunken hypocrite, what're you going to do when you hit Subic? Did you know I'm a Filipina-American? Before you start thinking your sick thoughts in your sick perverted mind, I never worked in bars, I was raised in Chicago. You navy officers are such scumbags. If you were a proper chaplain you would've saved my husband's foot, you wouldn't be drinking while under way, you'd do something to stop all the prostitution in the Philippines. I want to know what you're going to do about it!"

"About what, Mrs. Lebedeen?"

"*About all of it*, you drunken perverted hypocritical lying ineffectual cowardly foot-losing piece of—"

He had the headset off and he handed it to one of the radio men and said, "Please hang up on this person." Going back to his stateroom he thought he understood Major Lebedeen's character thoroughly at last and he felt very sorry for the man.

At the computer he hit the print command, then jogged down to the yeomanry to rip Banquette's final words from the spit-typing machine before anyone could read them. Back in the stateroom he cleared the desk and squared up the farewell in the center of it. He reread it . . . there was something wrong. Banquette would never do this without letting his wife know. So . . . ? A message to her? What if she responded? A nagging phone call from Manila to the ship was probably a lot cheaper than one from Pennsylvania. A message, then, somehow delivered to her, after he'd left the *Harding* . . . Shitcakes, with Mrs. Banquette and those reporters and who-knew-who so eager to see him, he'd have to shoot right off the ship the moment it docked. At least one good thing, the reporters wouldn't know him by sight.

The ninety minutes remaining before they docked were a tensely pro- longed time, during which he could only pace his room, recheck the duffel bag, pack the overlooked shaving kit, lock his door uselessly, worry, go to the head three times to nervously piddle. Twice he went out to see how close they were, and at first there were only the sea and the bunched-up jungle and the sky volcanically ash gray, the humidity, the diesel stink of the exhaust, and the dark forms of the other ships; the next time he could distantly make out the garbage-fire smoke funnels over the town of Olon- gapo, and he was afraid. Of what might be waiting. Even his pockets heavy with his hero monies didn't make him feel secure, just another burden of evidence against him, like the oppressive hat and uniform under the heat.

He lay in his rack, too sick with dread to move in the fluorescent- buzzing humidity.

BUMP.

It could be just one thing, so he leapt and took the duffel by its knot and, throwing it over his shoulder, he was through the door and down the P-way and descending the five ladders to the main deck and through a hatch, outside, running down the weather deck and wide-legging over cables and black tubing and arriving at the quarterdeck where the gangway wasn't yet down. After the purity of the sea and the jungle coast, he got a morbid feeling from the grayness of the docks and the grayness of the many ships silhouetted against each other with their jumbles of lines and masts and antennas, and the gray skyline of the town with the pillars of smoke segmenting the ashy look of the sky. He looked back up at the superstructure of the *Harding* with a surprising feeling of loss and imme- diate longing and he knew, as never before, that it was his home. Then he turned to the JO who was OOD and said, "How soon's the gangway going down?"

"Thirty minutes sir, but the liberty whistles aren't blowing for another two hours."

"That's a long time."

"Word's out you're eager to see your wife, sir." A smirk.

"Is it?"

"Service gangway's out, I'll radio and say you're coming down."

"Thank you."

He looked down and yes, there was a gangway of narrow wooden planks extending at pier level to the dock from an open hatch, and sailors were carrying rope coils and crates and lengths of black tubing man-to-man, shoulder-to-shoulder into the ship. He went back into the superstructure, seabag over shoulder, and went quickly down the ladders—as quickly with the bag on his back as the man who'd amazed him the first day—until he was at the pier-level deck, and then he found the open hatch with men stacking crates around it and more men with crates coming through. "Excuse me," he said to the chief, who waved him on, and with the privilege of an officer and a war hero, he was crossing the narrow gangway and the men coming from the dockside had to stop and back away to let him pass.

Once across, he dropped the bag and stood in the shadow of the ship for a moment to say his farewell to the sweep of it, from the twin derrick arms rising over the prow to the high block of superstructure to the confusion of mast-crosses and antennas to the tubular diesel stacks to the flat length of the fantail—good-bye—not home anymore—no home anywhere, once again—the ache of farewell. Then a sailor far above was saying, "Sewer Lines A and B backing up! You're supposed to connect A to portside before disconnecting B! We have fucking feces backing up on decks six through eleven!"

He hoisted the duffel bag and started away, happy to be free, to have money, to be Miles Derry again, despite the hat and uniform, which cooked him the moment he stepped out of the *Harding*'s shadow. While he still wore the uniform, he put its authority behind his purpose: he saluted a hurrying chief who stopped as though hitting a transparent wall, hand to forehead in obedience, and Miles dropped his hand and said, "Chief, what's the quickest way to the Manila airport? Is there a bus or anything?" The CPO turned and squinted against the morning sun, which was deadly through the hole it was burning in the gray ash of the volcanic sky, and Miles turned to squint toward the place the chief was pointing to. "There's a van that leaves for downtown Manila from in front of Quonset J-3 every hour, Commander. Costs nine dollars and takes about two hours. You can get a cab from downtown to the airport for about five bucks." He thanked the chief and walked in the designated direction and wondered where he would go. First plane out of Manila, it didn't matter where, preferably a country where ten grand was still a fortune—that ruled out any English-speaking place—but it didn't matter where he chose as long as he got out of here fast, before those reporters could get here, and damn! Somebody in the wardroom-cleaning detail might already be reading the note he'd left. Move fast. There might be orders already to the men in Quonset J-3 to stop the insanely benevolent chaplain who'd decided to risk his life on the shanty slopes of Mount Pinatubo. Portentously, the volcano commented from a hundred and fifty miles away: *Doooooooooom.* The heat and humidity and ashen sky reminded him of some bad days—Southern California, the closed smoky semen-and-Lysol air of the Little Pink Bookstore, the smog-choke outside. The United States was an ugly urban nation run by dick-heads like his father who made working people like Miles Derry suffer, and only very desperate Third World peasants wanted to go *there.* Where would he go? Maybe an island. Trade winds, palm trees. Hmm.

At the Quonset hut, he waited a nervous forty minutes with a group of enlisted and officers, navy and marines, for the van, and thank God he was ahead of the *Harding*'s liberty and that nobody here knew him though he expected, with a trotting heart, that the reporters would come looking for him at any moment. He paced, kicked the seabag, paced. When the gray van arrived, he was the first to move toward it—the others, respecting his rank and his jitters, deferred to his boarding first. He paid the nine dollars and proceeded to the long bench seat at the back of the van where he dropped the bag on the floor and hunched himself into the windowless corner with his cap visor down over his eyes and pretended to be asleep as the van drove off, and then he *was* asleep. He was dreaming they were back in the cold waters off the Aleutians, it was winter, white-sky winter, and the crew's lounge had a brick fireplace in the bulkhead, it was wide and high-manteled, with half a dozen logs crisscross-burning and the fire was roaring but when he went to it with his hands extended he half-tripped over Kruger, who was kneeling on the deck, wearing only his black-framed glasses and a slack-mouth vacant look, vigorously doggy-fucking one of the whores from the town, and Miles woke up. The air-conditioning in the van was shivering cold; he opened the seabag and dragged out the rolled-up officer's jacket and put it on. The row in front of him had windows and the Filipino world was a surreal contrast to the cold-metal interior of the American van: palm trees, rice paddies, heat haze, thatch huts, a brown lake with a herd of wide-horned water buffalo half submerged, mule-drawn carts, a pink bus crookedly weighted to one side passing them the other way. The sky was gray-brown with ash. Jungle shade, more heat-hazed rice paddies, jungle shade again, back and forth. His mind was numb and he was dozing and waking and each time he opened his eyes he felt a little safer.

An hour and a half went by.

The jungle shade opened for the final time and the shanties now were more numerous and they were lopsided against one another, fewer ones of thatch and more of wood or corrugated metal. The rain was starting. The windows were brown-streaked with wet ash and he watched the muddy suburb of slanted shanties blur past, naked children playing in the muddy alleys in the rain, men and women in gray raggy clothing idling in crossed-armed conversation in doorways or on porches of uneven planks. The traffic was heavier and slower, and the van crept along, and when the oncoming lane was suddenly moving faster a truck threw a wash of mud over the windows on that side and he dozed again.

This time when he awoke, it was because the lulling movement had ceased. They were stopped at a curb in building-shadow; the men in front of him were gathering up their seabags and stepping forward. Miles stood and stretched and looked out a window spotted with mud and ash and made out a boulevard congested with cars and jeepneys. Manila, downtown. The buildings showed the metal-and-glass modernism of the sixties, anachronisms more shabby than quaint. He hefted the bag and followed the others into the afternoon humidity. He walked for a while among the Filipino crowds, ignoring the raggy children who pursued him with their gum trays, piping in Tagalog. He walked among the people, watching their faces, reading any signs in English. He'd read about thirty signs before coming to the one in gold-colored letters screwed into black metal over a revolving door: PRATHET THAI. THE EMBASSY OF THE KINGDOM OF THAILAND. Of course he would need a visa before boarding a plane. Thailand, why not? He went through the revolving door, and the ancient bearings squealed. He nearly got stuck with the seabag, but finally pulled it through.

At the counter he requested the form, stood to the side filling it out. He made a checkmark in the tourist box, but wasn't sure what to write next to *DESTINATION(S)*. He thought a moment, wrote *Bangkok*. He thought another moment, wrote *Peacock Island*. He got out Banquette's passport and USN ID, tried to assume the serious look of the mustachioed photos, and then he went to the counter window, which had a gray-haired sleepy-eyed Thai woman behind it.

"Twelve dolla," she said, regarding the application form, but not yet the ID or passport.

After he'd paid she opened the passport, flipped pages, arrived at the ID page, looked at it only a moment, then flipped more pages and picked up a huge metal stamp and pistoned it violently onto a blank page. Only when she was tearing the carbons from the application sheet did she notice something that made her stop.

"Island no in country."

"Excuse me?"

"Cock of Pea Island. More sout, not Thai."

"Peacock Island isn't in Thailand? Somebody told me it was just off the Malay coast."

"Coast of Malay belong three country, Myanmar and Thai and Malaysia. Island of Pea of Cock belong Malaysia. You look map." She pointed to the wall at his right, covered with a ten-foot-square multicolored map of Southeast Asia. "Cannot go Bangkok to Cockpea. Must go Bangkok to Kuala Lumpur to Cockpea. But Thai have many island of beautiful also. Not need going Island of Cock. You stay Thai, have good time, not need Pea of Cock. You go Thai."

Thanking her, he pocketed the passport and ID, took the seabag by its knot and carried it carefully through the revolving door, and was back on the noisy street. From Bangkok he could get a flight to Kuala Lumpur and from there find a way to the island. But there was another thing, unreasoned, beneath the skin. Uneasy with what it might be, he threw the bag over his shoulder and walked through the crowds, vexed by the unknown matter . . . think . . . He'd wandered into a bad area. The street had turned to mud, the sidewalks were wooden boards, the houses were crooked shacks, there were children walking with him again, front and back, raggy shorts and shirts, chanting in Tagalog. It looked like Olongapo, there was a young prostitute in a too-tight blouse and dirty white miniskirt leaning in a doorway, there was a group of American air force boys in their blue uniforms laughing and smoking on a corner. He stopped, he would turn around—and then he saw it. It was a wooden stand like the one in Olongapo, there were a couple of bored-looking preadolescent boys sitting behind it, playing a kind of marble game on the countertop, and the shelves bore a row of dildoes and a large meshing of fuck baskets and a litter of the pussy toys like the one he'd left in the stateroom. He remembered Mrs. Banquette waiting in her suite at the Hotel Admiral. That was it. Banquette wouldn't leave without getting a message to her. Miles approached the stand and paid for one of the cat toys. It was exactly like the one Mrs.

Banquette had sent him, except that this one was new, it was pink and soft in his hand and the convoluted vulva of a rubber vagina bulged from its open mouth. He pulled out the artificial thing and placed it on the shelf so that the toy was just a stuffed animal like the one Banquette had given his wife. Then he put the cat in his pocket and handed out one-dollar bills to all the chanting children around him and then hurried away before the fly-boys down the block would notice where the chaplain was shopping.

He was back on the boulevard. The volcano gave a muffled cough, more distant here, not as loud as it had been at Subic. The sky was gray-brown except around the orange sun and his uniform was getting sticky with humidity and sweat. He waved a rattly Fiat cab to a stop, opened the door and threw in the seabag and got in and told the pucker-mouthed old man, "Hotel Admiral, please."

"Admero, okay."

He could leave the new pussy at the front desk with a note. No: any messenger coming this far would personally deliver it. So . . . what if . . . he thought about it a long time while riding in the cab . . . deciding . . .

He got out in front of the hotel and the driver was quick-nodding-happy to accept two American dollars and Miles pulled the bag out of the backseat and strode into the art deco lobby with red velvet walls trimmed in chrome and a front desk of green marble. Before he went there, he stopped at a floor-to-ceiling mirror, inspected his hat and mustache and uniform and seabag, saw the name BANQUETTE black-stenciled on the bag, noted also the black name tag white-stenciled J. BANQUETTE over his shirt pocket. He dropped the seabag, unclipped the name tag, put it in the bag, then dragged it over to the front desk, where he told the young blue-suited Filipino in glasses, "I'm here to see Mrs. Michelle Banquette."

"And sir your name it is?"

"My name is Miles." He paused, his name felt good in his mouth. "I'm an acquaintance of her husband."

"It is well, mister sir," said the clerk as he ran his finger down a computer printout. Miles saw the name *Banquette* and the clerk passed it, so Miles said, "That's it, suite six-nine-six."

"Ah, Mrs. Bankee. Must call." The clerk picked up the receiver and pressed the digits. After a moment: "Mrs. Bankee? . . . This be the down-stair. Is a man here for you. . . . What say? . . . No, not asking, am telling. Is a man here for you he is from army or sumteen. . . . Yes, yes, I make for him to go up, good-bye."

"Thanks," said Miles. "Can I—can I leave this bag behind the counter here? I don't want to drag it up there and back."

"Storing bag is one dolla."

He paid and then slung the duffel bag onto the counter, his memory flashing back to his final night at the Little Pink Bookstore, when he'd thrown the bag onto the counter and opened it and pulled out the items one by one and begun to reconstruct James J. Banquette.

In the elevator, he stood straight as he could, nervous, hands flat against his trousers, his palm over the bulge of the pussy toy in his pocket. He felt the way he used to feel when he was twenty-two, working in his father's factory, up for the assistant's assistant position that he would rum-and-Coke himself out of in the first week, having to ride the elevator to daily production meetings he was too zonked to follow, riding in the elevator thinking of it as something he had to get through before he could do what *he* wanted to do—

It was the same now, he wasn't crazy about seeing Mrs. Banquette, but he'd do his best by her, he'd refrain from congratulating himself, but he'd get it done. Quickly, and go.

Six flights up, the elevator doors parted creakily; the place smelled of ammonia as he stepped into the hallway. He walked a many-cornered route, reading numbers until he came to a teak door with 696 white-painted on it. He knocked. It felt good, finally, to be the one knocking and not the one knocked at; for a change, he was the man with the news. There wasn't an answer so he rapped again.

The door swung open.

The woman in the doorway was about half a foot shorter than Miles and her long dark hair fell straight all around her, over her arms and down her sides to the jean-packed curve of her hips, and her black bangs stopped just short of her black eyes, which were searching his face for a moment as though to find his depth. "Are you with Jim? I thought you *were* Jim, for a minute"—and her accent was a soft one of the Carolina or Virginia hills.

Miles could only look at her, this woman whose husband he was. This wife, this Michelle Banquette who'd written him letters full of pain, this woman who'd lived inside the marriage-lie created by her husband, a lie that was now to be extended by Miles Derry, this woman who deserved more than the pussy toy in his pocket. He felt guilt and—yes?—an instant attention to her that was surprisingly protective.

"Where is he, down there arguing with the cabdriver?"

"No, Jim isn't here."

"And who are you?"

"My name's—my name is Miles." The fresh truth of his real name felt extraordinarily good in his mouth.

"You a friend of Jim's?" Her dark eyes were searching his for his identity.

"I have a message from him."

"Oh. Well—you'd better come in and deliver it." She turned, with all that black hair whipping across her back, the end of the mane flying against the heart-shaped bottom packaged tightly in her jeans. "You want a beer or anything?"

"Thanks, I don't drink."

"A chaplain who doesn't drink?" So she'd noticed the collar crosses. "Are you a Mormon?"

"No, I'm in AA." He felt lousy about the lies he'd come to tell her, and it felt better to tell her a tiny portion of the truth.

She stopped in front of a small refrigerator and gave him a look. "You are? Wow—I'm in AA too. It's funny how the friends of Bill W. keep running into each other in the weirdest places. How long do you have?"

"Four years. What about you?"

"Two."

They were standing there looking at each other, the odd intimacy of strangers discovering a shared essence. Then she was leaning over the open door of the low refrigerator and her dark hair fell straight over her arms and shoulders to touch the floor and her tight round bottom was again of note, and it wasn't until she stood up with the bottles in her hands that Miles took in the suite. It was superb: mahogany paneling, carpeting as green as money, a foyer and a sitting room, a rectangle of sunlight from what must be the bedroom. She uncapped the bottles against an opener on the side of the fridge and she kept one of the 7-UPs for herself and handed him the other. "That's the only nonalcoholic they've got. It must be hard staying sober around here. You said you had a message from Jim?"

Miles felt clumsy as he took the bottle with one hand and looked down into her petite-nosed, smiling face with its intense coal-colored eyes as his other hand struggled in his pocket to bring out the toy. She looked down curiously at his work. Then he had the kitten out and was holding it up for her approval, but she put her hands over her face and said, "Oh my God." She wouldn't take it from him. "Not another one of *those* things."

Holding it up, he felt idiotic.

She took a long gulp of soft drink and turned and paced through the front room of the suite, shaking her head.

He placed the toy upon a barren desk against the wall, where the wide-mouthed object looked forlornly toward Mrs. Banquette. Miles took his hat off and placed it next to it, feeling he must stay longer, that there was no easy way out of the room.

"So," she said, "you know what those things are." From across a space occupied by a love seat and end tables and a coffee table, her dark eyes probed his own for a confession.

"I know what they are," he said.

"You think we navy wives don't talk about such things?"

He hadn't felt this awkward at any time on the ship. "I just brought it here because he asked me to."

"How long have you known Jim?"

"Not very long."

Her nod was short, suspicious, her arms crossing on her chest, her weight shifting to one hip. "So when is he going to be here? I've been waiting since last night."

Miles drew a breath. When he spoke, he looked past her, into the sunshine coming from the bedroom, as though the dead man might be waiting in there with the secrets he wanted no one to tell. "Jim went up to Mount Pinatubo. It's that volcano, you've heard it, haven't you? Well, it's killed a lot of people and made a lot of others homeless. Jim's the kind of man—he'd go up there and help them. If you haven't heard from him by tomorrow night, you should inform the navy. It's very dangerous, what he's doing, but—he had to do the Christian thing."

He felt awful about lying to her and wished he could tell her the truth, but knew it was impossible.

She was sitting on the couch, her hair falling all about her like a dark silky tent and her legs spread wide with her elbows on the knees and the 7-UP bottle held in the space between with both hands. Her expression had gone from dark-eyed suspicion to drop-lipped suspense to floor-staring disappointment. "You mean," she said, defeated, "all I get is that cat thing? I've been waiting here . . . I don't get it . . . I came here because I thought this was like a last-ditch . . . every time . . . it always turns out . . . "

Miles felt an ache of sympathy for her, and hated himself for having made her feel this way, for having reminded her what a disappointment her husband was, how unreliable, and Miles remembered the letter he'd written her from the ship, pretending to be Jim Banquette and promising to change—the poor woman had flown halfway round the world to see if it was true! And now Jim had disappointed her yet again, he wasn't here.

He told her, "I think Jim's changed a lot in the time I've known him."

"You said you didn't know him very well."

"I said I didn't know him very long—but I think I know him pretty well. I know he wants to treat his family better. He's—he's talked to me about those things."

"He has?" She wiped her nose with her knuckle; he realized how close she'd been to crying. "What kinds of things?"

"Mostly, how he wants to be a better husband and father. He's changed—he's won the Navy Cross, you know, that shows he's changed, and now he's up on that volcano helping people he doesn't even know—I'm not sure the old Jim would've done that."

She nodded and said, "When the marines said he'd saved that other man's life and was getting nominated for that medal I thought, Well, it must've been like a fluke, on account of Jim doesn't have the stamina for a thing like that, but it's nice for the kids to be able to think of their father like that, it changes the way the other kids treat them at school and all—but—what's he doing now? Is it something dangerous? He has a medical condition we don't like to tell a lot of people about, he has a small heart problem, you know, that's why he tires so easily and he always looks so pale . . . You going up on that mountain with him? Can you make sure he doesn't exert himself too much?"

Miles, who was sitting in an armchair across from her, didn't want to disappoint her further—he was remembering what she'd said in her last letter, how frustrated she was in her marriage, how she cried all the time, how Jim didn't seem to care who she was, how she tried to find the strength to hold everything together for the children, how much she wanted Jim to think about the man he was *supposed* to be. Her sensitivity and willingness to believe were the most engaging qualities Miles had seen in anyone in a long time, and, combined with her cute compact body, pretty face, and long hair, they made her an irresistible presence. He couldn't deceive her further, so he said "No, I'm not going to see Jim again. I'm leaving the country as soon as I—"

"He's not healthy enough to be saving people on volcanoes! He's always fatigued, sometimes he looks like a walking dead man—be honest, the last time you saw him, didn't he look dead?"

"Well—yes, he did."

Her dark eyes had become cloudy. "I hope Jim's changed. I flew all the way out here to *see* if he's changed. There was a different tone in his last letter, and now this medal and everything. I've been praying for a long time for Jim to change. I'm sorry," she said, fighting for control of her voice, "Jim and I have had a lot of—a lot of problems in our marriage, it sounds like he's told you, everybody has problems, but I've never really understood *why* he and I have so many. I used to drink because of our problems, but I don't do that anymore."

He wished he could tell her the truth, all of it, but he didn't know how to launch such a dangerous topic. They looked at each other, having created the easy space of incipient friendship.

"So you have four years," she said. "How do you stay sober around all those drunken sailors? It must be very difficult to be sober in the navy, you must be a very strong person." She gave him a shy, encouraging look.

Could he ever be strong enough to tell her the truth, all of it? She deserved it, the courtesy of the truth. His NA and double-A sponsors would've demanded that he tell the truth at this point, but he didn't know how to go about it.

Instead he found himself saying, "Would you like to have dinner with me?"

She considered this for a moment, then said, "It's a bit early, isn't it? I mean for you, not for me—this twelve-hour difference has me all upside down."

"I didn't have lunch. And—and I want to talk to you about Jim." Did he really? All he knew was that Mrs. Banquette had ceased to be an abstraction, that she was an attractive and sensitive woman who shouldn't be left alone in this hotel room with a pussy toy and a lie. He couldn't just go.

"You want to talk to me about Jim?"

"That's right."

"Well . . . okay. There's a restaurant in the hotel. Let me brush my hair." She went to the desk, which had a mirror over it, and reached into a big black purse and pulled out a hairbrush and shook all of her hair back so that it fell in dark undulations to her waist and she set about brushing it, watching herself sideways in the mirror, running the brush from the back of her head down to her butt, over and over, and then tidying the dark

bangs that fell just short of her eyes, and Miles watched with eyes unblinking and breath hardly moving, for he thought she was beautiful and troubled and she was his wife and she'd agreed to have dinner with him and he
felt the lurch of curiosity about a woman—*this* woman—as he hadn't felt
it in a long time. He watched her. When she was done and turned to look
at him it was to wait for him to lead, and he was eager to do so, rising for
the door, which he held open for her.

In the elevator on the way to the top-floor restaurant, she was a small
exotic female coming up to his shoulder, and he kept looking down at her
and she turned and aimed those dark eyes up at him and said, "What?" but
there was no way to tell her, not yet, that he was her husband and that he
would make a better job of it than her previous one and that he was wondering what it would feel like, what it would taste like, what it would mean
to kiss her. Crazy thought! What was he still doing here?

The doors separated creakingly, revealing the empty restaurant with its
rows of tables and chairs, and the dust floated through the late-afternoon
light coming through the windows and the first sound they heard was the
volcano rumbling *trooooth* and they selected—who selected?—wasn't she
in fact following where he led?—a corner booth.

"This okay?"

She nodded and slid in.

At the table, time and space lost their shapes just as completely as
during the long empty nights in his rack, but now the emptiness had
been occupied, fully, by Michelle Banquette, who was reading the leather-
bound menu that she held in both hands as though it were a hymnal. The
sunlight from the window was now strong enough to signify an opening
in the clouds and ash, and with the light at her back, she looked like a
novice reading her lifted book and her hair was like a flowing religious
hood. Miles was unable to move his eyes from her and had no way to
express, even to himself, everything he was beginning to feel—his being
with her in this place felt so natural as to be preordained, the logical
result of the intersection of his willpower and his possibilities. The crossing of his life with Michelle's had some deep unspeakable meaning that
he was already starting to value as so primal that he must hold onto it
and perhaps—perhaps even soon—begin to cherish it. Although
Michelle didn't know it yet, she and Miles had shared a life-changing
moment in a video arcade a long time ago and a long distance ago in San
Diego—it was a thousand times the size of anything he could've shared

with Robin, and it felt more momentous, even, than the ghost child he shared with Mary Lou.

The waiter came to them and food had to be decided upon, and Miles, who was suddenly very hungry, found that the hunger wasn't his largest feeling, so he ordered just-anything and then there was conversation, as though the words themselves were the real meal. She told him about her passion, the training of show horses and show dogs, the sixty-acre farm the Banquettes had in Virginia—Miles owned a farm!—and how she managed all the breeding and training her husband had no interest in, how she had two employees and took the animals to shows all over the Eastern Seaboard, and the roomful of trophies she had, and the money she made from stud services. She asked him about himself—did he have children?— and he told her about Kari, and she wanted to know about his wife, and he had to explain that he and Kari's mother were no longer together, and Michelle said she was very sorry about that, it was hard to keep a family together today—then she turned her head to the side and gave him an oblique look and said, "But you wanted to talk about Jim."

"I shouldn't've brought you that—that thing—I apologize."

She shrugged. "Jim doesn't know that I know what they are. He sent me one before, when he was in Amsterdam, he took out the disgusting part, the part he thinks I don't know about, and he sent me the stuffed toy as a symbol of our—of our love I guess—that's what he said, anyway. Sometimes I think my husband is a very twisted guy. So I just kept pretending I didn't know what it was, and I sent it back to him a few weeks ago—I was hoping it would make him face himself. I don't know what he meant by sending me *another* one. Maybe it's his way of telling me he's rediscovered his love for me, that he's changed. He's a different man, he's a war hero, he's out helping people on that volcano, right? I came here in hopes that he's changed. I just hope nothing happens to him. A volcano like that can explode at any minute, without warning, I think. I don't want him to take too many chances and strain his heart. How dangerous is this volcano? I mean, there's life insurance, but a father is more important to his kids than any half-million is."

"Half-million?" said Miles. "Dollars?"

"Yes. I'm glad Jim is making decent friends in the navy for once—four years without drinking is really impressive. I don't know for sure, but I think he was running around with some kind of bad crowd before. Did he ask you to—to look after me—until he gets to Manila?"

"Something like that."

"What did you want to tell me about him?"

She was looking at him with such sweet expectation that he felt it was impossible to tell her. "I'll tell you later," he said, wondering if he meant it.

The food came and as they started she said, "What made you stop drinking?"

"I got tired of waking up in jail and wondering how I got there. Then my father, who I've always hated, stuck me in a treatment center because I couldn't take care of myself anymore. I think he did it to prove to the world what a fuck-up I was."

She nodded. He was encouraged by the reaffirmation that you could tell a fellow AA the most outrageous truths about yourself and she wouldn't be shocked.

"When I drank, and when I did drugs," he continued, "I felt like I wasn't good enough for anything, for any of the positive things people have in this world. I was a bum. Even after I stopped drinking and using I was a bum for a long time. I was a bum until I—until I was in the navy. Before that, I never thought I could do anything important; now I feel completely different about myself. I feel I can do almost anything I want, go anywhere and do it. When I see something I want, now I think there's a chance I can have it." He looked at her, her cute petite face framed by bangs and long flowing hair, and he was wanting her, he was talking about her, and he was wondering if she knew it.

Without looking up from her food, she reached out and squeezed his hand on the table and said, "That's great," and although he recognized this as the patting reassurance you got at AA, the feeling of her hand on his, however brief, sent a lick of electric fire straight into his chest. Though still in uniform, eating with Michelle, he felt entirely like a civilian, and her acceptance of him made him feel that the civilian world might accept the man he'd become on the *Harding*, accept him in a way it never had before, that being One of the Guys might be as easy as being the man he was now.

"What about you?" he said.

She looked at him with expectant openness. "What about me?"

"What made you stop drinking?"

She looked balefully down at her plate. "I used to think it was all my fault. All of the problems with Jim. I used to think there was something wrong with me and that was why he didn't—I couldn't tell the difference between his problems and my problems. He'd go away for six months at a time, he'd always be volunteering for these six-month deployments when he didn't have to, and then, when he *was* home, he'd be so cold to me." In back of her words the volcano was speaking, but Miles was listening only to Michelle. "I used to think he was—out with other women, in the ports and everything. You say he's talked to you. I'm afraid to ask about that, I'm not going to ask, if he's told you things in confidence I'm not sure I want to know them. But I think he's changed, I'm here because I believe he's changed, and you said you thought he's changed, so I'm feeling very hopeful. What is it you wanted to tell me about him? You haven't gotten around to it."

He wanted to tell her the truth because he felt sympathy for who she was, a sensitive and wounded woman whose life had been one of disappointments and betrayals and trying to hold things together, a woman who'd struggled with drink, a complex and attractive woman. But there was no way he could tell her the truth in a restaurant—perhaps not anywhere. "I'll have to tell you later," he said. "After dinner—I don't think I can't tell you here, in public." Again, he wondered if he was actually going to tell her.

She looked at him with troubled alertness but said, "Okay . . ."

Then the bill was presented and he pulled out one of the five-thousand-dollar stacks the DISBO'd given him. He peeled off a hundred-dollar bill and laid it upon the check and as he was returning the money to his pocket Michelle Banquette said, "Do you always carry so much cash!"

"Only when I have to take good care of a friend's wife."

"You're an unusual man, Miles."

They smiled at each other.

At the elevator doors he was the one to press the down button, and once inside he was the one to press the floor button—hers—and as the elevator started down she said, "Did you notice what was on the menu?"

"What?"

"I mean the room service? Written on the menu? 'Comfort-girls, forty-five pesos.' They send them right up to a man's room. This country—I hope Jim doesn't do things like that."

"I know he doesn't."

When the door opened, there was no question as to his following, and they turned the maze corners and then they were at her door and she had the key out and opened the door into the darkened suite, turning on the light, and he followed. "Will Jim be here tomorrow, do you think? What did you want to tell me about him?"

She sat on the couch and yawned, the dragged-down face of jet lag making its appearance at last.

Miles took the armchair, very nervous now that the moment was before him, not wanting to spoil the friendship growing between them. "I'm not sure I *can* tell you."

"Why not?"

He could feel the sweat oozing out of the pores on his forehead, though the room was air-conditioned. He pressed his hands together. "Because telling you this is the hardest thing I've ever done in my life."

Her eyes were big and dark with alarm. She didn't say anything.

He told her, "AA says we have to be totally honest, right? In everything we do? Human beings can't live up to that all the time. But I think maybe I need to do it now—I want to do it now—I don't know if I can do it." His brow was wet and he could feel his armpits dampening too. He pressed his hands together hard. "Maybe I can do it with your help."

"What do you mean?"

"Well, I guess I'm hoping you won't throw me out after you hear this."

An overlay of confusion grew onto the worry on her face. "Is it that bad?"

"It's very bad."

"Why would I throw you out for something Jim did? I won't throw you out."

"It's something I did too. I don't want to hurt you; I want to tell you the truth—but gently—in stages, I guess. I don't really know what I'm doing. It's just that I like you a lot, and I think you deserve the truth, and I know the right thing to do is to tell it to you, but I don't know how. Maybe I shouldn't tell you at all."

The worry and confusion in her face resolved themselves into an arched indignation as she said, "What did you and Jim do, share some woman in Thailand or something? You guys are supposed to be *chaplains,* who's a woman supposed to complain to, who's going to believe a story about a husband who's a minister and can't be trusted? Whenever I suspect something, I'm never able to open up to any of my—"

"No, it's nothing like that."

"Well what is it then?"

"Michelle, you're better off without Jim. Jim—Jim doesn't like girls."

She was drawing back, shaking her head and squinting and saying, "What?"

"He doesn't like girls."

"Are you saying Jim is a—is a homo?"

"Yes."

"Why are you saying this!"

"Because he likes to have sex with other men."

"And you're saying you had sex with him? You said I was going to throw you out? Because of something Jim and you did?" She was sitting very straight and her eyes were dark and insistent and she was alert to every word of his.

"No, no, that's not it. I'm not a—I'm not gay. I like girls, Michelle. But Jim doesn't, he likes guys."

"How do you *know* that?"

"Do you know what an adult bookstore is?" He was tremendously uncertain of what he was doing, but he didn't know how else to say these things except to say them.

"Yes," she said with energetic disgust, "I know what those places are, those are those dirty places where they sell those dirty things like the one you brought me today."

"Do you know what happens in adult bookstores?" He could feel his face heating up, but he must go on. "In the backs of those places they have these little booths that lock, and they have forty channels of video porn, and in the walls between the booths they have these—these holes—they're called glory holes—and Jim—Jim likes to put himself through those holes, he likes to—"

"Why are you telling me such a disgusting thing!"

"I'm sorry, maybe I shouldn't tell you any—"

"How would *you* know all this? What's it all have to do with you?"

"Because I saw him do it—or, I mean, I saw him after he did it . . . He had a heart attack in June, Michelle, in San Diego, while he was doing it. I know about it, because I was working in the store and I found him afterward, when I was cleaning up—Michelle, I don't know how to tell you the rest, except just to tell you—I'm very very sorry—Jim is dead, he died in that video booth, before the ARG even deployed."

She was so agitated that she had to stand up and hold her hands out as though to halt him, and she said, "This is crazy—this is so crazy—why are you telling me this psycho stuff!—Jim's not dead, he saved that marine's life and he's up on that volcano saving other people's lives and he wrote to me from the ship—I have his last letter—"

"I'm the one who wrote that letter," Miles said, and he also stood up, trying to keep his voice down, to navigate between anxiety and the insistent necessity of truth. "I was the one you sent that cat thing to, and I'm the one who saved that marine's life. I was impersonating Jim, and I wrote to you how I was going to change, how I was going to be a better husband and father, how I was going to do what you asked, to think about the man I'm supposed to be. How else would I know all these things about Jim and you? You came to see *me*, not Jim, I'm the one who wrote to you. Jim died in that video arcade two months ago, and I'm not a chaplain, I never was a chaplain, I was the clerk in the store, I'm the one who found him dead, and I assumed his identity. I'm the one who went on the WESTPAC, not Jim. He doesn't exist anymore. I burned down the whole place when I left, with Jim's dead body in it, and I've been pretending ever since to be him. You admitted I kind of looked like him, we have the same mustache and eyes, you said when you first saw me today you thought for a moment I was him. I wanted to find some easy way to tell you everything, but—"

"You're a lunatic!" she yelled, her face dark and quivering and her eyes shining-wet. "You get out of here, you lying lunatic—"

"Please don't throw me out, you promised, Michelle, look," he said, growing as agitated as she was, reaching into the neck of his shirt with one trembling hand, then both hands, finding the clasp of the thing he'd had around his neck since that night in the bookstore, undoing and pulling out the dog tags. And he held them out dangling to her. "Read them."

Reluctantly she cupped her palm around them, brought them warily up to eye level. As she read them she started shaking her head and crying and she was screaming, "You get out of here, you psycho, you get the hell out of here—"

"Please—"

"Get out! Get out! Get out!"

And so he was through the door, in the hallway, shaking, ready to cry himself, not knowing what immediately to do, walking the maze until he found the elevator, pacing as he waited for it; he knew he couldn't leave the hotel, this would now become a prolonged struggle with uncertainty and to give it up now would mean returning to the old Miles, reverting to the way he'd been before the *Harding,* before the medal, before becoming a man who could tell her the truth, and so he could not leave. He went down to the front desk and got the seabag. He also got a room. Up in it, he arranged, on the dresser, everything he'd need for the morning, because he wasn't leaving her, he was going to see her in the morning. He got out the things: the dead man's liberty clothes, the guava-colored shirt and white shorts; the passport and the wallet; the telegram with the news of the *Reader's Digest* money; the two stacks of currency; the seabag itself, stenciled BANQUETTE. All of the evidence to corroborate his truth.

Lying in the unshifting, civilian bed, he felt an anxiety greater than that of the night prior to the Burmese mission; the fear of death, though awful in itself, was a simpler dilemma than the one that would confront him in the morning, when he went again to see Michelle Banquette. He felt he was finally a man, for he could not only do what was right—tell the truth—and accept every consequence, but he could also assume the risk, despite his fear, of pursuing what he wanted. And he wanted her. He wanted to make up to her for the kind of husband Jim Banquette had been, he wanted to take much better care of her. Was he crazy? He'd only just met her. But there was no other human being to whom the story of his life, especially the last two months, would be more relevant. And so he must talk to her again and risk telling more about himself. Whom else could he tell about himself? She was a sensitive person, she would eventually find him sympathetic, she'd see that he was telling the truth and that he wasn't a monster but had, in fact, protected her children from the truth—and they would still be protected, for the world could still be made to believe that the dead man had disappeared on the volcano—and because she wasn't just personally attractive but physically as well, and because his body couldn't forget the electric bolt that had passed from her into him when she'd touched his hand at dinner, he lay there fantasizing that she would love him, maybe not tomorrow but someday, perhaps soon, and they would go to Peacock Island together and be in love, and after a tropical honeymoon of sorts they would fly back to Virginia together, and they would live off the insurance money . . . he tried to look into the future but there was nothing to guess by . . . she might remain angry with him and try to have him arrested, that was the chance, that was the fear . . . he might have to flee, to run again, as he'd done so many times before, but he didn't want that anymore . . . through the night, as he lay fantasizing and fearing and dreaming and waking and sleeping and nightmaring, the volcano spoke its guttural wisdom to him, it made night sounds that spoke of love or jail or travel or peace or terror or triumph, the contradictory messages of anxiety. It was five-thirty A.M., a civilian time—he was back in the "real" world, with all the old rules he knew so well, and which he'd never been able to live up to. Well, maybe today. He couldn't go back to sleep so he rose and showered and put on the dead man's liberty clothes and sat in an armchair for an hour, hope and dread battling within his chest as the dawn lightened the room so gradually that he couldn't say when it had become day. He looked at his watch and it was 7:12 A.M.—civilian time, civilian time.

He put his evidence in his pockets and dragged the seabag into the hallway by its knot. Riding in the elevator he was more full of fear and hope than ever, and he knew only that he must take his chance and that he wasn't in control of her reaction. He dragged the bag out of the elevator and down the hall and around the corners, and he knocked at her door. He was sick of the sound of knuckles on a door—all those times it had unnerved him on the ship!—you could never tell what it meant. Not even now, when he was doing the knocking.

Opening the door, she was wearing the same blouse and jeans as the night before, and the downward pull of the jet lag on her face could only mean she hadn't slept at all, and her eyes were red enough to suggest what she'd been doing. She stepped back from him, her eyes magnetized to the sight of him. Her gaze traveled down his shirt and onto the seabag, which stood against his leg with the name BANQUETTE facing her.

"I wanted to talk to you again," he said.

She stopped walking backward and looked at him in paralysis.

"Can I talk to you?" he said. "Can I come in?" His heart, which had been flapping as though it were a thing with wings, settled itself as she looked at him steadily, not entirely trustingly—here was this weird man dressed like her husband, looking a bit like him—yet there was another shade to her look, a warm element, just a shadow left over from their friendship over dinner, and her gaze became a sad resignation as she motioned at the armchair. She took the couch, looking at him in terror and hope and curiosity and resignation.

He dragged the seabag in and sat in the chair. Before he could begin, she caught his eyes with her own and wouldn't let them go, and she said, "Tell me exactly who you are, tell me the whole truth."

"That's exactly what I came back to do." And he began telling it, how he'd made up the story of Jim going to Mount Pinatubo, and yes, he'd known it would be traumatic for her and her family to think Jim had died on the volcano, but it wouldn't be the awfulness of an erection poking out of a glory hole in an adult bookstore. She would've had the medal, after all, and possibly a second, the children would've had the myth of a father twice heroic—could still have it, she didn't have to tell anyone the things he was telling her, the world could still believe that Jim Banquette had saved the major and then died helping others on Pinatubo, and her children would be bound for a better destination than the dire facts that were buried in a heap of ash in a San Diego slum, on the fringe of the sewage swamps of the Tia Juana River. He told the truth as he'd lived it—the bookstore, the ship, himself, who he'd been and who he'd been able to become. He tried to tell her the truth in the order it had happened, but also filled in Mary Lou and Kari and his father and Doug Suveg; he told her about the bombed-out village and Father Ogleby; he told her about saving the major; he told her about her husband's secret homosexual life; he told her about the letter from Tuttleman and how he'd been approached by Tuttleman on Okinawa; he told her that he had endless sympathy for her; he told her he was very very sorry about Jim's death but that he thought she was better off without a husband like him; he told her how he'd tried to protect her and her children from the truth; he told her that he was taking a risk right now by trusting her with the truth, that he was vulnerable to her because she could destroy him. As he talked and as she sat there crying silently, he took from his pockets the things he wanted to show her. He placed them on the coffee table, and she looked down uncertainly at them: here was a block of hundred-dollar bills, here was another one, here was a wallet, here was a passport, here was a folded telegram, and he opened the wallet and pulled out Jim's IDs, he pulled out the pictures of Mary Lou and Kari, he unbanded the currency and fanned it out on the table, he unfolded the telegram and asked her to read it, he pointed to the pussy toy, which was staring at them from the desk across the room where he'd left it yesterday, he told her, as he had last night, that she had sent one not to her husband but to him, she had sent her letters to him, the letter she'd received in return had been written by him, the medal had been won by him, and he told her that she hadn't come to see her husband at all, but she'd come to see *him*, Miles.

She was sitting forward now as he spoke, the tears shining on her face as she shook her head and quietly squared the items on the coffee table, pretend-studying them with the dour pensiveness of an unhappy child.

And then, just as abruptly as he'd started talking, he was done. He sat there waiting.

When at last she spoke, in a voice tremulous and devastated, she

addressed the items on the table. "That explains it, why Jim was so different. It wasn't Jim at all." She raised her hand to wipe her nose with her
knuckle. "I always thought Jim was running around with other women. I
never knew the . . ." She looked at him, a perplexed and perplexing look.
Miles at first didn't understand what it meant, but as he kept looking into
Michelle's eyes he felt, passing between him and this woman, a kind of
imposed but, in its strange way, gratifying intimacy from the shared experience of bizarre and calamitous truths. "Yesterday," she said, blinking, "you
didn't come here planning to tell me the truth at all, did you?"

"No."

"What were you going to do after giving me that thing?" She pointed at
the pussy toy.

"I was going to take the *Reader's Digest* money and go to this island I
know about."

"But you decided to stay here and tell me the truth. Why'd you do this?"

He looked at her straight on: "I think you're a decent and sensitive person who deserves what's right."

They held each other's gazes again, and her lips parted a little, and
Miles could feel the electricity as though it were a circle enclosing them. He
enjoyed it as long as he dared, then spoke: "What did you do last night?"

Her eyes fell at last. "I didn't know what to do. I cried . . . I couldn't
believe the things you said, but somehow I knew they were true. They were
too crazy not to be true. I thought about calling somebody—the navy, but
I wouldn't know who to call or what to say to them—or I thought about
calling somebody back home, but I wouldn't know who to call there
either—who can I talk to about this? This is the most unreal, weirdest stuff
that's ever happened to me in my entire life." She shook her head and
wiped her eyes with her knuckles again.

"Mine too."

Again they were silent in the closeness that was growing between them
as they looked at each other without talking. Miles knew they were not yet
at a point where he might offer her a hug, but neither could they part. They
were alone in the middle of this mess, and they needed to keep talking to
each other.

"I thought about calling somebody," she said again, "but the only person I could think I needed to talk to . . . was you." She shrugged, looking
down, then looking at him again. The force of the deepening intimacy was
making it impossible for them just to sit there. There was a power building

from the things that had been said—all of the things since he'd arrived yes-terday—a power that neither of them could control or direct alone. Finally she said, "What do you want to do?"

"Will you have breakfast with me?"

She sat back; there was a pause. And then she said, "All right." She looked around the room, slowly, as though finding herself there for the first time. "Let me get myself fixed up."

He watched her brush her hair again. Inexplicably, it seemed a porten-tous, religious act. She was beautiful, and he thought these were the most serious moments he'd ever spent with another human being. What would they talk about at breakfast? Miles couldn't remember ever being more curious or expectant about a conversation. They would have everything to say to one another, and might never be done. It felt so strange and unreal and exciting, as though one world were dying at the moment that another was being created.

In the elevator she said in a tired voice, "Let's not eat here, I'm tired of being in this place, let's go out somewhere," and they rode down to the lobby. Miles told the bellhop they wanted a cab, and he and Michelle sat on a couch near the front desk and waited.

—eighty miles away, Mount Pinatubo groaned its volcanic agony—

The man on the couch wondered what man he would be after break-fast. It was possibly the most important breakfast of his life. He tried to imagine his way forward. He thought he could see a man who might be himself, a man going to Virginia with Michelle Banquette, living with her on the insurance money, the two of them inventing some acceptable response to the common if impossible-to-answer question: "So how did you two meet?" He looked hard into the future, and he might've been the man in love with her, going horseback riding with her on the farm—

—*One of the Guys, at last, a home and a family, but it was far from a cer-tainty yet*—

Alternately, the harder he looked, he might've been the man relaxing in the street café in Bangkok, alone, reading, in the *International Herald Tri-bune* about the explosion of a volcano across the South China Sea, the raining of ash and cinders on a place called Olongapo, its destruction and depopulation, the scattering of all ships from the Subic Bay Naval Station by desperate last-minute orders, a man reading a newspaper and imagining the disappearance and presumed death of a certain chaplain. Or he might've been the man in a secondhand peacoat, returning home by way of

Australia and North Africa, carrying a duffel bag over his shoulder, filled with treasures, walking up the oak-lined street on an Indian summer afternoon in Zincville, Illinois, not yet noticed by the four-year-old girl playing with her dolls on the lawn in front of the white clapboard house. Or he might've been these men and one more, the man perpetually in flight, forever aware of his willfulness and possibilities, always on his way to Peacock Island—

But then the woman put her hand on his, and she squeezed it in a first sign of proprietary relation, sending a lick of electrical fire into him as she'd done at dinner the night before, and the taxi was there, and Miles and Michelle rose together, and he was still holding her hand as they walked out of the hotel and into the tumultuous activity of the world outside.